Unmarked Graves

A Connor Fraser Thriller

Also by Neil Broadfoot

No Man's Land
No Place to Die
The Point of No Return
No Quarter Given
Violent Ends

Neil Broadfoot

Unmarked Graves

A Connor Fraser Thriller

CONSTABLE

CONSTABLE

First published in Great Britain in 2023 by Constable

A CIP catalogue record for this book
is available from the British Library.

ISBN: 978-1-40871-877-3

Typeset in Minion Pro by Initial Typesetting Services, Edinburgh
Printed and bound in Great Britain by Clays Ltd, Elcograf S.p.A.

Papers used by Constable are from well-managed forests and
other responsible sources.

Constable
An imprint of
Little, Brown Book Group
Carmelite House
50 Victoria Embankment
London EC4Y 0DZ

An Hachette UK Company
www.hachette.co.uk

www.littlebrown.co.uk

*For Mum – hopefully this'll put your
mind at ease about the edit.*

You thirst for blood, and with blood I fill you.

Inferno
Dante Alighieri

CHAPTER 1

It burst out of him, a deep, rumbling belly laugh that forced his broken ribs to grind together and opened the crusted scabs of blood that had formed around the cuts on his face and cheeks. The two masked men in front of him flinched, lowered their guns for a moment, then exchanged a glance and a shrug of the shoulders.

Their movement made Simon McCartney laugh even harder, tears from the pain it caused him rolling down his cheeks even as his laughter bounced and ricocheted off the corrugated roof and cold concrete of the room he was in. His bare feet slipped across the plastic sheeting on which the chair he was tied to had been placed and he rocked back. If his hands had been free and not bound behind him, he would have slapped his thighs and shaken his head as he fought for breath.

He was going to die. But he was damned if he would lose his sense of humour over it.

Strong hands landed on his shoulders and he was pulled forward, the shock of the chair's front legs hitting the hard stone floor stabbing fresh agony into his ribs. He dropped his head, still chuckling, only for the butt of a gun to be smashed into his face, throwing him back once more. He gasped for breath, but found it impossible as he was grabbed around the neck.

'Shut it, you fuckin' psycho,' his attacker hissed, warm, sour breath leaking out from behind the balaclava he wore. 'Now, are you gonna

1

start telling us how much you and Connor Fraser know, or do we need to cut a few more scars into that pretty face of yours?'

The man's eyes, framed in ragged eyeholes torn from the mask, told Simon he wanted the answer to be no. This was a man who enjoyed inflicting pain and suffering.

The problem was, as Simon had discovered, he was very, very good at it.

'Go on then.' He coughed as the pressure on his throat eased slightly. The words were hot, bitter with the tang of blood. 'Think you missed a few spots first time round. Tell you what, you'll never make it as a Turkish barber.'

With a grunt, the man released Simon's throat, took a step back, reached into his pocket and produced a Stanley knife. The handle was spattered with Simon's blood. He paused, took a moment to study the blade, turn it in the harsh strip-light overhead.

Simon knew the man was smiling under the mask.

He took a step forward, was stopped by the second man. 'This is fucking pointless,' he said. He was shorter than the first, less powerfully built, but there was something in his posture and voice that told Simon he was thinking three steps ahead. 'He's not going to tell us anything. We've wasted enough time on this. Come on, let's just fucking end it and get out of here.'

A third figure stepped from the shadows. He was smaller than the other two, and walked with an uncertain gait, but there was no doubt he was the leader of the trio. The sudden dipping of the other two men's heads and deferential shuffling backwards as the man walked forward told Simon all he needed to know.

'Aye, you're right,' he said. 'We can send the footage as soon as we've blown this pig's head off.'

Simon took a deep breath, swallowed the pain in his chest and the terror that arced through him like electricity. Memories cascaded through his mind in a confused jumble. Paulie King, gun clamped in his hand, screaming at the world as he scorched the air with the smell of gunpowder and blood. And then there was Connor Fraser. His friend. His brother. Lying in a heap at Paulie's feet. Was he alive or dead? Simon didn't know, had been dragged away before he could find out. But, in his desperation, he had left a message, a message only Connor would understand.

He prayed his friend had survived and found it. It was too late for him, but if Connor was still alive, Simon's killers would pay.

The thought caused fresh laughter to tickle the back of his throat. Laughter that died abruptly at the sound of a gun being chambered.

He looked up, saw the two armed masked men standing side by side, the shorter of the two now pointing a shotgun directly at his face. Behind him, the third man stood with a phone held up, the torch on as he recorded. That was why they were wearing masks, Simon thought, so no one who watched the footage would see their faces.

'Night night,' the man said, as he adjusted his feet slightly, readying himself for the gun to kick.

Simon closed his eyes. Thought of Donna Blake and all the things he hadn't said when he'd had the chance. Waited.

Waited.

CHAPTER 2

Three days earlier

They worked just a little too hard at being casual.

They were good, Connor Fraser was forced to admit. Very good. Almost the best he had seen. They wore mid-range suits with off-the-peg tailoring that was crumpled in all the right places. Their conversation was slightly forced and awkward, the almost-mirrored body language marking them out as work colleagues who were eager to make the right impression while on a lunch break. Even their speech patterns were right: stilted, slightly deferential, the feigned interest and enthusiasm of two relative strangers on temporary release from the desk jobs they hated, the jobs that provided the only topic of conversation they had.

'And did you hear about Erikson's latest fuck-up in accounting?'

'Oh, yeah, I did. Total idiot. If he spent as much time studying the accounts as he did Stacey's arse, he'd maybe get somewhere.'

Polite laughter. Shy drops of the head and enthusiastic nodding. Limited eye contact. Good, Connor thought again, as he followed them at a distance through the crowds in the St James Quarter shopping centre. Very good. Almost perfect.

Almost.

It was their eyes that gave them away. The sweeping gazes that scanned the vicinity and the horizon, picking out potential targets and threats. The slightly defocused look as they concentrated on their peripheral vision, even when they were avoiding each other's gaze. The way they locked on to security cameras or anyone who looked vaguely official as they wove through the crowds.

Eyes always give it away, Connor thought. And he should know. They were the same eyes that stared back at him every time he looked in a mirror.

The job had come in a week ago and, if he was being honest with himself, Connor was surprised it had taken so long. A gang had been making headlines by targeting jewellers in Edinburgh, raiding them at knifepoint at the end of the working day, when the staff were helpfully pulling all the four- and five-figure watches, necklaces and diamonds from their window displays and pooling them in the shop before they were locked in the safe overnight. Four shops, on Rose Street, Princes Street and George Street, had been hit, jewellery taken with an estimated value of £400,000. So it had been no surprise to Connor when his company, Sentinel Securities, received a call from Derek Maitland, owner of Maitland's, an 'exclusive jewellery and timepiece boutique' at the heart of the St James Quarter shopping centre on Princes Street. Sitting on the site of a former seventies concrete and harling monstrosity called the St James Centre, the Quarter was locally named the Walnut Whip due to its circular design and twisting metal spire. To Connor, it looked more like the track of a forgotten rollercoaster than a sweet treat from the 1980s that his gran enjoyed. Maitland's request to Connor, and Sentinel, had been simple: review the security at the Quarter and, specifically, his shop.

Connor had happily taken the assignment, partly as the case had caught his attention, and partly as an excuse to get away from the riot of cardboard boxes and bubble wrap that had taken over his flat in Stirling. Three months after buying a house in the city, the modifications to deal with Jen's mobility issues were finally complete, and it was moving time. And while Connor loved the prospect of living with Jen, the chaos that surrounded the move was making his teeth grind.

A few favours called in from DCI Malcolm Ford had given Connor access to the CCTV footage from the jewellery stores that had already been hit, and it hadn't taken him long to see the pattern. A man and a woman, dressed in mid-range suits, strolling past the store that was their target. Casual conversation, sometimes with coffee cups in hand, just two people out for a walk in the afternoon. Connor was forced to admit he was impressed – they almost blended in perfectly. But there was something in the way they moved, something that spoke to the savage, unevolved part of his brain, the part that still wanted to hunt his prey with a club, that Connor recognised. He began staking out Maitland's, waiting for them to take a casual walk past to check out the security. And just to make sure that the shop was their next target, Connor had instructed Maitland to take out adverts in the local press and on social media, highlighting the arrival of some very shiny, very expensive Swiss watches, favoured by movie characters with a penchant for English sports cars and drinks that were shaken, not stirred.

Now they had taken the bait. Connor smiled as the couple strolled past Maitland's with only one quick sideways glance. He would call Ford, tell him what he knew, let the police deal with it. Most likely they would come back tonight, tomorrow at latest. Now they had intel on what the security situation was, and were happy that there was nothing to stop them, they would want to strike quickly.

He was just reaching into his pocket for his phone when he froze.

They had turned, and were heading back for the shop. All pretence of casual strolling was gone, shed like a snakeskin. They were striding forward now, shoulders back, faces set, even as they slipped on face-masks. Nobody around them reacted – why would they? After the pandemic, slipping on a mask was just a routine part of life.

Connor's pulse quickened as he saw the woman reach into her jacket as she approached Maitland's. Her partner fell back, giving her a clear line of sight to the security guard, who had noticed them approaching and was readying himself to open the door for new customers. Connor got moving, covering the distance between himself and the shop as fast as he could. He saw the masked man look up at the disturbance Connor was making in the crowd of shoppers, saw his eyes widen in recognition of a threat. Beside him, his partner turned away from the door, the shopping centre erupting into a panicked scream of frantic movement as she pulled a machete from her jacket pocket. Without thinking, Connor hurled his phone at her as he broke into a sprint. The woman's head snapped up and her legs buckled as the phone hit her nose. She staggered back, clawing for her mask, pulling it down to stop herself choking on the blood that was now pouring from her nose.

Connor closed on her, grabbed the arm holding the machete and twisted as hard as he could against her grip. He felt something give in her wrist, heard a gargled cry of pain as the machete clattered to the floor. Behind him, he was dimly aware of a bolt being slid home, cursed silently as he realised the security guard was locking down Maitland's.

He was reaching for the machete when pain exploded in his ribs and he staggered to the side, his head slamming off the window of the jewellery shop.

'Bastard!' the masked man snarled at him, his voice carrying a level of vitriol only a Glasgow accent could fully articulate. 'You broke her fucking nose! I'll kill you for that!' He was pulling out of his jacket a machete identical to the one Connor had just prised from the woman's grip. His attacker held it over his head, ready to bring it down on Connor and split him in two. Connor braced himself against the window then lashed out, driving forward with everything he had and rugby-tackling his attacker. They landed on the cold stone floor in a heap, the man giving a frenzied cough of rage and surprise as the wind was driven from him. Connor dug his elbows into the man's chest and drove up, putting all his weight into the move. The man cried out as he flailed wildly, and Connor felt the machete cut the air in front of his face as the blade flashed before his eyes. He grabbed the man's knife arm, twisted, not stopping this time, finishing the job he had started with the woman and snapping his attacker's wrist. The sound of the machete clattering to the floor was the sweetest Connor had ever heard.

He leaned back, the man in front of him curling into a foetal ball of pain around his broken wrist. Connor reached down for the machete, then, satisfied his attacker wasn't a threat, turned to the woman. She was sitting propped against the jeweller's window, her face a mask of red that somehow matched the hatred in her eyes. She was grasping for the machete that lay just out of reach, her eyes flicking between it and Connor.

'Leave it,' he said, his voice as sharp as the blade he now held. 'You touch that thing, I'll break both your arms, okay?'

She glared at him for a minute, then sagged, the fight leaving her as the first sound of sirens drifted into the centre. Connor nodded once, looked through the window of the jewellery shop, saw the security guard standing there, all wide eyes and flushed, sweat-studded skin.

'Thanks for the help,' Connor mouthed to him, as he ticked off a small salute. 'Really, you were grand.' A thought occurred to him, and he turned back to the woman with the broken nose. 'Why change the pattern?' he asked. 'Why try your luck now instead of at the end of the day?'

She sneered at him, showing small bloodstained teeth. 'Didn't want to be predictable, did we?' she hissed. 'Get in one last hit, then off to Manchester, sell the gear there. Didn't expect you, though, did we?'

Connor shrugged, smiled. 'Sorry,' he said. 'Got a knack for being in the wrong place at the wrong time.'

CHAPTER 3

He hated the place in the way only someone who was born there could.

Standing there, Stirling spread out below him, a patchwork of stone and concrete that petered out as the Ochil Hills rose on the horizon, the warm breeze carrying the sounds of the city up to him, he could see it all.

And he despised it.

Not that he really remembered Stirling, or that the city had shaped his childhood in any meaningful way. No, it was more that it reminded him of what might have been, of roads, both literal and otherwise, not taken. Of a life he was cheated out of.

A life that had died with his father.

Conversation made it worse: the flattened consonants and elongated vowels of the locals he spoke to reminded him of his mother, and the accent that had coloured her voice despite more than four decades away from the place. He wondered if his father's had sounded similar, felt a sorrow-tinged fury at the realisation that he could not remember his voice. Oh, he could hear it: all he had to do was go online and find one of Dad's speeches, but that was different, like watching a replay of a football match instead of experiencing the event live. It was sterile. Emotionless.

Empty.

'Jonathan?' a voice from behind him enquired, shy and hesitant, almost as though the speaker had read his thoughts and was unwilling to intrude on his sorrow with her American accent. But she would. After all, that was why they were here, wasn't it? To intrude on his private grief, make it public, get answers to questions that had gone unanswered for too long.

He took one last sweeping look at the view, then turned his back on it. Amanda Lyons, his executive assistant, stood in the doorway to the observation deck, brushing back her long, dark hair as the wind tried to blind her with it. The warm tan of her skin suddenly made Jonathan yearn for California.

For home.

'Yes, Amanda,' he said. 'I take it they've arrived?'

She glanced back over her shoulder, as though she could see down the stairwell to check on their 'guests'.

They were in the Tolbooth, a large arts venue at the top of Stirling, close to the castle. The original meeting place of Stirling Burgh Council, the ornate baronial building had been renovated about twenty years ago and transformed into an arts and entertainment venue. Everything from music gigs to book festivals had been held in the building, and today, Jonathan Rodriguez was going to use it for another sort of entertainment, by bringing the media circus to town.

'Best not keep them waiting, then,' he said. They descended a narrow staircase, the sound of conversation, the hustle and bustle of cameras being set up and spotlights positioned rising to meet them. The room they had booked in the Tolbooth was a large, atrium-style space that could accommodate around forty journalists, all of whom would be plied with as much coffee and as many biscuits as they could endure. When planning this event, Amanda had suggested they hold it at the university, using Airthrey Loch at the heart of the campus as the backdrop. Jonathan had rejected the idea: it was too painful a place for him to visit.

Yet.

Amanda led him into a small anteroom behind the atrium where she had set up her laptop and printer. She crossed to the table, picked up a sheaf of papers, and handed them to him. 'Your speech,' she said. 'It'll run to eight minutes. Then we can open up to questions.'

He took the papers from her, then placed them back on the table.

'I'll do this one from memory,' he said, even as he saw unease tighten her face.

'You really think that's a good idea?'

'It'll be fine,' he said. 'Been rehearsing this in my head for months. Just do me one favour. Make sure the first question is from that reporter we spoke about.'

Amanda nodded, a smile playing at the corners of her mouth. 'Don't worry,' she said. 'I checked before I came up to the roof to get you. Donna Blake is here, and I've made sure she's got a nice cosy seat in the front row. You won't be able to miss her.'

CHAPTER 4

Connor's new phone started chirping the moment he slid the SIM card into it and powered it up. It wasn't surprising. After breaking his old phone on the face of a would-be robber, he had spent the next two hours with the police, patiently answering their questions on how he had prevented an armed robbery in the middle of the day in one of Edinburgh's busiest shopping malls. After finally agreeing a statement, he was released from Gayfield Square police station just off Leith Walk and headed back to the St James Quarter to retrieve his car. When he got to it, he pulled the SIM from his damaged phone and swapped it into a spare handset he kept in the Audi's glove compartment.

Security work. It was murder on his phone bills.

He checked the screen, saw he had seven voicemails and about twice that number of text messages, mostly from Jen, which ranged from 'Was that you in Edinburgh?' and 'Are you okay?' to 'Call me now. I'm worried. Love you.'

He winced at the last. Jen had been through enough in the last couple of years, from losing their unborn child to almost being killed in a hit-and-run accident that had left her with spinal injuries and mobility issues. The last thing she needed was him adding to her stress by going dark on her when he got into a dangerous situation. He was thumbing through his contacts list to her number when the phone rang. Connor cursed under his breath. The call was about as inevitable as it was unwelcome.

'DCI Ford,' he said, trying to keep his voice neutral. 'How are you doing today?'

A heavy sigh. When Ford spoke, he sounded tired, old. Connor could almost see him at his desk, hunched over the phone, rubbing at his eyes.

'I read the reports on your antics at the St James Quarter,' Ford said. 'Nice work. Though I do wonder when you're going to get it through your thick head that you're not a police officer any more and should leave the confronting of armed individuals to us.'

Connor closed his eyes, felt the machete blade cut the air in front of him. Shivered. How close had it come? Millimetres? How close had he been to serious injury? 'Didn't really have the time to call for back-up, sir,' Connor replied, forcing the thoughts down. 'Things just kind of got out of hand.'

'Story of your bloody life that, isn't it?'

Connor shifted in his seat. It was hard to argue. 'Look, sir, if—'

Ford grunted. 'Forget it. From what I've read and seen you did good work. Though I understand the Lothian area commander isn't too happy that you bagged two armed robbers who've been leading him on a merry dance around the city for the last month.'

'Just lucky,' Connor said. 'Anyway, sir, if there's nothing else, I really should be getting on the road home.'

A moment's silence on the line, just long enough to tell Connor that Ford was making some kind of decision.

'You been watching the news?' the policeman said eventually, sounding even more exhausted now.

Odd, Connor thought. It was unlikely Ford was talking about whatever headlines his antics at St James Quarter had generated, and since DCI Malcolm Ford wasn't the type to follow the latest celebrity non-story gossip, that left . . .

'You don't mean all that stuff with the university professor, do you? The Robert Balfour case?'

'That's exactly what I mean,' Ford said. 'His son could make life very difficult for us, and I need you to do me a favour.'

'Oh,' Connor said, the first glimmers of unease flashing in the back of his mind. 'And what would that be?'

Another pause, the sound of Ford drinking something. Connor would have laid even money on either coffee or whisky.

'I need you to look at the case. Coldly. Dispassionately. And then I need you to tell me if Jonathan Rodriguez is right in claiming that Central Scotland Police were involved in a cover-up back in the eighties and his dad really was murdered.'

The unease Connor had felt hardened into dread. He knew the case, of course – anyone who had been online or near a TV in the last month would. And it didn't make pleasant reading for anyone who wore a policeman's uniform in Central Scotland.

Back in 1983, Robert Balfour had been a professor of history at Stirling University. He was found floating in Airthrey Loch at the heart of the university campus on 22 July. His death was initially dismissed as a tragic accident: Balfour was known to be a heavy drinker whose marriage was collapsing around his ears. Interviews with his colleagues had shown that he had taken to drinking himself into oblivion in his office and sleeping there overnight. The consensus was backed up by a post-mortem examination that showed he had nothing in his stomach other than what was almost a bottle of whisky, and a contusion over his left temple. In a drunken stupor, he had apparently staggered out onto the campus, slipped and hit his head as he fell into the loch, where he had drowned. Tributes were paid and the death of a 'well-respected, talented and dedicated academic' was mourned.

But then, two months after his death, another story emerged.

It broke in an interview with one of Balfour's students that ran in the *Sunday Gazette*, one of Scotland's main Sunday broadsheets back in the eighties. In it, the student, Jamie Leggatt, alleged that Balfour's death wasn't a tragic accident but rather a state-sponsored execution. Leggatt claimed Balfour had told him he was being monitored by Special Branch due to his support for Scottish independence and his work to prove that Scottish resources were being used to prop up the rest of the UK. And while the allegations were dismissed by the government at the time as the ranting of an over-politicised student, they were enough to get the attention of senior nationalist politicians, who lodged parliamentary questions on the matter and demanded 'justice for Robert Balfour'. As the campaign gained momentum, it emerged that Balfour had been a key supporter of students who had protested against the Queen when she visited Stirling University in October 1978.

But while the story grabbed some immediate headlines, it struggled in the pre-social media, clickbait news landscape of the eighties and faded away, dismissed as just another conspiracy theory. Until last month, when Jonathan Rodriguez stepped onto centre stage.

Rodriguez had only been nine when his father had died and his mother, Elaine, had left Scotland to start a new life in America, where her sister had emigrated after marrying a US soldier. Rodriguez, who had taken the name of the man her mother had met and married in Los Angeles, had forged a career as a TV presenter and news anchor. He was a household name on the west coast of the US, where Americans welcomed him into their homes five mornings a week. And now, with the fortieth anniversary of his father's death looming, Jonathan Rodriguez had returned to Scotland to make a special documentary on Robert Balfour's death. It would include 'a series of explosive revelations that expose state collusion and a police-led cover-up' of what had happened. It was a huge story, US daytime-TV royalty visiting Scotland on a pilgrimage to discover the truth about his father's death. Press interest was so high that Rodriguez had called a conference in Stirling that morning. Connor vaguely remembered Donna Blake, his friend who worked for Sky News, mentioning it to him the previous day.

It suddenly felt like a long, long time ago.

Connor blinked, realised Ford was speaking. 'Sorry, sir, what was that? Signal got a bit patchy there.'

Ford sighed. 'I said, can you get to Randolphfield station? I can brief you on what we've got so far, and where this could go. I've got the chief constable crawling up my arse on it, but I need to know if there's any chance that what Rodriguez is alleging is true.'

Connor had known Ford for a few years now, had come to respect a policeman who put pragmatism before policy and refused to take the path of least resistance in pursuit of a quieter life. But, still, he was meant to be moving out of his flat this weekend, and into his new home with Jen. Could he really ask her to allow him to put his work before their relationship again? More importantly, did he want to?

He already knew what the answer was, and how the conversation with Jen would go. 'I'll be there in an hour or so,' he said, as he fired up the Audi.

'Okay,' Ford said, his tone telling Connor he wasn't happy with the response but wouldn't push his luck.

Connor killed the call before the policeman could say anything else, put the car in gear and started to drive. His plan was to get out of the underground car park, then phone Jen, tell her he was all right, and what Ford had just asked of him. He had his opening lines worked out, was just about to hit dial when his phone pinged with another text.

Connor felt a headache begin to form at the base of his skull as he opened the message and read it: *Just been at the presser for Jonathan Rodriguez. You will not believe what happened. Call me when you can, need to talk. Dx*

'Donna,' Connor muttered, as he pressed down on the accelerator. 'I should have bloody known.'

CHAPTER 5

Simon McCartney watched as Jen MacKenzie answered her mobile phone, felt the sudden urge to be elsewhere when he saw her straighten and smile, then slump forward and lean on her crutch as the conversation unfolded. He was too far away to hear what was being said, but he didn't need to. One of the advantages of being a police detective: he could read body language a mile off. And right now, Jen's body was screaming one word.

Disappointment.

He turned away from her, unwilling to intrude on her call, busied himself with the task at hand – packing books from a shelf in the living room of Connor Fraser's flat into a box to be transported to their new home. He had agreed to help Jen while Connor was at work and, from the look of her, that work would take longer than had been expected.

He looked around the flat, wondering again if it would ever truly feel like his home. When Connor had told him of his plan to buy a place with Jen, it had forced Simon to confront a truth he had been hiding from in the months he had been staying in Scotland: he didn't want to go back to Northern Ireland. He had initially taken leave of absence from the PSNI and travelled to Scotland to help Connor with a case but, as time passed, he had slowly come to realise that he was increasingly seeing Stirling, not Belfast, as home. He couldn't really say why. Other than Connor, Jen and Donna Blake, he didn't really know anyone in Scotland, and it wasn't as if his time in the city had been quiet or relaxing. And yet there was something about the place that had got under his skin. So he had come to a deal with Connor: he would rent the flat from him when he moved out, and put in for a transfer to Police Scotland from the PSNI. He had turned down Connor's offer of a consultancy job with his company, Sentinel Securities, but he wondered if that might be where he ended up when DCI Malcolm Ford heard of his plans to join Police Scotland.

He heard the click of Jen's crutch on the floor, turned to see her walking towards him, the knuckles of her left hand flushed with the effort of leaning on the crutch.

'That Connor, was it?' he asked. 'He okay after his heroics in Edinburgh?'

Jen's face twitched into a smile that didn't fit on her face. It looked fragile, cautious, almost pained. 'Says he's going to be a little later, got to see the police about a case. He's sorry, will get here as soon as he can.'

Simon nodded. 'No bother,' he said. 'Happy to help. And, besides, the faster I get the two of you out of my place and put it into some type of order the better.'

Another misplaced smile, then Jen's eyes slid away from his. She let out a deep breath, adjusted her grip on her crutch. Without thinking, Simon stepped forward, placed a hand under her elbow. 'Think maybe we should sit down for a wee bit?' he asked. 'Don't know about you, but I could do with a break.'

She laughed at that, and Simon heard the old Jen. Full of life and mischief, unwilling to let what had happened to her define her.

Simon lifted another box of books from the couch, then helped her to sit. He noticed she was sweating and flushed, and shifted position, trying to get comfortable.

'Bad today?' he said.

'Bad as any other,' she said, propping her crutch beside her and flexing her hand slowly. 'The joys of three ruptured vertebrae, a dislocated pelvis, broken ribs and a concussion.'

Simon winced internally. Jen didn't talk often about the hit-and-run that had almost cost her her life, and he respected her decision.

But, hearing the hard edge of resentment in her voice, he wondered if talking about it was exactly what she needed.

'Listen, you take a rest,' he said. 'I'll make us a cuppa, then I can crack on while you supervise.'

He jumped as she slammed her fist into the couch. 'Dammit, Simon,' she snapped, her voice cold and flat. 'I'm not a bloody cripple. I can do this!'

A moment of stunned silence and she looked away from him, sudden tears diluting the fury in her eyes.

'Jen, I'm sorry, I . . .'

She wiped her eyes, then held up a hand. 'No, Simon,' she said softly. 'I'm sorry. It's just . . . well, all of this,' she gestured around the room, 'and now Connor's too busy with work to help. And I'm . . . I'm . . .' She shook her head, as though the words were forming in her mouth but she couldn't bring herself to spit them out.

'It's all right,' Simon said. 'I get it. Moving in with someone is a lot at any time, but after everything you've been through? Course it's a big deal, especially when . . .'

She nodded, silent gratitude in her eyes. They had never talked about it, but Connor had told Simon enough for him to guess what she was feeling. She had been a personal trainer before she had been run over, her entire career dedicated to fitness and strength. Now her body was a traitor, unable to perform at the level it once had. The old Jen would have been juggling boxes and throwing furniture into vans, but the Jen her accident had made her was unable to do those things. And Simon could see that the realisation of that, and of what she had lost, was haunting her.

'I'm sure the big lad will be here as soon as he can,' he said. 'And when he gets here, we'll make sure he's got all the most awkward bastard bits of furniture to move, right?'

She sniffed a laugh, smiled at him. 'Bloody right we will,' she said, even as her eyes grew dark and serious. 'It's just work, though, isn't it, Simon? He's not using the job to avoid me, and us moving in together?'

Simon felt a sudden jolt run through him. 'Catch yerself on!' he snapped, just a little too loudly. 'The man's crazy about you. But you know what he's like about work, and if it's DCI Ford asking to see him, he can't really say no, can he?'

'I guess not,' Jen said, with a shrug. 'I just don't want him doing this out of pity, Simon. I told him that when I got hurt. And this,' she gestured around the flat again, 'this is a big step.'

'Sure it is,' Simon replied. 'But Connor wants to take it. With you. Believe me.'

'Yeah,' Jen said. 'Yeah.'

CHAPTER 6

Randolphfield police station was hunkered at the top of a low hill just off St Ninians Road, a squat concrete-and-brick monument to brutalist architecture, the dirt-stained grey of the walls made all the more depressing by a vibrant blue and silver 'Police Scotland' awning that hung over the main entrance.

Connor couldn't decide if it was meant as a message for the public or a warning.

He asked for Ford at the main reception desk, was met a few moments later by the policeman's junior officer, DS John Troughton. With his nondescript dark suit, conservative tie and haircut that looked like he'd had it since childhood, Troughton was the definition of 'forgettable'. Yet Connor had seen his work on a few cases, and had been impressed by his quiet determination and ability to chip away at a problem until he found the answer. He was, Connor thought, exactly the type of officer Police Scotland wanted these days – quiet, inoffensive, forgettable and efficient.

Hell, he'd probably be chief constable one day.

'DCI Ford will see you in his office,' Troughton said, by way of a greeting, then gestured for Connor to follow him through a security door into the heart of the station. Ford's office was on the first floor at the back of the building, just off a large room Connor knew would be used for major investigations. He passed a few officers who gave him an appraising look, again wondering why Ford had asked to meet him so publicly.

A question, he realised, that the conversation he had had with Donna Blake as he had driven here had only clarified in his mind.

'Ah, Fraser,' Ford said, as Troughton ushered him into the office. 'Take a seat, will you? You want coffee?'

The thought of drinking a cup of the volcanic brew Ford served gave Connor a vicarious caffeine rush. 'No, thanks, sir,' he said.

Ford shifted in his seat at the opposite side of a paper-strewn desk. 'Thanks, John. That'll be all.'

'Yes, sir,' Troughton said, unable to keep his disappointment out of his voice.

Ford waited for the door to close, then leaned forward, flat eyes on Connor. 'You're probably wondering why I asked to meet here, in front of my officers,' he said, his tone indicating that it was a statement of fact rather than a question.

'The thought did occur to me,' Connor replied. 'I mean, it's not like I've always had the best of relationships with Police Scotland, and I doubt the chief constable is going to be happy when he hears I've been speaking to one of his senior officers about a sensitive issue.'

Ford's face twitched into something that was more sneer than smile. It was common knowledge he was no fan of Peter Guthrie, Police Scotland's chief constable, but the naked contempt in his eyes at that moment surprised Connor.

'Jumped up little paper-pusher,' Ford said. 'More worried about how he can brown-nose the First Minister than getting any real policing done.' He cleared his throat. 'But, much as it pains me to admit, he's part of the reason you're here.'

Connor blinked. Interesting. 'Really?' he said.

Ford nodded. 'When Rodriguez started to make his claims about what happened to his dad or, more accurately, when he started to make his claims in the press, Guthrie contacted me. Asked what I knew about the case, then told me to do a bit of digging into it, see if there was any truth in the rumours. Said he didn't want any skeletons falling out of cupboards, told me I could use any resource I saw fit, including an independent third party. He initially suggested the investigative reporter DS Drummond knows, Doug MacGregor, but with her on leave and him God knows where, your name came up.'

Connor smiled. It made sense now. Guthrie might have been a brown-nosing bureaucrat, but he'd just proven himself to be a smart one.

'What?' Ford asked, noticing Connor's smile.

'Makes sense of a conversation I had on the way here, sir,' Connor said. 'With Donna Blake.'

Something hardened in Ford's eyes. 'What about Donna Blake?' he asked.

'Well, she was at the press conference Jonathan Rodriguez held in town,' Connor said. 'Seems he gave her the first question, which she used to ask him about what he hoped to get out of what he was doing, whether he wanted to see anyone charged. He gave a fairly noncommittal reply, from what she said, but then, when the press conference was over, his assistant asked her backstage for a further briefing with Rodriguez. That was when my name came up. Seems he'd been told by, ah, a source that I had been contacted by a senior police officer to look into the police handling of the case at the time. He then asked Donna if she could put him in touch with me.'

Ford stared at Connor, then leaned back in his chair, glancing up at a ceiling that might have been cured in nicotine stains over the years. 'Slippery wee bastard,' he whispered.

'If you mean Chief Constable Guthrie, I'm forced to agree,' Connor said. 'I take it you told no one else you were going to contact me before the fact so he must have told Rodriguez's people that you were bringing me in. Makes sense, I guess. Makes him look like he's not scared of the truth, and also underlines that anything I find, if there really is anything to find, isn't from an official police investigation so can be treated with a degree of scepticism.'

'Bastard,' Ford whispered again. 'I take it, though, that you're not going to get in touch with Rodriguez.'

'Not yet,' Connor said, his mind drifting to Jen and the growing need to get home and help her with the move. 'I've got other things to do, and I don't want to talk to him or Donna until I've had a chance to look at whatever case files you can give me.'

Ford took his gaze from the ceiling, focused on Connor. He leaned down, the sound of an old wooden drawer squealing open very loud in the quiet of the office. When he straightened, he was holding an old-style manila folder, bulging with what looked like photographs.

'Here it is. Balfour, Professor Robert J. Found dead in Airthrey Loch, Stirling University, twenty-second of July 1983. Cause of death was deemed to be misadventure after he fell into the loch while intoxicated.'

'You buy that?' Connor asked, as he took the file Ford offered him.

'I'm not selling,' Ford said. 'The question is, if I was, would you be in the market? Look, Fraser, I know there's going to be press attention on this, and it's clear Guthrie is already moving to cover his arse no matter what happens. I don't really care about that. But I care about this.' He pointed towards the file. 'Now, either Balfour's son is just looking for a way to justify his father's death or something nasty's going on here.'

He paused, looked over Connor's shoulder, as though seeing an old friend there. When he spoke again, his voice was low, hoarse with something more mournful than regret. 'I mean, it wasn't unheard of for reports to be lost, witnesses forgotten, statements changed to get the result that the powers that be wanted. But I don't care about that. If there's a case to answer in there, I want to know about it. Not because Rodriguez has brought Hollywood to town and whipped the press into a frenzy, not to give Guthrie a nice story to sell to the First Minister over tea and scones, but because it matters.'

Typical Ford, Connor thought. No matter how hard he tried to portray himself as the cynical, world-weary policeman who had seen it all, he could never fully hide his desire to see the job done right and justice served.

'Any hints as to where to start with all this?' Connor asked, as he started to leaf through the file.

Ford shrugged. 'Your call,' he said. 'But if I were you, I'd take a look at the statements made by Balfour's student, Jamie Leggatt, the one who first claimed there was more to the death. You may find you want to talk to him a bit more.'

Connor ran a quick calculation in his mind. Yes, Leggatt could indeed still be alive. He'd be pushing his sixties now, no age at all really. 'He's local?' he asked.

Ford grimaced. 'I'd hesitate to call Dundee local, but that's the last address we've got for him. Seems he took Balfour's lectures to heart.'

'How so?'

'He's a history lecturer in Dundee,' Ford replied. 'Seems Balfour inspired at least one of his students to follow in his footsteps.'

CHAPTER 7

He felt nothing. And, in acknowledging that, he felt it all.

The stiff collar of his shirt and his tie were choking him – a hangman's noose masquerading as formal attire. He swallowed the urge to loosen them, straightened his back, forced himself to look straight ahead at the one thing he did not want to see.

A marble plinth, about four feet tall, stood in front of him, a lectern off to its right. Around the plinth was what looked like a velvet tent, the front of which was pinned open, revealing a patch of some deeper darkness that seemed to mock the fingers of light that streamed into the room from the large windows in the ceiling.

Unable to bear the gaping maw, he looked down at what he was holding in numb hands that seemed to twitch in time with his heartbeat. He didn't remember picking up the pamphlet, felt tears burn his eyes and the noose around his neck tighten as he studied the face on the cover. Eyes full of humour and life gazed back at him and, in his mind, he could hear the voice that went with those eyes – soft, gentle, with just a hint of mockery.

Come on now. We both knew it would come to this one day. Eyes forward, there's still work to be done.

He looked away, swallowed the shard of ice that seemed to have formed in his throat, instantly regretted it as a fierce thirst gripped him. He wished he could just run away, flee this horror before it went too far and became too real. Knew he could not. Would not. Not when there was still work to be done.

A small, compact woman in a dark business suit caught his eye, nodded. He tried to remember her name. Diane? He'd spoken to her a few times over the last week, getting details of the ceremony right, talking about the life that had been taken far too soon, the life she would speak about in a few short moments. But how could she? he thought. All she knew was what he had told her, his memories and sanitised anecdotes. How could they convey what he had lost in a short speech delivered by a stranger?

She nodded to him again. 'Would everyone please stand,' she said, as a soft, orchestral tune he vaguely recognised started to play. He felt as though the sun streaming into the chapel was trying to push him back into his seat, and turned to see a room full of faces following his gaze towards the entrance doors.

An electric jolt of panic seized him as he saw the pallbearers enter the chapel, the coffin on their shoulders. He had wanted to carry it himself, wanted, needed, to feel the weight of it on his shoulders, but he had been told that the terms of the service had already been set, and that it was an express wish that he was not to carry the coffin at any costs.

He wondered how he should feel about that.

The pallbearers walked slowly up the aisle, a perverse procession in black, their faces somewhere between neutral and sympathetic. Again, the urge to run away seized him, sudden and almost over-powering. Instead, he leaned forward, grabbed the back of the hard wooden bench he had been sitting on, and squeezed until he felt the ancient, varnished wood begin to flex beneath his grip.

After what seemed an eternity, the pallbearers reached their des-tination and slowly lowered the coffin onto the plinth. Then they stepped away, bowed their heads and backed off, as though they had made an offering to an ancient, vengeful god.

Maybe they had.

The celebrant, Debbie, he suddenly remembered, spoke: 'Please,' she said as the music began to fade, 'be seated.'

A stolen moment for one last look around. He didn't know if he was consciously looking for her, but his eyes found her regardless. Sitting there, her beauty at once somehow accentuated and diminished by the grief etched onto her face. Not for the person in the coffin, but for him. She knew what this loss meant to him, what it would do to him. And in that moment, he loved and hated her for it.

He sat, forced himself to look ahead, unable to get the image of her face out of his head. Felt a maelstrom of emotions churn through him as flashes of memory danced across his mind's eye before they returned to her, always her.

He closed his eyes, felt the first tear slide down his cheek as the celebrant began to speak. Took a deep, hitching breath, then forced himself to focus on the coffin. Nothing more. The celebrant's words faded away, indistinct static washing through his mind. He felt the first spark of rage then, as cold and unyielding as the blade he had strapped to his ankle. He had seen the death certificate, knew that the official cause of death was 'cardiac arrest and vascular dementia', knew that for the lie it was.

This death was on Jonathan Rodriguez's hands. He had watched the press conference he had held that morning, barely able to suppress the urge to rip the TV from the wall and hurl it across the room. Rodriguez, with his preconceptions and notions of avenging his father's name, blundering back into Scotland like a toddler waddling into a sandpit, unaware of the monsters he was daring to wake from their slumber.

The weight of the knife on his leg seemed to intensify, anchoring him to the floor as the service droned on. He was dimly aware of music, and instructions to stand. He did so, eyes fixed on the coffin in front of him. A song began, one he had heard countless times over the years. It had been the backdrop to discussions on history, literature, art, life. Conversations that were never to be had again. In that moment, he decided he would play the song to his next victim before he plunged the knife into his heart and ended him like the animal he was.

There was, after all, still work to be done. And he would enjoy every moment of it.

CHAPTER 8

Before heading back to the flat, Connor took a short detour to the new house. It was less than ten minutes from his flat on Park Terrace, at the end of a short, gravelled lane that branched off from Windsor Terrace. It was typical of the architecture of the area, a grand old sandstone-and-granite villa, glowing a dull gold in the evening light. He had been lucky to find the place, only knowing it had come on the market thanks to a call from Robbie Lindsay, one of Connor's assistants at Sentinel. Looking back on it, Connor should have known better. He had made an offhand comment to Robbie about looking for a house in the area for him and Jen to move into and renovate, and two days later, Robbie had presented him with the details of the house he now stood in front of. Four bedrooms, detached, with a garage-workshop grafted to the side and a basement that would be ideal for a gym. When Connor had questioned Robbie on how he had found the place, he was met with a grin that, had he not known Robbie better, he would have mistaken for bashful. But he did know Robbie. A former call handler with Police Scotland, Robbie had joined Sentinel five years ago, and quickly proven himself a talented and creative investigator who could track down the most obscure facts with only the vaguest of clues.

'I, ah, I started looking for properties in the area, within five miles of your flat,' Robbie said. 'I cross-referenced that with recent death notices and the property pages. Didn't take long to find the place.

29

Seems a widower lived there, unwilling to leave though his wife had died fifteen years ago. I'm guessing the place is going to need a lot of work, but that's what you're looking for, isn't it? And the old boy's only family is a daughter in Canada, so I'm guessing she'll want a quick sale.'

It took only a few calls to get in touch with the daughter of the house's owner and then her lawyers. As Robbie had suspected, Margaret McAllister had no interest in holding on to the home her father, Paul Angus, had had for so long. From what scant detail he was able to glean from her lawyers, Margaret McAllister had fled to Canada to get away from her father, and wanted nothing more from him in death than she had in life. So a deal had been done and Connor had purchased the house.

And then he had learned what the term 'money pit' meant.

He had known any property he bought would incur expenses as he installed ramps, grab rails and all the other equipment he needed to make Jen comfortable as she continued her rehabilitation. What he hadn't counted on was buying a house that had not been troubled by a paintbrush or a hammer for many years. So, over the following months, Connor had gutted the house, from rotten floorboards and sagging stair risers to ripping out the kitchen and bathrooms. Eventually he had looked at the skip sitting in front of the house, had seen in it the remnants of the old kitchen units. It was worth it, he'd told himself. And, finally, it was done. All he needed to do now was finish packing up his flat and Jen's place, move in, and then maybe he could have a little peace.

He snorted. Peace? It was a nice idea, but futile, especially now that DCI Ford had landed him with a review of the Balfour case. Part of him wanted to turn the job down – with the media interest the story was generating and the machinations of the chief constable, there was no way he'd be able to do his work quietly. But when he had read the details of the case, of a bereaved mother packing up her son and heading for a new life in the United States, he had been reminded of the house he couldn't quite see as a home yet.

Was that why he had come here? he wondered. Or was he just using it as an excuse not to head home? He knew Jen was upset with

30

him, had heard as much in her voice when he had called her to tell her he would be late. But was there something more to it? The closer they got to moving, the more restless he found himself. And now here they were. A refurbished house, Simon set to move into his old flat, a new life beckoning. A life shared. Connor hadn't lived with anyone for almost eight years, not since his last relationship had imploded along with the rest of his old life in Belfast. Was that what scared him? The prospect of opening up? Sharing his life completely?

The vibration of his phone in his pocket roused him from his thoughts. He pulled it out, winced at the sight of the caller ID.

'Paulie,' he said slowly. 'How you doing?'

'Thought you were going to get back to me about that van,' Paulie King barked. 'Sorry, Paulie,' Connor replied, rubbing his eyes. 'Day got away from me a bit. Tomorrow still okay? Say nine a.m. at the flat?'

'Aye,' Paulie rumbled. 'Just make sure you're there, and not fucking around with your pal in the polis instead.'

Connor started. 'How did you . . .' He stopped himself. A lieutenant for Jen's father, Duncan MacKenzie, Paulie King had a reputation as a fearsome enforcer and a man who was not afraid to shed others' blood to get what he wanted. Connor had had a few run-ins with him over the years, and while Paulie's love of Jen had cooled the seething hatred he harboured for Connor, he knew that the man's patience was best not tested.

'Look, I hear things,' Paulie said. 'I know you went to see Ford today and it was probably about that story up at the university. I personally don't give a toss, but don't let it get in the way of getting Jen moved into that house, okay?'

'Aye,' Connor replied, as he pushed down a flash of anger. Getting into a pissing match with Paulie was pointless – especially when, deep down, he knew the man was right.

Connor ended the call, took a last look at the house. Tried to imagine him and Jen living there, making the place a home. Found the images that came to him were pale, distorted, like echoes of almost-forgotten memories rather than hopes for the future.

'Stop being an arse, Connor,' he muttered to himself, as he headed for the car. It would be all right, he told himself, as he got into the Audi and fired the engine. It was just nerves. He had never liked change, and moving house was a significant one.

He put the car into gear, glanced to the passenger seat and the folder Ford had given him. Looked ahead, out of the windscreen. He should get home to Jen, help with the packing. That was what he needed: routine, something familiar to calm his nerves. Some time with Jen. Maybe a workout.

And yet . . .

He sighed, reached across for the folder. Picked it up and started leafing through it. What was it Ford had said? *I'd take another look at Jamie Leggatt's statements.*

Connor found the pages he needed. Checked the dashboard clock. Told himself ten minutes wouldn't hurt.

Was still telling himself that forty minutes later when the light began to fade, and he switched on the reading light in the car.

CHAPTER 9

A knife is only truly yours once the blade has tasted you.

The memory of the words seemed to fill the room, scream from the sepia-stained shadows the streetlights cast into it. He could hear them whisper to him in the rasp of the blade on the sharpening steel.

After the funeral, he had returned home as quickly as he could, wanting to be away from the sympathy, the condolences and understanding that seemed to roll off the congregation in foetid waves, threatening to choke him more effectively than the noose-like tie around his neck ever could. He had exchanged a glance with her as he moved slowly but deliberately through the crowd, shaking hands, smiling, heading for the door. The look in her eyes told him she knew the pain he was feeling. He couldn't articulate how wrong she was.

Once home, he locked the doors, drew the curtains, retreated to his study and the laptop, then stripped off his suit and freed the knife from its leg strap. He retrieved the sharpening stone and oil from his desk drawer and began to work on the blade.

And that was when he had heard the words of a ghost, whispering to him from across a gulf of years, pulling him back to another place. Another time.

What, he thought with a sudden smile, would Jonathan Rodriguez think if he could see that scene? They had been in the woods behind Blairlogie, a small village just over a mile east of the Stirling University campus. They often went there for lessons that could never be found on a university curriculum – lessons that were all the more valuable for it.

He had been sharpening a stick when the knife slipped. There was nothing at first, just a sudden warmth running across his finger, but then the blood started to flow, rich as wine, and he lunged for the stream.

Balfour had followed him, inspected the wound when he had raised his hand from the water. A long, deep cut down his middle finger, almost as though he had been trying to sharpen it like a spear. He still had the scar. 'A knife is only truly yours once the blade has tasted you,' Balfour had said, nodding at his own wisdom, which only seemed to reveal itself when the stench of whisky was thick on his breath.

He blinked away the thought, concentrated on the matter at hand. The press conference had been well covered in the media, with video footage, reports and pictures. One, in particular, caught his attention, held it, as he recognised figures on the screen. The first was a tall, dark-haired woman talking to one of the reporters at the press conference. A quick trawl of Rodriguez's website told him the woman was Amanda Lyons, his executive assistant. The other woman, the one he recognised, was Donna Blake, a reporter for Sky TV. He clicked through the gallery to a shot of Blake and Lyons walking out of the room, shoulder to shoulder. He considered, then flicked over to the Sky website, and a piece Blake had written. It was mostly a wrap-up of the press conference, Rodriguez's claims that his father's death was a murder that had been covered up, dark vows to 'unmask the perpetrators with explosive revelations that would be detailed in the coming days'.

He paused his sharpening, considered the blade. Oh, yes, there would be revelations in the days ahead, of that there was no doubt. Somehow he doubted Jonathan Rodriguez would enjoy them. But to make sure of that, to make sure justice was served and the truth finally revealed, he would need an ally. A friend.

And, by appearing in those pictures with Rodriguez's assistant, Donna Blake had just made herself his number-one volunteer.

CHAPTER 10

The text arrived at just before 6 a.m. and, if he was honest, Simon had been expecting it to arrive earlier.

Early workout? Lawson's? Pads? Heading there now.

Simon eased himself up in bed. He had known this was coming since Connor had got back to the flat last night, had read it in his friend's distracted expression as they dismantled furniture and packed boxes, seen it in the moments when he would stop and stare into the middle distance, as though he had been unplugged from the world. Simon had tried to keep the evening casual, but he had seen the worry etched into Jen's face. She knew Connor as well as he did, could sense the change in him, the moment when a case would rise to the top of his thoughts and crowd out everything else.

And Connor Fraser's favourite way of clearing his head was hitting the gym.

It was, he had told Simon once, a legacy from his grandfather. A mechanic in Newtownards east of Belfast, Jimmy O'Brien had forged his body in a small, homemade gym at the back of his garage. When Connor had travelled to Belfast to study at the university, Jimmy had taken to training him, instilling a love of weight training and the discipline it required. It was one of the first subjects Connor and Simon had bonded over when they were partnered together in the PSNI, Connor taking Simon through training sessions and Simon repaying him by training him in mixed martial arts and boxing. Over the years, Simon had watched Connor evolve into a formidable fighter blessed with bulk and an almost freakish speed and grace. But there was also a rage in him, a fury he rarely spoke about that could, when ignited, drive him to obsession.

Simon made a mental calculation, then thumbed in a reply: *See you in 20 minutes. Just go easy on me, huh?*

He levered himself out of bed, winced at the soft groan and the covers moving next to him.

'Whoosat?' Donna Blake asked, her voice thick with sleep, her eyes still closed.

'No one. Got to go to work,' Simon said gently, leaning back over the bed to kiss her forehead.

'Call me later,' she said, snuggling into the covers again.

Simon watched her for a moment, her breath slowing and deepening. She had ended up working a double shift at Sky the night before, covering first the Balfour story, then a fire in an office block in Falkirk. Her parents had, reluctantly, agreed to keep her son, Andrew, with them overnight, freeing Donna to get a full night's sleep without having to worry about the school run the following morning. It also gave her and Simon the chance to spend some time together.

Simon smiled, watching her sleep as he dressed. It had started six months ago, after a case that had seen her kidnapped and held by a lunatic with a God complex. Simon often wondered if that was what had sparked things between them – the forced intimacy of facing a killer together or the realisation that he would do anything to protect her. Either way, they had gone through the looking glass, crossing the boundary between friendship and something more intense than Simon had known before. He had tried to keep things casual, keep the jokes going and the tone light, but he could see in her eyes that she felt the same way. And he wasn't quite sure what he thought about that.

He left the flat quietly, got into his car. Lawson's was little more than an industrial unit filled with weights, heavy bags and a martial-arts dojo. At that time of the morning, traffic was almost non-existent, and Simon made the journey to the industrial estate on the western edge of the city in fifteen minutes. He saw Connor's Audi already parked, wondered how long he had been there before he had decided to text.

He let himself into the dojo, found Connor hammering away at a heavy bag with a flurry of kicks and punches. The bag convulsed under the force of the blows, the chains holding it to the ceiling jangling as it bucked and swung.

'What did that bag ever do to you?' Simon called, as he took off his trainers then reached into his kit bag for his hand wraps and gloves.

Connor turned. 'Thanks for coming,' he said. 'Just wanted to get out of the flat, get a workout in before Paulie turns up with the van.'

'Aye, and I'm sure Jen loved you sneaking out,' Simon said, as he wrapped his hands.

Connor looked away, embarrassed. 'I'll be back in plenty of time,' he said.

'Aye, bloody right you will,' Simon said. 'Because if you're late, it'll be me who gets the blame, just like last night. What kept you, anyway?'

Connor shrugged, his eyes taking on the same disconnected look Simon had seen the night before. 'I got caught up in this case Ford has me looking into – you know, the one Donna was covering yesterday.'

'Oh, aye,' Simon said slowly. That he was seeing Donna was sensitive, especially as Connor had a knack of involving himself in cases that attracted the attention of the press.

Connor held up a hand. 'Didn't ask you here to get an insight into what she knows,' he said, 'but I got reading, and I think there might be something in Jonathan Rodriguez's claims that the police knew more about his dad's death than they let on at the time.'

'Oh,' Simon said, as he stepped onto the mats and dropped into a guard. 'How so?'

Connor smiled. 'Sparring first, then the case,' he said. 'But one question – how much do you know about Irish whiskey and petechial haemorrhaging?'

Simon was still trying to understand the question when Connor threw his first punch.

CHAPTER 11

Donna woke up about half an hour after Simon left, cursing herself for not rising when he did and reminding him that she needed to talk to Connor as soon as possible. She rose and headed for the kitchen, unable to stop herself creaking open the door to Andrew's room as she did so. It had been good of her parents to take him for the night, but still, even with Simon's presence, the flat felt somehow empty and incomplete without him.

When she got to the kitchen, she found the coffee machine primed and ready, filter in, urn topped up with fresh water. There was a small Post-it note on a mug to the left of the machine: 'Don't worry, I'll talk to Connor. But no promises. I'm the one sleeping with the enemy after all. Sx'

She took the note, smiled. Typical Simon. He used humour to mask what he was thinking, but she could see he was always one step ahead, working out all the angles on a problem, seeing it from everyone's perspective. It was a skill she admired, and one she wished she could have called upon yesterday when Jonathan Rodriguez had asked for his impromptu meeting.

She had been called aside by Rodriguez's assistant, a woman who wore designer clothes like a second skin and whose deep tan accentuated the clarity of her eyes, the intensity of her gaze. But even Amanda Lyons's heavy accent wasn't as stereotypically Californian as Rodriguez: tall and broad-shouldered, with perfect hair, teeth that gleamed and a tan that made her ache for a beachfront far from Stirling, he looked as if he had just walked off the set of his morning TV show. His smile was warm and welcoming, his gaze totally focused on her in a way that should have been disconcerting but somehow managed to be welcoming instead.

He had told her what he knew about Connor Fraser and her history with him, had shown just the right level of sympathy and gravitas when he touched on the murder of her ex, Mark, on a previous case. 'All of which,' he had said, 'tells me two things, Ms Blake. That Mr Fraser is a talented investigator who doesn't take his work lightly, and you don't back off from a story, no matter how difficult it might get.'

'And you expect this story to get difficult?' she had asked.

He smiled, humour flashing across brown eyes in which Donna was sure she could see the rim of contact lenses. 'If what I've been led to believe by sources is true, then it's as serious as it gets, Ms Blake.'

'Okay,' Donna said. 'So why tell me? And why call a press conference and alert other media to your story? Aren't you afraid they'll scoop you? After all, this is our patch, not yours. Reporters here are better connected, and you've just dangled a hell of a bone for them to chew.'

His smile widened as he nodded enthusiastically. 'Exactly, Ms Blake. And that's why I wanted to see you. Not only do you know Mr Fraser, who has been tasked to look into this case independently, but you're also a highly respected reporter. Getting this story out, telling the truth about my father, is more important to me than the headlines, so I wanted to talk to you, propose a . . . well, a partnership, if you will.'

'Go on,' Donna said warily.

'I have leads and access to information that you don't. But you have the contacts I don't. So I suggest we work together. My station back home, Channel 94, wants daily updates on what I'm doing here, along with collated footage for a wider documentary. Imagine what that would mean to your newsdesk – you reporting on a live investigation of a historical crime as it unfolds. And I'd give you the exclusive, no third parties.'

'Why?' Donna had asked, the vague shape of an answer forming in her mind as she spoke. 'If you wanted to do this exclusively, again, why call a press conference?'

'Because I want those who were involved in my father's death to know I'm coming,' Rodriguez said, the smile disappearing, as though a cloud had blotted out the sun. 'And the more press attention there is on me, the less likely they are to try to shut me up while I'm in the public eye.'

Donna had been unable to bite back the laugh. 'Seriously?' she said. 'You only gave the most general of statements about cover-ups and collusion, nothing to go on. Most of the reporters who attended will report this as the day the American TV host came to town, making big tabloid claims that ultimately will be dismissed as fake news. I know you've been unable to secure a meeting with any minister in the Scottish Government about your claims and, unless you've got something big up your sleeve, this story isn't going to last beyond the next news cycle. But you're claiming someone might be out to get you over this? Really? Come on, Mr Rodriguez.'

The smile returned to his face, colder this time, more calculated.

'I see your point. I'm giving you nothing to go on at the moment. So how about this? Meet me here at ten tomorrow morning, and I'll take you to meet one of the sources who contacted me. You can do it off camera, but if you think there's a story in it, I'll give you the interview and we can go from there. As for Mr Fraser, I'd appreciate talking to him, but I'll leave that to your judgement.'

Donna sipped her coffee, mulling over Rodriguez's words. She didn't like being used, and the fact that he had looked into her background so thoroughly rankled, but she couldn't escape the niggling thought that there was something here to be followed up. Even without his conspiracy theories it was a good story – US celebrity TV host returns to site of father's death on fortieth anniversary in quest for answers and closure. It was a no-brainer.

She looked at the clock on the kitchen wall: 6.30 a.m. Plenty of time to do a little digging, then head to meet Rodriguez in the centre of Stirling. She considered texting Simon, asking him again to talk to Connor, decided against it. She didn't want to put him between her and his best friend.

At least, not yet.

She poured another coffee, headed for her study, had been at her laptop for about twenty minutes, pulling up old stories about the Balfour case and Stirling University, when her phone buzzed on the desk. She frowned, annoyed at the interruption, then picked it up. Saw the message was from her newsdesk at Sky. Opened it. Felt her blood run cold as she read. She rocked back in her seat for a moment, mind racing. Then she keyed in an answer and sprang up, heading for her bedroom to get dressed.

And as she did, she couldn't help but remember Rodriguez's words: *I want those who were involved in my father's death to know I'm coming. And the more press attention there is on me, the less likely they are to try to shut me up while I'm in the public eye.*

She suppressed a shudder, pushed aside the memory. Instead she concentrated on the task in hand, mapping out the fastest route to Stirling University in her head.

CHAPTER 12

After an hour of sparring, in which Connor felt he almost held his own against Simon, they showered and changed, then headed back to the flat. They arrived just before 9 a.m., and Connor wasn't overly surprised to see that a van with the MacKenzie Haulage logo emblazoned on its side was already in the parking bay opposite the front door of the flat. He parked, Simon pulling up beside him, then clambered out of the Audi.

'Well, this'll be fun,' Simon muttered, as he looked at the van. Connor nodded, gave a thin smile. They'd both had their run-ins with Paulie King over the years, knew he wasn't a man to be trifled with.

They made their way down the stairs to the flat, found Paulie sitting in the half-dismantled living room, Jen beside him. A huge bouquet – roses, carnations, all of Jen's favourites – lay on a box that was acting as a coffee table.

'Why, Paulie, you shouldn't have,' Connor said, as he crossed the room and bent to kiss Jen's cheek.

'Don't be daft,' she said, punching his arm lightly. 'Read the card, they're not from Paulie. He's doing enough by helping us, isn't he?'

Connor grunted, reached for the card. 'Something to brighten up the clutter as you move. Don't let him leave you to do all the hard work. Gran x'

Connor smiled. Typical of his gran. She had developed a soft spot for Jen in the last few months, had been delighted when he told her they were moving in together. She had pressed him for details of the new house, gone easy with her jibes about making Jen 'an honest woman'. He put the card back, making a mental note to pay a visit to her at her care home in Bannockburn as soon as he could.

'So,' Paulie grumbled, as he set aside a mug of tea, 'now that you're finally here, where do you want to get started with all of this? Take the stuff out of here first, then move on to the other rooms?'

Connor turned, looked down at Paulie. He was a large, squat man, built for width rather than height. He was wearing a T-shirt and tracksuit bottoms, as though he'd taken his fashion advice that morning from an old episode of *The Sopranos* and was going for mobster-enforcer chic. His face was carefully neutral, and Connor knew that, for Jen's benefit, he was playing the role of a man whose life wasn't blighted by violence and death. But, again, it was in the eyes. Connor could see the killer Paulie was in that cold, unblinking gaze.

'Yeah, that would be great,' he said, aiming for casual, playing his own role. He knew it was pointless – Jen knew all too well who he and Paulie truly were, and how thin the line between tolerance and violence was but, nevertheless, it was a façade they maintained – just another lie to keep the world turning.

Paulie rose with a low grunt, straightening his shoulders and rolling his neck. Connor noticed scuffs on his knuckles and a slight bruising around his right forearm, wondered what he had been doing to earn them.

'Right,' Paulie said. 'We'll get started. You stay there, love, relax a bit.'

Jen rose, swatting Paulie aside as he bent forward to help her as she leaned on her crutch. 'Don't you start with this crap, Paulie,' she said, as she jutted her jaw towards Connor. 'I get enough of it from him. I'll do what I decide I can do, and neither you, he, nor this bloody stick will tell you otherwise.'

Paulie gave a laugh so warm and genuine it sounded obscene coming from him. 'Fair enough,' he said. 'Lead on.'

They worked for an hour, loading dismantled furniture into the van, Jen boxing up the last of the kitchen, mostly in silence, a dislike for small talk being something the four of them shared. But it was when Simon appeared at the van with a box of bottles that clinked as he moved that Connor had an idea.

'Paulie,' he said, 'what do you think of Clonshell's whiskey?'

Paulie paused, looked up at Connor, doing nothing to disguise his confusion. It made him seem younger somehow, as though he was a child in class just asked a difficult question.

'Irish cat's piss,' he said, after a moment. 'Wouldnae go near the stuff myself. Why? You thinking of getting me a bottle of it as a thank-you for helping with this?'

Connor smiled. 'Not quite,' he said. 'But it's not a brand a whisky lover would drink? Say someone with an appreciation for malts and the like?'

Paulie smiled. 'Fuck off!' He snorted. 'That's like comparing Buckfast and Dom Pérignon. Two totally different things. Why?'

Connor nodded. It matched what he had read in the reports DCI Ford had given him, and what he had spoken about with Simon at the gym. Robert Balfour had been found drowned in Airthrey Loch on the Stirling University campus. A post-mortem examination had reported that his stomach had been full of nothing but alcohol, a finding that was backed up by the two empty bottles of Clonshell's whiskey in his office, and another half-bottle on the bank of the loch near where his body had been discovered. But it was this fact that Balfour's student, Jamie Leggatt, had grabbed as proof his teacher had been murdered.

'Professor Balfour was a whisky connoisseur,' Connor had read in Leggatt's statement. 'He loved single malts, mainly from Speyside, never less than ten years old. There's no way he would have drunk something like Clonshell's, especially if he knew it was going to be his last drink.'

It was a tenuous reason to believe something sinister had been afoot, Connor thought. Yet it was one of those details that nagged at him, just like the petechial haemorrhaging found in Balfour's eyes. Ruptured blood vessels in the eyes were not common in cases of drowning, so why had they been found during the post-mortem examination of Robert Balfour? It was another detail that didn't quite fit the official story. And then there was the problem with Balfour's walking cane – a long, highly varnished ash stick with a ram's head sculpted into its handle. It had been found by the loch near the bottle of whiskey – but it hadn't started there. According to one of the reports Connor had read, a young constable had admitted moving the cane closer to the bottle 'for the purposes of easier evidence cataloguing'. The reports stressed that the young officer had been severely reprimanded, and Connor could almost have written it off as a careless mistake in a case where the cause of death was obvious.

And yet . . .

'I said, you gonna get lifting or just fuckin' stand there and ask about shite whiskey?'

Paulie startled Connor from his thoughts. He grabbed the end of the wardrobe they were loading into the van. 'Sorry, Paulie,' he said. He had just hefted the wardrobe to chest height when he saw Jen appear from the flat. Her expression was pale and drawn, and chilled something deep in Connor's guts.

He dropped the wardrobe, moved to her quickly. 'What's wrong?' he asked. 'Are you . . .?'

She shook her head, eyes locking onto his. 'It's Donna,' she said. 'I just flicked on the TV to see the headlines, and there she was, outside the university. They're saying they've found another body in the loch.'

Connor exchanged a glance with Simon, then Paulie.

'Go,' Paulie snarled, making no effort to keep the contempt from his voice. 'I'll stay with Jen, make sure this is done right. Just don't go getting yourself in any shit, Fraser. If you do, you're on your own.'

Connor looked at Jen, the resignation in her eyes hot rods of pain stabbing at his guts. 'Yeah, get going,' she said softly. 'You'd be no use to me here anyway – you'd only be thinking about whoever they found at the uni.'

Connor turned to Simon. 'You driving or am I?' he asked.

CHAPTER 13

Death had no place in daylight.

It was an opinion Malcolm Ford had formed over his years as a policeman. He could remember every dead body he had seen, every wound inflicted on the victims. And every crime scene he had visited, everybody he had seen, had hardened his belief that seeing such horrors in the cold light of day somehow intensified their impact. Violence and death were to be expected at night – they capered and played through the shadows – but in the daylight there was nowhere to hide from the savagery that lay at the heart of the human soul, and the sheer depravity that could be unleashed at any time.

He forced his gaze down, away from the placid silvered waters of Airthrey Loch, to the body at his feet. He had been found by a janitor heading into the university for his morning shift, the body tangled in reeds that grew on the banks of the loch. Whether driven by terror or a desire to preserve evidence, the janitor hadn't approached the body, and instead bolted for the nearest phone.

It was, Ford thought, lucky for him. He had met the paramedic who had arrived at the scene and turned the body over. Could see in the haunted, feverish glint of his eyes that he would never forget the sight that had confronted him. Ford couldn't blame him. It wasn't something he would forget either.

From eyebrows to chin, the man's face was gone. Not distended or bloated by the water, but gone. It was as though a bomb had been detonated in his mouth, and all that was left of his face was a bloodied crater glistening with scraps of flesh. Even after being submerged in the water, Ford could see flecks of brain and bone in the man's hair, the colour of which was hard to tell due to the viscera shot through it. Ford's stomach lurched as he looked down at the man's hands, the fingers clearly broken, the flesh a waxy grey.

'Well?' Ford asked, as he focused on the man kneeling beside the body.

Dr Walter Tennant turned away from it, as though he had forgotten Ford was looming over him as he worked. He blinked slowly, his glasses small and toy-like in his massive hand as he pulled them from his face and tapped them against his lips.

'Well, I'll have to make a full examination to be sure,' he said, 'but looks like he's been in the water for at least six hours. Cause of death appears self-evident,' he gestured towards the ruined head, 'but I don't want to jump to conclusions, especially as he smells as though he's been dipped in whisky rather than the loch.'

Ford growled thanks to the doctor, then turned, saw his detective sergeant, Troughton, standing beside his car, as though unsure what he was meant to be doing.

Ford walked towards him, saw the young policeman stiffen as he approached. 'Well,' he asked, 'we got anything useful from the body?'

'Ah, no, sir,' Troughton said, as he reached into the car for an iPad and started to tap on it. 'We got the call at just after seven twenty-one a.m. Report of the body being found was made by Jim Maitland, a janitor at the university. Officers who were first on the scene confirmed with the paramedics that it was a fatality, secured the location and called in the SOCOs, who are still searching the immediate locus. Initial search of the victim shows he either wasn't carrying a wallet or any other form of identification, or any items were washed away when he entered the water.'

Ford looked back to the loch. Calm and mirror-like, the only small ripples made by the wind. There was something in that, something—

He was interrupted by the trill of Troughton's phone. He turned back, watched as the detective took the call, his face tightening as he spoke, his eyes moving to Ford.

'Yes, of course,' he said. 'What? . . . Really? . . . Oh, okay. Thanks, Roddie.' He ended the call.

'What?' Ford said, even as the answer formed in his mind.

'Chief Constable Guthrie just signed in at the perimeter,' Troughton said, as though giving Ford a cancer diagnosis. 'That was Constable Grey, Roddie. Says the chief doesn't look in a good mood, but he's trying to impress his guest.'

'Guest?' Ford said, glancing down the hill to get a look at the chief's car.

'Yes sir,' Troughton said, his tone confused. 'Seems the chief isn't alone. He's got someone with him. Roddie, sorry, PC Grey said he recognised the man from that press conference held in town yesterday.'

Ford glared at Troughton. 'Press conference? You don't mean . . .?'

Troughton nodded. 'Yes, sir. It seems Chief Constable Guthrie has brought Jonathan Rodriguez to the site of a suspicious death.'

CHAPTER 14

The main entrance to Stirling University lay up a hill off a small roundabout on the Airthrey Road, close to Bridge of Allan. It was, Connor thought, probably why the police had left open the first section of the hill leading to the university – setting up a cordon directly off the roundabout would have created a traffic nightmare, especially with all the TV vans and press cars milling around the area.

Simon drove up University Road West, slowing as the cordon came into view. It was draped over what looked to Connor more like the entrance to a toll road than a university campus: two marked lanes leading into the campus, one leading out. The road was dotted with speed bumps, and three large security barriers had been lowered across it. He could see police officers making a human chain on either side of the road, ensuring no one wandered into the gardens of the university and stumbled onto the crime scene.

Simon pulled in behind a Sky News van about three hundred yards from the police cordon, bumping up onto the kerb and killing the engine. Connor had regretted agreeing to let Simon drive as soon as they got into the car. It was a small, overpowered hot hatch, which Simon had brought with him from Northern Ireland. He had affectionately nicknamed it 'The Pocket Rocket', while Connor had adopted the less affectionate 'The Roller Skate'. It was, simply, too small for someone of Connor's size. The sports seats were too narrow for his shoulders, the footwell too small for his legs. And the constant growl from the twin exhausts gave him a headache.

He got out of the car and stretched, grateful the journey had been relatively short. Simon was climbing out of the driver's side, a smile lighting up his face. Connor saw why. Donna Blake was walking towards them, looking camera-ready as ever. She was, Connor thought, doing a better job of hiding her emotions than Simon was, but not by much.

'Should have stopped to let you get some flowers,' Connor said.

Simon's smile widened. 'Catch yerself on,' he said.

'Well, well, well, fancy running into you here,' Donna said, eyes darting between Connor and Simon. 'Any reason for that, or is it just you couldn't wait to see me, Simon?'

Simon laughed, but when he spoke, his voice was calm, serious, and Connor saw something shift in his friend's posture as he took in the scene around him, gears changing from passer-by to professional. 'What we got?' he asked.

Donna shrugged. 'Not much. If you saw my report earlier, you know about as much as I do. Seems a body was found in the loch in the early hours. No official identification yet, but with the shit storm Rodriguez has stirred up about his dad being found in the loch, it's kind of hard not to see some sort of connection here.'

Connor was forced to agree. As a policeman, he had been trained to abhor coincidence. And a body being found in Airthrey Loch the day after Jonathan Rodriguez had alleged his father had been murdered and dumped in the same loch forty years ago was one hell of a big coincidence.

'Any word from Rodriguez?' Connor asked, a thread of unease shimmering in his gut. He knew Rodriguez had been told that Ford had asked Connor to look into his father's death, knew Donna wanted to talk to him about that. He had wanted to stay in the shadows until he had more information, but events seemed to have shown that up for the naive dream it was.

'Nothing official,' Donna said. 'Though I'm guessing we'll hear from him in some way at the press briefing the police have arranged in an hour's time up at the hotel on the campus.'

'Why's that?' Connor asked.

'Bit weird, actually,' Donna replied, a frown creasing her brow. 'We saw Chief Constable Guthrie arrive earlier, and I could have sworn Rodriguez was in the car with him.'

Simon spoke before Connor could open his mouth. 'What? The chief constable brought a civilian reporter into a live crime scene? Nah . . .'

'Can only tell you what I saw,' Donna said. 'It was just. . .' She trailed off as her attention was drawn over Simon's shoulder.

Simon turned and squared his shoulders, putting himself between Donna and the tall, pale young man who was approaching them.

'Ah, I'm ah, looking for Donna Blake,' he said, his voice thin and uncertain as he glanced between Simon and Connor.

Donna took a step forward, easing her way around Simon and giving him a pointed glance as she did so. *I don't need you to be my shining knight*, the look said. 'I'm Donna Blake. What can I do for you?'

The young man reached into his jacket, Simon tensing as he pulled a small, padded envelope from his pocket. 'Guy over there,' he said, gesturing to the crowd of bystanders loosely knotted around the police cordon, 'told me to give you this. Gave me fifty quid to do it. Said you'd understand.'

Simon's hand flashed out, grabbing the envelope before Donna could reach it. He ran his fingers over it, probing the corners and the seams, eyes falling on Connor, who nodded. Working as a police officer in Belfast, letter bombs were a fact of life, and checking for them was as reflexive for Simon as checking under his car for a little present left by unfriendly loyalists or republicans.

'What did this man look like?' Connor asked, as Simon handed the envelope to Donna and trained his gaze on the bystanders.

The young student shrugged, his eyes telling Connor he was coming to the conclusion that the fifty quid hadn't been worth the hassle. 'Average,' he said. 'Wore glasses and a hat, which he kept pulled pretty far down. Big, scraggly beard. Wasn't really paying attention.'

Brilliant,' Connor rumbled, the description doing nothing to help him. 'And what's your name, son?'

The student raised his hands, started to back off. 'Hey, I just wanted to make a quick fifty, not get the third degree. He said she'd understand the message. I've delivered it. I'm gone.'

Connor stepped forward, clamped his hand around an arm that, under the padding of the jacket, felt devoid of muscle. 'Sorry, not that easy. We'll need to talk to you some more.' He turned to Donna. 'What's in there anyway?'

Donna tore the envelope open, slipped her fingers inside. Her face creased with confusion and something Connor read as disgust as she withdrew a small square of battered leather and passed it to Simon. 'Looks like a wallet,' she said.

Simon opened it, his own frown mirroring Donna's as he looked up at Connor. 'What was the name of the student in the original Balfour case? The one you were telling me about this morning?' he asked.

Connor felt something chill in his guts as he tightened his grip on the messenger and glanced back to the crowd of onlookers. What had the kid said about the man who had given him the package? Average. Nondescript. Wore glasses and a hat. Beard. Useless. Based on that, he might as well have been looking for an individual blade of grass.

'Leggatt,' Connor said, pulling his thoughts back into focus. 'Jamie Leggatt. Hold on, you're not saying . . .'

'Bingo,' Simon said, as he pulled a picture-ID driving licence from the wallet and held it up for Connor to see. 'James Martin Leggatt. Oh, and one other wee detail. This wallet is wet, almost like it's been submerged in water. Think that's something we should tell DCI Ford about before the press conference or after?'

CHAPTER 15

He had to force himself not to run. Not because he feared being caught or identified, he had taken steps to ensure that could not happen, but because of the sheer electric thrill he could feel pulse through his body with every beat of his heart.

After dispatching his messenger, he had lingered just long enough to see the package delivered. He had not expected the reporter, Blake, to be accompanied by two men who, judging by the way they moved, were either military or police. He had dared to sneak a quick photo of the group with his phone, then turned and walked away, the adrenaline making his saliva thick and viscous in his throat, his excitement whispering to him to run as fast as he could.

It was done. The first steps towards justice had been taken. Blake would either understand the message he had given her, or she would work at it until she did. Either way, she was part of the story now, a front-seat observer to the history he was about to correct, and the wrong he was about to right.

A ten-minute walk took him back to his car, which he had parked on a residential street just off Airthrey Road. There were no CCTV cameras – he had checked weeks ago.

He eased himself into the driver's seat, looked around the street. No one. Sat forward, removed the holstered knife from where it lay nestled against his back. He dropped it into his lap, out of eye level, the low hiss of the blade drawing free of the sheath giving him a thrill of pleasure. *A knife is only truly yours once it has tasted you*, Balfour had said. For years, he had taken that as a universal truth, as immutable as the turning of the earth or the changing of the seasons. But after today, after sinking it into the chest of another living being, watching the shock and terror and disbelief kaleidoscope through their eyes as they realised their death was only moments away, he had learned a different, more profound truth.

A knife was only yours once it had tasted you. But, as he had learned, once a knife had tasted flesh, it wanted, no, *needed* more. It whispered to you, pleading, encouraging, beseeching. *Another taste*, it said. *More. I need more to remain sharp.*

He pulled his phone from his pocket, called up the picture he had taken of Blake and the two men with her. One was huge, a mass of muscle that radiated intent and power in the way he held himself, a man to be watched and approached with caution. The other was taller, slighter, but stood with a lithe grace and wary poise that spoke of years of training. Whether that training had been with military or police didn't matter. The answer was only a question away.

Whoever they were, they were part of the story now. And, as such, they would taste his blade. And when they did, he would make sure they suffered the same searing agony he had at the funeral.

CHAPTER 16

Ford arrived less than five minutes after Connor had called him, DS Troughton in tow. Connor brought him up to speed as Troughton gathered the wallet and envelope into an evidence bag, then turned his attention to the student who had delivered the package and was now looking as though he was about to be sick.

Ford said nothing, merely nodded as the muscles in his jaw clenched. Connor had seen this before, almost as if the policeman was trying to chew things over literally as well as figuratively.

'We'll pull the CCTV from whatever cameras we can find,' Ford said, after Connor stopped talking, 'see if Laughing Boy here can identify the suspect from footage. We'll need you three to give formal statements as well, and your prints to eliminate you from the forensic examination of the wallet.'

Connor saw an objection rise in Donna's eyes. He shook his head slightly in warning. The last thing any of them needed was her getting into a pointless argument with Ford and pissing him off.

'Can I speak to you for a moment, sir?' Connor said, eyes falling on Troughton. 'Privately?'

Evidently Ford read the unspoken message in his eyes. 'Let's take a walk,' he said, jutting his chin down the hill, away from the police cordon. 'Troughton, you secure the evidence and the witness, get those statements under way. Take the three of them back to the on-site situation room. You can work from there. And get someone to check in on Jamie Leggatt. Has he been seen? Does his description match the victim discovered this morning, that sort of thing.'

'Yessir,' Troughton said.

Ford started to walk away, heading back towards the university gates. Something in the set of his shoulders gave Connor the impression he was contemplating not stopping when he got there.

'So, what does this mean for my investigation?' Connor asked. There was no way to slip the question into conversation casually so he went for the direct approach. 'I mean, reviewing a cold case is one thing. Looking into a cold case that's probably linked to an active investigation is another matter entirely.'

Ford grunted. 'Aye,' he said. 'Though that prick Guthrie is doing a fairly good job of trying to mess up this case as well.'

'I heard about that,' Connor said. 'What the hell's he thinking, giving Jonathan Rodriguez access to a crime scene like that?'

Ford stopped, something between resignation and fury flitting across his face. 'He says he was in a breakfast meeting with Rodriguez when he was alerted to the body being found in the loch. Decided to bring him as the damage was already done, and as he's accusing the police of one cover-up, he didn't want to give him any ammo to accuse us of another. To be fair, he's kept Rodriguez and the woman he's working with away from anything sensitive, set them up in a conference room at the hotel and let them be. Oh, he'll be front and centre at the press conference, and no doubt Guthrie will make sure he gets his moment in the spotlight, but . . .' His eyes drifted back to the main gate of the university.

'So,' Connor said, 'do you want me to keep looking at the original Balfour case or not?'

Ford turned back to him, as though he'd just remembered Connor was there. 'Keep looking,' he said. 'But quietly. And if you find anything that might link that case to whoever was found this morning, I want to know about it. We'll make it official then.'

'Okay,' Connor said. 'In that case, I—'

He was cut off by the squawk of Ford's AirWave radio set. The policeman flinched, as thought he had forgotten he was carrying the thing, then fished it out of his pocket. 'Ford,' he said.

'Ah, DS Troughton, sir. Thought you'd want to know. We checked on James Leggatt as you requested. Officers called at his house this morning, found him there. Wasn't aware he'd lost his wallet, no explanation of how it got here, claims he hasn't been in the Stirling area for years. Local officers are checking his movements now to verify, and he's due to make a full statement at the Bell Street station later this afternoon after he finishes work at Dundee uni.'

Ford blinked at Connor, who shrugged. 'Okay,' he said into the radio. 'I'll be back with you in five minutes. Tell Tayside I want details of that statement pronto. Understood?'

'Yes, sir,' Troughton replied.

Ford pocketed the radio, looked back up the road. The muscles in his jaw were working furiously now, and Connor could hear the low rasp of his teeth grinding together.

'So,' the policeman said, 'if that's not Leggatt back there in the loch, then who the hell is it?'

'And why,' Connor added, 'did someone send us the wallet of Robert Balfour's number-one student?'

CHAPTER 17

The Stirling Court Hotel sat on the grounds of the university campus, not far from Airthrey Loch. Owned by the university, it hosted seminars and conferences, and offered accommodation to those who were visiting the Institute of Sport on the campus or tourists looking for a convenient base from which to explore the local area. But today it was performing a different function, hosting a press conference for Police Scotland.

It had taken Connor about half an hour to give his official statement to a uniformed officer who looked as if he hadn't yet completed puberty, let alone basic police training. But the young PC had asked all the right questions and kept the small talk to a minimum, almost as though he hated the administrative side of the job as much as Connor once had. When he had finished, Connor met Simon in a small bar just off the main foyer of the hotel, which was already filling up with reporters.

'Where's Donna?' he asked, as he slipped into a seat across a small table from his friend.

'Away getting set up for this press conference,' Simon said, 'staking out her place in the conference room with her cameraman.'

Connor nodded, a memory of a pale, doughy man flashing across his mind. He wondered if Donna's cameraman made everything he filmed look so good as some kind of reaction to his own shambolic appearance.

'So,' Simon asked. 'What's next? Doesn't seem like there's much to be gained by hanging around here.'

'Looks that way,' Connor agreed. 'We're not going to learn much from the press conference, and whoever sent that wallet to Donna is long gone, if they've got any sense. After all, why stick around when you can watch all this play out on TV?'

'Yeah,' Simon agreed, 'but something about that is bothering me.'

'The wallet?' Connor asked, seeing where Simon was going. 'I was thinking that myself. One, it targets Donna specifically. Not a member of the press, not the woman in the Sky van. Donna. Personally. Granted, whoever sent it might just have seen her name on the TV and taken a punt, but I don't like it. And then there's the wallet itself.'

Simon held up a finger. 'How did it get there?' Another finger. 'Did whoever's in the loch take it from Leggatt, or was it planted?' Another finger. 'Why put the focus on Leggatt like that? It rules him out as the victim but puts him straight in the frame as a suspect for the murder. Why? Anyone who can dump a body in a loch in the centre of a campus isn't going to be daft enough to leave their own wallet on their victim's person, are they?'

'Not very likely,' Connor said. 'So what? It puts the spotlight on Leggatt, drags him into this investigation, just like he was central in the original case forty years ago.'

'Too much to hope Ford will tell us what Leggatt has to say for himself?' Simon asked, his tone telling Connor he already knew the answer.

'If we want to know how he's connected to this, we're going to have to ask him ourselves. Or, more accurately, I am, as I'm guessing you're going to be sticking close to Donna, just in case.'

Simon's eyes hardened. 'You said it yourself,' he said. 'That wallet was sent to Donna. Specifically. If nothing else, it means someone connected to all this knows her name and has some kind of interest in her. After everything else that's happened, I'm not taking any chances with her safety.'

Connor couldn't argue. Just over a year ago, Donna had been kidnapped by a pyromaniac who felt he was doing God's work by burning down the world. It was after that incident, and another, when reporter Doug MacGregor turned up at the flat bloodied and beaten over a different story, that Simon and Donna's relationship had started to evolve into something more. They hadn't talked about it, but Connor knew Simon well enough to recognise that it was more than a casual fling for him. Which was very bad news for anyone who harboured any ambitions to hurt Donna Blake or manipulate her.

'Fair enough,' he said. 'Can you get a lift back from Donna if I take your car and see what I can get out of Leggatt?'

Simon broke into a wide grin as he reached into his pocket for his keys. 'Ah, you and the Pocket Rocket, all the way to Dundee,' he said. 'Great day for a drive. You'll be in love with that car by the time you bring her home.'

Connor took the keys from his friend, couldn't help but return his smile. 'Don't count on it,' he said.

CHAPTER 18

Simon had been to dozens of police press conferences over the years, facing the cameras, appealing to the public for information, parrying awkward questions from journalists. So as he watched DCI Malcolm Ford struggle to keep his face and tone neutral while he answered question after question with variations of 'The cause of death has yet to be established, enquiries are ongoing, the body has yet to be identified', he could sympathise with the policeman's plight.

That didn't stop him enjoying watching Donna work, though.

She was at the front of the hotel conference room that was being used by the police, to the left of Jonathan Rodriguez who, unsurprisingly, had the best seat in the house. He was opposite Ford, who sat at a long table with Chief Constable Guthrie to his left and a woman Simon guessed was from the Police Scotland communications team on his right. At the back of the room, arms folded like a bouncer, he had spotted Amanda Lyons, who was watching Rodriguez with a quiet, almost amused intensity.

Donna was on her feet, directing her question to the chief constable, whose immaculate dress uniform did more to project the image of a man painfully out of his depth than it did a senior law-enforcement officer taking command of a serious situation.

'Chief Constable, your initial press release said nothing would be ruled in or out until the post-mortem examination of the victim had been completed. However, my sources indicate that the victim had been mutilated and the clothes were heavily stained with blood. Can you comment on that? And do you think there's a specific link between this incident and the Robert Balfour case, which my colleague,' she tipped a pen towards Jonathan Rodriguez, who flashed his best on-camera smile, 'is here to investigate and which leaves Police Scotland and the former Central Scotland force with significant questions to answer?'

Simon wiped at his face to cover his smile as hectic colour rose in Guthrie's pasty cheeks and he tried to splutter his way through an answer. Donna's question had been like a scalpel, skewering Guthrie by describing whoever was found in the loch as a 'victim', revealing a key aspect of the investigation and neatly tying her reporting with the wider story her 'colleague', Jonathan Rodriguez, was covering. Connor had taken to teasing Simon that he was 'sleeping with the enemy', and at that moment, Simon was profoundly grateful that he was.

Guthrie's answer petered out into an awkward silence, and he shot a pleading glance at the woman sitting at the other end of the table. She nodded, rose to her feet as the reporters in the room erupted into a flurry of questions. They knew what was coming, and wanted to get the last word in.

'Thank you,' she said, her voice as pinched and serious as her expression. 'That's all we've got time for at the moment. We will issue further updates as and when we have them, and any interview requests can be lodged with the main press office.'

Ignoring calls from those in the room, she followed Guthrie and Ford away from the table and out of the room. Simon watched as reporters, photographers and cameramen started to pack their gear and shuffle towards the door. Some, he knew, would just set up again outside, the police cordon a backdrop as they filmed to-camera reports to be used in later bulletins.

He waited for a few moments, allowing the crowd to thin out a little, then worked his way towards Donna. She was still huddled in conversation with Jonathan Rodriguez. She turned as Simon approached, a smile in her eyes only.

'Ah, Simon,' she said. 'This is Jonathan Rodriguez. Jonathan, this is Simon McCartney, a – a contact of mine.'

Rodriguez accepted Simon's handshake with a warm, strangely gentle grip. He was about Simon's height, with hair as perfectly tailored as his suit and a smile that must have cost at least four figures. 'Pleasure to meet you,' he said, the vaguest hint of a Scottish accent poking out from the American bass. 'You're Connor Fraser's friend, aren't you? Is he here at all?'

Simon stiffened slightly. The man had done his homework, all right. 'Ah, no, I'm afraid not. He's been called away on other business,' he said.

'Ah,' Rodriguez replied. 'Pity. I'd like to talk to him about all this at some point. I understand we're working on the same thing – be good to compare notes.'

'Same thing?' Simon said. 'How so?'

'Well, I know Mr Fraser has been asked to look into my father's death, see if the police at the time missed anything. Peter – sorry, Chief Constable Guthrie – was good enough to tell me that earlier. I've looked into Mr Fraser and I know he's a good investigator who gets results. Since I'm here to look into my dad's death as well, I thought it would make sense to—'

He was cut off by the chime of his phone, which was echoed a moment later by Donna's. He gave Simon an apologetic smile, pulled his phone from his pocket, frowned at his screen, then looked at Donna, who returned his confused glance.

'What?' Simon asked.

'Take a look,' she said, offering him her phone. 'Text message. Not sure what it means, though.'

Simon took the phone. Read the message, his blood chilling in his veins.

Ms Blake. Mr Rodriguez. Jamie Leggatt. Dundee. Today. St Andrew's Double Cross. Saor Alba.

He tore his eyes from the screen, tightened his grip on the phone. 'I need to see Ford now,' he said, his voice louder and harsher than he had intended.

'Simon, what is it? What's wrong?' Donna asked, concern etching itself into the fine lines around her eyes and lips.

'Call Connor,' he said. 'Now. Tell him there's been a terrorist threat made on Jamie Leggatt's life. Codeword is legit. Tell him to secure Leggatt and find safe harbour. Now.'

He saw the excitement rise in Donna's eyes, tried not to hate it. She was, after all, a reporter, just doing her job.

'Codeword?' she asked.

'St Andrew's Double Cross,' Simon said, the words tasting sour in his mouth. He didn't have time for this. Needed to find Ford. 'Double Cross was the codeword used in the Birmingham pub bombings. It was IRA. Saor Alba is Gaelic for Free Scotland. So St Andrew's Double Cross is a Scottish twist on a viable code. Call Connor. Now.'

Before she could reply, he got moving.

CHAPTER 19

It was, Connor thought, almost as if they had choreographed their calls. No sooner had he taken Donna's uncharacteristically breathless call telling him about the threat than his phone began flashing with DCI Malcolm Ford's number.

'I take it you got Blake's message?' Ford asked, as Connor answered.

'Just off the phone with her,' Connor agreed. He was standing in front of Dundee University's School of Humanities, a blunt-faced granite building that Connor hoped was as well built as it looked.

'We've got officers en route,' Ford said. 'How close are you?'

'On site now,' Connor said. 'Just about to go in and find Leggatt, unless you're evacuating the building.'

Ford coughed. 'Not yet,' he said, his tone telling Connor he didn't agree with the decision. 'We've got a threat, with a bastardised code-word any arsehole with Google and half a brain cell could have come up with. Could be a bomb, could be anything. Chief doesn't want to spark a public panic so we do this quietly. Any hint of trouble, though, we evacuate the block, call in the bomb squad.'

Connor looked up at the building. It resembled the entrance to a seventies shopping mall, a steel revolving door encased in pine panelling.

'I'll find Leggatt, isolate him,' Connor said. 'Pass him on to your people when they arrive.'

Another grumble, as though Ford was trying to clear his throat and failing. 'Make it quick,' he said. 'And fuck the chief. If you see anything that looks out of place or you think poses any form of threat, pull the fire alarm and get everyone out as quickly as you can.'

'Copy that,' Connor said, then killed the call.

Through the revolving door and into the main reception area, where he was confronted by a small, stooped man who looked as though he wasn't so much sitting in his chair as being slowly eaten by it. 'Can I help you?' he asked, blinking up at Connor through small, circular glasses that glittered in the overhead lights.

'Looking for Professor Jamie Leggatt,' Connor said. 'My name's Ian Mason. I'm working on a joint paper with him.'

'Ah,' the old man nodded. 'Third floor. Office three sixteen.'

Connor nodded his thanks, tried to keep his pace steady but brisk as he walked along the corridor. He found a set of lifts at the end of the hallway, opted instead for the stairwell. If there was a bomb in the building, the last thing he wanted was to be trapped in a lift.

He sprinted up the stairs, found Leggatt's office. Knocked, found he was holding his breath, half praying there wouldn't be an answer.

'Yes,' an impatient voice called. Connor cursed silently, grabbed the door handle. He stepped into a room that would have been large if it wasn't for the books that lined the walls and stood in haphazard piles dotted around the floor. Beneath a large window there was a heavy oak desk, at which a tall, rangy man, with a thinning thatch of salt-and-pepper hair and thick-rimmed glasses, was sitting. As Connor stepped into the room, a question was furrowing his already deeply lined brow.

'Yes?' he said, tone wary. 'Can I help you?'

Good question, Connor thought. 'Professor Leggatt?' Connor said, the question rewarded with a small nod. 'My name is Connor Fraser. I'm, ah, I'm working with the police, sir. We believe a threat has been made against you. Officers are on the way, but I'd like to get you to a place of safety as soon as possible. Will you come with me, please?'

Leggatt threw up his arms, disturbing an untidy pile of papers on the desk in front of him. 'This again!' he shouted, his voice a frustrated growl, vowels elongating as though being north of the Tay had tightened his vocal cords. 'I told the police everything I knew this morning, which wasn't bloody much. I'm seeing them again later. And what do you mean about a threat on my life?'

Connor opened his mouth, closed it. What *did* he mean? And why was this man being targeted? 'We received word that someone might make an attempt on your life, sir. It may be related to the body found at Stirling University. Can you think of anyone who might want to hurt you?'

Leggatt blinked behind his glasses, then studied Connor as though he was trying to decide if he was genuine or part of some elaborate joke. 'No, I cannot,' he said, his voice thin and flat. 'As I told the police, I have no idea why my wallet would be on a body found at Stirling University, and I haven't been at the university for years. My diary will corroborate my movements over the last few days and . . .'

Leggatt leaned to the right in his chair as his voice trailed off. Connor heard the squeal of a drawer being opened. Felt an ugly bolt of terror as he heard a second sound: a soft, distinctive click. Opened his mouth to shout as he lunged forward, saw Leggatt look up at his cry.

The blast hurled Leggatt sideways and against the opposite wall of the room as the glass of the window exploded behind him. Connor was thrown back, landing in a heap on the floor as the force of the explosion blew him off his feet and the world screamed in his ears. He tucked instinctively and rolled with the force, felt debris pepper his back. Lay for a moment as he came to a halt, fighting back the waves of shock that told him to stay down, crawl away, get out of there. Opened his eyes and hauled himself onto legs that didn't feel like his own. Felt hot blood run from his nose and burn his lips with its iron tang. His ears rang, but he could vaguely hear a fire alarm screaming in the distance. It could have been coming from another planet.

He moved to his right, got to the heap of ruined flesh that had been the professor only moments before. He was lying against the wall, like a discarded doll, his legs and head at impossible angles, his thick glasses sitting squint on his face, the left lens cracked. There was a spatter of blood on the wall behind Leggatt's head almost, Connor thought, like some obscene halo. Connor crouched, felt for a pulse he knew he wasn't going to find. His stomach lurched as he realised the professor's right arm was gone, the force of the blast leaving nothing but a ragged stump, a hellishly white knot of bone peeking out from beneath the shredded flesh and gore.

He turned to the desk, which had been reduced by the blast to little more than a smouldering pile of wood. Forced himself to look past it, to the frame on the far wall, the web-like pattern of cracks in the glass seeming to accentuate the image he was seeing for the first time.

It had been a banner at some point. About three feet long, a foot high. A simple protest banner, daubed in paint, the message blunt. 'Saor Alba,' Connor read, as the door to the professor's office flew open and two uniformed officers charged in. 'No to the Queen.'

Connor could hear the officers talking to him, urgently asking questions. He ignored them as he pulled his phone from his pocket and read the text he had asked Donna to send him after her warning call.

Message is 'Jamie Leggatt. Dundee. Today. St Andrew's Double Cross. Saor Alba.' Simon thinks it's credible. Be careful.

Connor turned back to what was left of Jamie Leggatt. 'Credible,' he whispered, in a voice he barely recognised as his own. 'Yeah, I'd say this fits the bill.'

CHAPTER 20

After calling Connor with Simon's warning, Donna had bundled Keith into the Sky broadcast van and told him to get to Dundee as fast as he could. She knew she should have stayed to give the police a statement, knew also what Simon would say about her charging off into a potentially dangerous situation, found she didn't care. She could feel the story pulling at her, whispering into her ear, like a lover, compelling her to get to the scene, get the story out before anyone else.

Of course, it hadn't worked that way. In the days of social media, citizen journalists quickly flooded Twitter, TikTok and every other platform with jerky footage of smoke billowing out of a shattered window at a Dundee University building as sirens drowned their breathless, inane commentary. But all this did was intensify the adrenaline coursing through Donna's veins. Someone had sent her a warning. It had proved to be valid: a bombing on UK soil telegraphed with a coded terrorist warning. This was big. National big.

And whoever had carried out the bombing had invited Donna to take a front-row seat. Part of her flinched away from this, her thinking clouded with images of her son, Andrew. He had already lost his father due to Donna's pursuit of a big story. Did she have the right to put her own life in danger, risk making him an orphan left to the care of her parents? It was a question Donna had faced before. And her answer was always simple. This was her job. And she was damned if she was going to be the type of mother who taught her son that cowardice was a valid choice, that walking away from something you believed in when the stakes got high was a way to live his life.

They were on the M90, just crossing the Friarton Bridge, when Donna's phone pinged with an email alert. She grabbed it, a tension headache pulsing through her skull, aggravated by the static grumble of the van's tyres on the road. It was most probably Annie, her editor on the newsdesk at Sky, sending script lines, possible locations for filming and asking for an update. Which Donna couldn't give.

Yet.

'Keith, speed it up a bit, would you?' she said, as she opened the email app on her phone.

There was a moment when the world faded away, as though someone had grabbed the volume control and turned it all the way down. Her vision seemed to telescope onto the phone's screen. Part of her wanted to dismiss it as a crank email, the type that big news stories always seemed to attract from conspiracy theorists or armchair detectives who thought they had the answer to everything. But the subject line of the email told her this was no crank.

St Andrew's Double Cross. Saor Alba, it read.

She opened the email, aware that her hand was trembling slightly. Blinked once, felt something hot claw its way up her throat as she read:

Ms Blake,

By now, you will understand that I am not playing games, unlike Mr Rodriguez. He claims to have returned to Stirling for the truth about his father's death. Jamie Leggatt knew the truth, and that is why he had to die today. He will not be the last. I shall be in touch shortly, and together we can right a terrible wrong, and bring justice to those who would deny it. I believe the attached will dispel any doubts you have.

Saor Alba

At the bottom of the email was an attachment, a video file. Donna clicked on it. Her bowel gave a sickening lurch as her phone screen went blank, then flared to life.

The camera was trained on what looked like a framed banner on a plain manila wall. 'Saor Alba,' the banner read. 'No to the Queen.'

The camera lingered, then lurched left, panning around an office littered with books. Then it was moving towards an oversized desk covered with papers and yet more books. The camera swept over the desk, then dropped down to a drawer. A gloved hand stretched into the frame, holding up a Post-it note.

'My special delivery for Professor Leggatt is in this drawer, where I also found Mr Leggatt's wallet. The police will confirm this.'

There was a bark of laughter, harsh, discordant, like glass from a broken window raining down on concrete, and then the video ended.

Donna leaned back, struggling to breathe. It was as if her seatbelt had suddenly been yanked tight, constricting her chest and lungs. She closed her eyes, forced herself to be calm, think rationally.

'You okay?' Keith asked, from the driver's seat. 'Look like you've just seen a ghost.'

Donna opened her eyes. Everything seemed too bright, too defined, as though the world had just been flicked into HD. 'Drive faster,' she whispered, as she punched a number into her phone. 'We need to get to Dundee. Now.'

CHAPTER 21

Connor felt as though he had just been put through a heavy workout at the gym. His entire body pulsed with a deep, exhausted pain, and he felt that, if he were to lie down, he wouldn't so much sleep as just disconnect from the world and pass out.

He was sitting in the back of an ambulance parked outside the university, being fussed over by a paramedic so young and cheerful that she was sapping the last of Connor's strength. The police officers who had barged into what was left of Leggatt's office after the bomb blast had manhandled him out of the room and down the stairs. Connor had gone peacefully enough, his mind filled with the image of the ragged stump where Leggatt's arm had once been.

'You're fine,' the paramedic said, as she flashed Connor a smile straight from a toothpaste commercial, 'no sign of concussion, just a couple of superficial cuts and bruises. The ringing in your ears you mentioned should fade over time. There's no indication of damage to your eardrums. But take it easy for the next couple of days, okay? You've been through a hell of an ordeal, and you need to rest. Recover.'

Connor assured her he would, wondering if she could see the lie in his eyes. Someone had just detonated a bomb in his face and killed an innocent man in the process. Until he found whoever that was, resting was the last thing Connor would be doing.

He stepped out of the ambulance, into a chaotic fleet of fire engines and police cars. In front of him, he could see firefighters filing in and out of the university. Turning, he saw police officers lining a cordon, keeping back the scrum of bystanders who jostled for position as they held up their phones, desperate for a little memento of the drama unfolding in front of them.

He felt more than heard his phone ringing, smiled despite himself as he saw Simon's name flash on the screen. 'Before you say anything, I'm sure your car is fine,' he said, by way of a greeting. 'Parked her well away from all this, won't be a scratch on her.'

'Ack, catch yersel on,' Simon replied, as he gave a relieved chuckle. 'You all right, big lad? Saw some pictures online. Looks like it was a hell of a blast.'

Connor caught his breath, considered. There was something in that. Something about the size of the bomb, the blast radius, that banner . . .

. . . something . . .

'I'm fine,' he said, shaking himself from his thoughts. 'Just got a hell of a ringing in my ears and a few scrapes. I'll live. How are things there? I take it Ford hit the roof?'

'Could say that,' Simon replied. 'When I told him about the message, he looked as if I'd accused him of eating babies. Or being a politician. He's with the chief constable now, was muttering something about an emergency meeting with the First Minister. But, anyway, that's not why I'm calling.'

'Oh?'

Connor listened as Simon filled him in on the email Donna had just received. She had called him, sent over the video footage.

'Okay,' Connor said, as Simon stopped speaking. 'Send that to me, I'll take a look, call you back.' He ended the call, glanced back towards the crowd. All those people. All those phones.

Phones . . .

His own phone buzzed to tell him an email had arrived. He opened it, watched as the camera swooped around Leggatt's office. Felt bile rise in his throat as he saw the hand in front of the drawer and an ugly laugh filled his ears. Closed his eyes, saw the hellish white nub of bone where Leggatt's arm had once been.

'It's legit,' he said, as Simon answered his call.

'Thought it was,' Simon replied, his voice flat and emotionless. Connor knew the tone well. It meant his friend had left the room, and a cold, ruthless professional had taken his place.

'Donna still on her way up here?' Connor asked.

'Yeah,' Simon said. 'She needs to get footage and file a report from the scene.'

'Good,' Connor said, as his eyes drifted to the crowd again. 'I'll wait here for her, give her a lift home, make sure she's safe. Our bomber friend seems to have taken an interest in her and Jonathan Rodriguez. I'd like to discourage that.'

'Agreed,' Simon said. 'Rodriguez is still here on campus, I'll get him secured. I take it you're going to want to talk to him as soon as you get back here?'

'Oh, yes,' Connor said. 'I think it's well past time we had a little chat with Jonathan Rodriguez, don't you?'

CHAPTER 22

Jen collapsed onto the couch as her thigh began to spasm, her crutch clattering to the floor. She heard the heavy thud of footsteps, didn't need to open her eyes to know Paulie was charging into the room from the hallway, where he had been dismantling a bookshelf.

'You all right, hen?' he asked, his voice as close to tender as it ever got. 'You fall?'

Jen opened her eyes, swiped away a tear that rolled down her cheek. Forced a smile onto her face. 'I'm okay, Paulie, honestly,' she said. 'Just this bloody leg. Muscle spasms if I stay on it too long.'

Paulie glanced down at it as though he was trying to assess an opponent in a fight. Knowing his world view, she thought, he probably was. Paulie was a man of absolutes. If you were a friend, you were safe. If you were an enemy, you would be destroyed. There was no middle ground.

'Told you to take it easy,' he said. 'I can take care of stuff until Fraser gets back.'

Jen heard the sharpening of Paulie's tone when he mentioned Connor's name, ignored it. Opened her mouth to speak, was cut off by Paulie leaning over her and grabbing the TV remote. 'You sit there and relax,' he said. 'Watch a bit of telly. I'll make you a cuppa.'

She smiled her thanks at him, had to bite back a snort of laughter at the sight of Paulie lumbering around the kitchen, filling the kettle and retrieving cups from boxes. Growing up, Paulie had been her father's most trusted lieutenant, had become more after her mother had died of cancer. But there was always a lingering unease with Paulie, an almost subliminal realisation that violence and rage were his first language, lurking just below the surface, weapons ready to be unleashed.

The TV came to life, a familiar voice filling the room. Donna Blake was on the screen, standing in front of what looked like a police cordon, a building behind her, smoke wisping from one window a few floors up. 'Emergency services have yet to confirm the exact cause of the explosion,' Donna said, her face neutral, a caption reading 'Dundee University explosion' on the screen below her, 'but they have confirmed one fatality. Investigations are ongoing, and a report is being prepared for . . .'

Paulie snorted as he walked towards the TV, lowered his head and shook it.

'What?' Jen asked, confused.

'That man of yours,' Paulie said, with a sigh, 'he's got a hell of a nose for trouble, I'll gie him that.'

Jen blinked at Paulie, then turned back to the TV. 'Paulie, what . . .' And then she saw him. Just over Donna's right shoulder, lingering at the back of the shot, leaning against a tree, half turned away from the camera, arms folded, head sweeping from left to right across the crowd. 'Connor,' she whispered, the pain biting into her leg again.

'Take it he didnae tell you he was going to Dundee today?' Paulie asked.

'No,' Jen said, hearing the edge in her voice now, so similar to Paulie's. 'Last I knew, he was heading out to the university here, not up to Dundee with Donna.'

Paulie shrugged. 'Man like that, who knows where he'll end up? I'll get that tea.'

He moved back to the kitchen, leaving Jen to take her phone from her pocket. She felt a surge of anger as she saw there had been no messages. Connor had always been secretive about his work, as though trying to shield her from it. It had been worse since she was hurt, as though he was trying to protect her from the world. How much more, she wondered, was he shielding her from? What wasn't he telling her?

And how would his determination to split his professional from his personal life work when they were living together full-time? What would he say to her when he came home at night? *Evening, Jen. What? Work? No. Nothing eventful. Just ended up at the scene of an explosion at a university campus. One person died. I'm okay, though. You have a good day? What do you fancy for dinner?*

She unlocked the phone, keyed in a message to him, then deleted it, her concern for him and her anger battling in her stomach, making her feel sick. She wanted to know if he was okay, but another part of her, a part that had been growing for months, needed him to make the first move, to let her into all of his life, not just the parts he was willing to share because he thought they wouldn't hurt her.

With a snort, she threw the phone onto the couch, glared at it for a moment, then looked around the flat. Wondered if she was dismantling one life to build another, or just moving problems from one location to the next.

CHAPTER 23

Donna watched Connor circle Simon's car warily, dropping to his knees occasionally to inspect under the wheel arches. Then he stepped back, the muscle in his jaw fluttering, as though he was making a decision. His head moved slowly, his jade-green eyes focused and alert. He seemed to be trying to look through the street around them, to see something beyond reality. Donna had seen that look before, wasn't sure she would ever get used to it.

'Clear,' he said, more to himself than to her as he stepped towards the car and got in. She followed him, bundling herself into the passenger seat. When he'd approached her with the idea of travelling together back to Stirling, she hadn't taken much convincing: whatever was going on, Connor was at the centre of it, and if she was with him she'd have a front-row seat to the story.

They drove in silence as Connor navigated Dundee. The city had undergone a massive programme of building and regeneration over the last few years, with the waterfront being redeveloped and the V&A opening a museum there. The road network had also been upgraded and, from what Donna could see, made as complicated as possible.

Eventually they made it to the A90, the main road leading from Dundee to Stirling, and the traffic began to thin out.

'So,' Donna said, as she saw Connor relax a little in the driver's seat, 'what do you think is going on? Did Leggatt kill whoever is in the loch and then was killed for it by a third party, or is it something else?'

Connor's eyes darted from the road to her, a slight smile playing on his face. She held his gaze, unembarrassed. He had offered a lift to a reporter working on a national story: a few questions were to be expected.

'I don't know,' he said, as his eyes slid back to the road. 'But I know three things for a fact. Whoever planted that bomb knew what they were doing. That blast was just powerful enough to kill Leggatt and make a statement. Second, Leggatt was always the target, and our bomber wanted to lead us to him before he died, which is why the wallet was on the body, whoever that is.'

'And third?' Donna asked, after a moment's silence.

Connor's eyes fell on her again, no trace of humour on his face this time. 'Third, whoever is doing this has singled out you and Rodriguez as his messengers, which puts you at risk.'

Donna held Connor's gaze. 'Part of the job,' she said.

'Let me ask you a question,' Connor said. 'This guy Rodriguez. You've met him. He's obviously got pull with the chief constable to get the access he has and be told about my review of his dad's case, so who is this guy? And how is he so well connected?'

Donna let out a sigh. It was a good question, one she had been working on since she had learned that Rodriguez had visited the Stirling crime scene with the chief constable. 'I'm not sure,' she said. 'I mean, I looked into him, of course. Moved to America with his mother after his dad died, went into journalism after university. It was newspapers first, then a move into television and anchoring a morning show for one of the big networks over there. That gives him celebrity and pull, I guess, and we all know that Chief Constable Guthrie loves the limelight and a good headline. Whether that's enough for him to give Rodriguez the access he has, I'm not sure.'

Connor nodded. 'Something to look into, then,' he said. 'I'd like to know if—'

He was cut off by his mobile buzzing in his pocket. 'Damn,' he whispered, as he took one hand from the wheel and reached for his phone. 'Forgot to plug it into Simon's hands-free.'

Donna watched as he glanced at the phone's screen. He looked briefly at her, seemed to make a calculation, then answered the call.

'DCI Ford,' he said. 'Could I call you back in ten minutes? I'm driving, just need to—' He fell silent, his face blanching as white as the knuckles of his hand, which was gripping the steering wheel. When he spoke, his voice was a low growl. 'Yes,' he said. 'Understood. Thank you . . . Yes, I want to be there. I'll tell her, then bring her in later on.' He listened for a moment then ended the call. Dropped the phone into the side compartment, then shifted in the driver's seat, the car's engine growing louder as he bore down on the accelerator.

'Connor, what is it? What's wrong?' Donna asked.

His eyes never left the road. 'They identified the body in Airthrey Loch,' he said, shaking his head as if he was trying to deny what was happening. 'Ran the fingerprints as there wasn't much left of the face, got a match.'

'And?' Donna coaxed, after what felt like an eternity of silence. 'Who was it?'

He turned to her and she flinched instinctively. It was as though whatever he was feeling had stripped any humanity from his face, making it brutish, ugly, almost feral. 'It's Duncan MacKenzie,' he said flatly. 'Jen's dad.'

CHAPTER 24

He sat behind his desk, the order of service from the cremation in his hands, the only sound the soft spatter of tears as they hit the paper. He didn't remember bringing one home with him, wondered if she had delivered one. It would be, he thought, just like her. An act born of kindness, without considering the pain she had inflicted.

With an angry cough, he leaned forward, opened a desk drawer and put the order of service inside. Smiled as he closed the drawer slowly. Had Leggatt known what was happening in the second before the bomb detonated? Had he realised he was about to die? More importantly, had he understood *why*?

He took a swig of the whisky – Robert Balfour's favourite, not the rotgut he had died tasting – held it in his mouth, letting it scorch his tongue as he nudged the trackpad on his laptop and brought the screen to life.

The picture he had taken of Donna Blake with her two companions filled the screen. As he had expected, it hadn't taken long to identify them – it seemed they had a chequered history of popping up in stories Blake worked on. The walking mass of muscle was Connor Fraser, a director at a company called Sentinel Securities. A trawl of the company website gave the usual pitted biography, accompanied by a headshot that spoke of a man who hated being photographed. He had felt a thrill when he read that Fraser had been an officer with the Police Service of Northern Ireland before moving into the private sector, a thrill that had intensified to elation when he had identified Fraser's colleague.

Simon McCartney. A serving detective with the PSNI. His name appeared in press reports in newspapers produced in Northern Ireland, telling the story of a talented, dedicated police officer who had taken down drug-dealers, mobsters and thieves. He had made a call as soon as he had read this, was just waiting for the information to be collated and returned to him. Not that it really mattered if McCartney favoured the Falls Road or the Shankill, it was the symbolism that mattered.

A serving member of the PSNI, an agent of the Crown, killed due to his involvement with the Robert Balfour case? The synergy was almost too delicious to believe. It was almost as if there was a God, and He was helping in this bold pursuit of justice.

He knew that wasn't so: any lingering belief he had in a benevolent God had died in the crematorium. No, if there was a God, it was a mad, capricious, evil being, bent on inflicting pain and suffering on its creations.

At least, he thought, they had that much in common.

CHAPTER 25

Jen stiffened when she saw Connor walk into the flat, almost as if she could read bad news in his posture and faltering, unsure steps. Her eyes darted to Donna, who was standing just behind him. She had insisted on coming with him as a friend, not a reporter, not wanting Jen to face the news alone.

'Connor . . . what?' she asked.

Connor felt something hard form in his throat, fought to swallow it. Paulie stepped in through the patio doors, and Connor was suddenly very aware of the hammer he held in his massive hands.

He stepped forward, took Jen's hands in his. They were warm, soft, against his cold skin. He thought of Duncan MacKenzie, growing cool on a mortuary slab, and had to suppress a shiver.

'Connor, what is it?' Jen asked again, panic bleeding into her voice now.

'Jen, I, ah . . .' He paused, took a breath. Had a sudden memory of his gran whispering to him as a child, *Bad news is best given quickly, son. Big-boy pants needed.*

'Jen, I'm . . . I'm so sorry,' he said, his voice a whisper. 'It's your dad. I, ah, I got a call from the police a little while ago. He's dead. I'm sorry, Jen. I'm so, so sorry.'

There was a moment of utter silence, and Jen's face spasmed into a smile for a moment, as though Connor had just delivered a bad joke.

'What? I . . . I . . .'

He held her gaze in his. 'Jen, I'm sorry. They identified him about an hour ago. There's no doubt. It's him.'

'What? No. I just spoke to him last night, I . . .' She stopped, tears springing into her eyes. Connor took her in his arms, pulled her to his chest, aware of how small and fragile she was.

'I'm sorry,' he whispered, as the sobs began to rack her body. He buried his head in her hair, breathed in the smell of her. Closed his eyes. Wished the world would fade away.

'What happened?' Paulie rumbled, his voice a harsh rasp.

Connor snapped his head to look at Paulie, gave a quick, sharp shake. *Not now.* Too late.

Jen pushed away from Connor's chest, looked up at him. Something about the naked vulnerability in her face made her achingly beautiful. 'What happened?' she whispered. 'Where did they find him?'

Connor held her gaze. No point in lying about it: she'd find out soon enough. All he could do was try to downplay how MacKenzie had been mutilated.

'He, ah . . . It was your dad they found in the loch at the university this morning,' Connor said. 'I got a call from DCI Ford when I was on the way back from Dundee.'

'University?' Jen's eyes were clouding with confusion and, Connor thought, a fleeting glimmer of hope. 'Why would he be at the university? Dad's got no business there. It must be a mistake, it must . . .'

Connor tightened his arms a little. 'There's no mistake, Jen. I'm sorry, but it's definitely your dad. They got a positive identification. You've no idea why he would be there? Do the names Jonathan Rodriguez or Jamie Leggatt mean anything to you?'

She moved so quickly that Connor staggered back, almost lost his footing. Jen brought her arms up, shoved Connor in the chest, something harder and uglier than hate blackening her eyes.

'Stop treating me like a fucking witness!' she roared, as she took a step back. 'This isn't one of your cases, this is my *dad*. I know you don't give a fuck – you always made it quite clear what you thought of him. You probably caused it – that's what you do, though, Connor, isn't it, make sure those around you get hurt?' She raised her crutch, shook it at him. 'You, you . . .'

Then, as though whatever string was holding her up had been cut, she collapsed onto the couch, buried her head in her hands and rocked forward, guttural sobs shaking her body.

Connor took a step forward, felt a warm hand on his shoulder. Turned to see Donna.

'Give her a minute,' she whispered, as she offered him what he guessed was a comforting smile. 'Go on outside for a bit. I'll talk to her. I was the same when Mark died. Looking for someone to blame. Just give me some time with her.'

Connor looked between Donna and Jen, torn. All he wanted was to wrap his arms around Jen, shield her from the world, and yet . . .

''Mon,' Paulie said, as he stepped towards the patio doors. 'We can talk outside. Gie the lassies some time together.'

Donna gave a nod of encouragement, and Connor reluctantly followed Paulie into the garden.

'What the fuck happened?' Paulie snarled as he bounced the hammer in his grip. At the far end of the garden, Connor could see why he had needed it: a bench was half dismantled, propped up at an angle. Connor knew how it felt.

'I don't know,' he said. 'All Ford told me was that they'd had to use fingerprints and medical records to identify him. Face was mutilated. Teeth destroyed. I said I'd go in later and make the formal identification for the family. No way I want Jen seeing that.'

Paulie nodded slowly, his face suddenly very pale, his eyes black pits that seemed to absorb and smother any light that fell into them.

'Look, those names I mentioned,' Connor said, 'do they ring a bell? Would Duncan have had any, ah, business up at the university? Anyone been looking for him recently?' He let the question hang in the air, the rest of the conversation going unspoken. MacKenzie had been one of the biggest hauliers in Scotland, moving everything from industrial equipment to furniture. But he had used that network to ship other items as well, items that the police would find interesting if they were ever discovered.

'Naw,' Paulie said, after a moment. 'There's no' been any hassle recently that I know of. But I'll ask about, see if anything pops up.'

'Thanks,' Connor said, the word feeling clumsy and inadequate.

'Don't thank me,' Paulie replied. He squared his shoulders, and Connor thought for a moment that he was going to swing the hammer into his face. 'But I do want a favour in return.'

'What's that?' Connor asked, not sure he wanted to know the answer.

Paulie gave a small, tight smile that made Connor's skin crawl. 'When you go see his body, I want to come with you.'

'Why?' Connor asked. 'It's only a confirmation and signing some papers. One of us can handle it.'

'I fucking know that,' Paulie hissed. 'I dinnae gie a fuck about the paperwork. But I want to see Duncan's body. See what was done with him. That way, I'll know exactly what to do with the bastards who killed him when I find them.'

CHAPTER 26

In a strange way, the mortuary in the basement of Randolphfield police station always reminded Ford of a library. There was something about the forced quiet, the lowered voices, footsteps that sounded like insults and the stillness of the place that reminded him of the reading rooms and libraries of his youth. And, like those refuges where he could let the world fade away and grasp the simple opportunity to think, Ford found the place secretly relaxing.

Not today.

He was in Walter Tennant's office, a small, cramped room off the main examination area. He knew he should be using his own office, making sure the murder room was up and running, that detectives were being given assignments. But after the initial identification of Duncan MacKenzie as the body in the loch, Ford had felt the need to get away, find somewhere quiet.

Which had brought him here.

He looked to his left, at the window that gave onto the main examination room, the post-mortem table gleaming in the harsh overhead lights. How many bodies had he watched Tennant cut open there? How many horrors had he seared into his brain over the years? He looked beyond the table, to the wall of body lockers beyond. Felt a chill as he realised Duncan MacKenzie was lying in one, his faceless head mercifully in darkness.

Tennant had established that the cause of death was not, as Ford had suspected, the catastrophic injuries to MacKenzie's head. They had been caused later, by blunt-force trauma. The post-mortem report listed the likely weapon as a ball-peen hammer or a similar object with a small, compact head. The actual cause of death was a single stab wound to the heart, made by a long, single-edged blade. Death would have been nearly instantaneous, giving the killer all the time they needed to mutilate MacKenzie's face.

But, Ford thought with a shudder, although the killing blow had been quick, MacKenzie's death had not. Tennant had found other injuries on the body: ligature marks around the wrists and ankles, the fingers of both hands broken at every joint. Ford felt a thrill of revulsion at the thought: whoever had killed MacKenzie, they had taken their time torturing him beforehand.

But why? To blackmail him? Get him to reveal some secret? It was possible: MacKenzie may have been a respected haulier and businessman on the outside, but everyone with a warrant card knew he was one of the most feared gangsters in Central Scotland. But the damage to his face told Ford a different story. Tennant's report stated that the force required to obliterate the skeletal structure of a man's face was considerable, with more than a dozen blows required. To Ford, that spoke of a rage fuelled by hatred. It was personal. An act of revenge.

But, Ford wondered, revenge for what? And how was it connected to Jamie Leggatt?

He sighed, felt an all-too-familiar headache snarl behind his eyes. Too many questions. Not enough answers. And what was he going to do with Connor Fraser? He knew he was bringing MacKenzie's daughter, Jen, into the station to make a statement about the last movements of her father and, when he did, they were going to have a difficult conversation. Getting Fraser to look into a cold case was one thing, but now that cold case had been directly linked to his girlfriend's father, making the case personal for him. Ford knew he should tell Fraser to back off, let the police handle it. Knew also that it would be an exercise in futility to do so. He knew there was no love lost between Fraser and Duncan MacKenzie, but the man's death had injured Fraser's girlfriend. That, plus the killer having blown another man to hell in front of him, ensured that, one way or another, Connor Fraser would be at the heart of the investigation.

Ford felt only a sliver of guilt at this. In truth, he was envious of Fraser's autonomy, of his ability to duck the red tape that ensnared him and take the most direct approach to get answers.

And, Ford realised, they needed answers. Desperately. Two people were dead. And Ford had been a policeman long enough to know that theirs would not be the last blood spilled before this case was over.

CHAPTER 27

By the time Connor and Paulie stepped back into the flat, some-thing had cooled and hardened in Jen. The anguish and the sobs had vanished, and her eyes were hard and clear, the determination in them somehow amplified by the hectic colour of her skin and tear-fuelled puffiness. When she spoke, her voice was calm, flat, almost hollow.

Connor realised it reminded him of her father.

'So, what happens now?' she asked, her eyes fixed on Connor. It was as if Donna and Paulie had ceased to exist for her.

'Police are going to need a statement,' Connor replied. 'Last time you saw your dad, how he'd been in the last few weeks. Anything that might have been bothering him, that sort of thing. I can take you to the station, go through it all with you.'

'No,' Jen replied, her gaze hardening so much that Connor found it difficult not to look away. 'I can deal with that. Paulie,' her eyes flashed across the room like the glinting blade of a Stanley knife, 'you'll give me a lift to the police station?'

'Aye.' Paulie coughed, after a confused glance at Connor. 'If that's what you want, but I thought . . .'

Jen held up a hand. 'Connor's going to be busy,' she said, her eyes sliding back to him as she spoke. 'You're going to find who did this to my dad, aren't you, Connor? You owe me that much.'

Connor nodded, her previous words rising in his mind. *You*

probably caused it. That's what you do, though, Connor, isn't it, make sure those around you get hurt?

Was she right? Was he cursed to bring pain and suffering to those he loved? Or was she just lashing out in shock, trying to inflict the agony she felt on the man she loved?

He wasn't sure he wanted to know the answer.

'Good,' she said. 'And to save you some time, I can tell you what I'm going to tell the police. The last time I ...' she paused, the cold resolve in her eyes wavering for just an instant '... the last time I spoke to Dad was last night. It was when you were reading those bloody case files, Connor. He texted me, asked me how the move was going, if I needed anything.'

Connor considered. 'Was that unusual?' he asked. 'Wasn't your dad more likely to call you than text?'

'Mostly, he would call,' she said, after a moment. 'But if he was busy he texted. As long as he kept in touch. That was the most important thing to him.'

Connor felt another question tremble behind his lips, swallowed it. He wanted to know if the text had been different from any her dad had sent before – different phrasing, punctuation, language structure. But asking that would open up a Pandora's Box, one that held the very real possibility that the last message Jen had received from her father was actually from his killer, sent to her to create the false narrative that Duncan MacKenzie was alive and well.

'Right,' he said, forcing his mind back to the present. 'And the names I mentioned, Jonathan Rodriguez and Jamie Leggatt, they don't mean anything to you?'

She looked down, as though the answer might be in her lap. 'No,' she said. 'The only reason I know those names is your involvement with them over the last couple of days. I don't remember Dad ever mentioning them to me, though I suppose he might have. He did a lot of business with a lot of people over the years.'

'Don't you worry about that,' Paulie rumbled, his attempt to soften his voice painful in Connor's ears. 'I'll deal with it. I'll check our records at the office, see if they crop up anywhere. I'll do it as soon as we're done with the polis.'

Jen's eyes ranged over them, then fell on Donna. 'Can you keep this out of the press for a while?' she asked, her voice almost human now. 'Give me a little time to . . .'

Donna held up a hand. 'Of course,' she said, 'I won't report a thing until the police officially name your dad.'

If Jen saw the same calculation in Donna's eyes as she spoke that Connor did, she didn't show it. Donna was a reporter, a damn good one, and she had just been given a massive scoop on a huge story. No way would she merely sit on it.

'Fine,' Jen said, grunting softly as she rose to her feet and leaned on her crutch. 'Paulie, let's go.'

Paulie nodded, looked to Connor. 'Remember our agreement,' he said.

'No problem,' Connor said, the thought of delaying the viewing of Duncan MacKenzie's body for a few hours suddenly hugely appealing.

'So where are you going to start?' Jen asked him, the words a challenge.

'Rodriguez,' Connor said simply. 'He's at the heart of this, and I think it's well past time I had a little chat with him.'

He turned away from Jen, found himself reluctant to break her calm, empty gaze. At least it was something, some fleeting form of contact, no matter how tainted.

'I take it you'll want to come with me?' he asked Donna.

'Just try to stop me,' she said, as she grabbed her bag from the couch.

CHAPTER 28

A call to Simon established that Rodriguez had rented a house in Dunblane, a small, affluent town a ten-minute drive north of Stirling. Connor had visited a few times with Jen, heading to a pub close to the banks of the River Allan for lunch. But, like too many people, he mainly knew the town's name because of the massacre that had happened there in 1996: a plain-faced monster named Thomas Hamilton had stormed the primary school and shot dead sixteen children and one teacher.

It was, Connor thought, as he parked outside the address Simon had given him, a reminder that evil and the desire to kill held nothing sacred, not even the lives of children. And a coward with a gun could shatter countless lives, his one act of violence rippling out across the decades that followed, touching and tainting the lives of those who had survived and the families of those he had slain.

'So how do you want to handle this?' Donna asked from the passenger seat, jarring Connor from his thoughts. She had stayed silent since they had left the flat, and Connor was grateful for the chance to process the aftermath of his confrontation with Jen.

'Directly,' he replied. 'You can work out how you cover this with Rodriguez. Just try to keep me and Simon out of it. If I'm going to find whoever did this, the last thing I need is a camera in my face as I do it. And remember what you said to Jen. Not sure how quickly the police will release MacKenzie's name, but . . .'

Donna held up a hand. 'I gave my word,' she said. 'I won't run his name as the loch victim until the police announce it. But . . .' she paused, and Connor could see the faintest twitch of a smile '. . . that doesn't mean I can't do the background and have his bio and library shots ready as soon as his name drops.'

'Aye,' Connor said, as he unfastened his seatbelt and grabbed the door handle. 'Fair enough.'

The house was on a whitewashed row of terraced homes opposite what Connor thought was Dunblane Cathedral. There was no doorbell that he could see, so he knocked on the door, wincing as the sound echoed through the suburban quiet. After a moment, the door swung open to reveal a tall woman with long, brunette hair that seemed to accentuate the hazel of her eyes. Her face was slim, almost to the point of being gaunt, her cheekbones highlighted by subtle make-up that complemented a deep tan. Her gaze danced across Connor, a trace of a smile on her lips, as if they had shared a secret joke.

'Ah, I'm Connor Fraser,' he said, 'I'm here to see . . .'

'Mr Rodriguez. Yes, I know, Mr Fraser. I'm Amanda Lyons, Mr Rodriguez's executive assistant. Please, come in. Your associate is already here.'

She led them down a long corridor to a large, open-plan living and dining area. Simon was standing at a breakfast bar, a mug in one hand. He raised it slightly in salute as Connor and Donna followed Amanda into the room. Jonathan Rodriguez stood on the opposite side of the bar.

He turned as Amanda spoke, his smile flicking on like an overhead light as he did.

Aaaand action, Connor thought randomly.

'Ah, Mr Fraser, at last. Jonathan Rodriguez,' he said, leaning forward and offering Connor a hand as his smile intensified.

Connor shook the hand, thinking that the man in front of him was shorter than he appeared on television but somehow bigger as well, as though his personality was filling the room to make up for his lack of physical stature. 'Nice place,' he said, as Rodriguez let the handshake linger just a moment longer than he was comfortable with.

'Ah, yes,' Rodriguez said, making a show of looking around the room. 'My station back in the States arranged it for us. Cheaper than a hotel for an extended stay,' he said.

'And how long are you planning on staying?' Connor asked.

'For as long as it takes, Mr Fraser,' Rodriguez replied, his voice growing serious, his smile cold. 'After the events of today, I'd say there's definitely a story here, wouldn't you?'

'Hmm,' Connor mumbled, noncommittal. There was something unsettling about watching Rodriguez chameleon his way through moods and personalities, shifting seamlessly from genial host to grave announcer of bad news. It was, he realised, like switching channels on TV news: the story was the same, but the presentation was different on every channel.

'Why don't we all take a seat?' Amanda asked, gesturing to two sofas at either side of a large coffee-table in the seating area of the room.

'Of course, sorry, I should have offered,' Rodriguez said. 'And can I offer you anything to drink? Mr Fraser? Donna? As your friend Mr McCartney can attest, I make a mean cup of coffee.'

'No, thank you,' Connor said, not moving from where he stood. Beside him, Donna shook her head slightly. 'You said there's a story here. What made you look into your dad's death now, after all this time?'

Rodriguez took a deep breath, exhaled. When he spoke again, Connor felt as though he was seeing the real Jonathan Rodriguez for the first time.

'I was only nine when Dad, ah, passed away,' he said. 'He and Mum were having problems – I remember a lot of arguments – but when he died, it was like a tether had been cut. There was nothing left for her here so she moved us to Los Angeles, to be with my aunt Susan and her husband, Paul. But I always had questions about who Dad was, and the older I got, the more I was able to find out. His work at the university, his political activism, that kind of stuff.' He gave a rueful smile. 'I suppose you could say investigating my dad became my hobby. Some people collect stamps, some build Lego. Me? I collected everything I could about my dad.'

'Okay,' Connor said, thinking about the revelations to which looking into his own father had led him. 'I can understand that. But why did you come back to Scotland to make a documentary about him? And where are these "sources" you claim told you that your father's death was more than an accident?'

Something hard and ugly flashed in Rodriguez's eyes as they flicked from Connor to Donna. There was cold calculation in that glance, but Connor couldn't understand what the equation was.

'It was about three months ago,' he said. 'I knew the fortieth anniversary of Dad's death was coming up, and I felt there should be some sort of memorial of that. Amanda and I were working on an idea, a TV segment, a private trip back to Stirling, when the messages started.'

'Messages?' Connor said, noticing Simon and Donna tense slightly.

'Emails at first,' Amanda said. 'Short messages saying that the anniversary of Robert's death was coming up, and it was time to tell the truth about his murder. That's what I remember most about the early messages. They always referred to it as murder.'

'You've still got those messages?' Simon asked.

'Yes, of course,' Amanda said. 'If Jonathan agrees, I'm happy to share them with you.'

'Of course,' Rodriguez said. 'After all, we're working together, aren't we?'

Connor ignored the comment. 'So what happened?' he asked.

'Well, we emailed back, asking for details and an explanation of what was meant. And we got it. Over time whoever was mailing us sent us a variety of documents relating to my dad, his support for an independent Scottish republic, his campaigning and speeches. All stuff that was in the public domain. But then there were other items, pictures and documents that never made it to the public domain.'

'Like what?' Connor asked.

'Like this,' Amanda said, passing Connor an iPad. He took it, her eyes holding his as he nodded his thanks. On the screen was a black-and-white picture of a group of men. They looked as if they were on some type of camping trip, all in thick, military-style jackets, hats and combat trousers. At the front of the group, a man crouched, an ornate walking stick held in one hand, a long, wicked-looking knife in the other.

'That's my dad,' Rodriguez said, tapping the screen. But Connor wasn't looking at that. Instead, he was studying a man at the back of the group, holding one side of a larger version of the banner he had seen in Jamie Leggatt's office after he had been blown to pieces.

'Saor Alba,' he whispered.

'Yes,' Amanda confirmed. 'All the emails were signed off like that. It's Gaelic, isn't it? Means "Free Scotland"?'

Connor felt his head nod, unable to take his eyes from the iPad and the face he had seen. Was he right? He couldn't be sure, but the sudden thundering of his heart in his ears and the sick thrill of adrenaline catching at the back of his throat told him he was. He turned the screen back to Rodriguez, tapped on the man.

'Any idea who this is?' he asked.

Rodriguez peered at the screen, shrugged. 'No,' he said. 'None of the others in the picture were identified. Just Dad. Why?'

'Connor, what?' Donna asked, as though sensing something was wrong.

He passed the iPad to her. 'Guy top left, holding the banner,' he said, watching as her eyes widened and her face paled.

'Jesus,' she whispered. 'I mean he's a lot younger, a bit thinner, but that's . . .'

Connor nodded. 'Yeah,' he said, as he turned back to Rodriguez.

'Tell me,' he said. 'Does the name Duncan MacKenzie mean anything to you?'

CHAPTER 29

Paulie sat in his car outside Randolphfield police station, glaring up at the Police Scotland logo with unfiltered disgust. Given his line of work, it was no surprise that he hated the police, and over the years he had taken a savage joy in slipping through their fingers when he had stepped onto the other side of the law. He had stolen, killed and coerced over the years, and had always managed to stay one step ahead of those who wanted to cage him like an animal. But today his antipathy came from a different, more pragmatic place.

Today Paulie hated the police because they were forcing him to waste his time.

He had driven Jen here as requested, the entire trip filled with a fragile, charged silence. When he had looked over at her, he had been struck by how like her mother she was. The same defiant set of her jaw, the long blonde hair pulled back into a tight ponytail, eyes hard and clear, glaring out at the road, as though daring a car to pull out in front of them. When they had arrived, he had offered to walk her into the station, and she had turned on him with seething fury in her eyes.

'I can manage,' she said, her voice little more than a whisper. Then she blinked and dropped her chin slightly. 'Sorry, Paulie,' she said, the pain in her voice stabbing into his chest. 'Thanks. I'll be okay. But can you wait for me? Can't imagine this will take too long.'

'Course I'll wait, hen,' he said. 'You do what you need to do. They'll just want a statement on when you last saw your dad, anything un- usual, that sort of thing. Don't let them put words into your mouth, and if you feel uncomfortable, walk away. Just remember, you're here voluntarily.'

She smiled, a little of the old Jen peeking out in the dimples of her cheeks. 'Thanks, Paulie,' she said, then got out of the car. Watching her limp into the building, stooped forward on her crutch, Paulie felt an impotent fury. What type of world was it where an innocent girl like Jen could be so badly hurt?

The same type of world, he thought, that let her know a monster like him and have Duncan MacKenzie as a father.

He glanced again at the dashboard clock. Twenty-five minutes now. Twenty-five minutes he had been sitting there while the police played their games and filled in their forms. Twenty-five minutes in which whoever had killed Duncan MacKenzie had breathed free air without Paulie hunting them down.

He forced himself to be calm. She would be finished soon enough, and then Paulie would be free to hunt. He knew the police would interrupt him further – as one of Duncan's closest advisers he would be dragged in to make his own statement at some point – but that would be for later. Once he'd established the facts and created a time- line that suited him.

The last time he had met with Duncan, it had been at the head office of MacKenzie Haulage, which was at the heart of an industrial yard on the edge of Stirling, close to the M9. Paulie trawled through the meeting in his mind, found nothing that raised an alarm or hinted that MacKenzie was in some type of trouble. They had gone over a contract to transport fabrication equipment from Liverpool to Inverness. Then MacKenzie had reverted to his favourite topic – Jen moving in with Connor Fraser.

'That bastard doesn't deserve her,' he had spat. 'I mean, he's stood by her while she recovers from the accident, but she could do better than that fucking meathead, right?'

Paulie had murmured agreement, unwilling to stoke the fires of Duncan's hatred and set him off on another rant that involved ques- tioning Fraser's heritage. Paulie had little love for the man, but he had proven time and again that he cared for Jen and would do whatever was needed to protect her. That was good enough for Paulie.

Which all led him back to the same question: who had killed Duncan, and why? Frustrated, he pulled his phone from his pocket and dialled the haulage yard. Waited a moment until Janet, Duncan's secretary, answered. She had also been Duncan's lover for the last four months, and Paulie had been smart enough to go along with the lie that nothing was happening between them. Did she have a husband? he wondered absently. Was he a man prone to violence and revenge? And how would she take the news that her lover was dead?

'Hi, Janet,' he said, pushing the questions out of his mind as he concentrated on the lie he was about to tell. He would leave the police to tell her Duncan was dead. Right now he needed her helpful, not hysterical. 'Wondering if you can do me a favour. Boss wants me to check a couple of things out. We might have to move some meetings and do some follow-ups on work over the last couple of weeks. Could you take a quick photo of his diary over the last month, please, and send it over to me?'

'I could,' Janet said, her tone that of a teacher talking to a pupil who couldn't understand what they were being told, 'or I could give you shared access to his online diary for the fiftieth time and you could log in and look for yourself.'

Paulie ground his teeth, bit back his answer. He hated technology, couldn't understand why everyone wanted to make things more complicated than basic pen and paper.

'I'll do that,' he said, his voice calm as he reminded himself that the woman he was talking to was about to have her life shattered, 'but this is a bit of a rush job, so can you send the pictures to me?'

'Okay, okay.' She sighed. 'And if you're talking to Dun— ah, Mr MacKenzie, tell him to give me a call, will you? I expected him in the office this morning, got a few things to go over with him myself.'

'Will do,' Paulie said, the words flowing easily from his lips. 'And thanks.'

He ended the call and, less than a minute later, his phone pinged with the pictures Janet had taken. He opened the first – a standard shot of MacKenzie's diary, the one that always lay at the centre of his desk. Paulie knew he had a personal one for more sensitive matters, but for now, this was as good a place to start as any.

Janet had been thorough, taking pictures of the two-page spreads going back a month. Paulie felt a strange hollowness as he looked at MacKenzie's handwriting, realising he would never write another word. He scanned the pages, seeing nothing but the usual meetings with his drivers, suppliers and clients. He was so numbed by the minutiae that he almost didn't see it, scrolling past the image, then stopping, as though what he had just seen had taken a while to buffer in his mind. He flicked back, zoomed in on one entry for Wednesday a week previously.

'Bannockburn, 3 p.m.,' he read. 'For SA. Witches Craig.'

Paulie felt his pulse throb in his temples. 'Bannockburn. Witches Craig,' he whispered, his tongue suddenly thick and dry in his mouth. 'Jesus.'

He grabbed his phone, dialled. Waited, praying the police would keep Jen busy long enough for him to make the call.

'Fraser,' he barked, before Connor could speak. 'Need a favour. Now. Get onto your police pal, Ford, ask him if Duncan was stabbed with a long, single-edged blade.' He closed his eyes, remembered. 'About twelve inches. If he was, I might know where to look for the bastards that killed him.'

CHAPTER 30

It didn't take Connor long to confirm with Ford that Paulie had been right and a single-edged long blade had been used on Duncan MacKenzie. After Paulie's call, he stepped out of Rodriguez's rented house into a street so quiet that it jarred with the tumble of thoughts in his head. He phoned the policeman, ducked the questions on where he had come by the information relating to the knife, not wanting Paulie to get dragged into a police interview room when he was waiting to take Jen home.

After assuring Ford he would meet him for a debriefing as soon as he could, Connor stood for a moment, considering. Paulie had found something that gave him a clue to the murder weapon used on Duncan MacKenzie. But what was that? And how much of what he knew would he share? Connor had noted Paulie had said 'we' when tracking down MacKenzie's killers, but what guarantee did he have that the man wouldn't go charging off in search of revenge the moment he had driven Jen home?

Frustrated, he called up the image Rodriguez had shown him, which he had forwarded to his own email. A group shot, seven men including MacKenzie and Robert Balfour. They were in some kind of woodland clearing, their faces set and resolute in a way that only a mixture of youth and righteous zeal can produce. Connor studied Robert Balfour, who was obviously the leader of the group, crouched in front of them, a long, wicked-looking knife in his hand. Was that, he wondered, the same blade that had been plunged into Duncan MacKenzie's chest? And, if it was, who had wielded it? It stood to reason that it would be one of the other men in the photograph, but who were they? Judging from how young Duncan MacKenzie was, Connor guessed the picture had been taken at least forty years ago. Forty years, he thought, forty years since Robert Balfour had been found in Airthrey Loch, just like Duncan MacKenzie. And then there was the banner MacKenzie was holding in the picture – Saor Alba. Free Scotland. The same slogan he had seen in Jamie Leggatt's office just after he had been blown into the afterlife. The killer was obviously trying to say something. But what was it? And who was he speaking to?

He had dialled the number before he had consciously made the decision to do so, Robbie Lindsay picking up on the third ring.

'Boss,' he said. 'I heard about Jen's dad. I'm so sorry. Are you okay? Is Jen?'

Connor raised an eyebrow, felt the urge to ask Robbie how he was privy to classified information before it had been released, swallowed it. Since joining Sentinel Robbie had proven himself to be a shrewd and thorough investigator who had a knack for learning what other people didn't want him to know.

'Need a favour,' Connor said. 'I'm going to send you an image. I need to know who is in it, and anything else you can find out. Two of the men have already been identified, Duncan MacKenzie and Robert Balfour. But I need to know who else is in that shot. Also, run a background check on Saor Alba, any groups that might have used that slogan in the early eighties onwards.' He thought again of the men in the picture, their heavy military-style clothing and hats, expressions set and determined. He had seen men like that before, while working as a police officer in Belfast.

'Check paramilitary groups as well,' he said. 'And cross-reference that with Professor Jamie Leggatt, Dundee University.'

'Leggatt?' Robbie asked. 'That's the guy who got blown up in Dundee earlier on, isn't it?'

'Yeah,' Connor said, an image of Leggatt's bloodied, ruined stump where his arm had once been flashing across his mind as he spoke. 'The very same.'

'Okay,' Robbie said. 'Send me the image, and I'll see what I can do. What's the clock on this?'

'Soon as you can,' Connor replied.

'Right,' Robbie said. 'Will get back to you ASAP. But, boss . . .' His voice trailed off, and Connor could almost hear the question in the silence that followed.

'No, Robbie, I've no idea what's going on,' he said, as he turned in the street and looked back towards the house Rodriguez had rented. 'Something else,' he said. 'Run me another check. Robert Balfour's son, Jonathan Rodriguez. Career, background, anything that could link him with Chief Constable Peter Guthrie.'

'Guthrie?' Robbie said, surprise in his voice now.

'Yeah,' Connor said, as he stepped towards the door. 'Rodriguez seems to have some kind of special access deal with the chief. I want to know why. I'm going to ask him right now, but I need you to find out if what he'll tell me is the truth.'

'Copy that,' Robbie said, then killed the call before Connor could say anything else.

He pocketed his phone, took another step towards the door. Was just about to open it when it swung open to reveal Simon, his face pinched and grave. 'What?' Connor asked.

'Rodriguez and Donna just got another message,' he said. 'You'd better see this. I think whoever blew up Leggatt has just set the timer running on another bomb.'

CHAPTER 31

'It came in a minute ago, same as last time,' Donna said, as Connor stepped back into the room. She was offering him her iPad as she walked, her drawn, pale face giving the impression she was trying to pass him some perverse baton and absolve herself of any involvement in this nightmare.

'You both got the same message at the same time?' he asked.

Rodriguez nodded, but it was Amanda Lyons who spoke. 'More or less,' she said. 'The date stamps on the delivery times of the emails match.'

Smart, Connor thought, as he met her cool, almost detached gaze. Compared to Rodriguez, who was as pale and drawn as Donna, she was the epitome of calm.

'So what have we got?' Connor asked, as he took the iPad from Donna.

'Same as before,' she said. 'A message, that "Saor Alba" shit and an attached movie file.'

'What's on it?' Connor asked, his mind darting back to Jamie Leggatt's office.

'Easier if you just look for yourself,' Donna said.

Connor gazed down at the iPad. An email sat open, eight lines of text.

Ms Blake, Mr Rodriguez,

By now you will know of Duncan MacKenzie's death. It is only a small step towards justice, but a satisfying one. My next action will be more decisive, and much more instructive. For you, Ms Blake, it will give you a story. For Mr Rodriguez, it may shed some light on the real game that is being played here. Again, I attach a small amusement that will illustrate my resolve.

Ex 12: 42-51

Saor Alba

Connor looked between Rodriguez and Donna, got nothing but blank incomprehension in return. He went back to the iPad, saw the MOV file at the bottom of the email. Clicked it.

The file opened to an image of what looked like a small workbench. There was no clutter, just a row of tools in perfect alignment in the top right corner, what looked like a neatly bundled knot of wiring below them. The camera swayed slightly, and then a small item was pushed into the shot. Connor felt his breath catch in his throat as he heard the click from Jamie Leggatt's desk the moment before it exploded ring in his ears.

It was about the size of a paperback book, small and tightly constructed. Two greasy grey rectangles that looked like old-fashioned blocks of butter lay at either side of what Connor recognised as on old-style flip-top mobile phone. Various wires snaked from the phone to the grey blocks, which, Connor noticed, were studded with small obsidian dots that glittered in the light from the camera.

'Fuck,' he whispered, recognising the heads of what had been pushed into the grey blocks. 'Nail bomb.'

Off-camera, a tuneless whistling began, the tune so badly mangled Connor couldn't recognise it. Hands appeared from either side of the frame, and Connor realised that whoever had filmed this had done so using a body cam clipped to their shirt.

The bomb was picked up carefully in gloved hands, and placed gently into a large, Jiffy-style envelope that appeared in the frame. Connor watched, unaware that he was holding his breath.

The camera lingered on the sealed envelope for a moment. Then it was turned over. A large Post-it note had been placed across, obscuring the address that had been written on it. But it had been placed diagonally, just enough for Connor to read the EH postcode on the bottom line.

Edinburgh, he thought.

The Post-it note bore the same sign-off Connor recognised from the email: Ex 12, 42-51.

The whistling stopped, and then there was a hissing voice, so tight and nasal that Connor knew whoever was speaking was trying to disguise what they really sounded like.

'The cheque's in the mail,' the voice snarled. 'Saor Alba.'

The screen went blank as the clip ended, and Connor felt the world rush into the silence.

'We need to call DCI Ford, now,' Simon said, his voice a scream in the fragile quiet of the room.

'Yeah,' Connor said, mind racing. 'Because someone in Edinburgh is about to get a very nasty surprise through the post. The question is who? And why?'

CHAPTER 32

If he were a more charitable man, Ford would almost have felt sorry for Chief Constable Peter Guthrie. Since the call from Fraser alerting them to the film of a nail bomb being put into an envelope destined for somewhere in Edinburgh, Guthrie's life had become an endless succession of phone calls and competing demands on his attention, as everyone from counter-terrorism agencies to government ministers got involved.

It was, Ford thought, understandable. A credible terrorist threat on the Scottish capital would put the city into lockdown, with every piece of mail sent to official premises, from police stations and hospitals to government buildings, being carefully screened. But what about private addresses? What could be done to stop someone in a quiet residential street in Morningside or Stockbridge opening a package that would blow them into eternity?

It was a question that Guthrie was clearly wrestling with – and losing. But despite this, Ford found himself unable to summon sympathy for his boss. The man was a bureaucrat and a politician, put on the promotion fast-track, then given the job of running Police Scotland by a First Minister who liked to talk tough on law and order even as the service haemorrhaged officers driven to the brink by punishing hours and not enough resources. Ford had had a few run-ins with Guthrie over the years, and the opinion he had formed of him was only reinforced by what he was seeing now – the man was out of his depth, and people were most likely going to get hurt because of his ineptitude.

Ford tore himself from his thoughts, turning his concentration back to his computer and the footage Fraser had forwarded to him. He had run through the film more than a dozen times, poring over every frame for some clue as to who was doing this – and why. But all he had learned was summed up in the single frozen frame in front of him now: the image of a bomb that looked all too viable, out there somewhere, waiting to explode.

Was it, Ford thought, the same type of bomb that had been used to kill Jamie Leggatt, or was it even more lethal, designed to do even greater damage? Letter bombs hadn't been widely used since the end of the Troubles in Northern Ireland in 1998, yet there was something horribly familiar about it all to Ford. The bombs. The use of key words in warnings phoned in to journalists on news desks minutes before detonation. The creeping fear that no one was safe. Was this somehow linked to paramilitaries in Northern Ireland? And how did Robert Balfour and Duncan MacKenzie play into this? Or, he thought with a creeping dread, was it something simpler, someone on some messianic crusade? The reference on the note in the video was simple enough to decipher: Exodus 12, verse 42: *Because the Lord kept vigil that night to bring them out of Egypt, on this night all the Israelites are to keep vigil to honour the Lord for the generations to come.*

But what did it mean? The last thing Ford needed was a bomber on a mission from God.

He gave a frustrated sigh as he rubbed his eyes hard enough to make dark stars skitter across the blackness. Too many questions. He wanted to go home. See Mary, talk to her about anything that wasn't police work. Soak in the silence of their home as though he was slipping into a warm bath and washing away all the blood and pain he had seen.

'Sir?'

Troughton was hanging about in the door frame, as though afraid to step into the room. Ford could see excitement glitter in the young detective's eyes, dimly remembered feeling that way about a case himself.

'What?' he asked.

'Just had word, sir. Suspicious package has been intercepted at St Andrew's House in Edinburgh. Seems the security staff there got the alert we sent out, were extra careful screening the mail and they found it.'

Ford felt a spark of something like hope. Maybe no one would be hurt after all. 'Place has been evacuated, I take it?'

'Yes, sir,' Troughton replied. 'And the bomb squad is on the way now. Just wanted to give you the heads-up as the chief is making for Edinburgh now.'

Ford shook his head. Smiled. 'Course he is,' he said. 'Someone just sent a bomb to the headquarters of the Scottish Government. He'll be there to lap up the TV cameras, play the big hero and kiss the First Minister's arse. I doubt there . . . What?'

Troughton coughed, tried to bite back the smile that had been growing on his lips as Ford spoke. 'Sorry, sir, that's why I'm here. Been sent by the chief. He wants you in the motorcade with him. He's leaving in two minutes.'

CHAPTER 33

They scurried like ants on the screen in front of him, their panic bleeding from the television.

It was, he thought, intoxicating.

The story had broken about ten minutes ago, news channels cutting to live shots of people streaming out of St Andrew's House and collecting in shuffling, confused knots at muster points outside a police cordon, across the road from the building, in the shadow of Calton Hill.

'Security alert at Scottish Government HQ', the caption on the screen read, as a generic-looking reporter with a bad combover and too many teeth spouted inane facts to the camera, saying anything to fill time on air until he had some meaningful development to report.

They would have it soon enough, he thought. The stage was set. Everyone was playing the roles in which he had cast them, aware of it or not. He just needed the star of the scene to arrive. He flipped open the phone in his hand, closed it again. Told himself to be patient.

He looked back at the screen, another long tracking shot, the camera lingering on the blunt granite façade of the building, then zooming in to the main entrance, a rotating door with the Scottish Government branding above it. He sneered at that. Before St Andrew's House had been built, a prison had sat on the site, the Calton Gaol. At least that, he thought, was a more honest expression of the purpose of the building than its current masquerade as home to a government without the boot of Westminster firmly on its neck.

The building that would serve his needs well.

He saw her a few minutes later, at the corner of a shot, arguing with a police officer manning the cordon, pointing between him and a large, fat man with a camera hefted over his shoulder. She had made impressive time from Stirling, he thought, but from what he had learned of Donna Blake, he would have guessed that she had headed to Edinburgh the moment she had seen the film he had sent. It was why he had left part of the postcode uncovered – giving her just enough information to get into the general area and be on hand when the real games began.

He studied the screen, felt a pang of disappointment when he didn't see Connor Fraser or Simon McCartney anywhere. Not that it truly mattered. He would be seeing them soon enough.

He opened the phone again, felt a sharp thrill of adrenaline catch in his throat as he dialled the number. Thought again of the bomb, of the hours of work to perfect it, of the man who had shown him how to construct such a lethal device from a few bits of wiring, a small amount of plastic explosive and a mobile phone. He had learned those lessons well, and he thought that what was about to happen was a fitting tribute to the man who had been at once less and more than a teacher to him.

He closed his eyes, took a deep breath.

'Saor Alba,' he whispered, then hit dial.

CHAPTER 34

The drive to Edinburgh from Stirling usually took just over an hour. But after screaming along the M9 with sirens blaring, Chief Constable Guthrie's car made it in just over thirty minutes. Thirty minutes in which DCI Malcolm Ford almost regretted not believing in God or the afterlife.

The car was waved through the cordon, pulling to a stop just past St Andrew's House. Ford cursed under his breath as he spotted Donna Blake in the crowd at the other side of the cordon, talking into a camera. Of course she had been given a head start, he thought. Whoever was doing this was playing to an audience.

They got out of the car as a heavy-set man with a shaved head and dark eyes that didn't seem to blink marched towards them. Ford had seen him before, at the site of a car bombing in a village close to Stirling the previous year, found it impossible to remember the man's name.

'Chief,' he said, in a voice that sounded too gentle for his severe look. 'Sergeant Andrew Wilkins, bomb squad.'

Guthrie took Wilkins's extended hand with a wary look that told Ford exactly who was going to be in charge of this operation. And it wasn't Guthrie.

'What's the situation?' he asked, his tone expressing a confidence that wasn't matched by his body language.

Wilkins's eyes slid to Ford, as though asking a question. Ford simply shrugged, and Wilkins cleared his throat. 'Well, sir,' he said, 'we received a call from the security staff on the site, reporting a suspicious package had been delivered in the mail. We dispatched officers and evacuated the building. My men are in there now,' he jutted his jaw towards St Andrew's House, 'evaluating the threat level.'

'But we think this is a viable device?' Guthrie asked.

'We have to assume it is,' Wilkins replied, something hardening in his eyes. 'Especially in light of what happened at Dundee University yesterday.'

'Yes, yes, of course, of course,' Guthrie murmured in a distracted tone as he took in the scene around him. 'Well, keep me appraised, Sergeant. I'll be in the ops unit. The First Minister is at the parliament, and will want an update as soon as possible.'

'Of course, sir,' Wilkins said, his tone neutral as he shot another look towards Ford.

With a nod, Guthrie walked away, towards a large Police Scotland van with the words 'Mobile Command' plastered across its rear. It was, Ford knew, specially equipped with computers, communication devices and everything else that was needed to run a major incident from the scene.

He was just about to follow Guthrie when Wilkins's radio squawked. The sergeant unclipped it from his shoulder and clicked the reply button.

'Wilkins, go ahead,' he said, as Ford stepped closer.

'It's Jeffries, sir,' a reply came from the radio. 'We're in the post room now. We've isolated the device and, after examination, it looks like it's non-viable.'

Wilkins's jaw set, as though he had just bitten into something unpleasant. 'Repeat last,' he said.

'Device appears non-viable, sir,' Jeffries replied. 'The plastique is genuine, and the wiring is right, but there's no timer on the device and the phone doesn't have a battery attached, so there's no way it can be dialled to detonate. Looks like a nasty hoax.'

'Take all the necessary precautions, isolate the device and get it out here as soon as possible,' Wilkins said. 'I want a full sweep of the building made before we even think about letting anyone back in.'

'Copy that,' Jeffries said.

'What the hell?' Wilkins said to Ford, as he reattached his radio to its shoulder mount. 'Someone goes to all the trouble of wiring up a bomb, then doesn't leave a way to detonate it? It doesn't make sense.'

'No,' Ford agreed. 'But it does send a message.'

Wilkins was silent for a moment, then nodded. 'It lets us know that whoever sent it is the real deal,' he said. 'They've got the skills. They could have caused as much damage as they wanted at any time. They just chose not to. But why? What's the point of that? Why would—'

The blast came from nowhere, a primal, concussive scream that drowned Wilkins's words and sent both policemen staggering back. Ford whipped his head towards St Andrew's House, felt a moment of confusion as he realised the building was undamaged. But then he heard the screaming and, looking behind him, saw what had happened. On the opposite side of the street, smoke was belching from the bushes at the foot of Calton Hill. People were lying on the pavement and on the road like bloodied pieces of human rubble.

A bomb had gone off. Not in St Andrew's House, but in the bushes on the opposite side of the street, at the location that acted as a muster point for the staff who had just been evacuated from the building.

CHAPTER 35

'Jesus Christ!' Simon shouted, shattering the charged silence in the boardroom at Sentinel Securities. After alerting Ford to the threat, he and Connor had headed for Sentinel's office on the outskirts of Edinburgh, as Donna headed for the Edinburgh office of Sky News. They might not have known exactly where the threat was, but there was an unspoken agreement that they wanted to be as close to the action as possible.

Action that was now playing out on the wall-mounted TV screen in front of them, causing Simon to shout at the TV.

Connor watched as the camera jerked round from the blunt art-deco façade of St Andrew's House, back down Regent Road. Smoke billowed from Calton Hill, and Connor could see bodies around the epicentre of the bomb blast. He could see some people writhing on the ground, clearly hurt, but what troubled him more was the stillness of others.

Yet more lives he had been unable to save as he danced to some lunatic's tune, reacting rather than acting.

'Thank God,' Simon whispered, as Donna appeared on the screen. Her face was pale and tight, her eyes glittering with restrained tears and excitement. But when she spoke her voice was calm, distinct, professional, and admiration tinged Connor's relief.

'I'm reporting live from St Andrew's House in the heart of Edinburgh,' she said, 'where some kind of detonation has just taken place on the site where Scottish Government staff had congregated after being evacuated from St Andrew's House due to a bomb threat. We have no confirmed numbers for casualties as yet. It comes after a bomb was detonated at Dundee University, killing one member of staff.'

The camera panned away from Donna, zooming in on the site of the explosion rather than focusing on the injured people on the ground. It made sense, Connor thought. The last thing anyone wanted to see on the TV was bloodied body parts and people writhing in agony.

From what he could see, the main site of the blast was in a patch of messy shrubbery behind a low wall that separated the pavement from Calton Hill. Connor remembered going up the hill with Jen one day, visiting the observatory and the National Monument, an unfinished collection of columns that was designed to emulate the Parthenon in Greece and commemorate Scots who had died in the Napoleonic Wars.

Wars, he thought. Was that what this was? Another war, but being waged on different terms? With the bombings and the codewords and links to political sites, it had all the hallmarks of it.

He shook his head, some vague spark of recognition scratching at the back of his mind. He grabbed his phone, called up the last message from the attacker. That Bible reference – *Because the Lord kept vigil that night to bring them out of Egypt, on this night all the Israelites are to keep vigil to honour the Lord for the generations to come*: there was something in it. Something connected to Calton Hill. Something . . .

'And there's the slimy bastard, right on cue,' Simon snarled, rousing Connor from his thoughts. He looked back at the TV, saw Chief Constable Guthrie striding down Regent Road, as though drawn to the sirens of ambulances and the high-vis jackets of the paramedics who had arrived at the scene. Behind him, lingering at the cordon, Connor spotted Jonathan Rodriguez, who had hitched a lift to Edinburgh with Donna.

'That reminds me,' Connor said, leaning forward towards the conference table. He grabbed the phone and dialled Robbie Lindsay's extension.

'Robbie, Connor. You got anything for me yet on Rodriguez and his links to Guthrie?'

'I might have,' Robbie replied, his distracted tone telling Connor he was leaning into his computer screen, mining some obscure data from the internet in a way Connor couldn't understand.

'Quick as you can, Robbie,' Connor said, as he looked back towards the TV, thoughts of Calton Hill crowding into his mind again. *Because the Lord kept vigil.* Was it something he had seen? Something he had read? Something . . .

A memory flashed across his mind and he scrabbled for his laptop. Called up the search engine. Closed his eyes. Remembered that day with Donna. The National Monument.

Vigil . . .

He tapped in the search, found the page he was looking for. Called up a web page, which had another image of Calton Hill and Regent Road. Compared it to the images on the TV screen, and felt a cold, revolted excitement shiver up his back.

'Motherfucker,' he whispered.

Simon turned reluctantly from the TV. 'What?' he said. 'You got something?'

'The Lord kept vigil,' he said, turning the laptop so Simon could see the screen. 'It was a message. The bastard was telling us where he was going to detonate the bomb, what the real target was after all.'

'Jesus,' Simon whispered, as he studied the laptop, then turned back to the TV. 'It's the same place, isn't it? Almost exactly the same spot.'

'Yeah.' Connor remembered now. At the foot of Calton Hill, Jen had stopped for a moment, pointed out a nondescript patch of pavement diagonally across from St Andrew's House.

'Dad spent a lot of time here,' she had told him, then smiled at his confusion. 'Back in the nineties, when he was younger. Dad was never really political, but he hated Thatcher and the Tories for what they did to the miners. When they got back in, what, 'ninety-one, ninety-two, some activists set up a camp here, across the road from St Andrew's House, which housed the Scottish Office at the time. They were protesting against Westminster rule, calling for the recall of the Scottish Parliament.'

'And your dad was part of this protest?' Connor had asked.

'Yeah,' Jen replied. 'He was. Got a lot of pictures of him here back in the day. My God, Connor, his hair! But they didn't call it a protest.'

'Oh,' Connor had said.

'No,' Jen had replied. 'They called it "The Vigil".'

CHAPTER 36

It took Jen about an hour to agree her statement with the police, not that it told them, or her, much. The last time she had had any contact with her father had been two nights ago – a text message checking in to see how the move was going and a promise to catch up later in the week. The time before that had been the previous week, a lunch in Stirling. No, her father hadn't seemed preoccupied with anything. No, she wasn't aware of any change in his behaviour. Yes, it was natural for them to go for a few days without seeing each other. Yes, his somewhat fraught relationship with Connor Fraser was a factor in that. Yes, she would get back in touch if she thought of anything else that might be relevant. No, she did not want to speak to a family support officer or a counsellor.

She limped out of the station to Paulie's parked car, feeling her anger grow with each awkward step that sent a bolt of pain shooting up her back. She didn't want to be consoled or comforted or understood.

She wanted vengeance.

Paulie got out of the car as she approached, the chassis rocking as he moved his considerable bulk. He scuttled around to the passenger-side door, opening it for her.

'How'd you get on?' he asked, his voice so gentle it twisted in her ear.

'Fine,' she said, climbing into the car.

He nodded, seemingly satisfied, then returned to the driver's seat, the rocking of the car as he got in needling Jen's back with more pin-pricks of pain.

'Right,' he said, as he turned over the engine. 'Let's get you home, then.'

'No,' Jen said, the decision not made until the words were out of her mouth.

Paulie swivelled his massive head to her, confusion etched onto his face. 'What? You want to go to the new place? Your old flat? You just tell me where you want to go and I'll . . .'

'I want to go wherever you're going, Paulie,' she said, the idea hard-ening like ice in her mind.

'What? What do you mean?' Paulie asked, his tone betraying his confusion for the sham it was.

'You know damn well what I mean, Paulie. I know you. You'll have spent the last hour out here thinking of who might have wanted to kill Dad, and why. And I'm betting you've come up with a few ideas by now, haven't you? And you're just itching to test them out. So I want to go with you. See what we can find.'

Something between horror and disbelief flashed across Paulie's eyes. 'Jen, darlin',' he said. 'I really don't think that—'

'I don't care what you think!' she shouted at him, the words as hot as the tears that burned behind her eyes. 'Someone killed my dad, Paulie. Butchered him. You think I'm going to play the crippled wee girl and sit on my arse while you and Connor play the big men and go out looking for revenge? He was my dad, Paulie. Mine. The only family I had left. So I want to find the bastard that did this, and I want to look into their eyes as you do whatever the hell you want to them.'

The car fell silent, and Paulie looked at her as if meeting her for the first time. She returned his gaze coolly, unflinchingly, unwilling to be the one to look away first. And even as she did, there was another part of her, the part that cried out when the bones in her back ground together, the part of her that counted the hours between painkillers, that whispered she was wrong. That she should go home, lock the door and block out the world. But she knew that if she did that, if she gave in to the grief and the fear, it would overwhelm her, drown her in a deluge of sorrow she would never escape.

Paulie's jaw set, and he ran a huge hand over the bristle that covered his head. Then he puffed out his cheeks and exhaled, the sour smell of old whisky and older cigars filling the car. 'Okay,' he said. 'But you stay in the car. And you do exactly what I tell you. And if we find something I don't like, we leave. No questions asked. Understood?'

'Fine,' she said. 'So, where are we going?'

Paulie looked away from her, his shoulders sagging as he took hold of the steering wheel. 'You might find things out about your dad you don't want to know, Jen,' he said softly.

She felt a lurch in her guts. 'Paulie, I know he was no angel. I know he wasn't always on the right side of the law. I know he hurt people when he had to, probably had some killed too. But I need to know who killed him and why. So please . . .'

She trailed off and Paulie started the car. 'Okay,' he said. 'First stop is your dad's house. I need to check on something there.'

'What?' Jen asked, relief and unease washing through her at the same time.

Paulie gave a resigned sigh. 'I think this might be linked to something your dad was mixed up in years ago,' he said, 'so I need to go to his house and check.'

CHAPTER 37

Over the years, Robbie had come to love and loathe working with Connor Fraser in equal measure. On the one hand, working for the boss was never dull, and it gave him the chance to stretch his skills when he was asked for an esoteric piece of information or to find a pattern in the chaos that Connor seemed to attract, like a lightning rod in a storm. But on the other it forced Robbie to dance on the head of a moral pin: there were times when he had to cross a line to get to the information Connor needed. And there was just enough police officer left in Robbie to find that uncomfortable. On the occasions that he did cross the line, by hacking a secure database or accessing classified files from Police Scotland or another official agency, Robbie told himself he was serving a greater good, that the ends justified the means.

He hoped that would be the case this time as well.

He had been making slow progress on the picture Connor had sent him. Six men huddled in a woodland clearing, apparently on some wilderness camping weekend. As Connor had said, two of the men had already been identified: the banner holder, Duncan MacKenzie, and the man at the centre of the picture, Robert Balfour. But who were the other five who had been there that day?

He had worried that the picture was so old that any records he tried to access wouldn't be online but rotting slowly in some forgotten storage room. When he hacked Stirling University's files, though, he was pleasantly surprised to see that student names and details going back to the formation of the university in the sixties had been transferred online. Which gave him a starting point. He accessed the records on Robert Balfour, pulling up his biography as a professor of history lecturing at the university. Found his CV, which showed Balfour had studied at Edinburgh and St Andrews University. He then called up his class lists and got the names of students he had taught. Using Jamie Leggatt as a reference point, Robbie called up all the classes for the four years leading up to Balfour's death in 1983 that Leggatt was in, and was rewarded with a long list of faceless names. Any one of them could have been in the picture Connor had sent him, but how to narrow it down?

He looked back at the picture, considered. Connor had asked Robbie to cross-reference the image with Jamie Leggatt and any possible paramilitary groups, and Robbie could see the sense in that, given the composition of the picture. Was this a paramilitary training camp? Young men being taught how to wage a guerrilla war? It was possible, and the bombings in Dundee and Edinburgh added weight to the theory. But what war was being fought? And for whom?

He wrote a quick search algorithm, which would cross-reference the student names he had found with any reports of terrorist or paramilitary activity held online or in news or library archives. Then, with a familiar quiver of unease, he leaned forward again and began typing. He felt a flash of guilt at how easily he used a back door into the Metropolitan Police database and, specifically, the Anti-Terror Unit. He found their list of proscribed organisations, groups with views or motivations so extreme they had been outlawed, and set a program loose that would cross-reference the student names with them as well.

With nothing to do but wait, Robbie flicked across to his web browser and called up the Sky News site. There was Donna Blake, breathlessly reporting from the scene of the St Andrew's House blast. Robbie watched as the camera panned towards the ambulances and police vehicles that crowded the street, the wounded shielded by hastily erected screens to keep prying eyes away. A glimpse of Chief Constable Guthrie directing his men. So much random suffering,

Robbie thought. A bomb was a deadly, indiscriminate weapon. Jamie Leggatt had been targeted with a personalised letter bomb, yet the bomb in Edinburgh had been set off in public, in a large group of people. How had the bomber known his victim would be there, at that spot at that specific time, unless . . .

Robbie felt a sudden jolt, which caught his breath in his throat. He flicked between the Sky channel and his algorithm, then back. Saw the chief again. Odd that a chief constable would be on the ground at such a time. Unless, of course, he was playing to the cameras – the brave leader taking command. Robbie thought for a moment, then added another filter to the search.

His mouth dried and his eyes widened as the program began to spit names back at him. Names he recognised. Names that explained why Jonathan Rodriguez seemingly had Chief Constable Peter Guthrie in his pocket.

Names that could end the chief's career at a stroke.

The only question was, Robbie realised, were they names worth killing for?

CHAPTER 38

The drive to Duncan MacKenzie's home in Cambusbarron was, to Jen, like a journey into the past. She looked out of the window as Paulie drove, the years seeming to fall away as she recognised a pillar box, a corner shop, a play park, even a knot of trees on the road. How many times had she made this journey to see her father? And how many more times would she have to make it before the house was sold and there was no reason to make the trip ever again?

The house was on the edge of the village: an imposing Victorian manor. Knowing it was now empty, and that her father would never again open the door, seemed to accentuate the cold, blunt hardness of the limestone walls, and Jen suppressed a shudder as Paulie killed the Mercedes' engine at the kerbside.

'You sure you want to do this, hen?' he asked, as he leaned forward and looked up at the house.

She gave a small, humourless laugh. Digging into her father's past, exposing secrets he would never want her to know? No, this was the last thing she wanted to do. But someone had taken him from her, and she needed to look into their eyes and understand why in the moment before she handed the killer over to Paulie and whatever justice he deemed fitting.

'I'm all right,' she said, manoeuvring herself out of the car.

With a resigned sigh, Paulie followed her.

She walked up the short path to the front door, panic chilling her.

Was she ready for this? Walking into her father's empty home? The police had said they would need to search the property at some point. Would she disturb evidence, derail their investigation?

The realisation that she didn't care extinguished her panic, like a match being blown out. She was fumbling with her crutches and bag, looking for her keys, when Paulie joined her.

'Here, let me,' he said, producing his own key. She watched as he opened the door and stepped into the house, the alarm beeping a warning. He walked down the hall to the box mounted on the wall and punched in the code to disarm it. She knew Paulie would understand the significance of the code – it was her mother's birthday. Despite this, she was struck by the intimacy of Paulie having the key to her father's house and the code for the alarm. They had been close, confidants, friends and, occasionally, co-conspirators. How was Paulie feeling right now? His friend of more than forty-five years was dead, taken from them violently. How did a man like Paulie process grief like that?

'Need to go into your dad's study, hen,' he said, almost as though he had heard her thoughts and was answering them with decisive action.

She followed him down the hall then turned left to face the door leading to her father's study. Paulie didn't hesitate, just opened the door and walked in, like he owned the place. Jen took a deep breath, then stepped inside.

The grief hit her in the pit of the stomach, like a physical blow. Her father's study, which she remembered so well from when she was growing up. The walls lined with books, industry awards and pictures of her, her mother and various combinations of the three of them together. But what twisted a shard of ice in her stomach and brought tears to her eyes was the sight of her father's chair barricaded behind his desk. It was a large chair, rich burgundy leather, almost throne-like. Empty now, deprived of the man who had sat in it with her on his knee as a child, feeling as though she was in the safest place on earth, a place where her dad would always protect her.

Paulie, who had bent over the desk, looked up at her, his sharp gaze softening as his face contorted into something approximating sympathy. 'You okay, Jen?' he asked. 'If this is too soon, I can handle it. You can wait outside and I can—'

'No!' she snapped, the sudden anger cutting through the pain, like a torchlight slicing through darkness. 'No,' she repeated, more softly this time. 'Let's just get this done. What are you looking for, anyway?'

Paulie opened his mouth, closed it, and Jen could see calculation in his eyes. How much should he tell her? How much could he protect her from?

'Ah, a long time ago, your dad and I agreed to keep some, eh, items in storage for some people. Out at Bannockburn. We agreed that these items would be kept under the strictest lock and key. I had one key to access them, your dad had the other. I know my key is where it should be, what I want to know is if your dad's is where it should be as well.'

'Items?' Jen asked. 'What items? Come on, Paulie, don't piss about. What items are you talking about?'

'The type that can get you fifteen to twenty years, depending,' Paulie said plainly, his gaze cool and level.

She was about to ask another question when Paulie straightened and strode across to the bookshelf that dominated the wall behind her dad's chair. He scanned the rows of books, gave a small grunt, reached for one and turned back to the desk.

'How does a book help you find a key?' she asked. 'Paulie, what . . .?'

Paulie gave a smile that at once thrilled and terrified her. There was something cold and triumphalist in it, as if he revelled in knowing something she did not.

He opened the book, then froze, his face paling. 'Fuck,' he whispered.

'Paulie, what . . .?'

He blinked once as though reminding himself of who she was and what she was doing there. Then he held up the book for her to see.

It wasn't a book. Instead, it was a hollowed-out case that had been bound in a book cover and spine. The perfect place to hide a key in a room full of books. The problem was, it was also empty.

'They – they killed him for a key?' she said, her voice a dull whisper.

Paulie nodded, his eyes darting from left to right as though he was reading his words from a page. 'The door wasn't damaged, the alarm was on,' he said softly, more to himself than to Jen, 'so they took his house keys, must have got the alarm code from him. Took the key, then locked the house again, left it looking undisturbed to buy time.'

'Buy time for what?' Jen asked.

'Time to dig up the past and a whole world of shit,' Paulie said, as he ran a hand over his head, the short bristles of hair hissing.

'We need to talk to Fraser,' he said. 'I know who we're looking for. Or, at least, I know what tribe they belong to.'

CHAPTER 39

It took Jonathan Rodriguez just over half an hour to get to Sentinel Securities' offices at the Gyle in the west of Edinburgh. He had initially been reluctant to leave St Andrew's House and covering the story for his channel in the US, but Connor had convinced him with three words. And a promise.

He looked every inch the polished presenter Connor remembered from their previous meeting in Dunblane. The clear, unthreatening gaze that took in everyone in the room, managing somehow to single out each one of them. The perfect smile and the relaxed, casual set of his shoulders. But Connor could see anxiety beneath the veneer, could read it in the small twitches of his head, as though his shirt collar was a little too tight, the way he fiddled with his cufflinks and the soft flutter of a pulse in the smooth, tanned neck.

And then there were the eyes. Connor could always see it in the eyes.

'Thanks for coming, Mr Rodriguez,' Connor said, as he gestured for Rodriguez to take a seat at the conference table. 'You already know my colleague, Simon, and this,' he gestured to the chair to his right, 'is Robbie Lindsay, one of my investigators.'

'A pleasure,' Rodriguez said, as he unbuttoned his suit jacket and folded himself into the seat to the left of Connor. 'Though I have to say, Connor, your timing couldn't be worse. It may have escaped your attention but a big story's unfolding out there. My desk back in the

States wants me to cover it – gives them the chance to syndicate to other stations.'

'A story,' Connor said, reaching for a mug of coffee in front of him. He didn't want it, but he needed to play for time, draw out the moment. The more uncomfortable, the more unbalanced he could make Rodriguez, the better.

'Yes,' Rodriguez said, after a few seconds of awkward silence. 'So if you could get to the point of this, Connor, I'd be—'

'The point, Jonathan,' Connor said, leaning forward, 'as I said on the phone, is that I think you know a hell of a lot more about this story than you're letting on. So why don't we drop the bullshit pretence and get to the truth? And maybe, just maybe, you can give me something that will help me find the bastard doing this.'

Rodriguez squirmed in his seat. 'I don't know what you—'

'Marcus Guthrie,' Connor said. From Rodriguez's reaction, it was as though the name had a physical weight.

Rodriguez flashed a nervous smile, eyes darting between Robbie and Simon, as though he was looking for someone to defend him from what came next. 'What do you—' He coughed.

'Oh, I can't take the credit for that little gem,' Connor said, feeling a flash of guilt at enjoying Rodriguez's discomfort just a little more than he should. 'That was all Robbie's work. You see, I asked Robbie to look into that picture you were sent – you know, the one of your dad with Duncan MacKenzie and a group of men in some woods. I wanted to know who they were. But Robbie here, Robbie is very, very good at digging into things that bother me. And one thing that was bothering me was how you made Chief Constable Peter Guthrie roll out the red carpet for you when you got here. And when he was looking into that photo, and who your dad taught at Stirling University, guess who he found?'

'Marcus Guthrie,' Rodriguez whispered, his tone the voice of a sulking child.

'Exactly,' Connor said. 'Chief Constable Peter Guthrie's uncle. A student of your dad's and, from what Robbie's been able to dig up, someone with close links to the Scottish Liberation Brigade, whose motto just happens to be, you guessed it, Saor Alba. Nasty little group by all accounts, thought Scotland should be an independent republic, weren't afraid to spill a bit of blood to do it, either. But, Jonathan, they're a proscribed organisation, and anyone trying to get into the police who had a link to someone in the SLA would have been struck off. I'll have a word with the chief later to see who he bribed to make his uncle's past disappear so he could get into the police. But you knew that name, didn't you? And you used it to blackmail the chief into giving you access, didn't you?'

Rodriguez let out a long sigh, his gaze in his lap, as though fascinated by his fingers, which intertwined and released. 'Yes,' he said. 'It was in another of the emails I received from whoever got in touch saying Dad's death wasn't an accident. They gave me Marcus Guthrie's name, told me his link to the chief constable and that I should use it to get to the truth. So I did. But I don't see how that links to . . .'

Connor stood up and turned away from the conference table, exchanging a glance with Simon, the question they were both asking flashing unsaid between them. Whoever had killed Jamie Leggatt and set off a bomb at Calton Hill had wanted to keep Rodriguez close to the chief constable of Police Scotland. Why?

Connor turned back to Rodriguez, who fell silent under his gaze.

'Jonathan,' he said, his voice cool, as though this was a police interview room, not a corporate conference space, 'does the name the Vigil mean anything to you?'

Rodriguez looked up, with what looked like genuine confusion on his face. 'The Vigil? What? No, I've never . . .'

Connor held up a hand. In truth, he had expected as much. The Vigil had been a pro-Scottish Parliament demonstration that had begun at the foot of Calton Hill, across from St Andrew's House in 1992. It was non-party political, those attending coming from all corners of the pro-independence movement. With Jonathan's father, Robert, being found dead nine years earlier, there was nothing, other than his work on Scottish independence, to link it to Stirling and yet . . .

'It ties to the site of the bomb blast today,' Connor said. He looked for some glimmer of recognition in Rodriguez's eyes, got nothing but blank incomprehension in return.

'Okay,' Connor said, taking a different tack. 'You said whoever is contacting you gave you Marcus Guthrie's name. He's in the picture, just behind your dad. Did they give you any other names, anyone else who could help us with this?'

'No,' Rodriguez said. 'I've told you everything, Connor, I promise. Everything they've sent me, you've seen. Ask Amanda – she'll confirm I've been totally upfront with you on everything else apart from the chief's uncle.'

Amanda, Connor thought, the memory of Rodriguez's tall, dark-haired assistant springing into his mind. 'And where is Amanda?' he asked.

'Back at the house in Dunblane, maybe on the road,' Rodriguez replied, his previous confidence flickering back into his tone as the conversation moved to more comfortable territory. 'She said she had some research to do. We're filming at Bannockburn tomorrow, you see. Mum said Dad loved it there, what with the war memorial and everything, so she wanted to get some background in, take the car, scout for possible shooting locations. But I can let you have her number. I'm sure she'll give you anything you need.'

Connor was about to reply when his phone buzzed on the conference table. He flashed a smile at Rodriguez, then grabbed his phone. Frowned as he read the message from Jen. *We've got something linked to Dad. Paulie wants to talk to us. Meet us at the flat. Quick as you can. Do this for me, Connor. You owe me that much.*

Something about that last sentence gave Connor's guts an oily twist of unease. There was finality to it, almost like an ending.

He thought for a moment, wrestling with how to reply. Then settled on a simple *No problem, there soon* and hit send.

'Trouble?' Simon asked, as he looked up from his phone.

Connor shrugged. But, deep down, he suspected the answer was a resounding yes.

CHAPTER 40

They drove back to Stirling in silence, Simon at the wheel to give Connor time to digest what Rodriguez had told them. It was clear that Professor Robert Balfour's work for pro-independence groups was a part of what was going on, and it seemed likely that whoever had killed Jamie Leggatt and Duncan MacKenzie had been involved with one of those groups. It was the only explanation Connor could come up with for their access to the group shot in the woods and the use of the slogan Saor Alba, Free Scotland.

But what was the 'game' that the bomber insisted Rodriguez's investigation into his father's death was part of, and why suddenly turn on those the killer had obviously been close to at one point? Connor had left Robbie at Sentinel to use the information Rodriguez had provided to try to identify the remaining men in the picture. He wondered if one was the killer. Or had they been smart as far back as forty years ago, and made sure there was no record of them by having been the one who took the shot rather than being part of it?

He toyed with his phone as they drove, thinking of Ford. He should contact him, tell him what he had discovered. At the very least, the information on Guthrie and how Rodriguez had used his family's past to blackmail him for access to the case would be very useful to the detective. But Connor knew that, no matter how pragmatic a policeman Ford was, he was still a policeman. And any evidence that Connor presented to him about links to paramilitary groups would have to be fed into the official investigation. Statements would have to be given, evidence produced. All of which would take time.

Time Connor felt they did not have.

He was roused from his thoughts as Simon pulled the car to a halt in front of the flat. Paulie's car sat there, sleek and showroom-perfect as ever.

'Take it easy, big lad,' Simon said, as though reading Connor's thoughts. 'The man's here to help. Jen's message said he'd found something linked to her dad's death. If that helps us get closer to the lunatic running around blowing shit up, it works for us, agreed?'

'Agreed,' Connor rumbled, the last line of Jen's text replaying in his mind: *You owe me that much.* With everything that had happened, from her getting run over to losing the baby and them deciding to move in together, he couldn't argue. The question was, if she ever decided to present him with the bill in full, could he afford the price?

They stepped into the flat, found Paulie and Jen in the living room, which had now been mostly stripped. All that remained was an L-shaped couch Simon had asked them to leave. Jen was perched on one end, her crutches propped against the back. Paulie sat at the other, hunched over a can of Diet Coke that looked laughably small and fragile in his grasp. Jen looked up as Connor and Simon stepped into the room, made no move to stand and greet them.

'You've done some job clearing this place, so you have,' Simon said. Connor knew he had sensed the tension in the room when they stepped in. It was one of the things he admired and envied Simon for – the emotional intelligence to read a room and know what to say no matter the situation.

'We found something at Dad's house,' Jen said, ignoring Simon's attempt at levity. 'Or, rather, we didn't find something that should have been there.'

'What?' Connor asked, glad Jen was talking despite her business-like tone. Was it just shock? he wondered. A carapace of anger grown over her heartbreak at the loss of her father. Or was it something more?

You owe me that much.

Paulie sighed, stood up. Turned and looked out of the patio doors, as though all he wanted to do was step through them and close them on all of this, leave it for Connor and Jen to work out for themselves. 'There was a note in Duncan's diary,' he said, 'for last Wednesday. It set a meeting for Bannockburn for SA. It also mentioned Witches Craig.'

'Witches Craig?' Connor said. 'You mean the caravan park at the back of Stirling University?'

Paulie sneered at him as though he had just described *Mona Lisa* as a picture of a woman with her hands crossed in her lap. 'Aye. But it's also the site of the old Logie Kirk and the park gets its name from the Witches Craig hill. Which, in case you didn't know, was where it was rumoured a coven of witches used to live. Christ, Fraser, you're such a bloody tourist.'

Connor's anger rose at the jibe. He swallowed it. 'Thanks for the history lesson,' he said, 'but what the hell does all this have to do with Bannockburn, and Jen's dad?'

Paulie stared unblinkingly at him for a moment, then shrugged. 'SA. Saor Alba,' he said. 'I'm guessing you've heard that phrase a few times over the last few days. Well, it fits with Bannockburn. See, Duncan . . .' he paused, his eyes sliding to Jen, then returning to Connor '. . . Duncan was a bit wild in his youth. Didn't go to the university, but got sucked in by some of the students. Think he met them in the pub in Stirling. Anyway, he went to a few meetings of a group that wanted Scotland to be an independent republic, fuck the Queen, that sort of thing. Drifted away after a while but, Duncan being Duncan, he kept in touch. So when the group disbanded a few years later, they asked him to look after some equipment, put it beyond use, as the saying goes.'

Simon spoke before Connor could. 'Put it beyond use?' he said. 'That's what the paramilitaries in Northern Ireland said they'd done with their guns and other weapons after the end of the Troubles. You telling me . . .'

Paulie gave a slow, deliberate nod. 'They asked Duncan to store their guns and ammo for them. So he got me involved and we did, buried them in a lockbox in a quiet area of Ladywell Park in Bannockburn. The only people to have a key to the box, or know its location, were me, Duncan and the person who asked him to bury the weapons.'

'Who I take it you never met?' Connor said.

Paulie raised his hands in mock applause. 'No. Duncan said the folk handing off the guns were cagey, and that suited me fine. I knew where Duncan kept his key, went to the house to check earlier. It's gone. And whoever took it was very, very professional. You wouldn't know the place had been burgled.'

'I take it you've not been to Ladywell Park to check whether the guns have been dug up?' Connor asked, pushing back a shudder of revulsion as he did so. He knew the place, had taken his gran there for walks in the summer. How close had they been to those weapons?

'You think I'm fucking stupid?' Paulie snarled, eyes flicking back to Jen. 'Of course I haven't. Wouldn't be safe. Came back here and Jen messaged you.'

'Hold on,' Simon said. 'What did Rodriguez say? Wasn't his assistant, what's her name, heading for Bannockburn today?'

'Amanda,' Connor replied, remembering Rodriguez's words. *She's looking for filming locations.*

Would one of those locations be Ladywell Park? Connor wondered. And, if so, what would she find when she got there?

CHAPTER 41

Rodriguez's sudden disappearance from St Andrew's House surprised Donna, and puzzled her. He had accompanied her to Edinburgh after they had received the video of the bomb, and worked out a deal en route. In return for syndication and exclusive follow-up interview rights, Sky would let Rodriguez use Keith to film his reports for his station back in the United States. When they arrived on the site, and the bomb was detonated at Calton Hill, the deal seemed to work: Donna filmed her live feeds to the newsroom, and Rodriguez got his camera time when she was digging for the next angle on the story.

It was during one of those breaks in filming that Rodriguez disappeared.

'He got a call,' Keith told her, his doughy face grave, as though he were telling Donna her favourite puppy had just been run over. 'He didn't look too happy about it, but he agreed to get there as soon as he could. Lochee House, he said. That's where the Fraser guy has his offices, isn't it?'

'Yes,' Donna had replied, 'that's exactly where Sentinel Securities is based.' She let Keith drift off for more background shots, thoughts racing. What had Connor uncovered that demanded he see Rodriguez straight away and, more importantly, what did he have over Rodriguez that was powerful enough to drag him from the scene of a major story?

The answer came a few moments later, with a call from Rodriguez and an invitation to meet him for 'coffee and a talk'. Donna took a moment, then agreed. The bombing story was big, so big that Sky had decided to scramble one of the national presenters with household recognition and a six-figure salary to front the coverage. It didn't bother Donna. She was happy to let them be the face of the story for now: it gave her time to work out what was really going on and get the exclusive everyone else wanted.

She arranged to meet Rodriguez at the Scotsman Hotel on North Bridge, a ten-minute walk from St Andrew's House. Once the sprawling headquarters of the *Scotsman* newspaper group, the building had been converted into a hotel when the fortunes of the newspaper dwindled and it moved to other premises. The café at which Donna arranged to meet Rodriguez was located in what had been the main reception desk of the old *Scotsman*, and Donna wondered how many reporters and how many stories had walked across the polished tiled floors as she waited.

Rodriguez arrived twenty minutes later, the only hint that he was having a bad day his loosened tie and a strand of hair that had somehow managed to break free from the prison of gel that kept him immaculately coiffed.

'You left in a hurry,' Donna said coolly, arching an eyebrow as he sat down.

'Uh, yeah, sorry about that,' Rodriguez said, making a show of trying to catch the eye of one of the waiters rather than meeting Donna's gaze.

So he had something to hide, she thought. Interesting. 'What did Connor have to discuss with you that was so urgent?' she asked.

'Well, ah, it was about the messages I've been getting about Dad,' Rodriguez said, smiling as a waitress approached the table. 'He had some information on the picture of Dad I was sent, thought maybe I could help with it.'

'Oh, and what was that?' Donna asked.

'Nothing important, not really,' he said. He held up a finger as he ordered a coffee in a tone that indicated he wanted something a lot stronger, then turned back to Donna. 'He did have some interesting information about the bombing, though.'

139

'Oh, really?' Donna said, noting how smoothly Rodriguez had moved the conversation onto ground where he was comfortable. What had Connor found? she wondered. And what was Rodriguez hiding? She made a mental note to follow up with Simon and Connor later on.

'Yes,' Rodriguez said. 'It seems the bombing today was on the site of something called the Vigil. As Connor tells it, it was a demonstration set up to call for a Scottish Parliament back in the early nineties.'

'Interesting,' Donna murmured, even as she felt a flash of frustration at not being the first person to get at that piece of information. 'So you think that was the intended target all along, that the bomb sent to St Andrew's House was just a hoax to get people into position?'

'Looks that way,' Rodriguez said.

Donna chewed her lip, considered. 'Your dad did work on Scottish independence, didn't he? He was one of the faculty professors at Stirling who supported the anti-monarchy demonstration when the Queen visited the campus. You think there's a link?'

Rodriguez frowned as the waitress delivered his coffee, then made a discreet retreat. 'Possible,' he said, after a long slurp, 'but I don't see how it connects to Dad. He died in 1983, and the Vigil was set up nine years later, in 1992.'

Donna thought about this. Cursed internally. He was right: the timelines didn't match up. So if the person who was feeding Rodriguez information on his dad was the same person who had killed Jamie Leggatt and set off the bomb at Calton Hill, why use the Vigil as a reference point? Why?

Timelines.

Donna sat up straight in her chair, the suddenness of her move making Rodriguez freeze with his coffee cup halfway to his mouth. 'What?' he asked.

'Timelines,' Donna muttered. 'Tell me, Jonathan, when did you start to get these messages about your dad? When did whoever is contacting you tell you there was more to his death than just a drunken accident?'

A flash of confusion twisted Rodriguez's face, and he placed the cup on the table in front of him. 'Must have been, what, a month ago now? Not long after I came up with the idea to do the programme on the fortieth anniversary of his death.'

Donna's pulse quickened and she bit back the smile she felt quivering on her lips. 'So what came first?' she asked. 'Did you announce the programme and the messages began, or was it the other way round? And why did you decide to do this in the first place?'

Rodriguez gave a small, embarrassed smile. 'Actually, my mum gave me the idea,' he said. 'She always talks about Dad, drags out albums full of pictures of us in Stirling. It's almost like she's trying to keep alive the few childhood memories I have of Scotland. But we were talking one night, and she pulled out a picture and said she couldn't believe Dad had been gone forty years this year. And that's when the thought hit me. An anniversary show marking the forty years since his death.'

'The US audience,' he dropped his gaze, and Donna saw calculated guilt in the move, a way to foster sympathy, 'well, they love their Scottish history. So the story was a slam dunk. My producers loved it, and I ran with it. The announcement on social media sparked a wave of interest and here I am . . .'

Donna felt frustrated excitement bubble up in the back of her throat. How could he not see it? 'So the announcement came first,' she asked slowly. 'You announce that you're doing an investigative piece on your dad's death and after that the anonymous emails start, claiming it was something more than an accident?'

'Well, yeah,' Rodriguez agreed, 'must have been a week after. But why is that important?'

'Narrative,' Donna said, after a moment. 'Your announcement of an investigation must have rattled some very old, very dusty skeletons in cupboards. Remember what the messages said? This is part of a wider game? There's a truth here and an injustice to resolve? Sounds to me a lot like someone is very, very keen to have their side of your dad's death told, and only their side. Christ, they've been leading you by the nose with this drip-drip of information from the start.'

'Okay,' Rodriguez said slowly. 'But I don't see how that changes things. I've still got a story to cover.' He gestured over his shoulder, as though pointing back to Calton Hill. 'Today proves that.'

'Yeah,' Donna agreed, 'it does. But it also proves there's another story here, one our killer doesn't want told. And I'm very interested in finding out what that is, Jonathan. Aren't you?'

CHAPTER 42

The silence of the flat screamed at her. And it took all the self-control Jen had not to scream back.

After Paulie's revelation about the arms cache at Bannockburn, Jen had ordered him, Simon and Connor out of the flat. The awkward glances the three men exchanged as she spoke fuelled the cloud of rage that was washing through her mind like static.

'Look, I don't need you three protecting me,' she snapped, shocked to hear her dad in the harsh, flat tone of her voice. 'We want to find out who did this. Going to Bannockburn is the next step. I'll only slow you up,' she held up a crutch as though punctuating the point, 'so go. Find something we can either use or give to the police.'

She saw Connor take a step towards her, then stop. The helpless pain in his jade-green eyes twisted something in her guts, and she felt heat rise behind hers. 'Call me, tell me what you find,' she said, forcing her voice to be kinder now, gentler.

'Promise,' Connor said. He led Paulie and Simon out of the flat, the sound of the door clicking shut like a gunshot. Then she was alone, the silence crowding in on her, forcing her to face all the things she had been running from since Connor had told her that her father had been killed.

Orphan. The word rose suddenly in her mind. She was an orphan now. Her mother had died years ago, when Jen had been just a child, taken by cancer. But as much as that had hurt, as much as that had opened up a chasm in Jen that she could never truly fill, she had still had her dad to cling to. And while Duncan MacKenzie could be aloof at times, never wanting to show Jen his own pain when she was trying to deal with hers, she had never once questioned the depth of his love for her. He had protected her from his world, the world he lived in with Paulie, a world filled with guns and violence and pain. It was, she thought, one of the reasons he had hated her being with Connor. Since they had first met, Connor's work had provided a bridge back to the world that Duncan had worked so hard to shield Jen from. And he had been right, hadn't he? Since knowing Connor, Jen had almost been killed, lost her mobility and fitness, and miscarried a baby she hadn't known she wanted until she was told it was gone. She knew somewhere deep down that none of this was Connor's fault, that he was merely reacting to the situation he was presented with, but a part of her wanted to blame him. She knew that if she stopped, if she gave the silence time to soak into her, the grief would catch up with her. She could feel it quivering in her chest, a tidal wave crashing against a storm wall. If it breached that wall, if she let it, she knew she would start crying and never stop. So, no. Better to blame Connor. For now. Make him the focus of her rage, blame him for what had happened to her father and—

She stopped, snapping forward in her seat so fast that her back screamed in protest. Spat an expletive into the silent flat even as she cursed her own stupidity. What had happened to her father? She had been told only that his body had been found in the loch at the university campus, that he had been injured before he died. Why? She grabbed her phone, opened the last message she had received from him. He had texted her, asking how the move was going, promising to see her soon. She scrolled back, the superficiality of their texting chats making the grief swell in her chest. They had spent so much time talking but saying nothing, and now she would never get the chance to speak to him again.

She stopped scrolling when she came to a picture message. It had been her dad's way of answering her when she had asked a week ago if he was free for lunch. He had sent her a picture of his desk in his study at home, papers strewn across it.

144

Sorry, he had written in the message that accompanied the picture. *Drowning in paperwork. Feels like I'm a student again. Catch up when I'm a bit freer?*

Jen felt a shiver of revolted excitement. At the time, she had dismissed her dad's message as one of his typically bad jokes – he made no secret of his disdain for mainstream education, thought studying was a waste of time when life could teach you everything you needed to know by getting out into the world. But now, looking at that message *Drowning. Feels like I'm a student again*, she wondered if he had been trying to tell her something.

Her stomach lurched and she shambled towards the toilet, the thoughts crowding into her mind. Had her dad known he was going to die in Airthrey Loch? Was he trying to tell her so?

She got to the toilet and vomited, bile spattering into the bowl as a massive pressure built up in her temples and threatened to split her head open. Was she imagining this? Trying to find some other rabbit hole to fall down instead of confronting the fact that her father was dead, and she was now alone in the world? Or was she right? Had he known he was going to die, and was he trying to send her a message?

She wiped her hand across her face, flushed the toilet. Collapsed around the toilet seat, the porcelain cool against her cheeks. Forced herself to breathe. Then, when she felt more under control, she took out her phone. Read the message again, a cold certainty hardening in her mind as she did so, the words *drowning* and *student* jumping out at her.

She opened the picture of her father's desk. Zoomed in and scrolled around. Was there something on it? Something he was trying to tell her? Something . . .

She froze, her breath catching in her throat. Pinched and zoomed the screen to confirm her eyes weren't deceiving her. When she realised they weren't, she felt the urge to scream again.

Her father had left her a message. No. Not a message. A plea. A demand.

Avenge me.

CHAPTER 43

Ladywell Park was a sprawling public park in Bannockburn, not far from the care home where Connor's gran stayed. He felt a hollow pang of conflicted guilt as he followed Paulie's car through Bannockburn to the car park outside Ladywell, struck at once by being so close to his gran without seeing her, and not wanting any part of what he was involved in to touch her life.

The car park was mostly deserted, peppered with a few stereotypical family estate cars or SUVs as dogs were walked or children played with. Yet Connor could feel the same nervous energy that radiated from Simon in the passenger seat, the cold hyper-vigilance that made the world into a series of snapshots in his mind, moments to be analysed for threats or enemies.

And, as he was learning, those enemies could be anywhere.

Connor glanced across at Simon as he pulled in behind Paulie and killed the engine of the Audi. Simon said nothing, merely nodded, the snap of the magazine being driven home into his gun more eloquent than anything he could say. They got out of the car, Paulie glancing up at them briefly before turning his attention back to the main entrance to the park. 'About a ten-minute walk.' He stuffed his hands into his pockets, rounded his shoulders and set off.

'Hold on, hold on,' Connor called, and Paulie turned to him, an expression of disgusted impatience twisting his face.

'What?' he spat.

'Don't you think we should talk about this before just charging in?' Connor asked. 'Whoever knew about the lock safe is aware you'll have a key as well. If they've been here, which seems likely, hasn't it occurred to you that they may have left a few, ah, surprises for us, that they might even be waiting for us? We'd make tempting targets to test those buried guns on.'

Paulie's face twisted into a tight, almost feral smile. 'Be nice to get my hands on the bastards,' he growled. Then he took a breath, looked over his shoulder then back to Connor.

'Look,' he said, his voice less predatory now, 'whoever knew about the arms dump knew that Duncan and I had keys to the lock safe. They've got Duncan's key. So they've either been here and got the guns or they're on their way. If they've been, we know they're armed and dangerous. If they've not, we can assume they will be at some point, in which case we can stake the place out and wait for them. Either way, we need to know if the guns are still here. So I'm going in.'

'And what if they've booby-trapped the place, like Connor said?' Simon asked.

The smile crawled back onto Paulie's face. 'I'm lighter on my feet than I look,' he said. 'And, besides, I know what to look for. I'm guessing you do too. So keep your wits about you, don't be a stupid cunt, and we'll be fine.'

Without waiting, Paulie turned and lumbered off towards the park. Connor exchanged a glance with Simon, shrugged, then followed.

He caught up with Paulie, fell into step with him, Simon bringing up the rear.

'So you've no idea who might be doing this?' Connor asked.

'No,' Paulie said, not taking his eyes from the path in front of him. 'Duncan was more involved with the students than I was. I just made the arrangements to bury the guns for him. Pretty obvious he told someone else about it, and whoever that is, they decided to take the guns and shut Duncan and Leggatt up about them.'

'The guns,' Connor said, as the thought occurred to him, 'what were they planning to do with them?'

'Have a tea party – what the fuck do you think?' Paulie barked.

'You work it out. Duncan told me there was a group of what you'd call radical nationalists at the university. Seems the professor that was found in the loch, Robert Balfour, was the ring leader. Took them out into the woods behind Witches Craig, fed them anti-Unionist texts, talked about Wallace, the fight for Scottish independence, that sort of thing. Way Duncan told it, he was an admirer of the IRA, believed armed struggle was the only way to gain freedom. But when Balfour died in the loch, the group kind of drifted apart, and Leggatt asked us to bury the guns.'

'Why bury them?' Connor asked. 'Why not just get rid of them?'

Paulie blinked as though he couldn't quite believe Connor's naivety. 'You don't get it, do you?' he asked. 'Once someone's had a gun in their hand or a cause to fight for, they never get over it. Oh, they can pretend they've seen the light and reformed, pretend to live an ordinary life. But they never forget. It's like an alcoholic. They can stop drinking for years, but all it takes is one bad day and they're reaching for the bottle again. These boys? All it'll take is one bad headline too many and they'll be dusting off the guns, painting their faces blue and looking to send the English homeward to think again.'

'I still don't understand it,' Connor said. 'Why now? And what about these references to a bigger game and a lie being exposed? What is the killer trying to tell us?'

'Not my problem,' Paulie said. 'All I'm interested in is getting my hands around the bastard's throat and paying him back for what he did to Duncan. After that . . .' He shrugged.

They walked for another ten minutes, Paulie leading them off the concrete path that snaked around the park and into thick underbrush. He moved with a fluid grace that belied his bulk, and Connor could see by the constant swivelling of his head that he was scanning the landscape as he moved, alert to any dangers.

He stopped at a huge silver oak tree, its branches gnarled, arthritic fingers stretching for the sky. Did a slow turn, nodding to himself.

'Aye, this is it,' he said. Connor looked across at Simon, who had already taken up a defensive position about ten feet away. He was standing with his hands crossed at his waist, covering most of the gun he held. Connor knew the safety of that gun would now be off, and Simon would use it at the first sign of trouble.

'Shit,' Paulie hissed.

Connor walked behind the tree, found Paulie crouched next to the trunk, sweeping dead leaves and branches away from it.

'They've got them,' he said, pointing towards a small depression at the trunk, the swept-away foliage showing a hole that slanted diagonally into the tree.

Paulie pulled a small torch from his pocket, shone it into the hole. Something glimmered there, and Paulie leaned forward. Connor felt a warning die in his throat as Paulie's arm disappeared up to the shoulder. He fumbled for a moment, then pulled back and lifted what he had found into the light.

'Huh,' he said. 'Wasn't expecting that.'

Connor found it hard to argue. What Paulie had pulled from the hole in the tree trunk was a long, wicked-looking knife with a single-edge blade. Connor had a sudden image of the picture Duncan had been in, with Robert Balfour at the front, holding a blade that looked almost identical to this one.

Identical, that was, except for the mobile phone impaled on the tip of the blade.

Connor leaned forward, pulled the phone free. The blade hadn't been pushed all the way through, leaving the screen to jump and flicker, like an insect caught on flypaper.

'Now who do you think that belongs to?' Paulie asked.

A thought flashed across Connor's mind, and he pulled out his own phone.

'What you doing?' Paulie asked.

'Playing a hunch,' Connor replied, as he found the number he was looking for and hit call.

He felt a chill skitter across his shoulders as the phone with the shattered screen began to vibrate and ring.

'Oh, aye,' Paulie said. 'Smartarse. So who were you just calling?'

'Amanda Lyons,' Connor said. 'Jonathan Rodriguez's assistant. He sent her out to Bannockburn on a location scout. Guess she found more than she was bargaining for.'

CHAPTER 44

After agreeing to meet Donna later in the day to compare notes, Jonathan Rodriguez found himself adrift in Edinburgh. It was, like Stirling, a city that was largely a stranger to him. And, like Stirling, that lack of familiarity did nothing to cool his hatred for the place.

His father had died before Jonathan had been able to form any real memories of him, and all he could recall of the man was his presence: a warmth and strength that made him feel safe; the smell of whisky and tobacco trapped in a tweed jacket Jonathan remembered snuggling into when his father picked him up. But there were other feelings too, feelings Jonathan hated, which made him secretly glad his father had died. The jangle of stress arcing through his parents when they were in the same room, the sharp, discordant shouts that made the young Jonathan's bladder quiver, the slamming of doors and clatter of the drinks cupboard when his father had lurched into the house late and drunk.

When his father had died, Rodriguez had revelled in the peace that descended on his mother and the house they shared. And his mum made sure he never felt as though he was missing something with being in a one-parent home. It was only later, after their move to America, that he had become curious about who his father was, mostly due to his new stepfather Michael, whose insistence that Jonathan could rely on him for anything he might need of his old man ensured he never did.

So, he began to research his father, first in the pictures and news clippings he found in the bottom drawer of his mother's bedside table, then in the school library and online. Slowly, he came to know a man who had been a respected academic, a historian with a love for Scots history and a belief that his country should be free. He had worked for the nationalist movement, spoken at rallies, even considered running for office. Jonathan had found an article from *The Scotsman* in 1981, a picture of his father, microphone in hand, addressing a flag-waving crowd on the esplanade outside Edinburgh Castle. The caption below the article read: 'Professor Robert Balfour regales the crowd with tales of Scots kings at Edinburgh Castle as part of a protest calling for the reopening of a Scottish parliament.'

And from that picture, Jonathan's hatred of Edinburgh had been born. Only two years before his death, with Jonathan just seven years old, his father had thought a protest and a picture opportunity were more important than being at home with his son and wife. Jonathan had no plans to be a father himself, but he hoped if the day ever came he would be less selfish with his time than his own father had been, and immune to the siren call of a city miles from his home.

Home. The thought was sudden and urgent. What was he doing here, thousands of miles from home, chasing ghosts, trying to understand a man he had never known? He felt hot embarrassment at the memory of Donna's words, of her clear, undeniable assessment that he had been drawn into a game and was being shown only what a killer wanted him to see. But what, he thought, was the killer trying to tell him? That there was more to his father's death than a simple accident? If so, what did the killer have to gain by exposing this? And why did—

His phone chirped in his pocket, and he reached for it. Felt a repellent excitement thrill through his veins as he read the 'No Caller ID' message on the screen. Was the killer reaching out to him? He had only ever been in touch via email or video file before. But, after two bombings in two days, was he escalating? Did it mean an endgame was in sight? And an answer to his questions?

He hit reply, his finger not quite steady.

'Jonathan Rodriguez,' he said, the afternoon sun suddenly bright and harsh to his eyes.

'Mr Rodriguez? You don't know me, but my name is Jen MacKenzie. My father was Duncan MacKenzie. He – he was the man found in Airthrey Loch the other day. I'm calling as I've found something that might be linked to his death and I need to see you about it. Could we meet?'

CHAPTER 45

It was, Robbie thought, like being asked to put a jigsaw together and only given a picture of what the finished puzzle was like halfway through. Once you had it, the pieces made sense, and putting the picture together became inevitable, with enough time and patience.

And in this case, the picture that let Robbie make sense of everything was Connor's mention of the Vigil.

After Connor, Simon and Rodriguez had left, Robbie had gone back to his computer and put together a search that cross-referenced articles mentioning the pro-parliament Vigil on Regent Road with the names of Robert Balfour's students. It didn't take long for one name to ping onto his screen, a name with which Robbie was vaguely familiar.

Angus Kirk.

Robbie called up the associated article, was surprised to find it was from Stirling University's history archives. The article had been uploaded in 2017, but referred to an event that had taken place in 1992, a hundred days after the Vigil on Regent Road had been set up. Those who had organised the Vigil drafted the Declaration of Calton Hill, which called for the setting up of a Scottish parliament that was accountable to and voted for by the people. There was a long list of signatories to the document, one of whom was the late Angus Kirk, who had died of a heart attack a few years ago. Robbie flipped over to an image search, cross-referencing Angus Kirk with the Vigil as search terms. He was rewarded with a picture of a group of people standing in front of what looked like a large shed, painted blue and white, with a Saltire flying above it. In the centre of the group stood a slight, severe-looking man with a rapidly receding crown of curly dark hair and glasses that almost seemed to be welded to his face.

'Activist Angus Kirk takes his stint at the Vigil in Edinburgh, after signing the Declaration of Calton Hill,' the caption accompanying the picture read. Robbie flicked back to the photograph Connor had sent him, of Robert Balfour and MacKenzie in the woods, and scanned the faces.

Yes, there. In the second row, to the right behind Balfour. There were about twenty years between the Balfour picture and the image at the Vigil, but there was no mistaking that the same man was in both. It was something about the eyes, the glasses magnifying the intensity of the gaze. The passing of two decades might have forced Kirk's hairline further up his forehead, but it did nothing to dim his gaze.

Robbie leaned back, bit his lip. Angus Kirk. Still, the name nagged at him, like a half-remembered song. But not from the news, from something he had worked on at Sentinel. Something . . .

He sat upright suddenly, lunging for the keyboard. Accessed the internal Sentinel database and found what he was looking for. Sir Angus Kirk QC. A lawyer practising at the High Court in Edinburgh, he had asked Sentinel to carry out a security review of his offices after he had helped a local MSP beat charges of sexual harassment levelled at him by his office staff. Robbie pulled up the file. A summary of the case against the MSP, Ronnie MacRae, was appended to it. MacRae was broad where Kirk was lean, with a pendulous gut and a face that looked as though it had suffered from a landslide that was dragging his features down to the double chin that threatened to spill over his shirt collar. Robbie flicked back to the Balfour picture, scanned it. Found one figure at the far right of the picture, lurking beside a tree, scowling at the camera. There was the first hint of the double chin in that image, and shoulders that spoke of strength rather than gluttony, but something in the eyes told Robbie it was the same man. He ran another search, cross-referencing Balfour's students and, sure enough, Kirk and MacRae were listed.

Robbie felt a thrill of excitement arc through him. He delved deeper, exploring the connection he had found. It didn't take him long to identify the rest of the men: they were all linked to Kirk and MacRae in one way or another. But it was the last name that surprised Robbie. It perhaps explained why Chief Constable Peter Guthrie, and the men in the picture, had been able to cover up his uncle's involvement with the Scottish Liberation Brigade.

He reached over for the phone, punched in Connor's number. Smiled as he thought of Connor's reaction to the names he had found, wondered what it would be like when Connor confronted the last man in the picture, Lord Advocate Donald Byrne, about what he had found.

CHAPTER 46

After making a sweep of the area around the tree to make sure there were no booby traps or clues, Connor drifted away from Paulie and Simon to call DCI Ford and bring him up to speed. Simon didn't envy Connor the call: telling Ford that not only were guns out on his streets but he was looking at a possible kidnapping wouldn't be the easiest of tasks.

Guns on the streets.

Simon glanced at the exposed hole under the tree trunk, then back to Paulie, who was bouncing the blade they had found in the arms dump in his hand, as though trying to assess its weight or effectiveness. The thought did little to put Simon at ease.

'So, Paulie,' he asked, trying to keep his tone casual as he jutted his chin towards the tree trunk, 'what was in there anyway?'

Paulie looked up at him, as though waking from a dream. He glanced at the knife one more time, something like disgust flashing over his eyes. 'Guns,' he said simply. 'What the fuck I look like, an expert? They asked us to wrap them, make sure they were watertight. We stripped them, serviced them, then sealed them up.'

Simon felt irritation itch at the back of his throat. 'Yeah, but were they big guns? Hand guns? What are we looking at here?'

Impatience darkened Paulie's face and he glanced away, towards Connor. Simon knew that Paulie wanted to be gone from the scene well before the police arrived, wondered how much longer he would hang around.

'Mostly handguns,' he said, 'not much different from that cannon you carry around.'

Simon nodded. He had a Glock 17, standard issue for PSNI officers. Powerful. Efficient. Deadly. 'Mostly handguns,' he said. 'So there were bigger guns in there as well?'

'Aye,' Paulie said, looking down the tree trunk as though the guns were still there. 'Big things, looked like rifles with a tripod on the barrel. Had a name to do with hair. Barnett or something, Leggatt said.'

Simon felt his mouth go dry as a horrible thought slithered through his brain and took root. 'Barrett,' he said softly, as he held his hands up to his chest. 'Would have been about this long, black, sighting scope, large mag in front of the trigger and a shoulder stock?'

'Aye, that's it,' Paulie said. 'Why?'

Simon ignored the question, swore instead. He knew the weapon all too well. The Barrett M82 rifle had been used during the Troubles in Northern Ireland by a group called the South Armagh Snipers. Members of the IRA, the Snipers used the rifles to target British soldiers and police officers in Armagh, south-west of Belfast. The problem with the Barrett was its power: bullets could rip straight through soldiers' body armour. The thought of such a weapon on the streets now was a nightmare.

'Hold on.' A thought had occurred to Simon. 'You said guns. So there were no explosives in the lockbox you buried?'

'If there were explosives, I would have mentioned them, wouldn't I?' Paulie said. 'What – the guns not enough for you?'

'It's not that,' Simon said, trying to push the thought of sniper rifles from his head. 'Whoever dug this up will presumably want to use the weapons, right? Why else kill Duncan for the key? But if there were no explosives in the cache, then the person who blew up Jamie Leggatt and set off the bomb in Edinburgh isn't relying on this as his only supply of weapons.'

'Aye, okay, so?' Paulie grumbled, a surly confusion in his tone.

'So someone who can access the explosives our killer can wouldn't need to rely on some guns that had been buried for twenty years, would he?' Simon said, the idea hardening in his mind as he spoke. 'Which means there's more to this than just getting some guns. Pulling this arms dump means something else. It's another message. Just like the Edinburgh bombing and putting Duncan's body in Airthrey Loch.'

Paulie grunted, spat. Then he held up the blade they had found where the guns should have been. 'You think this is the blade that killed him?' he asked.

'I don't know,' Simon said. 'But it's similar to the one in the picture. Not sure if it's the same blade as the one Robert Balfour is holding in the picture with Duncan, but it's another message, isn't it? Our killer's trying to tell us something about Duncan, Balfour and Jamie Leggatt.'

'I fuckin' hate puzzles,' Paulie said, his tone so blunt and resigned that it was almost comical.

Simon was about to reply when he heard footsteps. His head darted up, his gun following in one smooth motion.

'Jesus, Simon, don't shoot, it's me!' Connor said, as he stepped back into the clearing.

Simon lowered the weapon slowly. 'Sorry, big lad,' he said. 'Paulie's been telling me some tales, got me a little jumpy, you know?'

Connor glanced at him with a question. Simon dismissed it with a short shake of the head.

'Ford's got a team en route,' Connor said. 'Paulie, you should make yourself scarce. I'll think up some bullshit about how we found this cache. We've not got time for you to be answering endless police questions now.'

'Oh, aye,' Paulie said, his tone wary. 'And what have you got time for me to be doing?'

'First, check in on Jen,' Connor said. 'Got a text from her when I was talking to Ford. Seems she's found something in her dad's messages, something she wants to follow up. Given how she's reacted to her dad's death, I don't want her doing anything, ah, rash.'

Paulie smiled. 'So, you want me to babysit her while you deal with the cops?' he said. 'You know she'll have your balls for that? Girl hates to be coddled.'

'I can live with that if it keeps her safe,' Connor snapped, his tone making Simon tighten his grip on his gun again. 'There's a nutter out there with bombs and now guns,' Connor continued. 'He's already killed two people, and now it looks like he's kidnapped another. We keep Jen and the people we care about safe until we get him, clear?'

'Aye,' Paulie rumbled. 'I'll make sure she's safe.' He lumbered off towards the path without another word, the blade swinging by his leg as he moved.

Simon watched as Connor studied Paulie's retreat, could almost hear his friend counting the man's paces. He gave a small nod, almost as if answering a question he had asked of himself, then turned to Simon. 'I didn't want to say in front of him, but I got another call as well,' Connor said. 'Robbie's made some headway on the other names in the picture.'

'Oh?' Simon said. He wasn't really surprised – Robbie had proven himself to be one hell of an investigator.

'Yeah,' Connor said. 'A real *Who's Who* of civic life in Scotland from what he says, including the Lord Advocate. Which might also explain why Guthrie was able to hush up his family's chequered past, and his oblique involvement in all of this.'

Simon felt the vague shape of some insight rise in the back of his mind, then sink again, as though swallowed by a rising tide. 'Christ,' he muttered. 'Bombs, sniper rifles, top lawyers and policemen. What the hell have we got involved in here, Connor?'

Connor started. 'Sniper rifles?' he asked, glancing over Simon's shoulder to where the guns had been buried. 'You don't mean . . .?'

Simon nodded slowly. 'I'll tell you in a minute,' he said. 'You were right about keeping the ones we care about safe. Let me call Donna, make sure she's okay. Then I'll tell you all about the fun and games that have just been dug out of that hole.'

CHAPTER 47

It took less than two hours to make the guns operational, which, despite himself, annoyed him. Not because he needed them – they were, after all, incidental to his plan – but because their condition, after more than twenty years of being buried, meant MacKenzie had done his job well. And that meant facing up to the fact that, whatever other sins he had committed and failings he had had, Duncan MacKenzie had, on some level, been a professional.

The irony was not lost on him. After all, if MacKenzie had shown the same professionalism in other matters as he had with the guns, none of this would be necessary, would it? The past would have remained dead and forgotten, history left as it was intended, written by the victors. But, no, Balfour's son had decided to embark on a quixotic crusade to tell the story of his father, the tragic university professor who campaigned for his country as he descended into alcoholism, conspiracy theories, the loss of his family and, ultimately, his life.

Looking back, he should have seen what was going to happen much sooner. It was, after all, obvious. On every camp Robert Balfour had taken them to, every 'training mission'. as he put it, he was never without his hip flask. He was professional enough to put it away when they were handling blades or weapons, but once the practical work had begun, once he began his campfire stories of a Scotland free from the shackles of the Union and the 'obscenity of the blood-soaked monarchy', the hip flask would appear, flashing in the light from the fire as Balfour held court, his accent thickening and his words slurring as the night wore on. Of course, nobody really cared back then – it was always about the camaraderie of the moment, the fact that they were joined by a common purpose, fighting the good fight.

It was only now, looking back, that he could see the seeds that had been sown on those forbidden trips. Only now he truly understood the reason for Balfour's fondness of the bottle and enthusiasm for those camping trips.

It was, he thought, with a sneer, one of the things Balfour had had in common with MacKenzie. That, and the fact that they had both had to die for their sins.

He picked up one of the rifles, revelling in the pristine sheen of the metal and the cold, dead weight of it in his hands. One pull of the trigger, one round, and he could blow a hole through someone's chest from almost half a mile away. And while he was no marksman – others in the group had proven much more efficient in that regard than him – part of him ached to test himself. To put Connor Fraser or his policeman friend, McCartney, between the sights and pull the trigger.

But no. To indulge himself in such a way was amateurish. And dangerous. He had retrieved the guns and, in so doing, left another message, another breadcrumb for Fraser and his friends to follow.

He hoped Fraser was as intelligent as he was beginning to suspect he was, hoped it wouldn't take him too long to find the excavated arms dump, the blade and the phone he had left at the scene. He had not asked for this, had been forced to act when Jonathan Rodriguez had decided to dredge up the past and led him to stand in a crematorium as the only person who had meant anything to him was consigned to flame.

It had been forty years since a Balfour had caused pain and suffering. But, he had come to understand, there was a comfort to be had in that. After all, he had been taught that God was jealous and would punish the children for the sins of their fathers.

And, as he had learned, Robert Balfour had indeed sinned. And for those sins, he would ensure that his son Jonathan, and all those close to him, died.

CHAPTER 48

Connor and Simon sat in the car outside the flat, too tired to speak. Ford had arrived on the scene at Ladywell Park about fifteen minutes after Connor had called him. They met him in the car park and walked him back to the abandoned arms cache, the detective's mood darkening as Connor would only tell him that 'third-party sources and a search of MacKenzie's records' had led them to the discovery. Not telling Ford that it was Paulie who had put the pieces of the puzzle together grated on Connor, but he and Simon had agreed that the further they kept Paulie away from the police, the better. It was the same reason they agreed to be vague on the type of weapons that had been stored there – if the authorities found out that high-grade sniper rifles were on the streets, police, the security services and even the Army would be called in. And if that was to happen, Connor had the feeling that the killer would fade into the background or, worse, start picking off targets as though he was back in South Armagh. And Connor didn't want that. He wanted the killer focused on whatever twisted mission he had, thinking he was setting the pace even as Connor closed in.

After being shown the empty cache, and what was left of Amanda Lyons's mobile phone, Ford had called DS Troughton and ordered him to issue a missing person's alert for Rodriguez's assistant and to send a patrol car to the house she was renting with Rodriguez in Dunblane to see if there were any clues to be gleaned. He called in forensic teams and additional officers to cordon off the area, then stopped, sighed and turned to Connor. 'Get out of here,' he said. 'Once again, Fraser, you've given me a hell of a shit sandwich to deal with. The bureaucracy of this is going to take hours to sort, and the chief is going to hit the roof when he finds out. So go. I'll get all the ducks in a row, but I want you at Randolphfield tomorrow for a formal statement and debrief, okay?'

Connor had considered this for a moment, turning over what Robbie had found out about DCI Guthrie's chequered family history and his potential links to the Lord Advocate.

'Sir, it might be better to meet at a more, ah, neutral location,' he had said. 'There are a few details you need to be appraised of, and it would be better done outside the police station.'

Ford had frowned, opened his mouth, then closed it. When he spoke, his voice was flat, defeated, the voice of a man at the end of a very long, very bad day.

'Fine. For now, I don't want to know. Got enough to deal with. Get out of here. Your place. Tomorrow. Ten a.m. Don't stand me up.'

Connor agreed and he and Simon had left. The light was fading as they pulled up outside the flat, Paulie's car sitting in the driveway, low and gleaming and predatory.

'Sorry about this,' Connor said, as he killed the engine. 'With everything that's been happening, getting out of here and leaving you in peace is taking longer than I thought. I'll see if Jen wants to stay at the new place tonight, give you some time alone.'

'And who says I want to be alone?' Simon asked, a slightly strained smile playing on his lips. 'Don't worry about it, Connor. Jen and you have enough to be getting on with.' He held up his phone, waggled it. 'I've already texted Donna. Chinese food and a bottle of wine at her place tonight. Gives me a chance to catch up on her as well, see where she is on all of this.'

'Hell of a story for her,' Connor said.

'Aye,' Simon agreed. 'Just wish I could make sense of what the bloody hell is going on. Way I see it, it's all tied to Robert Balfour and his wee band of Scottish rebels back in the day. From what Robbie said, that was a pretty high-powered group, with members going on to be politicians, teachers and influential lawyers. So is one of them our killer, desperate not to have Balfour's boy dig up their sordid past as wannabe paramilitaries? I mean, it's pretty clear Guthrie's uncle pulled some strings to keep his nose clean, but what if someone else in that group prefers the more, well, direct approach to making the past go away?'

'Maybe,' Connor said, the word feeling clumsy as he spoke it. 'But there's something else going on here as well, I think. Why the arms cache? Why blow up Jamie Leggatt and detonate that bomb on the site of the Vigil in Edinburgh? And why grab Amanda Lyons? It's all very public, very showy, if your goal is to keep things quiet and the past hidden. There's something we're missing here, something I . . .' His voice trailed off, the sound of the leather steering wheel squealing as he squeezed it filling the car.

'Tomorrow,' Simon said. 'Get yer head showered tonight. See Jen. Relax. Regroup. We'll see Ford tomorrow, tell him everything Robbie's found.' He paused, then added, 'We're going to get this bastard, Connor, promise. And then we'll put the fucker in an unmarked grave for everything he's done to you and your family.'

Connor turned to Simon. Smiled. His best friend, a man who operated from a simple moral imperative – fuck with my loved ones and I will end you. At that moment, he was profoundly grateful to have Simon at his side.

They said their goodbyes and Connor let himself into the flat. Jen was sitting on the sofa, Paulie hanging out of the patio doors, a halo of smoke curling around his head. He turned as Connor entered the room, nodded a welcome, then flicked the stub of his cigar into the deepening shadows in the garden.

'I'll leave you to it,' he said, voice unusually uncertain. He paused for a moment, then seemed to make a decision. 'Left that item from today in the garden for you, I don't want it near me.' He headed for the door.

Connor frowned until he realised what Paulie meant. He watched Paulie leave, listened as the front door slammed, then moved towards Jen and crouched in front of her.

'How you doing?' he asked, hoping the words weren't as inadequate and stilted as they sounded to him.

She flashed him a fragile smile. 'Getting there,' she said.

'You said you had some kind of lead about your dad?' Connor said, hating himself for shattering the brief illusion of normality with his question.

She nodded, and he thought he saw something harden in her eyes. 'I looked back at the messages Dad sent me,' she said. 'Found one from a week ago.' She shifted in her seat, pulling her phone from her back pocket, then unlocked it and passed it to him. 'I found that.'

A picture of a cluttered desk, the message from MacKenzie below: *Sorry. Drowning in paperwork. Feels like I'm a student again. Catch up when I'm a bit freer?*

'Okay,' Connor said slowly, with rising unease that his lack of understanding would anger Jen.

'The message,' Jen said, as she took the phone back from Connor. 'Drowning. Feels like I'm a student again? Dad was never a student, never got past high school. So was he trying to tell me something?'

'Jen, I . . .' Connor said. She was reaching, that was it. Looking for something, anything, to keep her busy. Looking for a cause of her father's death rather than the fact of it in all its horrible finality.

'Look,' she said, handing him back the phone. 'I zoomed in to the desk, and look there, in the far-right corner.'

Connor took it, pinched and zoomed as he tracked across the desk. Just paperwork, invoices and receipts and . . .

He looked up at Jen suddenly, then back at the phone.

'Jesus,' he whispered.

'Exactly,' Jen replied, cold triumph in her eyes.

Connor looked back at the image. Tucked behind a billing invoice, the corner of an old newspaper article peeked out. Connor couldn't read the full headline, but he could make out 'Stirling Professor'. But more interesting was the list of names that ran down the left-hand margin of the newspaper, scrawled in MacKenzie's blunt, industrial capitals. Six names. Six names Connor recognised. The same six names Robbie had identified as the men in the picture of MacKenzie holding the flag in the woods. And below that, another name and a note: 'Rodriguez must know? PC 11 a.m. PST.'

Connor looked back to Jen. 'PC?' he asked.

'Dad's shorthand,' she replied, 'for phone call.'

Connor looked back at the image: '11 a.m. PST.'

PST. Rodriguez, Connor thought. 'PST,' he said. 'Pacific Standard Time. In the US, Los Angeles. So . . .'

'Yeah,' Jen said. 'It might be a guess, but I'm thinking Dad spoke to Jonathan Rodriguez by phone before he even set foot in Scotland.'

'But why?' Connor asked, mind racing as he tried to fit this new information with all the parts of the puzzle he already had.

'I don't know,' Jen said, her voice hollow now, business-like. 'But I'm going to find out. I'm meeting him tomorrow, ten a.m. Want to come with me?'

CHAPTER 49

Simon watched as Donna played with her food, struck by how similar she was to her son, Andrew. She sat across from him, a plate of sweet and sour chicken in front of her, her head leaning on one hand as she pushed rice and chicken around the plate with the fork in her other. The wine he had poured her sat undisturbed in front of her.

'Penny for them?' he asked.

'Wh-what?' She raised her head, her face blank, the way she looked when she had just woken from a nap. She blinked, seemed to remember he was there, then gave him an embarrassed smile. 'Sorry,' she said, laying down her fork and reaching for her wine. 'Sorry, Simon. Just caught up in my head. This bloody story . . .'

Simon nodded. It wasn't surprising. In the time he had known Donna, he had come to understand that what made her such a good reporter was her ability to crawl inside a story, see it from the inside out. The problem was, such an approach was all-encompassing, immersive, obsessive. And that could cause problems, especially when the story poked at wounds that were still fresh for Donna.

'You know they'll be doing everything they can to find her,' Simon said softly, as he picked up his wine. A 2016 Bordeaux he had picked up on the way to Donna's flat. Connor had teased Simon about being a wine snob, but he saw it as knowing what he liked, and being willing to pay extra for it.

'I know,' Donna said, her eyes sliding from his as she spoke. She cleared her throat, took a slug of wine. Simon didn't need to ask her to know the movie that was playing in her head. About a year ago, Donna had been kidnapped by a religious zealot who had believed he was on a mission from God. A mission that involved killing innocent people. Simon and Connor had rescued Donna, but Simon knew that the ordeal still troubled her – he'd held her in the aftermath of enough nightmares to know that the memories were still too close for comfort. Memories that the kidnapping of Amanda Lyons would bring to the surface.

Donna gave a frustrated cough, took another swig of wine, as though trying to swallow the unpleasant memories.

'Ack,' she said, as she reached for the bottle to refill her glass. 'It's not just that. It's everything about this bloody story. Nothing quite adds up, and I've been so busy covering the latest line that I've not been able to dig into what's really going on.'

'Oh?' Simon asked, shaking his head as she tipped the bottle towards his glass. 'Like what?'

Donna set down the bottle, took a sip of wine. Considered the glass for a moment. 'Rodriguez mostly,' she said. 'Some of the things he's done. At the press conference the other day, he told me he wanted attention on him so anyone who didn't want him revealing the truth, whatever that is, about his dad wouldn't take a pop at him. But then he tells us that someone, most likely the killer, had been in touch before all this, feeding him information about his dad. So why would he be scared that his source would kill him when he was doing everything they wanted and covering the story?'

'Hmm,' Simon muttered, thinking it over. 'Good point. You think he's playing some kind of double bluff? Trying to show whoever has been feeding him information that he's got the media buy-in to do something with it, that he's the golden goose that should be left alone?'

'Maybe.' Donna shrugged. 'But it's not just that. Part of his initial deal with me was that he'd prove he was on the level by taking me to meet a source of his. That never happened, what with the bombings and the way the story unfolded, but who is this source? Everything he's been given has been done anonymously so far, via emails and texts. So who was he going to take me to meet? Or was that just more bullshit to get me onside?'

A thought that had been in the back of Simon's mind since Duncan MacKenzie's body had been found at Stirling University jostled its way to the front. 'About that,' he said. 'Why does he want you involved in this anyway? He's a big-name US TV reporter with the ear of the chief constable. Everything that's happened has made sure he's the face of this story, so why is he so desperate to cosy up with you? And why is his source, if it's the same person who killed Duncan and sent those bombs, so keen to talk to you personally?'

'Personally?' Donna said. 'But the emails and texts with the footage of the bombs were sent to both Rodriguez and me.'

'Yeah,' Simon agreed, 'they were. But Jamie Leggatt's wallet was addressed to you personally and hand-delivered. Why? Why not send that titbit to Rodriguez, like the killer has done with everything else?'

Donna pushed away from the table, started to chew her lip slowly. 'Good point,' she said, her tone contemplative. 'You know, you're not so bad at this, McCartney. Not just a pretty face, after all.'

'Aw,' Simon said, feeling heat flush his cheeks. 'You noticed.'

'Don't worry,' Donna said, a smile creeping onto her face, 'I'll not tell anyone. Your secret is safe with me.'

Simon raised his glass in a toast, relieved to see some of the tension drain from Donna's shoulders and brow. But even as he did, the thought nagged at him: why had the killer sent that wallet, the wallet that had put them on the track of Leggatt and on a collision course with a bomb, to Donna alone? Why had—

He was cut off by the chirp of Donna's phone on the kitchen counter. She gave him an apologetic smile, then rose and grabbed it. Simon felt a flash of guilt as he hoped it wasn't her parents telling her that Andrew was fussing and wanted to come home. It wasn't that Simon didn't like spending time with the boy, he loved his energy and playful nature, but at that moment all he wanted was some time alone with Donna.

She answered the call, back stiffening as her voice became clipped, business-like.

'Jonathan,' she said, flashing a look over her shoulder at Simon, who nodded understanding. Jonathan Rodriguez. Were his ears burning after their conversation?

'Yes, yes, I . . .' Donna stopped, blinked, turned to Simon again, her face somewhere between relief and confusion. 'Okay, yes. Yes. That is good news. Thanks for letting me know. Yes, I know Jen. Yes, yes, I can be there. Night.'

She ended the call and peered into the blank face of the phone, as if looking for an answer there.

'What?' Simon asked.

'Rodriguez,' she said, turning to him. 'Seems he's had a call from Jen MacKenzie. Thinks she's found something that ties him to her dad's murder, wants to meet him tomorrow at ten a.m. to discuss it. He wants me there.'

'Interesting,' Simon said. 'As a reporter, or to hold Jen back?'

'Dunno,' Donna said, clearly distracted.

'What else?' Simon said, remembering the call. *That is good news.* 'What else did he say?'

Donna blinked as though roused from a daydream. When she spoke, Simon had the sudden impression that she was in mild shock. 'Oh,' she said. 'Yeah. It seems Amanda Lyons turned up in Dunblane about an hour ago. Lost her phone while out location scouting in Bannockburn, so stopped to get a replacement on the way back to the house.'

Simon felt the shock he had read in Donna's gaze wash over him. 'What? So she's back? Unharmed and unaware of what's been going on?'

'Yeah,' Donna said, brow furrowing as she spoke. 'All seems a bit convenient, doesn't it? But, believe me, it's one more thing I'll make sure to ask about tomorrow.'

CHAPTER 50

Connor woke with a jolt, took a minute as the disorientation and hammering in his chest faded and he remembered where he was.

After his conversation with Jen the previous night, and the revelation that Rodriguez had been in touch with her dad before his death, he had offered to take her to the new house, thinking that, even though it was still relatively empty, a night there would be preferable to the chaos in the flat. But she had refused, saying she didn't want to taint their new home by dragging their current problems into it with them.

'Let's get this sorted out about Dad,' she had said, her tone hushed as she refused to meet his gaze. 'Then we'll get into our house. A new start, for both of us.'

And before he could protest, she had left, saying she was going to stay at her old flat that night and 'sort my thoughts out before meeting Rodriguez in the morning'. Connor had stood in the flat, feeling as though he should try to stop her but not knowing how. And, before he could decide, she was gone, leaving him alone.

Feeling the walls close in on him, he had headed out into the garden, where he was joined by Tom, the stray cat that had adopted him and Simon as her providers and servants about a year ago.

'What a fucking shit show,' he had muttered to the cat, who watched him with impassive eyes. He had been wondering how he could break his appointment with Ford the following morning to accompany Jen to her meeting with Rodriguez when his phone had rung. Simon wasted no time in telling him about his talk with Donna, Rodriguez's possible motives and the reappearance of his assistant, Amanda, whose phone had been found at the arms cache in Bannockburn. They had quickly formulated a plan: Simon would contact Jen, ask that he and Donna go with her to the meeting with Rodriguez. It made sense, and made Connor's life easier: Jen wouldn't be alone with Rodriguez, and having Simon with her might just throw the man off balance, make him reveal something he shouldn't.

With the arrangements in place, Connor had found himself at a loss. He paced the flat, the buzzing, chaotic nature of his thoughts seemingly amplified by the emptiness of the rooms around him. Finally, he had given in and headed out for a run, taking in a six-mile loop that left him physically exhausted but mentally aggravated. There was something in what Jen had said, something about her dad's last message to her, that nagged at him, like a half-remembered lyric to a favourite song. *Drowning in paperwork*. Had MacKenzie known he was going to be killed? Had he been trying to send Jen a last message? And what had his scrawled note meant? *Rodriguez must know . . .*

Know what?

He had set up camp on the sofa with his laptop, a throw blanket draped over his shoulders. He searched through Sentinel's files and the information Robbie had pulled together on the men in the picture. A scandal-hit MSP, the uncle of a police chief constable, a now-deceased lawyer and a Lord Advocate. All men of power and position, but would one of them be willing to kill to protect the life they had built? And there was something else about the image of Robert Balfour and Duncan MacKenzie, something Connor felt he was missing.

Something . . .

As he worked the problem over, he had fallen into a deep, dreamless sleep. He only started awake when Tom began mewing at the patio doors, demanding her breakfast. He hissed at the pain in his neck from sleeping sitting up, his head lolling to one side.

He got up, fed Tom, then went into the garden. It was a clear, crisp morning, and Connor felt his mind clear as he started to work his way through a set of bodyweight exercises: press-ups, burpees, squats, sit-ups. He finished by using the ornate, exposed stone of the wall that made up the back of the garden as a climbing frame, grabbing rocks as handholds and performing sets of pull-ups until his shoulders and arms burned from the exertion.

By the time Ford arrived at ten, Connor was showered, caffeinated and felt more like himself. Unfortunately, whatever morning routine the policeman had been following didn't appear to have had the same effect as Connor's: his skin was pale, almost grey, and there was a glittering intensity to his gaze that spoke to Connor of a lack of sleep.

'You want some coffee?' he asked Ford, as he led him into the flat.

'Aye, please,' Ford said, as he took in the room. 'You just about done getting this place sorted out?'

'Yeah,' Connor said, a vague hollowness echoing through him as he spoke. He had loved this flat. It had been his refuge when he had returned home after a disastrous stint as a police officer in Belfast. And now he was getting ready to move on, move in with Jen. Share his life with her. Whatever that meant.

He poured Ford a cup of coffee, topped up his own, then gestured at the couch.

'So,' Ford said, as he eased himself into the seat, 'what was so sensitive that you couldn't tell me about it at the police station?'

Connor took a swig of his coffee, decided on the direct approach. 'I take it you've noted the, ah, special access that Chief Constable Guthrie has been affording Jonathan Rodriguez?'

Ford stiffened in his seat. 'Yeah,' he said, his voice tight. 'He's not crossed the line in involving a member of the press in an active investigation but he's come hellish close. Brushed me off with some bullshit about "operational necessities" when I confronted him about it.'

Connor choked back a laugh. 'It's an operational necessity, all right,' he said. 'Necessary to keep him in his job.'

'What?' Ford said, his gaze sharpening, becoming almost predatory. 'What do you mean?'

Connor took a breath. 'We were provided with a picture,' he said slowly. 'It showed Jonathan Rodriguez's father, Robert, with a group of men we've now identified. One of them was Duncan MacKenzie, and another was a man called Marcus Guthrie, whom we've ascertained was Chief Constable Guthrie's uncle. Rodriguez has told me that he was given this picture as a way of blackmailing Chief Constable Guthrie into giving him, ah, special access to the MacKenzie murder investigation.'

'Special access?' Ford asked. 'But why?'

'Saor Alba,' Connor said. 'It seems that the group in the shot were part of some splinter group that believed direct action was justified to gain Scottish independence. Guthrie's uncle's involvement in such a group would have precluded him taking a role in the police when they did their security checks, and Rodriguez was using that against him.'

'Shit,' Ford whispered, as he leaned back in his seat. Then, before he could hit the back cushion, he jerked forward again.

'What?' Connor asked.

'Marcus Guthrie,' he said, reaching into his pocket for his phone. 'I know that name. I just . . .' He trailed off, his fingers working the screen of the phone. Then he stopped, a strange, bitter triumph somehow making him seem younger and more alive than he had been minutes ago.

'There you go,' he said, passing the phone to Connor. 'I knew I recognised that name. This came round a few days ago. Standard all-org email that HR sends out for such occasions.'

Connor looked at Ford's phone, saw a standard Police Scotland email, the title of which was 'Guthrie, Marcus, Supt (retd): Arrangements'.

'He was a policeman?' Connor muttered, stunned. Then he read on.

The funeral of Superintendent Marcus Guthrie will be held at Stirlingshire Crematorium, Bannockburn, on 3 August at 2 p.m. All off-duty officers are invited to attend. Family flowers only, donations to the Police Federation.

Connor read the email again, then looked up at Ford. 'Hold on,' he said. 'That date?'

'Yes,' Ford said, a small, cold smile pulling his lips thin. 'He was cremated just two days before MacKenzie's body was found in Airthrey Loch. That sound like a coincidence to you, Fraser? Because if it is, it's a fucking huge one.'

CHAPTER 51

Simon and Donna picked Jen up at her flat, Simon grudgingly driving Donna's car instead of his own. With its low suspension, bucket
seats and an engine that rocked the chassis every time the accelerator was blipped, they agreed it wasn't the best mode of transport for
a woman recovering from the spinal injuries that had left her with
limited mobility.

They drove in silence for a few minutes, Jen in front, Donna in
the back, passing the new-build estates sprouting up around Stirling
like patches of kit-form weeds as they headed north towards the A9.
Simon was driving down the slip road to merge onto the bypass when
Jen finally spoke.

'They're formally naming Dad today,' she said, as she stared out of
the window.

Simon shot Donna a look in the rear-view mirror and she leaned
forward, close enough for Simon to feel the heat from her body. 'You
ready for that?' she asked.

'Not got much of a choice,' Jen replied, bitter humour giving her
voice an off-key lilt that Simon found disturbing. 'Troughton called
this morning. Said they wanted to release Dad's name as part of an
appeal for information. If it helps find whoever killed him, then . . .'
She shrugged, went back to studying the landscape.

'You know that the press are going to come calling when his name
gets out,' Donna said. 'Your dad was a well-known businessman in

the area, as well as, er, everything else. If you want, we can work on a statement from you, put it out on the PA wires so all the news agencies get it, with a line at the end saying you'll be making no further comment. It won't dissuade everyone, but it might get them to back off a bit.'

'And I'm sure Paulie and I can deal with anyone else who comes knocking,' Simon added. He had hoped that such a blatantly sexist remark, implying that Jen needed their protection, would prompt some kind of response from her. Instead, she shrugged again, turned to give him a weak smile.

'They're releasing the name at four, so it's available for the six o'clock bulletins,' she said. 'If we can work something up beforehand, Donna, that would be great, thanks.'

'Not a problem,' Donna said. 'We'll do it as soon as we've finished with Rodriguez and his assistant.'

They arrived in Dunblane a few minutes later, Simon finding a space outside the house Rodriguez and Lyons had rented. He was again struck by the tranquillity of the location, a quiet, well-tended suburban street, the neat homes facing a church nestled in manicured grounds. He had found himself wondering what it would be like to live in a place like this, to find his own home with Donna instead of taking Connor's place. Jump into his new life in Scotland with both feet rather than just dipping a toe in.

'Ack, one step at a time,' he muttered.

'What?' Donna asked, a smile on her lips, as though she had read his thoughts.

'Nothing,' he said, pushing back the urge to reach out for her. 'Just talking to myself.'

'Best watch out for that,' Jen said as she got out of the car. 'Folk will get the wrong idea about you.'

'They always do,' Simon replied, with a smile.

They walked up the short path to the front door, which opened as they approached. Amanda Lyons stood there, looking as if she was ready for a TV appearance, or a fashion shoot. Her hair and make-up were almost too perfect, and the suit she wore might have come straight from a hanger in some exclusive boutique. Her dark eyes strafed across the three of them as they approached, her face arranging itself into a smile so welcoming it seemed vaguely predatory.

'Good morning,' she said brightly, as she ushered them into the house. 'Jonathan is in the lounge, and we've got the coffee on.'

They stepped into the open-plan living and dining area, found Jonathan Rodriguez sitting at the dining table, which was strewn with the morning's papers. Unsurprisingly, the headlines were all concerned with the bomb attack at St Andrew's House. Donna had checked the wires before leaving her flat and had updated the piece she had written for Sky's website – nine people hurt in total, two of whom had what had been described as 'life-changing injuries'. It was, Donna thought, a miracle that no one had been killed. Or, she was forced to admit, some precise calculating by whoever had planted the bomb.

Rodriguez rose from his seat, raising his mug of coffee in salute. 'Morning to you all,' he said. 'Just catching up on the coverage of yesterday's fun and games. Seems my report got picked up by a few of the papers, and you did some good work online, Donna.'

Donna gave Rodriguez a smile that told Simon she was treating him as an interview subject, not a colleague. 'Jonathan, this is Jen MacKenzie, Duncan MacKenzie's daughter,' she said. 'I believe we all have a few things to talk about.'

Rodriguez's smile faltered, then regained its previous intensity. 'Yes, of course,' he said, leaning forward and offering Jen his hand. 'We spoke yesterday. I'm sorry for your loss Ms MacKenzie. I'll help you in any way I can.'

'You can start by telling me why you were speaking to my dad before you came to Scotland,' Jen said, the bluntness of her tone making Simon wince internally. He knew the type of anger that went with that tone, had seen it in Connor enough times to recognise it.

'Ah, yes,' Rodriguez said, as he slid back into his seat, gesturing for the others to sit. 'It's somewhat delicate, as it relates to the story Donna and I are working on at the moment and—'

'We're working on the same story, maybe not together,' Donna cut in. 'Anything you've got to tell me, you can say in front of Jen. Whatever the hell is going on, it cost Jen's dad his life. I think that earns her full access, don't you, Jonathan?'

Rodriguez's smile intensified as he gave Jen his best sympathetic look. 'Of course,' he said. He exchanged a glance with Amanda Lyons, who was circling the table, pouring coffee from an oversized cafetière. He shook his head when she offered him a top-up, gazed into the mug as though he could see his next words there.

'When I was first contacted about what happened with Dad, the picture of him in the woods with those other men was one of the first items I was sent,' he said. 'No one else was named, but your dad was pointed out in the picture, and I was also sent a link to a news article about his company, MacKenzie Haulage. So, naturally, I reached out to see what he could tell me.'

'And what was that?' Jen asked.

'Not a lot, to be honest,' Rodriguez said, with a shrug. 'He met some of Dad's students at a pub in Stirling, where he was working on the door at the time. Seems there was a fight one night, and your dad broke it up. He impressed some of the boys, and they invited him along to one of their weekend camps so he could train them in self-defence and the like.'

'And that's where he met your dad?' Simon asked.

'That's what Mr MacKenzie told me,' Rodriguez agreed. 'Seems Dad took to him a bit, taught him about Scottish history and his beliefs around Scotland being independent.' He paused, sadness clouding his features. 'It's funny, Ms MacKenzie. In a lot of ways, your father knew my dad better than I did.'

Simon saw Jen tense at those words, decided to step in. 'Mr Rodriguez, one of the notes Jen found relating to your conversations with her father referenced the other men in the picture. We now know they're some pretty influential people. Did you speak to any of them before you came to Scotland?'

Another glance from Rodriguez towards Amanda Lyons. 'Well, I spoke to Chief Constable Guthrie, of course,' he said, with an embarrassed shrug. 'But the rest of them I was planning to meet when I was here. As a matter of fact,' he turned to Donna, 'one of the men I hoped to meet was the contact I was going to take you to see. You know, before all this, well . . .' His eyes flicked to Jen as his voice trailed off, and Simon felt a flash of gratitude for Rodriguez's sudden show of tact.

'And who was that?' Donna asked.

'Ronnie MacRae,' Rodriguez replied. 'He's a member of the Scottish Parliament. I thought we could go and see him together. I'd emailed him, and he was happy to talk about being one of Dad's students.'

'I wonder how happy he would have been to talk when he found you'd brought a local TV reporter along,' Donna said, her face impassive. Something about her tone told Simon she was re-evaluating Rodriguez and not liking the conclusions she was forming.

Simon let the silence stretch out, then turned his attention to Amanda Lyons. 'Sorry, Ms Lyons,' he said, with a smile, 'almost forgot, I wanted to have a wee word with you as well.'

She gave him a look of perfectly manicured confusion. 'Me? Not sure what else I can add, Mr McCartney. I work closely with Jonathan, and he knows everything I do.'

'I'm sure he does,' Simon said, enjoying her discomfort as he spoke. It was a classic interview tactic when dealing with more than one person: change the subject and focus of the interview abruptly, throw everyone off balance and see if they say anything they shouldn't.

'So how was Bannockburn?' he asked. 'I understand you lost your phone there yesterday.'

Amanda's face darkened, before returning to its previous good humour. 'Oh, yes, that,' she said, as though Simon had just reminded her of a good joke. 'All quite embarrassing, really, but I went through it all with the police last night. I was out location scouting at Bannockburn, you know, for shots we could use when we're talking about Professor Balfour's love of Scottish history, and somehow I lost my phone when I was out.'

'Location shoots,' Simon said. 'Anywhere in particular? Maybe Ladywell Park?'

Lyons shook her head. 'I'm not sure where that is,' she said. 'No, I was at the Bannockburn Visitor Centre, you know, where they have the monuments and the displays about the battle. Took a walk around the grounds, must have dropped my damn phone somewhere. When I realised I'd lost it, I asked the staff at the centre to look out for it, then headed into Stirling to get a replacement. Went to some shop in the centre of town, in the shopping centre there.'

Simon nodded. 'The Thistles,' he said.

'Yes, that was it. Got a new phone. Different UK number, but my normal US number is diverting to it, and I can access my emails, so not a total loss.'

'And the police didn't tell you where your old phone was found?' Simon said.

'No,' she replied. 'Only that it was found at the scene of an active investigation.' She gave a small shudder, one hand rubbing at her neck. 'But the thought that someone stole my phone to place it at such a scene, well, it's horrible, isn't it?'

'Yes,' Simon agreed, a thought forming in his mind. 'Absolutely horrible.'

CHAPTER 52

Ford stayed with Connor for another hour, going over what had happened in Bannockburn and what had led him and Simon to the arms cache. Connor felt a vague unease at lying to the policeman about Paulie's involvement in what had happened, but pushed it aside with the thought that the ends justified the means.

It was, he knew, another lie. But it was one he found he could live with.

After Ford left, he headed out into the garden to retrieve 'the item' Paulie had referred to the previous evening. It didn't take long to find: the knife had been carefully wrapped in plastic sheeting and tucked behind a large bluish-purple shrub close to the wall at the back of the garden. Connor took it into the flat and unwrapped it, feeling another pang of guilt. Another piece of evidence he was withholding from the police in the hope it would be of more use to his investigation than theirs. And what, he wondered, did that mean? Simon had promised that whoever was behind this would be dealt with, but how far would Connor go to deliver that justice?

He laid it on the coffee table in front of him, swallowing a snarl of revulsion. Was this the knife that had been used to kill Duncan MacKenzie, the same knife he had seen in the picture of Duncan with Robert Balfour and his band of acolytes?

Connor retrieved his laptop and pulled up the picture of Balfour and Duncan. Zoomed in on the knife and examined it, comparing it to the blade on the table in front of him. It was difficult to tell precisely, but they both looked the same – just over a foot long, with a single-edged blade. The handle in the picture was obscured by Balfour's clenched fist, but Connor guessed it was about the same length as the one on the blade in front of him – maybe six inches in total, made from some dark, hard wood that had been stained almost black by years of varnishing and polishing.

He stood and went to the kitchen, grabbed a pair of nitrile gloves and snapped them on before picking up the knife. It was heavy but beautifully balanced, feeling natural in his grasp. He waved it gingerly, feeling it cut through the air, and the memory of another knife flashing before his eyes as he disabled a would-be armed robber sprang into his mind's eye.

There were no signs of blood or viscera on the blade, which gleamed in the light streaming through the patio doors. The handle was ornately carved to look like knots of rope bound together. At the top of the handle, an amber jewel had been set into the brass cap and Connor could make out some kind of engraving there.

He grabbed his phone, switched on the torch and inspected the engraving. But it was useless: the glare of the light flared back from the polished brass, making everything unreadable. With a curse, Connor stood and walked towards the patio doors, angling the blade so he could read what was written there.

He eventually made out two words, which meant nothing to him. A memory of Paulie sneering at him, *Christ, Fraser, you're such a bloody tourist.* He smiled, walked back to the coffee table and his laptop. Punched in the words he had found and hit search.

It didn't take long for the answer to appear on his screen: *Ne obliviscaris,* Latin for 'Forget not'. Connor sat back, considering. It made sense. Whoever was behind this had a grudge with what had happened with Professor Balfour forty years ago, and wanted some perceived injustice addressed. They forgot nothing and wanted revenge.

Connor leaned back into the screen, kept scrolling down. Stopped when he found another entry for *ne obliviscaris,* a common use of the phrase. He took what he had found, cross-referenced it with the names of the other men in the photograph with Balfour and Duncan

MacKenzie, cursed when he couldn't find a match. In frustration, he began another search, this time cross-referencing Bannockburn. Felt excitement crawl across his skin when he got a result, a possible connection between the knife and the arms dump.

Another search, this time using the phrase on the handle and a description of the knife told Connor it was a ceremonial Highland dirk, a blade used by the Scottish clans in the eighteenth century.

He placed the dirk on the table again, sat back as thoughts and ideas crashed through his head. The killer was trying to send a message: was the dirk part of that message? It made sense, and the motto on the handle, 'Forget not', seemed to enforce that. But was there something more? Something deeper? The killer's sign-off, Saor Alba, Free Scotland, seemed to indicate that, and when added to the motto Connor had just found . . .

He grabbed his phone again, dialled. Got an answer on the third ring.

'Robbie, it's Connor. Do me a favour, pull up everything you can on Clan Campbell, family motto *ne obliviscaris*. I know they fought at Bannockburn, but I want anything else you can get, including if they're affiliated to anyone else in that picture of Balfour and MacKenzie.'

Robbie confirmed his instructions and asked, 'Anything else you need, boss?'

'That picture,' Connor muttered, his eyes drifting to the laptop screen.

'What?' Robbie asked.

'Oh, sorry, Robbie, just thinking. That's all for just now. Let me know what you get.'

He ended the call, Robbie all but forgotten by the time he had laid his phone back on the table.

That picture.

And then it hit him. What he had missed, what had been nagging at him. He swore softly under his breath, felt a twist of excitement that was soured by the embarrassment of not seeing what had been staring him in the face.

There were six men in the picture. Three dead, MacKenzie, Balfour and Kirk, three still alive. Powerful, connected men. If and how they were connected to the deaths of Robert Balfour, Duncan MacKenzie and the bombings in Dundee and Edinburgh were questions for later. Right now, Connor had a more pressing question he wanted answered.

Who was the seventh person there that day? The person who wasn't in the photograph, the one who had taken it?

CHAPTER 53

After his conversation with Connor, Ford headed for Randolphfield police station in Stirling, calling Chief Constable Guthrie as he drove. He wasn't overly surprised when the chief's mobile diverted to his answering message. After all, a man like Guthrie considered himself too important actually to talk to his officers. Ford left a short, curt message that was just this side of polite, which included the name of Guthrie's uncle and a strong recommendation that Guthrie clear some time in his diary for a meeting. His phone pinged ten minutes later, just as he was pulling into his parking space at the police station. A text message, almost as curt and to the point as Ford's message to Guthrie had been.

My office. As soon as you get back. Leave the fucking attitude in the car park.

Ford smiled, got out of the car and looked up at the blunt, closed face of Randolphfield police station. Was Guthrie staring out of one of those windows on the top floor, he wondered, waiting for him to arrive? He hoped so.

He headed into the building, took a side trip to the canteen for what passed as coffee, then the lift to the executive suites on the top floor, where Guthrie had requisitioned an office. A secretary he vaguely recognised looked up when he stepped through the door, her gaze sharp and accusatory, and Ford wondered how much of Guthrie's reaction to his message had been directed towards her.

186

'Chief's expecting me,' Ford said, gesturing towards a second door that led to Guthrie's office.

'Yes, he is, go on in,' the secretary replied.

Ford nodded his thanks, stepped to the door. Didn't bother knocking, just walked straight in. Anger flashed through him as he saw Guthrie sitting barricaded behind a desk, wearing a uniform that he somehow made look like a child's costume.

'DCI Ford,' he said, his eyes sliding over Ford's shoulder to the door and the secretary behind him. 'Please, come in. Close the door behind you.'

Ford did so, forcing himself not to slam it. Then he sat in front of the chief, not waiting for an invitation. He saw disdain shimmer across Guthrie's face, felt a warm satisfaction bloom in his guts at the sight.

'You wanted to see me about something related to my family?' Guthrie said, with a calm conviction that didn't make it to his eyes.

'Yes, sir,' Ford said. 'More accurately, I'd like to speak to you about your uncle, Marcus Guthrie, his links to Professor Robert Balfour, suspected paramilitary activity and how you're being blackmailed by his son, Jonathan, to give him privileged access to a live murder investigation. You got a preference as to what order we take all that in?'

Guthrie opened his mouth, closed it. Looked down at his hands, which were knotted on the desk in front of him, knuckles white as he tightened his grip. He took a deep breath, let it out in a shudder as he shook his head. Then he looked up at Ford. Any illusion of authority had gone, replaced by a small, broken man who was finally facing up to some unpleasant truths about himself.

'Your parents, are they still alive, Malcolm?' he asked.

Ford blinked. Not what he had been expecting. 'No, sir,' he replied. 'Mother died about twenty years ago now, Dad went five years later.'

'Hmm,' Guthrie mumbled, nodding as if this was the correct answer to a question Ford hadn't understood. 'That's good. So you were an adult when they died. You had time with them.'

'Yes, sir,' Ford agreed, confusion diluting his anger at the policeman who had jeopardised a live investigation in a petty attempt to hide some dirty family secrets.

'I wasn't as lucky,' Guthrie went on. 'See, my parents were killed when I was seven. Car crash, just outside Perth. I was in the car, don't remember anything about it. But they died instantly, and I ended up going to live with my aunt, Dorothy, and her husband, Marcus, my dad's older brother.'

'Sir, I'm not sure how this is relevant. I know that Mr Rodriguez was using your . . .'

Guthrie held up a hand. 'It matters because it's context,' he said, his voice suddenly tired. 'Aunt Annabel and Uncle Marcus raised me as their own son. And I loved them fiercely in return. It was Uncle Marcus who suggested I study politics at university, then get onto the fast-track with the police. Everything I am today, I owe to him. He was a remarkable man, yet he always struggled to fit in.'

Ford's anger reignited, like dying embers suddenly given air. 'And it was also Uncle Marcus who asked his pal the Lord Advocate to help doctor the family history,' he said. 'Make sure his involvement with Professor Balfour's university band of radicals didn't stop him from getting into the police or keep you out of that chair?'

Guthrie stiffened, his face paling. He leaned forward, voice little more than a whisper. 'Yes, Uncle Marcus may have helped with that. He believed that the indiscretions of his youth shouldn't hamper his chances, or mine.'

'So that's why you helped Rodriguez, was it?' Ford asked. 'You didn't want your uncle's past "indiscretions" coming to light? It wouldn't look very good on his record, and it would also raise questions about your job, wouldn't it? The chief constable who allowed his family to cover up their past to make sure he got the top job. Wonder what your pal the First Minister in Bute House would think of that?'

Guthrie brought his hand down, slamming the desk hard enough to make the computer sitting on it jump slightly.

'It wasn't like that!' he said, voice shrill now. 'Well, it was. But when Rodriguez got in touch with me, Uncle Marcus was ill. He hadn't been well for years, heart disease and vascular dementia, and the shock of all that from forty years ago coming out in the press would have killed him and Aunt Annabel. I just wanted to make sure they were comfortable. They deserved that much.'

Ford thought back to the all-staff notice he had shown Connor Fraser, the message that informed police staff of Marcus Guthrie's cremation.

'Did Rodriguez contact him?' he asked, trying to soften his tone. 'Was that a contributing factor to his death?'

Guthrie stared at him, naked contempt and pain in his eyes. 'No,' he said. 'I mean, he knew that Rodriguez was planning a story on his dad's death, had seen that much in the news, it was one of the few things he actually took in and understood. But as far as I'm aware Rodriguez never contacted him directly. He, ah ...' he coughed something watery off his chest '... Uncle Marcus fell in the garden at home. Cracked his head open. He held on for a few days, always was a fighter, but ultimately ...'

Ford nodded, sympathy cracking the façade of his contempt for the man in front of him. 'Sir, I have to ask, did you compromise the investigation into Duncan MacKenzie's death at any time? Did you share any confidential details with Rodriguez?'

'No,' Guthrie said, his tone flat. 'I agreed to give him as much access as I could, and access to the files on his dad's death from back in 'eighty-three, but nothing more. You may not think much of me, DCI Ford, but I'm still a policeman. There are some lines even I won't cross.'

Ford gave a thin smile. 'And have you spoken to anyone else involved with your uncle back when they were at Stirling University? Discussed the case with them, given them a heads-up as to where Rodriguez's story might have been going? Because if you have, you might have given one of these men a motive for murder.'

'No,' Guthrie said. 'I mean, I saw Ronnie MacRae at Uncle Marcus's funeral – he was there as Uncle Marcus was a constituent of his. But Donald weren't there – probably thought better of it, given Rodriguez's story.'

Donald, Ford thought, wondering how many people were on first-name terms with the Lord Advocate.

'And you've had no further contact with Rodriguez? No further requests have been made of you for access?' Ford asked.

'No, not since St Andrew's House,' Guthrie said. 'Not that I'm going to be much help for him now. Once we're done here, I'm going to report myself to Professional Standards and recommend Deputy Chief Constable Dalwhinnie take over while I'm placed on administrative leave.'

Ford blinked, shock robbing him briefly of the power of speech. 'What?' he said, after what felt like an age. 'But what about all the stuff you said about protecting your uncle's memory? What about your aunt, Annabel? I thought . . .' He was remembering Guthrie's words: *I just wanted to make sure they were comfortable. They deserved that much.*

Past tense.

'Yes.' Guthrie nodded, as if reading Ford's thoughts and confirming the conclusion he had come to. 'Aunt Annabel passed away last night. Heart attack apparently, very peaceful, I'm told. So you see, DCI Ford, there's no need for me to lie any more. I'll face the consequences of my cowardice and, if it helps fuck up Rodriguez's story or lead to the bastard who's doing all this, so much the better.'

CHAPTER 54

She died as she had lived.

Defiantly.

He had known that she had to die from the moment he had seen her at the funeral. At first he had thought he could contain the maelstrom of emotions and memories that she triggered in him, but as time went on and he focused on his mission to drag the truth kicking into the cold light of day, he had found himself distracted by her, by the thought of her at the funeral, her beauty transcending years and her own grief, her soft eyes telling him that she, and she alone, understood what his loss meant. He had found himself pausing while working on the bomb for Jamie Leggatt, pliers held frozen above the device he was working on, as the thought of her dragged him into a whirlpool of memory, back to a time forty years ago, when her skin was smooth and unlined, and her eyes shone with passion instead of grief.

It was then he realised, in a moment of clarity that was at once joyful and soul-crushing, that she would have to die. Another martyr to the cause.

Another life that Robert Balfour's actions had ended.

The decision made, he had agonised on how to kill her. The poetry of using one of the guns retrieved from the arms cache was undeniable and alluring, but he could not bring himself to desecrate her body in such a way. He had briefly regretted leaving the dirk at the site for the police and Connor Fraser to find, knowing that one slash across her throat would be enough, but again, he could not bear the thought of the blade tasting her flesh, no matter how much it might have hungered for it.

The answer came to him as he finished the bomb for Leggatt and addressed the envelope he had encased it in. Looking at the name, he knew what he would do. He would tell her the truth of who he really was, where he really lived. Not the truth she had helped keep secret. No. He would unburden himself upon her, tell her the secret he had kept for forty years, the secret they had all built their lives around, and then he would put his hands round her thin, delicate neck and end her.

She let him into the house with a welcoming, open smile. He was, after all, a lifelong friend, more even than that in their long, long history. She had ushered him into the house, asked how he was, offered her sympathies and told him how she had looked for him at the wake after the funeral. He had smiled, thanked her and then, when she had busied herself with making tea and presented him with a cup, he had begun to tell her his story. The story of a lie that had been told forty years ago, of why Robert Balfour had had to die, and why Jamie Leggatt had been blown – literally, he hoped – to Hell and why he had detonated a bomb in a crowd of people outside the home of the Scottish Government. And as he spoke, he watched her face grow pale, accentuating the lines and creases the years had etched into her skin. And in that moment, he had known that her death was not murder, but an act of kindness.

She had rocked back in her chair when he had finished talking, her eyes wide and filmed with tears, her face pinched as though she had sucked something sour. She lifted her cup of tea, hand shaking so badly that the china chinked musically against the saucer, then lifted it to her face.

She moved so quickly he did not have time to react. One minute, she was sitting before him, and then his world descended into a scalding shriek of agony as she hurled her tea into his face. Then she was on him, clawing at his face, her thin body a mass of foetid, furious energy as she hissed curses at him and promises that she would kill him for what he had done.

He rocked back in his seat, seized her wrists. Pushed her forward with all his strength. She hit the floor with a dull, excruciating thud and rolled away, and he lunged forward instinctively.

When he rolled her to face him, her eyes were wide with an animalistic, incredulous fury. She clawed at her chest with a hand that had become a frozen, palsied talon, and her mouth was twisted into an agonising sneer as she gasped for breath.

He stood up, wiping his face as he used the pain from his burned skin to argue against helping her. He had come to kill her, and it was obvious that that was what he had done. He watched for what felt like an eternity as she bucked and writhed on the floor, fighting to grasp the life that was seeping from her with every second. She had always had a weak heart, and it hurt him to realise he had killed her by breaking it.

Eventually, the writhing eased and was ended with a long, gargling rasp. He forced himself to look away as he saw darkness bloom in the crotch of her dress, her bladder giving way as her body died.

He waited for a few moments, looking down at the woman he had loved and helped give him a life, the woman he had been forced to kill. Then, when he could no longer bear the silence of the room, a silence that seemed to judge him, he carefully cleared away the cup he had used, then retraced his steps as he had been trained, obliterating any evidence of his presence.

He wasted a moment on a whispered goodbye, then, satisfied that the stage was adequately set, let himself out of the house and disappeared into the night. He walked with his head down, finding the gloom soothing, calming. And as he walked, he thought of her final moments as her heart betrayed her and her life came to an end. It was not the death he had planned for her, but it was enough. Another loose end tied off, another danger from the past neutralised.

One more message, he thought. That was all it would take. One more message to push Rodriguez, Donna Blake and Connor Fraser right to the edge of the cliff. And there, just before they fell, he would force them to watch as he killed Simon McCartney, and everything he stood for.

CHAPTER 55

The call from Ford had been brief, business-like and as close to panicked as Connor had ever heard the policeman. He told Connor about confronting the chief over his deal with Jonathan Rodriguez, and his decision to confess to being blackmailed.

'Which means,' Connor said, after Ford had stopped speaking, 'that the deputy chief constable is going to want to review every stage of the investigation into Jamie Leggatt and Duncan MacKenzie's deaths. And that's going to be a headache for everyone.'

'A headache we've not got time for,' Ford agreed, his agitation bleeding into his voice. 'There's a lunatic with bombs and guns out there. The last thing I need is to get caught up in a case review while he's planning his next move.'

Connor noted Ford's use of *we*, pushed it aside. That he was seeing Connor as a partner in the investigation, rather than a necessary evil or a problem to be solved, showed how rattled he was.

'Agreed,' Connor said. 'I'll keep looking into this. I've still got the files on the original Balfour case that you gave me to review. Maybe there's something in them that I can use.'

'Look into Ronnie MacRae as well,' Ford said. 'He was at the funeral for Guthrie's uncle while his pal, Byrne, stayed away.'

Connor remembered the list of individuals identified in the picture of Balfour and MacKenzie. 'He's the MSP, isn't he?' he asked. 'Interesting that he'd go to the funeral if the Lord Advocate decided to stay away. And speaking of the Lord Advocate, you had any contact from him yet?'

Ford coughed a growl down the phone. 'Not yet, but I'm sure it's coming,' he said. 'No way a fuck-up this big doesn't come to his attention, either through official channels or others. He'll have his hands full, though.'

'Yeah,' Connor agreed. 'The First Minister will have a shit fit about this, and Byrne will have to deal with that, Guthrie's screw-up and keeping his own nose clean.' He paused, the thought rising again in his mind. 'You think that's what all this is about? Someone in that picture trying to keep the past buried, a past our bomber pal is keen to see dragged into the light?'

'I'm not sure,' Ford replied. 'I mean, it makes a certain sense, but how much damage does it really do to anyone involved? So they were students, radicalised by the teaching of a history professor known for his nationalist sympathies who helped an anti-monarchy protest almost fifty years ago. Would you go to this length to keep that quiet? Wouldn't you just put your hands up, blame it on a misguided childhood and move on? And there's something else too, something about the way MacKenzie was killed. The savagery of it.'

'It's personal,' Connor said. He had thought the same – to obliterate a man's face completely, to wipe away any identifiable features, took determination, rage, hatred even.

Identifiable features. Connor paused, random thoughts coalescing in his mind as connections formed. A sudden flash of the would-be robbers in Edinburgh, the woman snarling up at him: *Didn't want to be predictable, did we?*

And then it was gone, and he realised Ford had stopped talking.

'Sorry,' he said, 'random thought. Leave it with me. I'll find Simon, see how he got on with Rodriguez and Lyons, then pay Mr MacRae a wee visit.'

'And how are you going to manage that?' Ford asked. 'With all this going on, I doubt he'll be in a talkative mood.'

Connor smiled, consulted his watch. 'Ah, but you're wrong,' he said. 'It's Monday, a constituency day. Mr MacRae is paid to be talkative today, paid to be there to listen to his constituents.'

Ford snorted a laugh. 'One small problem with that,' he said. 'Even with you moving, you're not in his constituency, unless the boundaries have shifted since I last looked.'

'No,' Connor agreed, 'they haven't. And you're right, I'm not in his constituency, but I know a man who is. And I'm sure I can persuade him to let me borrow his name for a wee while.'

Wariness crept into Ford's voice. 'Oh, aye, and who might that be?'

'Let me put it this way,' Connor said, the idea taking root in his mind. 'You ever look at me and think I was more like a Paulie than a Connor?'

CHAPTER 56

Donna's broadcast van was waiting outside Jen's flat as Simon pulled up, Keith busying himself unloading a camera and a tripod.

'We'll do a quick to-camera chat. Then I'll write up your statement and get it to the wire service, try to get other reporters off your back,' Donna said to Jen, as Simon killed the engine. 'And if you feel uncomfortable at any time, we can just spike the whole thing, okay?'

'Okay,' Jen said. Simon turned to her and, for the first time, he saw grief on her face rather than anger. She looked exhausted, ground down by not only the loss of her father, but the fury she had sustained to shield herself from it. He felt a pang of sympathy for her, lanced through with a cold, hard hatred of whoever had done this to her.

'I'm gonna stick around out here,' Simon said, as they got out of the car. 'I'm not good around cameras, and I want a bit of time to think. I'll go for a wee stroll. Just text me when you're done and I'll head back to get you, Donna.'

'Why? Where are we going?' she asked.

'You heard yer man Rodriguez,' Simon said. 'He was going to introduce you to Ronnie MacRae. Be rude not to keep that appointment, even if Mr Rodriguez can't make it.'

A slow smile spread across Donna's face as she shook her head slowly. 'Well, don't you know how to show a girl a good time,' she said, her voice slightly mocking.

'And don't you forget it,' he said, then turned and walked away.

The estate Jen's flat was on was typically anonymous: wide tree-lined streets broken up by patches of grass and cars parked end to end. Simon knew there was a playpark nearby so headed in that direction, letting his thoughts wander. It was a trick he had picked up when he was in uniform and studying for his CID qualifications back in Belfast. Whenever he had a problem he couldn't solve, he would walk the beat, let his mind drift, the facts washing over his conscious mind like waves crawling up a beach. Sometimes those waves would leave something behind, a detail or piece of information he had initially missed but his subconscious knew was important.

He replayed his conversation with Jonathan Rodriguez and Amanda Lyons. They had given the appearance of being helpful and honest and, Simon had to admit, Rodriguez's brief show of contrition at blackmailing Chief Constable Guthrie had been a nice touch. But what had interested him most, what had played on his mind since leaving Dunblane, was Amanda Lyons's story about losing her phone at Bannockburn. Simon had no doubt that, if he was to check her credit-card records and CCTV cameras at Bannockburn and in the Thistles shopping centre in Stirling, he would see Amanda Lyons just as she had described, first touring the visitor centre, then heading into town to replace the phone she had lost.

But it was the phone that bothered Simon. Or, more specifically, the loss of it. He had watched her at work before, knew that, like most people these days, her phone was rarely out of her hand. It made sense: she had said her US number was diverting to the phone, and her emails were being forwarded to it. Her phone was an invaluable tool in her work, which was part of the problem. If she had been scouting for filming locations as she had claimed, would she really have had her phone in her bag or a pocket, and not out taking pictures and notes? Would she really not have noticed it was gone, and would she really have been as calm as to ask staff to look for it, then head off to a store to buy another?

It was possible, but there was something about the idea that Simon didn't like. Which left him with two possibilities. Either whoever had taken the phone had been a skilled pickpocket and lifted it from Lyons when she had been distracted by something at the visitor centre or, more worryingly, she had willingly given it to someone.

But there was a problem with that as well. Why? Why would she willingly give her phone to someone who, as far as he and Connor could tell, had been responsible for at least two murders? Was she being blackmailed in the same way Rodriguez had blackmailed Chief Constable Guthrie, or did she feel she owned the killer in some way, either for giving them the information that had put her and Rodriguez on to the story in the first place or for something else? He took out his own phone, pinged himself a text message: a reminder to look into Amanda Lyons more closely when he got a free minute.

Simon sighed, felt an all-too-familiar itch in the back of his mind. He was missing something, he could feel it, something he had seen or heard and hadn't realised its importance. He strolled on for another couple of minutes then looped back towards the flat. It was a bright, warm day, and he was happy enough to wait outside in the sun.

He turned the corner back onto Jen's street, stopped dead as an icy rush of adrenaline chilled his blood and turned his breath acidic in his lungs. Donna's car was sitting in the spot where he had parked it but was listing towards the driver's side at an alarming angle. Simon felt his senses reach out, straining to see or hear anyone nearby. An image of one of the rifles Paulie had described from the arms cache flashed across his mind, and Simon felt his skin crawl in suppressed panic. Was a sniper's sight being levelled at him now?

He ducked and pulled his gun as he crouch-walked to the car, using the other parked vehicles as some form of cover from the road. Futile, but better than nothing. He kept his head swivelling as he moved, trying to take in every detail, see potential threats. He got to the car without incident, circled it slowly. The problem was obvious; both tyres on the driver's side of the vehicle had been slashed, leaving the car to sit on its alloys.

'Shit,' Simon said, straightening slowly. The work of kids, or something more? A message from the killer? Probably. After all, young vandals wouldn't just target one car, especially when there was a tempting TV van parked in front of it.

Instinctively, he inspected the car for any explosives, checking under the wheel arches and underside of the vehicle as he had been trained to do in Belfast. He breathed a sigh of relief when he found nothing. But, then, why target her car? Why commit an act as petty as slashing a couple of tyres when . . .

He stopped dead when he saw it. A small envelope tucked under one wiper on the windscreen. It was standard letter-sized, too small to hold a bomb, but more than adequate for holding something noxious and deadly. Simon reached into his jacket pocket and pulled on the gloves he found there. Donna often teased him about carrying forensic gloves with him, but to Simon it was as natural as carrying his phone or wallet. It was just something he did.

He reached out slowly, warily, and picked up the envelope, his mouth drying as he read his name scrawled across the front in blood-red ink. He squeezed the envelope gingerly, felt a hard, familiar shape. He took a deep breath, prayed he was right, then tore the envelope open and tipped out the contents into his hand.

It was about the length of a lipstick, but much slimmer, with a tapered head that narrowed to a wicked point. Simon knew the type of bullet all too well: it was a 5.56 NATO cartridge, the type used in the Armalite AR-18 rifle that had once been favoured by paramilitaries in Northern Ireland.

He turned the bullet slowly, looked at the tip of the shell. Smiled coldly as he read the one word that had been engraved there. Whoever had carved the word into the bullet had done so with impeccable care and precision – the letters were distinct and perfect.

Five letters. Five letters that made up one name. His own. The message was simple: this bullet is for you, Simon.

Simon closed his hand on it, squeezed. Felt a rush of panicked excitement as thoughts and ideas screamed through his mind. Finally, whoever was doing all of this had made a mistake, given him something concrete he could work with. Not the message, but the way in which it had been delivered. He looked around again, wondering if the person who had left it for him was still nearby, watching him. He straightened his shoulders, tossed the bullet into the air, caught it.

'Game on, motherfucker,' he said. 'Fucking game on.'

CHAPTER 57

Connor had been on his way to Ronnie McRae's constituency office in Lenton Barns when Simon had called to tell him about the slashed tyres on Donna's car and the message left on the windscreen. He had driven on to Jen's street warily, his mind filling with thoughts of the sniper rifles that, until recently, had been buried at Ladywell Park. He parked, saw Simon push himself off Donna's car and walk towards him casually.

''Bout ye?' Simon said, as Connor got out of the Audi. He looked casual, almost relaxed, but Connor could tell from the glitter in his eyes and the set of his jaw that Simon was on full alert.

'More importantly,' Connor said, his eyes falling to the envelope Simon had in his right hand, 'how are you doing?'

Simon held it out to him. 'Not the first death threat I've had,' he said. 'Doubt it'll be the last. But it's interesting, isn't it?'

Connor took the envelope, examined it. Felt fury burn through him like acid when he saw Simon's name scored into the front in angry red slashes. First he'd had a bomb blown up in his face, and now someone was targeting his friend? He remembered Simon's comment about finding whoever was behind all this and putting them into an unmarked grave. It was a sentiment Connor found himself agreeing with more strongly with every passing minute.

He tipped the envelope upside down, the bullet falling into his palm. It was cold and heavy, a small fragment of death. He squinted, read Simon's name on the bullet, the fury he felt squeezing at his temples.

'NATO round,' Connor said, forcing himself to focus. 'For the AR-18?'

'Aye,' Simon said. 'And who do we know used to like that particular rifle?'

'Well, it was favoured by the IRA back in the day, and then there was ...' He caught Simon's train of thought. 'You thinking this is related to Belfast?'

'Got all the hallmarks,' Simon said, as he took back the bullet. 'Arms dumps, letter bombs, weapons favoured by paramilitaries, including some very, very deadly sniper rifles. And then there's this.' He flipped the bullet like a coin, caught it. 'How many times have we seen death threats like this?'

It had been common enough in Northern Ireland both during and after the Troubles – paramilitaries would send their targets bullets as a warning and a way of keeping whole communities afraid. And now here was another warning, delivered in a language that Simon and Connor, both of whom had served in Belfast, would understand.

'So what are we thinking?' Connor asked. 'That Balfour armed his students with weapons he got from Belfast? I guess it makes sense – he advocated direct action to gain independence – but then why was he killed? Something went wrong with the IRA or whoever he was dealing with? If that's it, why did Duncan MacKenzie and Jamie Leggatt have to die forty years later?'

'I don't know yet,' Simon said. 'But it gives us another line of enquiry, doesn't it? Add this to some ideas I've had about Amanda Lyons and her phone and I think—'

He was cut off by the sound of a door creaking open, and Keith lumbering out of the door to Jen's apartment block. A moment later, Donna followed him, her heels clacking loudly on the concrete as she walked.

'What the hell happened to my car?' she asked, as she approached them, her eyes darting accusingly between Connor and Simon.

Simon gave her his best disarming smile. 'Bit of tyre trouble, that's all. Some idiot trying to make a point. I'll fix it – already put a call in to a local garage to get a couple of new tyres.'

'But I ... I ...' Donna said, as though trying to decide between fury and resignation.

'How'd it go with Jen?' Simon asked. Connor had to bite back a smile when he saw the ease with which Simon made the bullet he was holding disappear. It was so subtle and deft, in direct contradiction to his attempt to change the subject away from the damage to Donna's car.

Donna shook her head, brushed a strand of hair away from her cheek as she tore her gaze from her car. 'She's been through a hell of a lot,' she said, her voice suddenly tired. 'Christ, I hate this part of the job, the death knocks. Just hope the statement we've given to PA will keep the vultures away from her door for a while.' She turned to Connor. 'You should go and see her, Connor.'

Connor looked to Simon, who nodded. 'Go on,' he said. 'Call me when you're done. I'll get Donna's car sorted out, then we can start looking for the wanker responsible for all of this.'

Connor glanced towards Jen's flat. Felt something cold and oily turn lazily in his guts as he remembered her words after he had told her about her father's murder. '*Find whoever did this, Connor. You owe me that much.*' The coldness in those words, the hatred, had unnerved him. Donna said Jen needed him, but for what? Support? Love? Or something harder: as a weapon of revenge?

As he walked towards the door of the flat, Connor found he wasn't sure he really wanted to know.

CHAPTER 58

Paulie couldn't remember the last time he had shed tears. He had cele-
brated when his father had died, satisfied that the world was better
for the passing of an abusive alcoholic who routinely used his wife
and son as punchbags on which to vent his frustrations at his petty,
wasted life. He remembered no tears when his mother died either,
only a vague relief that she was free of the cancer that had stalked her
through her final years, robbing her of her dignity and independence.
He was, he thought, a typical Scot, taught to repress his emotions, to
swallow them and ignore them.

And yet, sitting in the silence of his living room, his iPad at his side
on the couch, Paulie King wept.

It had been a simple enough task to get access to the police files
and the pathologist's report on Duncan MacKenzie. Paulie knew
more than a few police officers, and one detective sergeant in particular who had a taste for late-night casinos but no talent with the
cards. He was so deeply in debt to Paulie now, from the money Paulie
had loaned him and the words he had had with the casino owners to
keep the sergeant's kneecaps in one piece, that he would do anything
Paulie asked. So Paulie had asked for the file on MacKenzie.

And when he had seen the post-mortem pictures of the body,
he had wept for the man who had been his friend and employer for
decades.

It was the savagery of it that appalled Paulie most. Not the grotesque, bloodied chasm where Duncan's face had been caved in, but the methodical nature of the torture he had endured. Every finger had been broken, and there were indications that he had been cut in several areas across his chest, arms and legs. Paulie could almost see it – Duncan tied to a chair, screaming against a gag in helpless fury, writhing to be free as he was tortured.

Paulie picked up the iPad again, looked at the image of MacKenzie's body. Forced himself to look at it clinically, like a surgeon judging the work of one of his peers. He wanted to remember the injuries so that, when the time came, he could inflict them on whoever had done this.

And thanks to the post-mortem report, Paulie thought he had a place to look. He had seen that type of torture before, watched as it was inflicted in an industrial warehouse. That time, it had been a warning, a message to a man who had been dealing drugs where he shouldn't. Paulie had thought at the time that the display had been performative, a show for the visitors from Scotland. But he knew now that it had been more than that.

It was a statement of intent.

He closed the file, flicked over to his work app, his fingers feeling fat and useless as he navigated the various screens on the iPad. He hated technology, struggled with anything more complicated than his mobile phone, but with the MacKenzie Haulage office closed on compassionate grounds following Duncan's death, he had little choice.

He found his email, then toggled over to his calendar app, and clicked on a box that let him view Duncan's diary overlaid with his own. He knew there must be a way of searching for what he was looking for, but also knew it was beyond his capabilities to work out what that was, so he merely started scrolling back, looking for confirmation of what he had suspected from the moment he had discovered the arms cache had been dug up and the weapons taken.

It took him a few minutes but, just as the urge to throw the iPad against the wall was becoming irresistible, he found it. One entry, from three months ago. An entry that made sense of the torture inflicted on MacKenzie before he had died. Paulie let out a shaking breath, a mixture of excitement and nausea churning in his stomach.

He stood and crossed to the large table that sat against the back wall of the room, its surface cluttered with various bottles of whisky and other spirits. He poured himself a large whisky, raised it in a toast.

'I'll get them, Duncan, I promise,' he said, his words sounding strangely flat in the emptiness of the room. 'I'll kill every one of those fucks, I promise.'

CHAPTER 59

Connor could feel Simon glancing at him as they drove out towards Lenton Barns, knew his friend wanted to ask him about his conversation with Jen, help if he could. The problem was, Connor wasn't sure what he was feeling. Stepping into the flat had been like stepping into a hurricane of emotions – one minute Jen was cold, then furious, then distraught, then dejected. She had pushed him away when he had first tried to hug her, then collapsed into his arms, as though she had lost the ability to stand up.

Their conversation, what there was of it, had been brief and perfunctory. She needed the case to be solved, for whoever had killed her father to be found. Only then, she said, could she find some peace, lay her father to rest and move on with her life.

The question Connor had wanted to ask was if that life included him. He was still haunted by her words *You owe me that much, Connor* and all the unspoken meaning and finality that went with them. So he had swallowed the question, made promises that felt hollow even as he spoke them, then left. He had called Paulie on the way to the car, told him about the bullet left on Donna's car and asked him to check in on Jen when he could. Connor didn't believe that whoever had left the bullet would do Jen any harm, the specific message for Simon told him that much, but he wanted to be thorough.

You owe me that much.

So they drove in silence, the urban sprawl petering out as they headed for the more rural village of Lenton Barns. Connor knew the place well: he had worked a case at the church there a little over a year before, and when he drove down the wide, open high street, he was pleased to see that the physical scars of that case had healed – shattered windows had been repaired, smoke-damaged stonework cleaned.

If only everything was that neat and simple, he thought.

MacRae's office was at the end of the high street, next to a small butcher's which had a painter's table outside the front window, displaying an array of eggs and vegetables for sale. But while the butcher was vibrant and cheerful, the red awning glowing in the afternoon sun, somehow amplifying the colours of the produce on display, MacRae's office was dour and almost bleak by comparison. To Connor, it looked almost like an estate agent's premises, with MacRae's name stencilled on the window above the portcullis logo of the Scottish Parliament. Strip blinds hung in the window, pulled shut against the day, almost like a barricade.

'So, how do we play this?' Simon asked, as he got out of the car and surveyed the front of the office.

'Straight on,' Connor said. He had called before heading for Jen's flat, made an appointment to see MacRae using Paulie's name and address. Not that Paulie would ever consider contacting his local elected representative about anything, but his address and, more specifically, his postcode gave Connor the pass he needed to get in to see MacRae as one of his constituents.

They stepped into the office, which was gloomy and strangely cool. A sprightly looking woman glanced up from the paperwork strewn on the desk she sat behind, her large, owl-like glasses catching the light from the desk lamp and flashing silver. 'Yes?' she said, her voice a soft Highland lilt. 'How can I help you?'

'Paulie King,' Connor said, keeping his voice soft and as friendly as possible. 'I called earlier. I have an appointment to see Mr MacRae about a planning application that affects my property?'

The woman nodded, glanced down at the desk. 'Ah, yes, Mr King. I have your appointment here. Though you are a little late . . .'

Connor gave another smile, ignoring the rebuke that hardened the woman's lilt a little. 'Sorry,' he said. 'Car trouble. Had to get my friend Freddie here to give me a lift.'

The woman's magnified gaze flicked to Simon, then back to Connor. 'I see,' she said. 'Well, he's waiting for you in his office. Please go in.' She gestured to a door at the far end of the room, gazed at them expectantly, like a teacher trying to chivvy on tardy pupils.

'Thanks,' Connor said.

The room he and Simon stepped into was large and windowless, the only light coming from powerful, industrial-style strip lighting that hung from the ceiling. Connor was vaguely reminded of a major investigation room back in Belfast. The walls were covered with pictures of MacRae at various points of his career, being sworn in at Parliament, meeting other famous politicians, attending ribbon cuttings, tree plantings and other civic events. But what caught Connor's eye was the banner that hung on the wall behind MacRae's desk. A banner he had seen a version of before, in another office, just before a bomb had killed a man in front of him.

A banner that read Saor Alba.

'Good afternoon, Mr, ah, King.'

Connor snapped his attention back to the desk, and the man who was levering himself up from behind it. He was as broad and stocky as he was in the picture from the woods, but he had added a sizeable beer belly and lost most of the thick dark hair he had had forty years ago.

Connor stepped forward, took the extended hand. MacRae's grip was cool and rough, as if he had the callused hands of a manual labourer, not those of a politician.

'Ah, sorry,' Connor said, as MacRae withdrew his hand. 'Wee bit of a mix-up there. My name's Connor Fraser. I'm here to speak to you about your old history professor, Robert Balfour, and the deaths of Duncan MacKenzie and Jamie Leggatt. I used Mr King's name so we could do this discreetly.'

MacRae jolted to his full height, grey eyes darting warily between Connor and Simon. 'I have nothing to say on that matter,' he said, his face blank, his tone clipped and formal. 'Any questions you have can go through my solicitor. Now if you will . . .'

'Your solicitor?' Simon said. 'That would be the late Angus Kirk, yes. Former university pal of yours, shared your taste for camping and fireside stories with Professor Balfour, yeah?'

MacRae blinked, as though dragging himself from a memory. When he spoke, his voice was low, almost bewildered. 'Who are you, exactly?' he asked.

Connor held up a placating hand. 'We're not with the police officially,' he said. 'I work for Sentinel Securities, whom I believe you know. I was there when Jamie Leggatt was killed, Mr MacRae, and I knew Duncan MacKenzie. We just want to ask you some questions, see if we can make sense of any of this. But if you'd prefer, we can do this more publicly. I believe you were in contact with Professor Balfour's son, Jonathan, and were going to be a part of the programme he's making about his father's death?'

MacRae pulled his face into a sneer, then sighed, his shoulders dropping. 'Hardly,' he said. 'I was contacted by his assistant, a woman named Angela, I think, to be interviewed about his father.'

'Amanda,' Connor corrected, as MacRae retreated behind his desk. 'So you didn't actually agree to go on camera and speak to Jonathan?'

'No, it never got that far,' he said. 'We had some initial discussions, and she asked what I remembered about Professor Balfour before he died.'

'And how much do you remember?' Simon asked.

MacRae straightened in his seat. 'The man was a giant,' he said. 'Made me the politician I am today.' He gestured to the banner behind him.

'And that's a nationalist, yes?' Connor asked.

The sneer returned to MacRae's face, and he held up a finger. It was stained yellow, and Connor noticed flecks of ash on the lapel of his jacket. So he was a smoker, a heavy one.

'Oh, no,' MacRae said, 'I'm an independent now. I still believe in Scottish independence, but my views were too, ah, extreme for the modern, moderate, don't-rock-the-boat government. So I resigned the party membership, and sit as an independent nationalist.'

Despite himself, Connor was interested. 'And what exactly does that mean, sir?'

A smile appeared on MacRae's lips, almost as though Connor had given the right password to grant him access to the man's inner thoughts.

'It means, Mr Fraser, that I can continue Professor Balfour's work in arguing and fighting for an independent Scottish republic, free from the shackles of a corrupt Union and the obscenity that is the monarchy.'

'Right,' Simon said, his tone noncommittal.

'Oh, come on,' MacRae snapped. 'You don't agree? Balfour was right when he helped us students protest against the Queen visiting the university all those years ago. Did you see the coronation? Sickening. There are parents struggling to feed their children, our health service is on its knees but, hey, public money is no object when it comes to "celebrating" an old man inheriting a fancy hat. Scotland is better than that.'

Connor ignored the obviously well-rehearsed diatribe. 'So you wouldn't be ashamed to be associated with Professor Balfour and some of his more, ah, unorthodox teachings?' he asked.

'You mean the training camps?' MacRae said, his matter-of-fact tone surprising Connor slightly. 'No, of course not. Those were just the adventures of a misspent youth. I've never believed in violence as a tool for political change, I've campaigned peacefully all my life.'

A thought hit Connor. 'Including being at the Vigil at St Andrew's House?' he asked.

MacRae nodded. 'Yes, I did my stints there when the campaign was ongoing. But why—'

Connor spoke quickly, wanting to keep MacRae off balance. 'Did you believe Jamie Leggatt's claims that there was more to Professor Balfour's death than a mere accident? That he was silenced for something he knew?'

MacRae grew very still, his grey eyes turning hard and unblinking. His right hand strayed towards his suit pocket, then stopped. Connor made a bet with himself that he was reaching for a packet of cigarettes.

'I don't know,' he said, his voice low, thoughtful. 'I mean, it wasn't without precedent, the Secret Service keeping tabs on prominent nationalist campaigners at the time. But despite all his rhetoric, Professor Balfour was, ultimately, an intellectual. Yes, he took us on the camps and trained us in armed struggle, but I think he believed that to resort to those methods would highlight the weakness of his arguments. He wanted to win the battle of the minds, not the war on the streets.'

Another well-rehearsed speech. Either he had been expecting a visit like this, or MacRae was a more talented politician than anyone had given him credit for.

'We've got a photograph of you in the woods with the professor, some students and Duncan MacKenzie. Did you know MacKenzie well?'

'Not really,' MacRae said simply. 'Met him at a pub, and he just kind of got dragged into stuff. Was handy with his fists, taught us how to box, stuff like that. Didn't take the professor long to fill his head with thoughts of the Lion Rampant and storming the fields of Bannockburn, but other than that . . .'

Bannockburn. Interesting. Connor pushed the thought aside, wanting to stay on track. The photo. One more question. 'Mr MacRae, can you remember who the seventh person there that day was?'

'Seventh?' MacRae said, eyebrows knotting.

'The person who took the picture,' Connor said, feeling his guts tighten as he spoke. He was on the verge of something important here, he could feel it.

MacRae's brows knotted tighter, deep grooves appearing in his forehead. 'Well, let me think. There was me, Duncan, the professor—'

He was interrupted by a sharp knock at the door, and the appearance of his secretary. She was strangely pale and fidgeting in a way that gave Connor's nerves a hot, foetid squeeze.

'Diane, what?' MacRae said.

'Line one,' she said, her voice totally devoid of its previous singsong lilt. 'You're going to want to take it. It's Helen. She just found Donald. He's . . . well, he's . . .' Her words were broken by a deep, hitching gasp for breath.

MacRae looked at Connor, then picked up the phone. His face drained of colour as he spoke, as though someone was turning the colour balance down on the picture Connor was seeing. After a moment, he placed the phone down with one shaking hand. It told Connor everything he needed to know.

'Donald,' he said. 'As in Donald Byrne. The Lord Advocate?'

MacRae blinked, nodded slowly, his movements made jerky by shock. 'Yes,' he said. 'Oh, sweet Jesus. That was his wife, Helen. They just found him. He's . . . he's . . .'

'Dead,' Simon said, his voice flat.

The word was like a slap to MacRae's face. 'Yes,' he said, his voice hard now. Cold. 'They found him in his office. Seems he,' a wet intake of breath that promised tears were not far behind it, 'he, ah, hanged himself.' He shook his head, as though trying to ward off the image in his mind. When he looked to Connor, his eyes were glistening, imploring. 'Why would he do that? You don't think it's connected to all this, do you?'

'Yes,' Connor said softly. 'I'm afraid I definitely do.'

CHAPTER 60

He hated the airport.

More accurately, he hated the people that crowded there. Parents shepherding whining children, lovers holding hands as they drifted along in their own little bubbles of ignorance, harassed business travellers who had managed somehow to perfect a look of impotent constipation as they strode towards the departure gate, as though getting there before everyone else would somehow hasten the departure of their plane.

He knew another, more final, way to hasten their departure. He imagined it sometimes, to amuse himself.

'Dominic? C'mon, man, catch yourself on. Car hire is this way.'

He blinked, turned. Saw Miles standing beside him, bouncing softly from foot to foot, a ball of excited energy, impatient to get on with the task. Normally, he was a quiet, sedate man, content to float through life, but not when there was work to be done.

Not when there was blood to be spilled.

They made their way to the car-rental desk, had no problem getting what they needed. An anonymous people-carrier, nothing too flash, nothing too fast. A car that would be looked at and forgotten almost as quickly as it had been seen. From the information he had been given before jumping on the flight from Belfast, Dominic didn't think they would need any other form of transport on this trip, which he found strangely disappointing. He had always loved stealing cars, a habit he had developed in his youth, and there was little that beat the thrill when a car to which you did not have the keys roared into life and you knew it was yours.

They drove out of the airport, found a layby just before the slip road to the bypass. No security cameras here, perfect for their needs. Not that it really mattered. After all, they were just tourists trying to get their bearings. Which, Dominic thought, was true enough.

He reached into the bag between his feet, pulled out the two mobile phones he had purchased at Belfast Airport before boarding the flight for Edinburgh, bought with the same cloned credit card with a false name that they had used to rent the car.

He slipped a SIM from his wallet, inserted it into the phone and powered it on. The phone pinged almost immediately with a text message. Dominic opened it, smiled at the message and the attached image.

'Good news?' Miles asked, from the driver's seat.

'Oh, aye,' Dominic replied, turning the phone so Miles could see it. He read the message, lips moving silently, then nodded his approval.

'Very nice,' he said. 'We get to do a bit of sightseeing and kill a pig. Nice way to spend a couple of days.'

'Aye, isn't it just?' Dominic agreed, as he leaned forward to access the car's satnav and input the address he had been given. And as he did, he found himself hoping that Simon McCartney wouldn't be there when they arrived, that he would present them with more of a challenge than just opening the door to them.

After all, the kill was made sweeter by the hunt.

CHAPTER 61

After the meeting with MacRae, and the revelation that the Lord Advocate, Donald Byrne, had been found dead, Connor felt as though some breaker had tripped in his head. Too much was happening too quickly, fresh information piling in on top of what he already knew, making it impossible to come to any conclusion. His mind felt like a card dealer, shuffling the deck, dealing various hands, then sweeping them away before he could make sense of it all.

He sent a message to DCI Ford without expecting an answer, knowing that the policeman's focus would be on the Lord Advocate's death. Was it really a suicide? If so, why would Scotland's top lawyer and legal adviser to the government suddenly decide to end his life? Was it, as Connor had said to MacRae, connected to what was going on?

Probably. But again, why?

He was grateful when Simon said he was going to head off to see Donna and check something with her. But it left Connor with a dilemma. Should he head back to Jen's flat, or should he give her space? Their last conversation had left him feeling strangely numb, as though a distance was growing between them that he could not stop. Would it take presenting her with the head of her father's murderer to bring them back together? Or was that just another excuse for him to avoid her and the growing unease he felt whenever he remembered her words: *You owe me that much.*

He thought of heading to the flat, but the idea of sitting in the place when it was a half-gutted shell that was still a riot of packing made his head hurt even more. So he eventually headed for the new house, the thought of its relative emptiness and silence suddenly appealing.

He let himself in and made his way to the open-plan living-dining area at the back. It looked out onto a large swathe of lawn bordered by high privet hedges, and Jen was already planning a patio and a fire-pit for the area.

The idea of it, and the thought of sitting with Jen, enjoying a glass of wine on a summer's evening, seemed very far away.

He stepped into the garden, smiled despite himself when he saw the bench Paulie had been dismantling at the flat sitting in the middle of the lawn, perfectly rebuilt. He walked to it and slumped onto it, his laptop bag at his feet. He closed his eyes and tilted his head to the sky, trying to concentrate on his breathing and the breeze on his face. He needed to calm himself, think through everything that had happened, start being proactive instead of reacting as the next situation developed in front of him.

The ping of an arriving text message shattered his moment of calm. With a frustrated grunt, he opened his eyes and grabbed for the phone. It was a message from Robbie, telling him he had completed his research on Clan Campbell and the dirk, as Connor had asked, and had mailed it all over to him.

Connor reached for his laptop bag. Robbie was shaping up as a valuable asset for Sentinel Securities, but there were times when Connor wished he was just a little less efficient and fast-working.

He booted up the laptop, tethered it to his phone, then accessed his secure email. Robbie's communication was at the top of his inbox, sitting atop a long list of unopened emails relating to ongoing work with Sentinel. Problems for another day, he thought, as he opened Robbie's and started to read.

Boss,

I checked into Clan Campbell as you asked. As you said, they fought at Bannockburn with Robert the Bruce when he defeated the English in

1314. Got a long and storied history as one of Scotland's biggest clans, based mostly up in Argyll. Bad blood between the Campbells and the MacDonalds, probably due to the Massacre of Glencoe. I've attached a link, here. I've not found any pertinent familial links between the Campbell clan and Balfour, MacKenzie, MacRae, Leggatt, Kirk, Byrne or Guthrie, but I'll keep digging.

Hope all of this helps. Let me know what else you need,

R

Connor sighed. 'Anything else I need,' he muttered. 'How about a motive and a suspect to pin all this on?' He skimmed over Robbie's email again, the blue text showing the link to the Massacre of Glencoe catching his eye. The name was familiar to him, some event in history that he had no doubt been taught about in school and forgotten. He smiled as he heard Paulie's mocking words in his ear: *Christ, Fraser, you're such a bloody tourist,* then clicked on the link.

It took him to the PDF of a chapter of a book, *Devil's Gallop,* by a writer whose name Connor vaguely recognised. The chapter told how, on 13 April 1692, more than a hundred Argyll soldiers led by a Captain Robert Campbell rose up against the men and women who had been sheltering them for almost a fortnight and, on government orders, massacred them. Connor read of families being 'shot or bayoneted, their blood staining the snow red. Children were gunned down as they pleaded for their lives. Families were lined up against dung hills and cut down.' Almost forty people were killed, primarily because the head of their clan, the MacDonalds, had been slow in pledging his allegiance to the new king and queen, William and Mary. The book stated that the massacre was considered an outrage as it violated the Highland code of hospitality, which obligated clans to provide food and shelter when asked for it and defend their guests if required.

Connor sat back in the chair, thoughts running through his head. Balfour had been involved in the anti-monarchy protest at Stirling University: was this linked to it? He thought back to the picture, of Balfour sitting in the middle, the dirk proudly displayed. Why would he be using a knife with the Campbell name on it? And why had that knife been left at the abandoned arms cache, Amanda Lyons's mobile phone impaled on it?

He closed his eyes and rocked his head back, screwing the palms of his hands into his eyes, hard enough for sparks to skitter across the darkness. There was something here, something in the joke he had made to Simon about his relationship with Donna, and how he was sleeping with the enemy, just like in Glencoe. Glencoe, where Highland rituals and customs demanded hospitality and shelter be offered when needed.

Hospitality.

It was a whisper at first, the barest echo of an idea at the back of his mind. He opened his eyes and leaned forward, straining for the thought. What was it Leggatt had claimed about Balfour's death? That the bottles of whiskey found at Airthrey Loch and in Professor Balfour's office were a cheap brand he would never have drunk?

Irish cat's piss, he heard Paulie hiss in his mind. *Like comparing Buckfast and Dom Pérignon. Two totally different things.*

'Two totally different things,' Connor whispered, as he called up the image of Balfour on the laptop, the Campbell dirk held proudly in front of him. The dirk from the same clan as a man who had, on state orders, turned against his fellow Scots and killed them, just like . . .

Connor felt his world freeze as an avalanche of thoughts crashed through his mind. He gasped, almost as if at a physical rather than a mental onslaught. Forced himself to slow down, think it through one step at a time. What had Ford said when he had asked him to look into the original murder inquiry? *It wasn't unheard-of for reports to be lost, witnesses forgotten, statements changed to get the results the powers-that-be wanted.*

The powers-that-be.

MacRae's words now: *It wasn't without precedent, the Secret Service keeping tabs on prominent nationalist campaigners at the time.*

Connor grabbed for his phone, fingers numb. His senses felt supercharged, almost as if the mixture of excitement, adrenaline and sudden understanding had opened his eyes to another world operating just beyond the one he existed in.

The phone seemed to ring for an eternity, but Connor could barely hear it over the rush of thoughts in his mind. But then it was answered, and he spoke in a rush.

'Robbie? Connor. Great work on the Campbell background. One more favour to ask. Amanda Lyons. Yes, Rodriguez's assistant. Can you run a check on her? As deep as you can and as fast as you can. Education, work history, all that? Send it to my mobile? Great. Thanks.'

He rang off as quickly as he could, feeling as though talking to Robbie was slowing his thoughts down. Then he called the image of Robert Balfour back up again, staring at the blade.

Sleeping with the enemy. The results the powers-that-be wanted. The Secret Service keeping tabs on prominent nationalist campaigners.

Glencoe.

It made sense now. And if Robbie found what Connor thought he was going to when he dug into Amanda Lyons, it would prove that the blade left at the arms cache was a message, and that the killer had taken the Campbell family motto, *ne obliviscaris*, 'Forget not', to heart.

The killer had no intention of forgetting. And he was going to make sure that no one else did either.

CHAPTER 62

Simon over-revved the car as he drove back to Lenton Barns, the deep, angry growl of the engine somehow mirroring his thoughts.

The conversation with Donna had, understandably, not gone well. She'd pushed him on why her tyres had been slashed, had been less than satisfied with Simon's vague reply that it was a mistake, the killer targeting her vehicle in the belief that it was his. He could see in her eyes and read in the set of her jaw that she didn't believe it, that she knew there was more to it than that. But what was the best way to tell your girlfriend that someone had left a bullet with your name on it under her windscreen wipers? Especially when that girlfriend was a journalist who specialised in investigating difficult stories, and asking awkward questions of people who preferred to stay out of the limelight? The last thing Simon wanted was Donna chasing down an angle on a bullet death threat and getting caught in the crossfire. So he had lied, telling himself that he was only trying to protect her. She had gone along with it, partly because she wanted to get back to work on the immediate story, partly because she knew he wouldn't tell her any more.

Still, he wondered how much damage he had done to their relationship, and what, if anything, he could do to repair it.

He had thought about asking Connor to come back with him to Ronnie MacRae's constituency office after he had left Donna's flat, decided against it. He could see that his friend needed time to think through everything that had happened, and since the bullet had been delivered specifically to Simon, it meant the killer was focused on him rather than Connor.

Which was just fine with Simon.

He parked outside MacRae's office. The blinds were still drawn tight against the day, but there was a feeling of emptiness about the place that Simon had not felt before. He got out of the car, wasn't surprised to find the door to the office was locked. He tried the buzzer, waited, ears straining for an answer as he glanced casually up and down the street.

No CCTV cameras. Good.

It made sense that MacRae had left for the day – learning that an old friend had taken his own life was enough to dampen anyone's enthusiasm for work. But when that friend happened to be Scotland's leading lawyer, and you yourself were an elected member of the Scottish Parliament, the loss took on another aspect. Ronnie MacRae might be mourning his friend, but Simon was willing to bet that he was also trying to work out the political consequences of Donald Byrne's death.

Satisfied that no one was going to respond to the buzzer, Simon walked away from the office, ambling up the quiet street. He reached into his pocket and palmed what he needed, then headed back to the door, where he dropped to tie his lace. He glanced around the frame, saw no contact points or wiring that would denote an alarm. There was no alarm on the outside of the building either. And why would there be? Lenton Barns was a small, quiet village, the type of place where everyone knew everyone else and break-ins were someone else's problem.

He stood up and walked to the door, lock picks ready. A moment to locate the lock and tumblers and he was in, pushing the door softly behind him. He stood in the silence, holding his breath and waiting to see if he had been wrong about the office being alarmed. But no alarm sounded, no wall-mounted panel flashed into life, demanding a disarm code. Satisfied, he pocketed his lock picks and walked towards the door leading to MacRae's office, calling up a mental image of the place. MacRae had talked with pride about his time studying with

Professor Balfour, and the Saor Alba banner that was pinned to the wall proved he was a man who liked his mementos.

Which led Simon to ask, what other mementos did he have in that office?

He opened the door and stepped inside, taking a moment to glance up at the banner. It was the same as the one Duncan MacKenzie had been holding in the picture with Balfour, and identical to the one Simon had seen in the video of Jamie Leggatt's Dundee office before it had been blown up. Was it a badge of honour? Or an act of defiance? MacRae had said his political views had grown too extreme for his party so he had been forced to resign and sit as an independent. Was the proud display of the banner, and the adoption of the values it represented, a way of sticking his finger up to the party that had rejected their extremism?

Simon turned away from the banner, took in the rest of the room. It had the bland, almost anaesthetised aesthetic of a waiting room. Two cheap chairs stood in front of MacRae's desk, which was bare apart from a laptop computer sitting in a docking bay and a large monitor. Simon stepped towards the wall to the left of MacRae's desk, studying the various pictures of MacRae doing what a politician does – shake hands and smile uncomfortably at the camera. He saw nothing that interested him, just variations on the theme of middle-aged men in suits that did nothing to disguise their expanding guts, so he turned his attention to MacRae's desk. He approached it and eased himself into MacRae's chair, which was a lot more expensive and plush than the seats on the other side of the desk. He looked at the laptop, toyed with the idea of logging on, discarded it when he saw the Scottish Parliament logo on the corner of the machine. That meant it was a networked computer, linked to the parliament, which meant the security would be robust. Simon had no doubt he could crack it in time, but it was time he didn't have. Not when someone was out there, ready to put a bullet in him at any point.

Instead, he reached for the top drawer of the desk, wasn't surprised when he found that it was locked. He pulled out his lock picks again and sprang the drawer. There was nothing out of the ordinary there, just the usual smattering of pens and Post-it notes you would find in any office drawer, along with a Zippo lighter and a half-finished packet of cigarettes. Simon was about to close the drawer and look elsewhere when he spotted something poking out from underneath the cigarettes. He pushed aside the packet, frowned at what he found.

A key.

Simon pulled it from the drawer, inspected it. It was old-fashioned, the metal dulled by years. It looked like an old latch key, with a long neck and a small, machined head. Simon glanced around, saw nothing that would need such a key, and a quick check confirmed that it would not fit the desk drawer he had pulled it from.

So what was it for? A lock somewhere else? In MacRae's home, perhaps? But if so, why leave it here? Why not take it with him?

Simon leaned back, considered. Found his eyes wandering back to the banner. The banner that was tacked to the wall at eye level.

Eye level when he was sitting down, that was.

He stood up, a vague thought whispering in his mind. Stepped around the desk and walked towards the banner. When he was standing in front of it, it was about shoulder level. Wasn't that low for a banner that MacRae was so proud of? Shouldn't it be higher, given a position of more prominence?

Unless . . .

Simon leaned forward, saw that the banner had been threaded with twine at its corners and looped over hooks that were screwed into the wall. He reached for the left-hand top corner and unhooked the twine, letting the banner fall away from the wall. A smile twitched his lips when he saw the metal face of the wall safe that was behind the banner.

The lock gave a strangely satisfying *thunk* as Simon turned the key he had found, and the safe swung open. He looked inside, saw what looked like a pile of money in front of a sheaf of papers and documents. Simon took a second to draw out his phone and take a photograph of the safe's contents as they were: a visual reference he could use when he reloaded the safe after he had emptied it.

That done, he pulled the money and the documents out. The money was tightly bound rolls of twenty-pound notes, each totalling a thousand pounds. There were twenty rolls in total. Simon set them aside, wondering why a local MSP would need access to £20,000 in cash at all times. Then he turned his attention to the bundle of documents.

The top layer was mostly bland paperwork, bank statements, certificates of insurance for the office and a car, a small ledger detailing expenses and the like. But below that, there was more, a stack of what looked like old photographs and letters, the paper stained yellow by the passage of time.

Simon shuffled through them, slowing as he recognised one. It was a copy of the picture he had seen Duncan MacKenzie in with Balfour, the group huddled in the woods, Balfour at the centre, the teacher with his students. He flicked through, finding variations on a theme – members of the group posing with knives, frozen in time as they made fires or grinned into the camera.

But then he came to one image that was different from the others. And he froze. Simon blinked, felt something click in his throat as he swallowed. Forced himself to count the number of people in the image. Six. The same as all the others. But this time, there was a different face. The photographer had stepped out from behind the camera, and Simon could tell from the others in the picture that Balfour had taken this particular photograph.

A photograph of a dead man holding a rifle, the rest of the group huddled tightly around him, faces intent as he taught them how to handle the weapon.

A dead man who was known for his love of sending bullets as messages.

A dead man Simon knew all too well.

CHAPTER 63

Connor almost collided with Paulie's car as he backed out of the driveway. His plan was to head for Dunblane, and hope that Robbie came back with the information he needed by the time he got there.

'Shit!' he hissed, as he hammered on the brakes and the car lurched to a halt. He felt the seatbelt dig into his chest as it tightened, fumbled for the release. Sprang out of the car, adrenaline and shock making his saliva thick, viscous and bitter, like acid waiting to be spat at whoever was in front of him.

'Paulie, what the fuck?' he said, as Paulie's stubble-shaven head emerged over the roof of his car.

'Sorry.' Paulie raised his hands. It was a diffident, somehow submissive gesture that didn't fit with what Connor knew of him.

'Look, I've got to be somewhere,' Connor said. 'Can whatever this is wait until later? I know I've got to speak to Jen, but this isn't the time.'

'Jen?' Paulie said, his features arranging themselves into a more familiar disapproving scowl. 'Naw, this isnae about her. I need your help. Found something out. Would have found it sooner if you'd taken me to see Duncan's body like you promised.'

Connor frowned, confusion and curiosity washing away his anger at the barb. 'What the hell are you talking about?' he said.

'Probably better if we do this inside,' Paulie said, gesturing towards the house. 'Can we go in?'

Connor sighed. Paulie being in his home was becoming an all too familiar occurrence.

'Yeah,' he said. 'We can use the garden.'

Connor led him through the house, back into the garden he had left only a few minutes before. Paulie ambled in, nodded silent approval at the bench he had constructed.

'Look, Paulie, I'm in a bit of a hurry, so can you tell me what's going on? You said something about Duncan's body, what did you mean about—'

'You ever run into paramilitaries in Belfast?' Paulie asked, ignoring Connor's question. 'You know, IRA or one of the splinter groups that replaced them when the Troubles ended?'

Connor opened his mouth, closed it, his mind flashing back to Belfast and a small-time thug called the Librarian. Connected to the IRA by family. Connor had crossed paths with the Librarian and beaten him to a pulp when he had threatened his girlfriend at the time. The incident had led Connor to leave the PSNI, his girlfriend and his life in Belfast.

'A little, why?' he said, dragging his thoughts back to the present.

Paulie sighed, as though some massive, invisible weight had just been dropped onto his shoulders. He reached into his pocket and pulled out the stub of a cigar, put it into his mouth, then thought better of it. When he spoke, he kept his eyes on the cigar.

'I should have seen it sooner,' Paulie said, voice heavy with regretful anger. 'But it wasnae until I saw what they did to Duncan that I understood. See, we did some business in Belfast and Derry back in the day, travelled over there, did some deals and moved some, ah, merchandise that wasn't exactly legal.'

'Like guns?' Connor asked, something cold and heavy dropping into his guts.

'Aye,' Paulie said. 'Like guns. Anyway, we were over there one time, working with a gang of boys in Belfast who claimed to be with the Real IRA. Easy deal, we were picking up some guns and shipping them south to the Republic in MacKenzie Haulage vans. But these boys were keen to impress, you know? Showed us the town, made sure we never paid for a drink or a meal. But they wanted to show us they meant business too.'

'What happened?' Connor asked, sure he didn't want the answer.

'We got taken down to the docks one night, to a warehouse they owned. Found a wee lad there, strapped to a chair. Poor wee cunt had shat himself with fear, was already in a bad way when we arrived. They said he'd been caught dealing on their patch, and they had him there so he would tell them who his supplier was and who he was working for. There were rumours there was more to it, that the boy had knocked back the advances of one of the main guys and embarrassed him.' Paulie shook his head, sighed. 'Gay, Protestant, Catholic, Black, white. All just easy labels and reasons to inflict pain.'

'They tortured him?' Connor asked, remembering how the IRA and other paramilitary groups dealt with anyone committing non-sanctioned crime on their turf.

'That's one way to put it,' Paulie said, as he rolled the cigar between his fingers. 'Started with his fingers, broke every one of them, asking questions after every one. Then it was the knees and elbows, then they took a knife to his arms, stripped the skin off and poured whiskey into the wounds.'

'Just like what happened to Duncan before he was killed,' Connor muttered, as the acrid tang of bile scalded the back of his throat. 'So you think what happened to Duncan was some kind of message? Punishment? For what?'

'The guns,' Paulie said, his voice weary. 'I looked at Duncan's diary, found a trip to Belfast scheduled a couple of months ago. Got me thinking, what if he went back there to cut another deal and something went wrong? So they followed him back here and killed him.'

'So they tortured him and he offered the guns cache as a way out, as some kind of compensation?'

'Maybe,' Paulie said, with a shrug. 'Or maybe whoever was in Saor Alba who Duncan was working for already got there and took the key. Either way, it doesnae really matter, does it? What matters is Duncan was tortured in the same way as that wee boy in Belfast by terrorists we were moving guns for. Seem like a coincidence to you? So I need you to check in with your Belfast polis pals, see if they know anything.'

A question Connor didn't want to ask reared in his mind. He swallowed, realising he was too far through the looking glass to stop now. 'What about Duncan's face?'

'What?' Paulie said, the hand rolling the cigar suddenly becoming very still. 'What the fuck are you talking about?'

'You said Duncan was tortured in the same way as the kid in Belfast,' Connor said slowly. 'OK, fine. But why smash his face in afterwards? Why obliterate his identity? That's personal, old-school stuff, desecrate a body so badly that the family can't have an open coffin at the funeral or say goodbye at the funeral home. Why do that? To slow down the identification? And why plant Jamie Leggatt's wallet on him in the first place? How did the killer get that?'

'How the fuck do I know?' Paulie snapped. 'Look, Fraser, this is the only lead I've got. Are you going to help me or not? Or are you going to piss around thinking about lost wallets and Duncan's missing face? So they fucked him up. Maybe it was to slow down the identification of the body, who knows? All that matters is they made him suffer, and now I'm going to make them feel the same agony.'

Connor looked up with a start, an idea flashing across his mind. An idea that connected Jamie Leggatt to Duncan's body and the torture he had endured. 'Feel the same agony,' he muttered.

'Fuck off,' Paulie grunted, swatting the air in front of him as though dismissing Connor. 'I thought you could help me with this. My mistake. I'll deal with it myself. Go over there and tear Belfast apart for these fucks if I have to.'

'You won't have to,' Connor said, a memory of the bullet delivered to Simon filling his mind. 'If I'm right, they're already here. And they're coming for us to make sure the killer's story is finally told.'

CHAPTER 64

Ford had never met Donald Byrne, Scotland's Lord Advocate, in life, but he was getting to know him in death.

As he had expected, Deputy Chief Constable Susan Dalwhinnie, a short, humourless woman with a Yorkshire accent as thick as the glasses she wore, had ordered a case review in light of Chief Constable Guthrie's admission that he'd allowed Jonathan Rodriguez to blackmail him for access to the MacKenzie murder investigation. She was, understandably, worried that the investigation had been compromised, with any prospect of a prosecution fatally wounded. Ford understood, and the request from Dalwhinnie's office for a full report on the matter was what he had expected. But, still, it infuriated him, the need to pause and look back, to pore over previous decisions when a murderer was on the loose.

But then the news of Byrne's suicide had reached Ford, and his priorities had shifted. With Byrne featured in the picture of Robert Balfour and Duncan MacKenzie in the woods, it was too much of a coincidence that he had decided to take his own life just at the time the police were looking into his past and his links to a controversial professor with some radical ideas about Scottish independence and how to achieve it. So Ford locked himself into his office, told DS Troughton that he was not to be disturbed, then started digging.

The biographical information on Byrne that he found on the Crown Office's website was little more than three paragraphs, detailing Byrne's time studying at Stirling University before moving to Edinburgh, his work on the Court of Session, High Court and the UK Supreme Court. It was a prestigious résumé that showed a dedicated lawyer slowly working his way through the profession to become Scotland's top lawyer. Was that, Ford wondered, why he had decided to hang himself in his office? A career brought down by his historic links to a murdered businessman who operated on both sides of the law, links that Jonathan Rodriguez's documentary promised to expose? It was possible, but Ford thought it unlikely.

He toggled from his web browser into the Police Scotland system and called up the case file on Byrne. He felt as though he was looking over another officer's shoulder and stealing the answers to a test by delving into an investigation that was not his, but he told himself it was necessary, that somehow it was all connected to Stirling University, Jonathan Rodriguez and the discovery of Duncan MacKenzie's body.

The initial report was almost as brief and to the point as the biography of Byrne. Officers had been called to the Crown Office's headquarters on Edinburgh's Chambers Street after Byrne's secretary, Diane Winters, had entered his office and found him hanging from a chandelier by his belt. Security staff on site had cut him down and attempted CPR, but it was too late. The attending officers called the duty doctor to attend the scene and confirm that Byrne was dead.

Ford clicked on another folder marked SOC Images and found a list of thumbnails, images taken by scene-of-crime officers documenting the scene. It showed him a large, bright room with floor-to-ceiling windows, a huge, dark-wood desk sitting in the centre. Above it hung the chandelier, the ragged cut end of the belt dangling from it. Other images showed Byrne's body as it had been found. He was lying on the floor of the room, his shirt ripped open to the belly, probably, Ford guessed, by the security guards and paramedics who had tried to save him. His face was horrible, ashen purple, his eyes and tongue bulging obscenely and distorting his features. Ford could guess what had happened. Byrne must have stood on his desk, tied his belt to the chandelier and round his neck, then stepped into the void. He remembered a case, years ago, when a depressed father of two had walked into the woods and done the same. He had taken his belt, looped it around the branch of a tree and stepped off the small mound of earth he had been standing on. Ford, who had been in uniform at the time, was sent to the scene and noted that the man's fingers were bloodied, his neck a churning of scratches as he clawed for air. He wondered if Byrne had changed his mind in the same way, fought for life in those last seconds as the world darkened around him and his lungs screamed for air.

He zoomed in on the picture, focusing on Byrne's hands, which were lying by his sides, palms up. The fingers were clean of blood, though pulled into palsied talons. So he hadn't fought for life, hadn't changed his mind. He was about to close the image, move on to another, when something caught his eye. Just below the cuff of Byrne's left wrist, there was a small mark, like an ink stain. He zoomed in, squinting. To his surprise, it was a small tattoo, two words, poorly rendered in the blue-green ink that Ford usually associated with prisons.

'*Regnum defende*,' he muttered, as he read the tattoo. He flicked back onto his web browser, wondering why and when a man who had committed his life to the legal profession had decided to get a cheap tattoo. A drunken night out? A midlife crisis? Or was it something more personal, something more meaningful?

Ford punched in the words and hit search. Waited less than a second for the answer to appear on his screen.

'Jesus Christ,' he murmured, as he read the translation of the words.

And then, he understood. What was it Fraser had said? *You think that's what all this is about? Someone in that picture trying to keep the past buried, a past our bomber pal is keen to see dragged into the light?*

He leaned forward, accessing the Police Scotland database again, armed with a new piece of information to search with. They had been looking at it all wrong, he thought, cursing himself. It wasn't the past the killer was trying to bring to light, if Ford was right; it was an organisation. An organisation whose motto Donald Byrne had tattooed on his inner wrist, exactly where it could easily be hidden by a watch.

Just, Ford realised, as Byrne had hidden the truth about himself. No wonder he had decided to take his own life rather than have his mask ripped away.

CHAPTER 65

Connor could see that the arrangement he had made with Simon to wait for him at the house wasn't sitting well with Paulie, who was pacing around the garden, trailing cigar smoke behind him like some demented steam engine. He could sympathise with Paulie's need to act rather than wait, he shared it, but Simon had said he had found something important.

And one thing Connor knew about Simon was that he rarely exaggerated.

He arrived at the house about fifteen minutes after he had called, the snarling growl of his hot hatch announcing his arrival. Connor opened the front door, watched as Simon circled round to the boot of the car and leaned in for something. Then he jogged to the door, a sheaf of papers in one hand, clapping Connor on the shoulder as he did.

'Big lad,' he said, and Connor could hear excitement in his tone.

'You okay?' Connor asked. 'You seem awfully chipper for someone who had a special delivery of a bullet earlier today.'

Simon smiled. 'Aye, but I know which group sent that little love letter now,' he said. 'Is there a place we can talk?'

Connor led him through to the kitchen area, felt Simon tense beside him as he saw Paulie through the patio doors.

'He came asking for a favour,' Connor explained. 'Seems to think there's a Belfast link to all of this. He and Duncan did a bit of work for

233

the IRA back in the day, moving guns and stuff. Would explain the bullets and the arms dump, wouldn't it?'

'Yeah,' Simon said slowly, and Connor thought he could hear disappointment in his voice, almost as though he had ruined the punchline to some joke he was about to deliver.

'What did you find?' Connor asked, as Paulie lumbered into the kitchen, flicking the stub of the cigar over his shoulder as he moved.

'Well, I went back to MacRae's office, wanted to have a wee look around,' Simon said, his eyes straying briefly to Paulie before focusing on Connor. 'Found a wall safe he had hidden behind that Saor Alba banner, and this was in it.' He lifted the bundle of what Connor could now see were photos. He shuffled through them before handing them to Connor.

'See anyone you recognise?' he asked.

Connor looked down, saw the group of men in the woods huddled round another figure, who was holding a rifle. Studied the face, which was familiar despite being years younger than Connor had known it.

'Think beard and a scar down the left cheek,' Simon said.

Connor frowned. And then it hit him, and he felt a jolt of recognition. 'Jesus Christ!' he said, head whipping to Simon, who was starting to smile. 'That's Ryan Walsh!'

Simon nodded. 'Aye, Wrecker Ryan. Remember him? IRA hitman turned gangster. Killed, what, five civilians who he thought were collaborating with the police. Then turned to enforcement and armed robbery when the Troubles were over. Loved a wee bit of intimidation, did our Wrecker. Don't think I've enjoyed a drink more than the one I had the night I heard he had been killed in prison.'

Connor blinked, trying to take in this new information. Ryan had been a feared paramilitary in Northern Ireland, a man who was as happy killing for a cause as he was for cash. He was always on the most wanted list of the PSNI, a man who, if sighted, was to be approached with extreme caution. He had eventually been caught and jailed and subsequently died when a Unionist called John Garrison had decided to slip a sharpened toothbrush between his ribs.

'What the hell was he doing in Stirling forty years ago?' Connor asked. 'And how the hell did he know MacKenzie and Balfour?'

Simon's grin grew wider. 'I called a pal back in Belfast, pulled in a favour. Seems that back in the eighties, when Wrecker was just a pup, he made it a little too hot in Belfast – he kneecapped a police inspector's son after a bar fight. He was known to have family over in Port Glasgow. I'm guessing he drifted over this way to disappear, and fell in with Balfour. There were rumours that the IRA were trying to train radical Scottish nationalist groups for armed struggle at that time, to attack the British on two fronts, so it makes sense.'

Connor nodded. It made sense all right. Of the bullet delivered to Simon, of the bomb left for Jamie Leggatt, of the bomb being detonated in Edinburgh. It read like a paramilitary playbook.

'Is that what this is all about?' Connor asked, putting it together as he looked at the picture. 'Somebody in that picture was worried that Rodriguez's poking about would expose their links to a known terrorist, so they started picking off everyone in the group before they talked?'

'It fits, doesn't it?' Simon agreed. 'They all went on to be influential people – two top lawyers, a politician, and a prominent local business-man. Christ, it sounds like the Lord Advocate took his own life rather than have that little skeleton in the closet see the light of day. Or did he kill himself because he knew the killer, knew he was coming for him, and wanted to die his way, rather than like Duncan did?'

Connor shook his head. There was still something missing. The involvement of Ryan Walsh explained a lot as it proved a link to para-militaries, but who had contacted Rodriguez with the information about the group in the first place, and why? And still there were his questions over Amanda Lyons, the Campbell dirk and what the killer was trying to say.

He was startled from his thoughts by the buzz of his phone. He handed the pictures back to Simon, then stepped out into the garden, Paulie taking his place.

'DCI Ford,' he said, as he answered the call. 'I'm glad you phoned. We've just found something that—'

'Fraser,' Ford interrupted. 'If asked, this call never happened, okay? I'm calling you to arrange a follow-up interview pertaining to the blackmailing of Chief Constable Guthrie, understood?'

'Understood,' Connor muttered, as he felt a shiver of unease.

'I've been reviewing the case notes and evidence collected in relation to the death of Donald Byrne,' Ford started, his voice cold, business-like. 'It looks as though he took his own life, no foul play. But I think I know why. I think he was afraid of a secret getting out, something that would be very uncomfortable for him to be out in public in light of the documentary Rodriguez is doing about his father, his politics and his death.'

Connor nodded. It chimed with what Simon had just discovered. But how had Ford found out about Ryan Walsh being part of the group and training them with guns?

'Okay,' Connor said. 'I think I know where you're going with this. Simon just found evidence that a known paramilitary operative was working with Balfour to train his students with firearms and the like. I'm guessing that's what Byrne was afraid would be exposed – that he spent his youth training with the IRA. But how did you find that out from crime-scene photos, sir?'

There was a pause, and Connor could almost feel Ford thinking at the other end of the line. When he spoke, his voice was slow, contemplative. 'That's not what I found, but I think it makes even more sense now. No, I found a tattoo on Byrne's wrist, Fraser. Small, innocuous, easily hidden. It was two words, *Regnum defende*.'

'*Regnum defende*?' Connor said, the phrase familiar. 'Latin for "Defend the realm"? But hold on that's . . .' He stopped speaking, the revelation temporarily robbing him of speech.

'Yes,' Ford said. '*Regnum defende* is the motto of MI5. So tell me, Fraser, why would someone who was working for, or going to work for, the British Secret Service to "defend the realm" hang out with fellow students who wanted to break up the realm he was going to defend? Either that's a hell of a shift in his political thinking, or something else is going on. Either way, I can understand why he would want to take his own life rather than see his career ruined by the revelation that he went from terrorist wannabe to MI5 to the highest legal job in Scotland.'

'Yeah,' Connor mumbled, lost in thought. It was like being handed your first pair of glasses: everything that was blurred and indistinct suddenly snapped into brutal, hard-edged focus. He understood now. Knew he had to get to Rodriguez and Amanda Lyons as soon as possible.

He realised there was a silence on the line. Ford was waiting for a response to a question Connor had not heard. 'Sorry, sir?' he said.

Ford sighed, impatient. 'I said, I'm going to be tied up with this case review of Guthrie's work, which will end with him formally stating he was blackmailed, and an arrest warrant being issued for Jonathan Rodriguez in relation to that. So you have that long to get to Rodriguez, work out what the hell is going on and find whatever madman is doing this. Understood?'

'Totally, sir,' Connor said, a certainty growing in his mind. He should have seen it when he learned about Glencoe, and the clans sleeping with the enemy.

He ended the call, headed back inside. A sliver of worry sliced through him as he saw Simon's pale, slightly dazed expression.

'What?' he asked.

'You tell him,' Simon said, nodding to Paulie.

'What?' Connor asked again.

'The boy in that picture,' Paulie said, jutting his chin towards Simon and the sheaf of photographs he held, 'what did you call him? Ryan Walsh? Said he grew a beard, had a scar down his cheek?'

'Yeah,' Connor said slowly.

'Well, one of the guys we met in Belfast had a beard and a scar down his cheek. Might not mean much, but . . .'

Connor felt as though he had been punched in the gut. 'You sure?'

'I watched him torture a wee boy half to death. Him and two of his goons. Think they were called Miles and Dom. Doug? Whatever, sounded like a brand of cheap cigarettes. It was them and him. So yes, I'm fucking sure,' Paulie said, his voice angry. 'But it couldnae be him, could it? After all, you said he died in prison.'

'That's what we were told,' Connor agreed, another thought rising in his mind. 'That's what we were told.'

CHAPTER 66

Jonathan Rodriguez opened the door to the house in Dunblane with his typical wide-eyed, tooth-flashing good humour. But Connor could see worry pinching the corners of his eyes, and his healthy tan had paled somehow, as though it was wearing off.

Had he realised that his blackmailing of Chief Constable Guthrie could result in consequences more serious than a slap on the wrist, Connor wondered, or was there something more?

He ushered Connor and Simon into the house, gestured they should sit down. Connor stayed standing, wondering again if he should have been more insistent that Paulie joined them. He could play bad cop to Simon's good cop pretty effectively, but it would have been a different game entirely if Paulie was with them: good cop, stony-faced psychopath.

'Good to see you again,' Rodriguez said, as he settled into the couch. Simon took the one opposite him, Connor standing sentry between them, Rodriguez's eyes darting towards him nervously.

'If you're looking for Amanda, I'm afraid she's not here. Said she wanted to check a few things out, get some local colour. We're thinking of filming at the university in the next couple of days.' His smile faded, as he dropped his head. 'I'm not looking forward to that.'

I'll bet, Connor thought. Though he wondered what Rodriguez's reason was. Not wanting to visit the place where his father's body had been found, or not wanting to revisit the scene of his own crime in blackmailing Chief Constable Guthrie.

'Mr Rodriguez, did you know that your father was consorting with known terrorists, and using those terrorists to train his students in the use of firearms?' Connor asked, his face as impassive as his voice.

Rodriguez's mouth fell open and he glared up at Connor, naked shock on his face. 'What?' he stuttered. 'No, of course I didn't. Was that what was happening in those pictures I was sent? No, I had no idea.'

'It's okay, Jonathan,' Simon said, his tone soothing. Mr Good Cop. 'We understand that this is a bit of a shock. So let's go back to the start. The pictures you received, can you tell me . . .'

Connor's phone pinged in his pocket. He nodded towards Simon, who returned the gesture and got back to talking to Rodriguez. They needed him to see Simon as a confidant, a friend, someone he could trust compared to the blunt, abrasive Connor.

Connor headed into the hall as he pulled out his phone. It was a text from Robbie – *Got that background on Amanda Lyons for you. Can email briefing or talk you through it.*

Talk you through it, Connor thought. Robbie code for *I want to talk about this as it could be big and I want to be part of the investigation.*

He dialled Robbie's number, didn't have to wait long for the reply. It took Robbie less than five minutes to tell him what he had found out, and by the end of the call, Connor was wondering how he could stop himself grabbing Rodriguez and trying to slap some sense into him.

He walked back into the room, Simon and Rodriguez turning to him.

'Everything all right?' Simon asked. It was a tactic they had developed in the PSNI: after receiving new information, Simon would ask the question, clear the stage for Connor to dictate what happened next.

'Mr Rodriguez, when did Amanda Lyons start working with you?'

Rodriguez frowned, glanced across at Simon, who was leaning forward, hands on his knees. 'I, ah, not that long ago actually,' he said, confusion lightening his tone and somehow making him sound more

Scottish than American. 'About a month ago. She came from print journalism. Not as a reporter, as an administrator, PA to the newsroom, that sort of a thing. She worked for the *New York Journal*, I think. Why?'

'Was this before or after you decided to make the documentary about your father and announced it to your viewers?' Connor asked, his mind filled with the thought of the dirk and Lyons's phone impaled on it.

'About the same time, maybe just after,' Rodriguez said.

'Course it was,' Connor replied. 'Would it surprise you to know that Amanda Lyons is still working at the *New York Journal*, Mr Rodriguez? She's sixty-three years old, ready to retire. Lovely woman, one of my colleagues had a chat with her earlier. Tell me, did you do your due diligence on Ms Lyons and check her references and work history, or did you just see a pretty face who said all the right things and take her on the spot?'

Colour rose in Rodriguez's cheeks. He made to stand up, then changed his mind when Connor straightened his back and folded his arms over his chest. 'Look, Amanda, or whoever she is, and I, well, it was never like that. We never ... I mean, well, we ... Look, this must be some kind of mistake.'

'It's no mistake, Jonathan,' Connor said. 'No more of a mistake than her phone being found at a cleared-out arms dump in Bannockburn.'

'What the hell are you talking about?' Rodriguez asked.

'She told you she lost her phone, yes? That she went to Stirling to get a new one? Well, the phone she lost or, more accurately, the phone that was stolen was found at the site of a weapons cache that had been buried for your father years ago. Her phone was impaled on the end of a dirk, a Campbell dirk to be exact. Do you know what the Campbell clan is famous for, Mr Rodriguez?'

'What? What do you mean? No, no, I don't. Look, this must be—'

'At Glencoe, they slept with the enemy before they killed them,' Connor said. 'I don't mean sex, though I'm not sure I believe that your relationship is platonic, but they slept with their enemy before they slaughtered them. The phone being left at your dad's arms cache was a message from our killer – you're sleeping with the enemy, she's not what you believe. Pretty accurate, don't you think?'

'If Amanda's not, well, Amanda, who the hell is she?' Rodriguez asked, defiant anger and impatience in his voice.

'I don't know,' Connor said. 'But I'm betting it was her idea to come to Stirling for location shooting, wasn't it? So whoever she is, she wanted you here, and wanted to be in on whatever communications you were being sent from your contact.'

'But why?' Rodriguez asked.

'That I don't know yet,' Connor admitted. 'She could be helping the killer, she could have another agenda. But whatever it is, she used you like a pawn in her game. A game that has seen two people killed so far, maybe your father as well. Tell me, when you spoke to Jamie Leggatt, what exactly did he offer you?'

'Leggatt? How did you know—'

'Phone records,' Connor said. 'We had "Amanda's" number, so it was easy enough to get her records. And one of the calls she made was to Dundee University, more specifically, the extension of Jamie Leggatt. You remember him, don't you? He's the man I watched get blown to pieces a couple of days ago.'

Rodriguez blinked, looked towards Simon, a silent plea for help tattooed over his face. Simon merely sat there, watching him squirm.

'I didn't know she had contacted Leggatt – at least not once we got to Scotland,' he said.

'So you spoke to him from the States?'

Rodriguez nodded. 'Yes, a conference Zoom call. Amanda set it up. He was the first one to mention that Dad's death wasn't an accident. He put me on to his statements at the time about the whiskey they claimed Dad had drunk before he died, that it was wrong, then that his cane was in the wrong place and that he thought the Secret Service was watching him for his anti-Unionist teachings. That gave us the hook for the story – a bit of international intrigue always goes down well with the viewers. We had planned to interview Leggatt on camera, but with the body being found at the university, things just happened too fast.'

'And you were too busy getting your special access from Guthrie to tear yourself away and actually look into the story, follow up leads, get to the truth?' Simon asked, his voice surprisingly cold.

241

'Look, I'm sorry about Guthrie, I am,' Rodriguez said. 'But it was his idea.'

Connor exchanged a glance with Simon. 'What was his idea?' he asked.

'The whole blackmail line. He said he wanted to get away from the case, didn't want to be a part of it. Said that if he said I was blackmailing him, he'd have to step away from it. He said I'd get into a bit of trouble, but he'd take care of it, call in a favour with his friends, make sure I never faced charges.'

'His idea?' Connor said. 'So you're saying it wasn't blackmail at all?'

'God, no,' Rodriguez said. 'When I found out about Dad's links to his uncle, I contacted him, asked if he wanted to meet and discuss it. He was enthusiastic, and when we got to Scotland he was on the phone almost as soon as we got off the plane, offering us full access to police files. And when that body was found in the loch, he contacted me, insisted we tag along when he visited the crime scene.'

'Okay,' Connor said, mind racing. 'You said when you got to Scotland he was on the phone. Was that to you or "Amanda"?'

Rodriguez seemed to fold into his seat a little. When he spoke, he sounded like a child admitting he had cheated on a test. 'Amanda,' he said at last. 'Or whoever she really is.'

'Course it was,' Connor said. 'I think "Ms Lyons" will have a really interesting story to tell.'

'Question is,' Simon asked, 'if she's gone dark, how the hell do we find her?'

'Easy,' Connor said, a smile spreading across his lips. 'We ask your girlfriend for a favour.'

CHAPTER 67

They arranged to meet Donna and her cameraman, Keith, at Stirling University as she had an appointment to interview the principal about student safety and safeguarding in the wake of Duncan MacKenzie's body being discovered in the loch. It was, Donna told them, a puff piece to show the university as a caring institution that was committed to the safety of its students. She had agreed to do it as, before she joined Sky, Donna had spent some time lecturing at the university and felt she owed the principal a favour.

The plan was simple. Connor asked her to wrap the principal's interview into a wider piece on the murder investigation, with cuts back to Rodriguez's press conference from a few days ago woven into the report. And the shots from the press conference would focus on 'Amanda Lyons', with reference to how she been instrumental in bringing Rodriguez to Scotland. In return, Connor had promised her an exclusive line on the chief constable and what Rodriguez had told him. He felt a tinge of guilt that he hadn't run his plan by DCI Ford, but he didn't want to give the policeman the chance to talk him out of it. He needed Lyons's face on people's TV screens. Hopefully, the exposure would drive her out of hiding, force her to either get in touch or make another move.

'So,' Simon said, from the passenger seat, as he ended a call he had made when they'd got into the car, 'Darren owes me a favour, is going to do a little more digging, see what he can find about what happened to Ryan Walsh, and if Paulie's right. Will give me a call back. So, what are you thinking? How the hell does all this fit together?'

Connor mulled this over. A picture was developing in his mind, but it wasn't fully formed yet, as though he was in a dark room and some of the lights weren't working. Hopefully, the information DCI Darren Michelson could dig up for them in Northern Ireland would help.

'If we take it that Paulie's right,' he said, 'and Darren confirms that Ryan Walsh is somehow still alive, I think he's the one who's been feeding Rodriguez the information about his dad and what he got up to. He got wind of the documentary, and decided he wanted to keep his name out of it. Best way to do that would be to control the narrative, push Rodriguez in the direction of the other members of the group and have him ask them difficult questions. Puts them off balance and gives him time to pick off the rest of them.'

'You think that's why he planted Leggatt's wallet on MacKenzie's body?' Simon asked. 'To lead us to him?'

'Partly,' Connor said. 'And partly to send a message to the others. Think about it, an MSP and the Lord Advocate would be a lot harder to get to than a university lecturer. Taking Leggatt and MacKenzie out first would be like working your way up the chain, taking out the relatively unprotected targets, and sending a message to the others – I'm coming.'

'I dunno,' Simon said, shifting in his seat. Connor glanced over, saw that he had drawn his gun and was holding it loosely in his lap, pointing at the floor. 'I mean, it makes sense, but if it is Walsh, and he's killing folk to keep himself out of the limelight, why detonate that bomb in Edinburgh? And why at the site of the Vigil you told me about?'

'I was thinking about that,' Connor said, his mind drifting back to Jen. 'Jen told me her dad spent a bit of time at the Vigil across from St Andrew's House when it was running in the nineties. MacRae admitted to spending time there as well. So that's two members of Balfour's group who were at the Vigil. Now that might just be their sense of political duty in campaigning for a parliament, but Duncan never struck me as someone who acted for principle rather than profit. So what if it was something else? What if he was using the Vigil as a meeting place? Easy enough to lose yourself in the crowd, and if you just so happened to run into a like-minded old friend there, so much the better.'

'But meet for what reason?' Simon asked, frustration leaking into his voice. 'And why would Walsh want to bomb the place?'

'He's trying to tell us something,' Connor said. 'Remember the messages he sent to Donna and Rodriguez? What did he say in them? This is part of a wider game. There's a truth here and an injustice to resolve. Whatever that truth is, the Vigil is part of it.'

'And you think Amanda, or whoever the hell she is, is working with Walsh to tell that story.'

'Maybe,' Connor said, thinking back to the dirk that had been used to impale her phone. As a history professor, Balfour would have known about the Campbell clan's history and the massacre at Glencoe. Something was nagging at him about that, something . . .

'The timing fits,' he said. 'Rodriguez announces his documentary, and Lyons drops into his lap, the perfect person to help him realise his vision. She arranged for him to talk to Leggatt, who kicked this off by claiming his dad's death was no accident back in the day. And then he . . .'

Connor trailed off as a thought crossed his mind, random bits of information coalescing to create something new. A memory of Ford now, telling him about the tattoo he had found on Donald Byrne. A tattoo that bore the motto of the intelligence service, MI5.

'What if . . .' Connor whispered, sitting up straighter in the driver's seat.

'What if what?' Simon asked. 'Come on, Connor, don't keep me waiting.'

'It's what you said . . .' Connor was feeling for the idea as he spoke '. . . about the timings of the killings. MacKenzie, then Leggatt. The man who was running guns for paramilitaries and the man who claimed that the government had had a hand in the murder of a radical nationalist who had helped support an embarrassing protest against the Queen. Now who would benefit from those two people being taken off the playing board?' He turned to Simon. '*Regnum defende*,' he said.

'MI5?' Simon said, his eyes widening. 'Come on, Connor, that's a bit of a stretch, isn't it? I can buy that Walsh is killing folk to keep them quiet. I can even buy he wants to put a bullet in me because I'm a cop, but why would MI5 get involved?'

Connor shook his head. 'Do me a favour,' he said. 'Back seat, my bag. The file Ford gave me, the case notes from the original Balfour death inquiry. Find Leggatt's statement, would you?'

Simon grunted, holstered his gun and reached into the back of the car, straining to grab for the bag. After a moment he reached it, then opened the file and began to rifle through the pages. 'Anything particular I should be looking for?' he asked.

'Try to find his statements on Balfour's death,' Connor said. 'He made some claims about it being more sinister, that Balfour was killed to shut him up.'

'Okay,' Simon said, 'I remember that. What are you getting at?'

'I'm wondering . . .' thoughts of the Campbell dirk Balfour had used were rising in Connor's mind again '. . . if maybe Leggatt was right. Balfour was shut up. But maybe not for the reason he thought.'

CHAPTER 68

They met Donna at the loch, the grey waters shimmering and glinting, like the skin of a moving seal as the wind played across it. The forensics teams and police cordons were long gone, but Connor could see their echo in the way passers-by would glance nervously at the loch or point excitedly. Crime scenes, he thought, could be cleaned up, made almost as they had once been, but the scars never quite healed.

'So, what's all this about?' Donna said, as they approached her. Connor noticed her eyes skim from him to Simon, her gaze softening as she saw him, and for an instant, he felt as though he was intruding on a private moment, then experienced a stab of melancholy - Jen used to look at him in the same way.

'Amanda Lyons . . .' Simon said, then went on to tell Donna what they had learned about her, and that giving Rodriguez access to the MacKenzie investigation wasn't blackmail but had, in fact, been Chief Constable Guthrie's idea.

'Okay,' Donna said slowly, her brow furrowing as she processed what she had been told. 'We got any ideas about who Amanda really is, and why Guthrie is so keen to keep Rodriguez close to a police investigation?'

'I was hoping you might be able to help with that,' Connor said. 'It would be a real shame if you were to call Guthrie and put some difficult questions to him. And if you could get Lyons's face on air and online as much as possible, it might help flush her out.'

Donna smiled. 'Oh, I'd be happy to ask Mr Guthrie some questions he doesn't want to answer,' she said. 'And putting Lyons in the story is no problem, but who do you think she is? Someone working with the bomber?'

'Possibly,' Connor replied. 'It would make sense, if it wasn't for her phone being left at the arms cache. That's either very sloppy, or very deliberate, and I'm starting to think it was deliberate. She fakes her identity to work with Rodriguez, then provides a solid link with the bomber by dropping her phone at the arms cache? Doesn't add up, unless . . .'

'She didn't drop it,' Simon said, cutting across Connor, his voice fast and sharp as he made the connection. 'She dumped it. She told me that the first thing she did after "losing" her phone was to get another, to make sure she was getting calls and emails forwarded from her US number. She wanted another phone. A clean one. Which means she dumped hers because she knew or at least suspected it was being monitored.'

'So,' Connor said slowly, as he followed Simon's train of thought, 'she went to Bannockburn not to scout filming locations, but to find the arms cache, which she was told about by the bomber? Something tipped her off that her phone was being monitored so she left it with the dirk impaled in it as a message? "I know you're watching me"? She picks up another phone to keep her lines of communication open, then heads back to Rodriguez in Dunblane to make sure her cover is still in place. Happy with that, she disappears before we arrive?'

'Okay,' Donna said, excitement glinting in her eyes. 'All this is great, but none of it is fit to print or broadcast at the moment. It's all conjecture and theory. What have we got that's concrete? Who is she?'

Connor smiled, then felt a rush of embarrassment at not thinking of it sooner. He had been too distracted by Duncan's death, the threat on Simon's life and Jen's reaction to him to think clearly. 'We've got her phone number,' he said. 'At least, we've got her original number, the one tied to the phone she dumped in Bannockburn. I can ask Robbie to back-trace that, see if it shows anything up.'

'I want to know what you get the moment you get it,' Donna said, her gaze hard. 'This is shaping up as a hell of a story, and I want the exclusive on it.'

'Of course,' Connor said, with what he hoped was an easy grin. He caught the look Simon gave him, knew what he was thinking. At some point they would have to tell her about the threat that had been made on his life, and the bullet left on her windscreen. But hopefully, by the time they had told her, Walsh had already been caught.

'Okay,' Donna said, after a moment in which she studied them both. 'I'll do this interview with the principal and get on to Guthrie. I'll take him head-on, not go through the press office.'

'You think he'll talk to you?' Simon asked.

Donna smiled. 'Oh, he'll talk to me, all right,' she said. 'I can be very persuasive.'

'Amen to that,' Simon said, with a grin.

They split up, Donna and Keith heading for the main university building, Simon and Connor wandering back to the car park. They were halfway there when Simon's phone began to ring. He pulled it out, turned it to Connor. 'DCI Darren Michelson', the caller ID read.

'Darren, 'bout ye?' Simon said brightly. 'You're quick getting back to me, you—'

Connor couldn't make out what was said, but he could hear a harsh, clipped voice. He watched as Simon's face paled, his eyes widening, something in his gaze making Connor very aware of how exposed they were standing on a path with open grounds around them.

'What?' he said, as Simon ended the call and stared at him.

'Big lad,' Simon said, his voice almost shocked, 'we have stepped into one very, very big lake of shite. Let's get the hell out of here. Darren says he's going to send me some documents over, but let's go find a pub. I've got a story to tell you, and I'm going to need a drink to do it.'

CHAPTER 69

To Ford, it felt as though a thunderstorm was raging in his skull, threatening lightning that would split him in half. Part of him wondered if that would be such a bad thing.

He had been immersed in the case review for the deputy chief constable, going over the MacKenzie case, making sure that Guthrie's compromised position with Jonathan Rodriguez hadn't put the investigation, and the possibility of any future prosecution, at risk. But as he worked, what he had learned about Donald Byrne gnawed at him. Why would the Lord Advocate have a tattoo that related to MI5? A record check showed that he had never served with the organisation, having spent his career working in the Scottish legal system. So why have it? A midlife crisis? The action of a devoted fan? Why?

He was working through the problem when his phone rang. Distracted, he picked it up from his desk and thumbed answer as he lifted it to his ear. When he heard the voice at the other end of the line, he cursed himself for his sloppiness.

'DCI Ford, it's Donna Blake, Sky News,' she said, her voice just polite enough to tell him she was pissed off and this wasn't going to be a casual chat.

'Ms Blake, you know as well as I do that all media requests need to go through our main Comms office. I'm afraid I can't speak to you,' he said.

'Oh, I know that,' Donna said. 'It's standard procedure. Procedure your chief's been following very, very closely as he's been ducking my calls for the last twenty minutes. Got to say, the man cannot dictate a voicemail message for shit.'

Despite himself, Ford smiled at that. 'The chief is a very busy man. I'm sure the comms team can—'

'Oh, I'm sure he is busy,' Donna said, her voice suddenly cold and hard. 'Busy lying to you all about his little arrangement with Jonathan Rodriguez and access to the MacKenzie murder investigation.'

Ford's headache snarled again. 'What do you mean, lying?' he asked.

So Donna told him. About how it had been Guthrie who had approached Rodriguez and offered him access to not only the files on his father's case but the live investigation of Duncan MacKenzie's death. And as he listened, Ford felt his mood grow darker, the thunderclouds in his mind blackening and becoming murderous.

'Do me a favour,' he said, when Donna had stopped speaking. 'Give me one hour with this before going to Comms or doing anything with it. I'll get you an answer, I swear. And if Guthrie won't give it to you, I'll go on the record myself.'

'Really?' Donna asked, naked surprise in her voice.

'Really,' Ford said, anger coiling in his guts. The little bastard, he thought. The slimy, limelight-grabbing little bastard.

Donna agreed reluctantly, then ended the call. Ford put his phone down, looked at it, fought back the urge to smash it against the wall. Instead, he reached forward and grabbed for his landline, pressing the button that connected him to the chief's secretary and the office he had commandeered in the Randolphfield station.

'Tracey?' he said, when the call was answered. 'It's DCI Malcolm Ford. Is he in?'

'He is,' Tracey said, her voice low, even and tinged with boredom. This was a script she had read from many times before. 'But he's tied up in meetings all day. He won't be able to—'

Ford ended the call, stood up and started walking. He found it impossible to wait for the lift, opted instead for the stairs, taking them so quickly that he found himself gasping slightly as he walked into Guthrie's office.

Tracey looked up, confusion creasing her already crevassed brow. 'I told you he was busy, that he . . .'

Ford ignored her, just kept walking. Got to the door to Guthrie's office and walked straight in, not bothering to knock. Guthrie, who was sitting at his desk, phone cradled to his ear, whirled around, indignant surprise on his face. 'What the—' he said.

'You lying bastard,' Ford hissed. Somewhere deep inside, the policeman he had been trained to be, the one who had been drilled at Tulliallan, had taken exams and risen slowly up the career ladder, screamed in almost feral outrage at addressing a senior officer in such a way. But he deserved it, Ford knew. And so much worse.

'Sir, I'm sorry, he just . . .' Tracey bustled into the room behind Ford.

Guthrie's eyes took in Ford, seemed to read his mood. He muttered an apology into the phone, then hung up slowly.

'It's all right, Tracey,' he said, his voice cautious. 'Nothing to worry about. You can leave us to it.'

Tracey beat an uncertain retreat, the sound of the door clicking shut like a gunshot.

'You want to tell me what that little outburst was about, Detective Chief Inspector?' Guthrie asked, emphasising Ford's rank as he spoke.

'It's about you being a lying shit,' Ford said, surprised by the sheer level of fury he felt towards Guthrie. What he had done was selfish, a betrayal of everything a policeman should stand for.

'What – what do you mean?' Guthrie asked, his voice wavering slightly.

'I mean your cosy little arrangement with Jonathan Rodriguez,' Ford said. 'You told me he was blackmailing you, using your uncle's connections to Saor Alba and Professor Balfour to make sure he got a front-row seat at our investigation. But that's not the truth, is it? You invited him in. You offered him access. Why? To try to burnish your career, make yourself look good. Everyone knows you're only using the job as a step into politics, somewhere you can be even more of a prick than you are now. But I didn't think you'd risk letting a killer go free just to earn a few fucking headlines. Jesus!'

Guthrie seemed to collapse back into his seat, his face growing pale. He looked away from Ford. Then he gave a very small laugh. He shook his head, as though remembering something that was at once funny and immeasurably sad.

'Take a seat, Malcolm,' he said softly.

Ford felt a ripple of confusion sour his anger. 'I'm not staying,' he muttered. 'I only came here to tell you I know, and I'm going to make sure everyone else knows what you've done. A reporter from Sky is going to call you. I'd probably answer with a resignation statement if I were you.'

Guthrie nodded, as though he had been expecting this. 'Malcolm, please. Sit down. This isn't what you think it is, at all. There are some things I need to tell you. Things I should have told you before. That's my mistake, my hubris, and I'll admit to it. But, please, let me explain.'

'Explain what?' Ford snarled, his anger reigniting. 'That you're an ambitious media whore who puts his image before police work?'

'I didn't have a choice,' Guthrie said, his voice tired now, as though he had spent the last hour trying to explain a simple problem to a reluctant pupil. 'I was under orders.'

'What? What orders?' Ford asked.

Guthrie rubbed his eyes, then settled an even gaze on Ford. 'I'll get to that,' he said. 'But first, let me tell you about my uncle, and Professor Robert Balfour.'

'What about them?' Ford asked, curious despite himself.

Guthrie smiled again, the memory of the secret joke returning. 'I'll get to it,' he said. 'I'll tell you all of it. And to do that, I need to go back a bit. You remember the protest against the Queen when she visited Stirling University in 1972?'

Ford nodded. 'It was in Balfour's file,' he said. 'And Jamie Leggatt mentioned it as well. Students protested when the Queen visited campus. The reports state that, as a militant nationalist, Professor Balfour helped the students by supporting them and giving them access to certain areas on campus.'

'See, that's where you're right and wrong,' Guthrie said. Ford could hear relief in his voice, almost as if he'd been holding on to this information for a long time and was glad, finally, to be sharing it.

'What do you mean?' Ford asked.

'Well, he did help the students, that's right,' Guthrie said. 'But Professor Robert Balfour was no crown-hating militant nationalist, Malcolm. Far, far from it.'

CHAPTER 70

Simon's choice of venue was the Curly Coo, a small, cosy pub on Barnton Street, a five-minute walk from the centre of Stirling. It surprised Connor, as the Coo had a reputation for its huge and exotic selection of whiskies, and Simon McCartney fancied himself as something of a wine snob. But when they arrived Simon ordered two large whiskies from a distillery Connor had never heard of, then leaned over and talked to the barman who had served him.

''Mon,' he said to Connor, as he turned away from the bar. 'We can use the back room. Quieter there.'

Connor followed Simon through a door and up a narrow flight of stairs that led to what looked like a secondary bar. He led Connor to a table at the far end of the room and sat down.

'Okay,' Connor said, sitting opposite him and taking the whisky he offered. 'You want to tell me what's going on, and what Darren found out?'

A smile twitched at the corners of Simon's mouth. Then he lifted the whisky, offered a silent toast and took a large swig.

'So Darren pulled a few favours and ran Ryan Walsh's name for me,' he said, his voice slightly huskier than normal, as if the whisky had somehow singed it. 'First thing, he's alive. And he's been living across here for the last seven years under an assumed identity.'

Connor clenched his hand on the glass he was holding. 'What? But we both saw the reports at the time. He was stabbed in prison.'

'Yeah,' Simon agreed. 'That was the official story. Seems that his injuries were greatly exaggerated. He was stabbed, and they used that to get him out of prison and set him up over here.'

'But why?' Connor asked, confusion warring with a twisted excitement. They had a name, at last. A person to pin everything that had happened on. And, more importantly for Connor, he had a killer to present to Jen.

'Well, that's where it gets a bit interesting,' Simon said. He gave his glass a wistful look, then pushed it aside. 'Darren's got a few friends in the intelligence services, thanks to his counter-terror work. Says he had to pull in a lot of favours, but it seems that someone put in an appeal on his behalf, under the terms of the Good Friday Agreement, and pushed it through.'

Connor considered this. He knew of the Good Friday Agreement, which had ended the Troubles in Northern Ireland, and the clause within it that allowed for the early release of 'political prisoners' from both the loyalist and republican sides. But that had been years ago, and he had never heard of an appeal being made for a release under the terms of the Agreement after that time.

'But who would have the juice to do that, and why?' Connor asked.

Simon smiled, lifted his glass in another toast. '*Regnum defende*,' he said.

Connor blinked, felt a mix of realisation and astonishment bulldoze its way through his thoughts. 'Jesus,' he whispered. 'Donald Byrne?'

'May God rest his recently departed soul,' Simon agreed. 'Seems the late Lord Advocate quietly lobbied the government for Walsh's release, and got it. Darren's going to send over what documents he can, but he wants to know what the hell is going on as soon as possible. This could be big for him as well.'

'I'll bet,' Connor said, his mind racing. 'So Byrne lobbied to get Walsh freed from prison and moved to Scotland with a new identity. What do we think? That Walsh contacted him, threatened to expose their connection if he didn't help get him out?'

'Makes sense,' Simon agreed. 'I'd say being known to have consorted with a recognised terrorist might have made his job as Lord

Advocate a little bit on the difficult side.'

'Okay,' Connor said. 'Let's say that's true. Why had Walsh come out of hiding and started to pick off the members of Saor Alba? To protect his new life and identity? If that's the case, why did he contact Rodriguez and start feeding him information in the first place? Why not just go deeper under cover and wait the whole thing out? After all, Rodriguez didn't have a lot to go on, just some old police reports and Jamie Leggatt's claims that the security services were somehow behind Professor Balfour's . . .' He trailed off, looking down at the whisky in his hand even as thoughts of Duncan MacKenzie's ruined face flooded his mind. 'Jesus,' he whispered.

'What?' Simon asked, leaning forward.

'Leggatt got it wrong,' Connor mumbled, the thought crystallising in his mind. He forced himself to focus on Simon. 'The whiskey. He said that the whiskey bottles found in Balfour's office after he died were the wrong brand, that Balfour was a whisky snob and wouldn't have been seen dead drinking such a cheap brand. Paulie said it was like comparing Dom Pérignon and Buckfast, an insult to whisky.'

'So?' Simon said, making no attempt to conceal his confusion.

'That's exactly what it was,' Connor said. 'An insult. Just like taking Duncan MacKenzie's face off. These killings were personal. Walsh wanted to disrespect both men, torture them in different ways. So he force-fed Balfour cheap rot-gut whiskey and took Duncan's face to make sure his body couldn't be seen by his family.'

'Okay,' Simon said slowly, 'I see that, but why torture him? For the location of the key to the arms cache?'

'I don't think so,' Connor said. 'I'd guess Walsh would have been able to lay his hands on guns fairly easily, thanks to his connections in Northern Ireland, so why waste the time torturing MacKenzie for the location of guns that had been in the ground for years? No, there's something else to that. He wanted MacKenzie to suffer for something else.'

'Like what?' Simon asked. He finished his whisky, his eyes falling hungrily to Connor's untouched glass.

'That's what I don't know yet,' he said. 'We're still missing something. What's Amanda Lyons's involvement in this for a start?'

'Nothing from Robbie on tracing her?' Simon asked.

'Not yet,' Connor said. 'Come on, let's get out of here and I'll give him a—'

He was interrupted by his phone. He pulled it from his pocket, exchanging a glance with Simon.

'His ears must have been ringing,' Simon said, with a shrug.

Connor gave Simon a smile. Felt it curdle and die on his lips when he read the caller ID.

'What?' Simon asked.

Connor turned the phone to him to show him the caller ID – 'Paulie. MB'.

Simon frowned. 'Something on the crowd from Belfast?' he asked.

'No idea,' Connor said, before answering the call.

'Fraser, it's me,' Paulie said, his voice low and urgent. 'Got a call from Jen. She says some strange-looking men were sniffing around your flat earlier. I'm there now, having a look around. Only thing out of place is one of those shitty hybrid Volvos. So unless your neighbours have decided to go green, there's a strange vehicle in the area.'

'What?' Connor said, forcing himself to remain calm. 'Why did she call you? Why did—'

'How the fuck should I know?' Paulie snapped. 'Point is, she was worried. Called me. I'm here. She's safe, won't come out till I give the all-clear. But I could do with— Ah, shit!'

Connor was on his feet before he was aware of moving. 'Paulie, what?'

'Two men moving back towards the flat, they must have been walking around the block, looking for another way in. I don't give a fuck where you are, but get here, now. And don't come naked.'

'Naked': Paulie's term for being without a weapon. 'Paulie, what's going on?' he asked, swallowing the empty helplessness he felt.

'I know these two,' Paulie whispered. 'They were there with Walsh the night he tortured that wee boy in Belfast. Dominic Milligan and Miles something. Heavies and enforcers. These fuckers never go anywhere without a gun and a blade, and I'm betting they're not here for tea and cakes. I'll do what I can to keep them away from the flat, but one against two isn't good odds when the bullets start flying. So get your arse here. Now.'

Connor ended the call, saw worry etched on Simon's face.

'What?' he asked, as Connor started running.

'We have to get home, now,' he shouted over his shoulder, as he took the stairs back down to the main bar three at a time. 'Seems we've got visitors. Two thugs from Belfast.'

'Belfast?' Simon said. 'Fuck. Go, go!'

CHAPTER 71

It was less than a five-minute drive to the flat, and Connor cut that time almost in half. He forced himself to ease off the accelerator as he turned into the street, not wanting to announce their arrival.

'Look,' Connor said, his voice tight as he pointed to a vehicle parked at the side of the road. 'A shitty hybrid Volvo, just like the one Paulie mentioned.'

'Park here,' Simon said, pushing the car door open before Connor had pulled fully to a stop. He slipped out and, crouching low, moved towards the vehicle.

Connor parked and got out. Every sense was straining for something, anything. But there was nothing, just the normal sounds of suburbia. He looked across the road, towards the small track that led to the back of the house, which sat above his garden flat, and the parking area.

'What do you think?' he asked, as Simon walked up beside him, his phone in one hand.

'Won't know until we get in there,' Simon said, pocketing it after fiddling with it for a moment. 'Paulie could have led them away, could have killed them, or they might have got to him. Either way, we're going to know fuck-all standing here. We take it slow and easy. Cover the angles – you take the left side, I take the right. You see anyone other than Paulie, me or Jen, put them down.'

Jen. The mention of her name stabbed at Connor, like a cold blade.

Was she safe, barricaded in the flat? Or had she been taken, a pawn in Walsh's twisted game? Another, darker, thought twisted through his mind, seductive and insidious. What if she had been hurt?

'They sent that bullet to you,' Connor said, as he drew his gun. 'You know they'll be gunning for you.'

Simon smiled, dark and predatory. 'Just gives you more time to get to them if they're concentrating on me,' he said. 'Now come on, let's go.'

They moved slowly, the soft crunch of the gravel almost painful in Connor's ears as they walked. The path took a gentle right turn that led into the forecourt in front of the flat, and Connor took a deep breath as they slid around it. The normality of the scene that unfolded in front of him was like a gut punch. It was his courtyard, the gravel perfectly raked, Paulie's car sitting gleaming beside Simon's hot hatch. He looked over to Simon, who was scanning the scene intently. He twitched his shoulders in a shrug, then pointed to the steps leading down to the front door. 'I'll keep point, you check it out,' he said, drawing his gun and adopting a standing guard, one finger up the barrel, gun half raised.

Connor went down the stairs, gaze sweeping them as he did. No signs of blood, no fresh scuff marks showing someone had been dragged up them. He got to the door, felt a rush of relieved confusion as he saw no damage to it, either. He pressed it with one finger, found it was locked. Was about to knock when he heard the rattle of the chain and the sound of the lock being released.

He stood back, raised his gun. The door opened a crack, an eye peering around it as a gun barrel slid from the darkness.

''Bout fucking time,' Paulie rumbled, as he withdrew the gun.

Connor forced himself to exhale, lowered the gun. 'Paulie,' he said. 'What the fuck is going on?'

Paulie looked over his shoulder, then stepped through the door. 'Fucked if I know. I saw these guys walking towards the flat. Managed to get up the driveway before they did. Barricaded us into the flat, was going to blow the fuckers away if I saw them on the CCTV and one came to the door. But nothing.'

'Are you sure it was them?' Connor asked. It was years since he would have seen either man.

'I'm not fucking stupid,' Paulie growled. 'I know what I . . .'

A high, piercing whistle cut across Paulie's voice, followed by Simon saying, 'Connor,' in a tone that spoke of nothing but trouble.

Connor turned, took the stairs as quickly as he could. Saw Simon facing two men, one taller than the other, both armed. They were strangely barrel-chested, even though the taller of them had a drawn, almost gaunt face. Something about that nagged at Connor, but he pushed the thought aside.

'Dominic and Miles, I presume,' he said, raising his own gun and cursing himself as he did so. They wanted Simon. Easiest way to get him? Spook Jen or someone else close to Connor, then sit back and wait for them to come running. Stupid, he thought, as he tightened his grip on the gun. Fucking stupid.

The taller man's face twisted into something that was more leer than smile, nodded slightly. 'Pleased to meet you, Mr Fraser,' he said. 'And you, Mr McCartney. Or do you prefer Detective Inspector?'

'I'd prefer you to away off down the fucking road,' Simon hissed, his voice as cold and hard as the gun he held in his hands.

Dominic's smile intensified. 'I'm afraid we can't do that, Simon,' he said, his tone all empty regret and sarcasm. 'See, we've been sent to get you and, believe me, the man we work for is not one to be disappointed.'

'How is Wrecker Ryan?' Connor asked, playing for time. He was aware of Paulie lumbering up behind him, could almost feel the radiating presence of the shotgun he held as Paulie tried to work the angles. They were trapped. Two armed assailants in front of them, covering the only access point to or from the flat. Limited cover. So the only real options were to shoot it out here or retreat back into the flat and fight it out there. Which wasn't a realistic option with Jen inside.

'Mr Walsh is just fine,' Miles snapped. His accent was rougher than Dominic's and his eyes squinted and widened in a way that made Connor wonder if he was on something more than mere adrenaline.

'Thanks for confirming who you're working for,' Connor said. 'But, still, what Simon says goes. Fuck off. Now. Police are on the way, so you might be lucky enough to get out of here in time.'

Dominic shook his head. 'I doubt that, Mr Fraser. If you'd reported an armed incident, this place would be crawling with officers already, and we'd hear the sirens. But nothing. No, I think you got Paulie's call and came running. Thanks for that.'

Connor winced again at his own stupidity.

'Better the pigs aren't here,' Paulie growled. Connor could hear gravel crunching as he stepped to his side, knew he was trying to get a better angle. 'Means we can deal with you fucks properly. Then you can take us to Walsh. I've got business with him.'

Dominic sighed, the despair of the gesture cut through by the savage glee in his eyes. 'This is pointless,' he said, almost to himself. 'Miles . . .'

A frozen moment, almost as if someone had pressed pause on the world, and then there was an explosion of frantic movement. Miles's free hand flashed upwards, and Connor saw something hard and metallic glint in the sun.

'Grenade!' he shouted, as he dodged to his left. There was an explosion of noise as Miles and Dominic opened fire, the world becoming a scream. Connor hit the deck and rolled, trying to keep his eye on the men in front of him while searching for the grenade. It landed about a foot from his face and Connor felt his blood freeze and a scream try to crawl its way up his throat. But nothing happened, and it took him a split second to understand why.

'Decoy!' he shouted as he saw the blue markings on the body of the grenade, markings that showed it was an inert device most commonly used in training exercises.

He felt a bullet singe the air above his head, flinched as another dug into gravel inches from his face. He risked a glance behind him, saw Paulie advancing, nothing but fury in his face. He fired, and Connor saw Dominic fly off his feet and hit the gravel. Miles cried out and lunged for his friend. Connor took the opportunity and levelled his gun centre mass, pulled the trigger. Miles folded almost double, his forehead dropping as his legs flew up and he was lifted from his feet.

'Thank Christ,' Connor said. 'You both—'

'Fuck!' Paulie spat. Connor spun round, saw Dominic sitting up, his face a rictus of pain. Connor studied him, his bulky shape, suddenly realised he was wearing a bulletproof vest. He reached into a pocket, and another shape flew through the air. Though this time, Connor realised with icy clarity, it was no dummy.

'Flashbang!' he cried, as the concussion grenade landed between him, Simon and Paulie. The detonation was devastating, overpowering. Connor felt his ears rupture and the world jolt sickeningly beneath him as the concussion from the blast and the blinding light tore at him. He had a sense of Paulie, who had been further away, staggering, holding his gun, the sound of the shot he made muted by the screaming ring in his ears. Tried to fight the blackness that seemed to be crawling into the edges of his vision, like ink dropped into water. Found his legs wouldn't work when he tried to stand up, get to Simon, who Miles had reached and was dragging away.

Get up! his mind screamed. But even as it did, the darkness closed in and Connor fell to the ground. There was a sharp moment of agony as the gravel dug into his chest and face and the impact drove the breath from his lungs.

And then there was nothing.

Nothing at all.

CHAPTER 72

Connor snapped awake, the world rushing in on him like an attacker intent on doing him serious harm. His head was a sick scream of agony, which felt as though it would explode at any second. There was an instant of blind confusion: he was on the floor in his flat – had he been on a night out, staggered home drunk? And then he saw Paulie's face loom over him, and realisation flooded him in a foetid rush.

'Simon!' he barked, as he sat up, the world lurching around him as he did.

Paulie's hand fell on his shoulder, the gesture surprisingly gentle. 'Take a minute,' he said. 'You got a hell of a hit from that blast. You've only been out for a couple of minutes, but it'll take you a while to shrug it off.'

Connor nodded, almost toppled back to the floor as Jen barrelled him into a fierce hug. 'You fucking idiot,' she said into his chest, her voice caught somewhere between laughter and tears. 'What the hell are you doing, getting hurt like that?'

Despite everything, Connor felt something unclench within him, soothed and eased by the warmth and fervour of her embrace. He let himself fall into it until, reluctantly, he pushed her away gently. 'I'm fine,' he said, feeling as if the lie was written all over his face. 'Promise. Just another day at the office.'

'Police will be on their way,' Paulie said, before Jen could speak.

Connor nodded. Forced himself onto his feet, then helped her up from the floor.

'We'd better get moving,' he said, wincing at the way the words echoed painfully in his head as he spoke them.

'What?' Jen said, her voice a whisper of disbelief. 'You can't go back out there! Those men have guns and bombs, for God's sake. Let the police handle it. Connor, you can't!'

'I've got to,' he said. 'They've taken Simon. That's my fault. And if I wait here for the police, I'll never find him in time.'

'But – but . . .'

'Jen,' he said, as whatever her hug had unknotted in him clenched tight again, 'I have to.'

Her face hardened, her gaze sharpened by the tears that threatened to fall. 'I can't do this any more,' she said. 'Dad's dead, and now you're determined to follow him. I said I wanted you to catch his killer, but not if it means you getting killed in the process.'

Connor opened his mouth, closed it. A maelstrom of emotions raged in him, more agonising than the after-effects of the flashbang grenade. But what could he say to her? How could he tell her he loved her, but he had to find Simon?

'I'm sorry,' he said, then headed for the door.

He climbed the stairs from the flat, Paulie behind him. Felt hot tears bite at the back of his eyes as he looked down at the gravel. the scrapes and char marks telling the tale of the violence that had gone before. In the distance, he heard the first wail of a siren.

'Let's get going,' Paulie grumbled.

'Yeah,' Connor said. 'I'll call Ford, try to buy us some time. Last thing we need is every police officer in Stirling looking for us.'

He took out his phone as he walked briskly along the drive, heading for the Audi parked on the street. Stopped dead when he saw the text message alert on the screen, Simon's name on it.

'What?' Paulie said.

Connor ignored him, opened the message.

Even in peace time, you always check under the car. Check mine. Did the same for these boys, just in case. Log in is 1711357, password is our old local. But you'll not need this, as feck-all will go wrong.

Connor looked at the time stamp of the message, made a rough calculation. Remembered Simon having his phone in his hand as they stood outside the flat. Connor hadn't heard the message arrive as their phones were on silent. Standard practice when they were going into a dangerous scenario.

He walked across to Simon's car, which was parked beside Paulie's. Crouched and checked under the wheel arches. Smiled when he saw something, reached under the car to grab it.

'What the hell are you doing?' Paulie asked.

Connor held up a small metal object, about the size of a Zippo lighter. 'Even in peace time, you always check under the car,' he said. 'It's what Simon drilled into me in Belfast. Always check under the car in case someone has planted something nasty under there. Or something really helpful. Like this.'

'A tracker,' Paulie said softly.

'Exactly,' Connor agreed, as he got moving again, excitement and adrenaline chasing away the agony in his head. 'Simon's message told me he's put a tracker on Dominic and Miles's car. With this,' he held up the device he had found, 'I know the brand of tracker he used, and he's given me the ID. So all I have to do is log onto the website, hit the ID and we've got a trace.'

'I take it this is your way of telling me I'm driving?' Paulie said, deadpan.

Despite himself, Connor laughed and handed over the keys to the Audi.

'Fuck me, this must be serious,' Paulie said, the ghost of a smile on his lips.

CHAPTER 73

When Ford saw the report of shots fired in Stirling, he wasn't surprised to see that the address the disturbance was reported at belonged to Connor Fraser. Ford had learned that the man had an almost supernatural talent for attracting trouble and resolving it.

The problem was that, this time, he didn't know just how deep that trouble was.

He stood outside the flat, watching the SOCO teams examine the forecourt. They had found bullet casings, a dummy grenade and the shattered remains of a flashbang grenade in the centre of a patch of scorched gravel. But there was no sign of Fraser or his friend, Simon, and Fraser's girlfriend, whom Ford had left with Troughton in the flat to finish interviewing her, would say only that he had left. There was an almost matter-of-fact quality in her reply that made Ford wonder if she was suffering from shock, or that this, on top of the brutal murder of her father, had been too much for her and she was shutting herself away from the world as a way of coping.

Ford felt tempted to do the same.

He turned away from the SOCOs and walked back down the small driveway that led to the road. Saw another cordon there, police officers keeping back a growing crowd of onlookers. He wasn't surprised to see a Sky van parked at the kerb, made a bet with himself that Donna Blake was somewhere nearby. He thought of his last conversation with her, and his promise to give her a quote about the chief constable and his behaviour with Rodriguez. It was, he thought, with bitter irony, lucky that this shootout had happened – Blake was obsessed with breaking the next live story, being the first on screen with it. This bought Ford a little time to decide how much of what Guthrie had told him he would tell her.

And how much he would keep secret.

He pulled out his phone, sighed as the fantasy of just throwing it onto the road and driving home to Mary played across his mind like a well-loved movie. Then he shook his head, found Connor Fraser's number and hit dial.

'DCI Ford,' Connor said, his voice strained and tired. 'How can I help you this afternoon?'

'I'm standing outside your flat, Fraser,' he said. 'Any idea why that would be?'

'Probably to do with that backfiring exhaust,' Fraser said.

Ford took a breath, released it. 'I take it there's no way you're going to come in and do this properly, officially?'

'Sorry, sir, I can't,' Fraser replied. 'They've got Simon. I can't be slowed down by official channels right now.'

Official channels, Ford thought, a memory of his conversation with Guthrie flashing across his mind. It's all about them, isn't it? 'Look, Fraser, there's more going on here than you know. A lot more. It would be better for everyone if you stepped back, let us deal with it.'

'Would you if it was Troughton or another of your men?' Fraser snapped back, his voice defiant.

'No,' Ford said. 'No, I guess I wouldn't.' He looked around, making sure he was out of earshot of anyone. Tossed a coin in his head, even though he knew he had already made the decision. 'Look, I'm not sure this is going to help you, but if you're going to do this, there's something you need to know.'

'Go on,' Connor said, interest raising his voice slightly.

'This is totally off the record, okay?' Ford said. 'I spoke to Guthrie about his cosy little arrangement with Rodriguez and access to the MacKenzie case.'

'He was blackmailing the chief, wasn't he?' Fraser said.

'No,' Ford replied, still not quite able to believe what the chief had told him. 'He was following orders.'

'What?' Fraser asked.

'He was ordered to pull Rodriguez into the investigation, use it as a way to keep him close and control the story he was trying to tell about his father's death,' Ford said.

'But who could order that?' Connor asked, distracted. 'Who can give the chief constable orders except . . .'

His voice trailed off, and Ford could almost hear the pieces of the puzzle fall into place for Fraser down the line.

'The Lord Advocate,' he said. 'Jesus. But why?'

'To cover something up,' Ford said. 'According to Guthrie, Balfour's little group wasn't a radical nationalist group after all. Not really. And the Professor didn't believe what he was teaching those kids.'

'What?' Fraser asked.

'It all started with the protest against the Queen in 1972. Balfour wasn't helping the students to protest against the monarchy, he was helping them so he could get their names. They'd caught wind of the anti-monarchy, anti-Union sentiment running around the university, and wanted to do something about it.'

'Who wanted to do something about it?' Fraser asked.

'*Regnum defende*,' Ford said, a sudden memory of Byrne's cheap tattoo flashing across his mind.

'MI5?' Connor said. 'Jesus, you're telling me Balfour was an MI5 agent?'

'More like contractor,' Ford said. 'Way Guthrie tells it, they approached him, paid him to find out who were the big movers who protested against the Queen and were agitating for independence. He painted himself as a champion of the cause, pulled the kids in, put them through training, then blackmailed them with that past into working for the government against independence.'

A moment's silence while Fraser digested this. And then: 'Is that why Walsh was involved? Balfour and the intelligence services wanted to get intel on Scottish links to paramilitaries in Northern Ireland? How they were getting the guns in, what their capabilities were?'

'Probably, yes,' Ford replied.

'Jesus,' Connor said. 'So Walsh is killing everyone in the group for betraying the cause and . . .'

'What?' Ford asked. Sensing that Connor had just made some sort of connection.

'Duncan,' Connor said after a moment. 'Walsh caved his face in. We thought it was in revenge. It was, but what if it was more than that, more literal? Like you two-faced bastard. You betrayed me. It's why he tortured him, forced Balfour to drink cheap rot-gut whiskey when he killed him. Humiliation and revenge.'

'Okay, I can see that,' Ford said. 'But it doesn't change the fact that you need to be very fucking careful. There are a lot of people who don't want this coming out.'

'I'll bet,' Fraser replied. 'With the new talk about abolishing the monarchy and Scottish devolution under threat from Westminster, finding out that a key member of the independence movement was actually working against independence and for the Union would pour rocket fuel on the nationalist movement. Christ, they'd probably slap on the woad and sack York for the fun of it.'

'Aye,' Ford agreed, the image somehow cheering to him.

'But why did Walsh target the Vigil site?' Connor asked. 'There's never been any indication it was ever anything but a sincere political movement.'

'I don't know,' Ford said, spotting Donna Blake across the road. 'Ask him when you find him. But, Fraser, do me one favour?'

'Anything,' Connor said.

'Try not to make too much of a mess. And if at all possible, save some of him for us, would you? I'd be very keen to talk to Ryan Walsh about all the shite he's brought down on my home town.'

CHAPTER 74

Donna saw Ford pacing around on the other side of the police cordon, phone pressed to his ear. She made a mental note to call him and chase the comment he had promised her on the chief constable, then turned back towards the driveway that led up to Connor's flat. A dark sliver of unease slid through her stomach as she watched the police officers standing guard there.

There had been reports of gunfire and vehicles leaving the area at speed. This had brought the armed officers who were currently standing sentry, but what had happened? She knew Simon had been keeping something from her about her car tyres being slashed: was this part of it? Or had whoever had killed Duncan MacKenzie decided Connor and Simon were getting a little too close to the truth and decided to take them out of the equation?

She reached for her phone, dialled Simon's number again. Panic rose as the phone rang on before switching to voicemail, just as Connor's had done moments before. Closed her eyes when she heard Simon's voice telling her to leave a message, felt a sudden dread that she would never hear his voice again.

'Donna? Donna?' She started, blinked, saw Keith had walked up beside her. She hadn't even heard him coming. 'You good to go? Got a nice set-up shot, you in foreground, the police officers in the background. Should show off their guns nicely, get us a good terror-in-suburbia vibe.'

She gave him a smile that felt hollow and fragile, then forced herself to concentrate on the task at hand. She was a reporter. Her job was to report facts others didn't want found.

She was pocketing her phone when the thought hit her.

She turned to Keith, gave him a smile that felt a lot more comfortable. 'Sure,' she said. 'But let's make this quick. I've got another lead to track down on this, and a phone call to make.'

CHAPTER 75

The tracker showed that Miles and Dominic were heading east, out of Stirling and into the countryside, which was peppered with towns and villages.

'Any idea where they could be going?' Connor asked, looking up from his phone.

'What the fuck am I – psychic?' Paulie grumbled, eyes not leaving the road. 'They're heading towards Fallin and Throsk if they stay on this road, or they could go down to Falkirk or Kincardine. Long as they can keep your pal Simon quiet, they could drive wherever they want. That Volvo may be a shit bucket, but it's an anonymous one, and unless there's CCTV on your street or some curtain twitcher took down the licence number, the police won't be looking for them.'

Connor felt a stab of panic at the mention of Simon's name. The bullet delivered to him was a fairly unambiguous statement of what Walsh wanted to do to him. But if that was the case, why had Miles and Dominic not just put a bullet in his head on Connor's forecourt? Why drag him away?

His thoughts were interrupted by the sound of his phone ringing through the car's stereo system. He glanced at the dashboard, saw Robbie's name flash on the caller ID.

'Robbie,' he said, answering the call. 'What you got for me? Any luck with tracing Amanda Lyons, or whoever the hell she is?'

'Not yet,' Robbie said, the frustration evident in his voice. 'I used the number you gave me to do a scrape of her mobile information, texts, emails, calls, that sort of thing. Hit a bit of a wall. The level of encryption I had to work through to get to any of her information was almost Biblical. I mean military-grade stuff.'

Connor smiled, felt another box tick in his mind. What was it Ford had told him about Guthrie saying he was being blackmailed by Rodriguez? He was just following orders.

Maybe he wasn't the only one.

'So what have you got for me?' Connor asked.

'Well, I managed to track the phone she's using now by mast pings. Last call was made three minutes ago. Closest mast to it is in a wee village called Throsk.'

Connor's head snapped up. He exchanged a glance with Paulie.

'It's about five minutes away,' Paulie said. 'I know where they're taking Simon.'

Connor tried to put this together with what they knew. Was Amanda working with Walsh? Had this been the plan all along? To use Rodriguez and lure Simon in to kill him? 'Robbie, keep working on it,' he said. 'And get in touch with DCI Ford, tell him what you've found. Be sure to tell him about the military-grade safeguards.'

Connor ended the call, looked across to Paulie. 'You said you know where they're going?' he asked.

'Throsk,' Paulie said. 'There's an industrial estate on the outskirts of the village. Isolated wee place. Duncan has a unit there, off the books. Uses – sorry, used it to store some less than legal items.'

'Like guns?' Connor asked.

'Aye, and some explosives as well,' Paulie agreed.

Connor nodded. Was that Duncan's final humiliation? Had he been tortured to reveal the location of his personal arms cache, the weapons and explosives Walsh found there used to blow up Leggatt and the site of the Vigil?

'Jesus Christ!' Paulie spat. There was a moment of weightlessness and the car swayed violently to the right, then Connor's seatbelt bit into his shoulders as the car slewed into a skid. Connor looked up, saw why Paulie had cried out. In front of them, two large black SUVs were parked across the road, blocking it.

Paulie brought the car to a stop, the smell of scorched rubber biting into Connor's nose, bitter and acrid. He pulled out his gun, held it low. Had Dominic and Miles realised they were being followed, turned back to confront Connor and Paulie? If so, who was in the second car? Reinforcements?

Connor felt his breath catch as he watched the passenger door of the SUV on the left swing open. Out of the corner of his eye, he saw Paulie shift the Audi into reverse.

'They start shooting, shoot back and I'll get us the fuck out of here,' Paulie muttered.

Connor nodded. Waited. Felt his jaw drop open as a figure emerged from the car, dark hair whipping in the wind. What was it Robbie had said? *Last call was made three minutes ago. Closest mast to it is in a wee village call Throsk.*

'Connor?' Amanda Lyons called. 'Sorry for stopping you like that. Got a moment? I've a favour to ask.'

CHAPTER 76

It didn't surprise Donna that Jonathan Rodriguez wasn't happy to see her when she arrived at the house he was renting in Dunblane. What had he said when they first met? *I want those who were involved in my father's death to know I'm coming. And the more press attention there is on me, the less likely they are to try to shut me up while I'm in the public eye.*

She understood what that meant now. What she didn't know was if Rodriguez himself did.

'Donna, this really isn't a good time,' he said, as she followed him into the house. 'I've got the network breathing down my neck, and now Amanda's missing with all her research and production notes, I'm really in the shit.'

'I'll bet you are,' Donna said, deadpan. 'Especially since your cosy little arrangement with Chief Constable Guthrie is at an end and you've served your purpose for Amanda, or whoever the hell she really is.'

Rodriguez's face pinched, part anger, part shame. 'What are you talking about?' he said.

'When we first met, you said you got the idea to dig into your father's death because your mum mentioned it was the fortieth anniversary of his body being found in Airthrey Loch. But that's not quite true, is it?'

Rodriguez cleared his throat, eyes moving left and right as he sought to avoid Donna's gaze. 'I've no idea what you're on about,' he said.

Donna smiled. 'Of course not. What was it you said when you held that press conference in Dunblane? That you wanted those involved in your father's death to know you were coming? But they already did, didn't they? I'm betting you told them during that first call with Jamie Leggatt.'

'What? I – I . . .' he stammered.

Donna held up a hand. 'You said it yourself, Jonathan. You told me it was Amanda who lined up that first Zoom call with Leggatt when you first started this story. It was her who gave you the idea for it, wasn't it? How did she sell it to you? That the fortieth anniversary of your father's death was coming up, a death shrouded in mystery? What better than a son coming home to investigate it, a quest for truth sparked by a heart-to-heart with his dear old mum? It's a great line, and I bet you jumped at it.'

'It wasn't like that,' he said, petulant defiance in his voice. 'When Amanda came to work with me, she asked about my background and Dad's name came up. She was interested, said to ask my mum about it, see what she could remember. Then we developed the pitch, and she contacted . . .' He trailed off.

Donna saw a revelation brighten his eyes. 'She had it all to hand, didn't she? The anti-royal protests, the stories from back in the day when Leggatt claimed your dad was assassinated. All right to hand. How long did it take her to put you in touch with Leggatt?'

'It was quick,' he admitted. 'But she was good. Professional. It never occurred to me . . .'

'That she was leading you by the nose to do exactly what she wanted?' Donna said. 'And when she set up that call with Leggatt, how active was she in it? Did she take the lead in the interview, or was it you? I'm betting it was her. Did she say anything odd in that interview, anything out of place?'

Rodriguez's brow knotted as he looked at her. 'No, not really. Though there was one strange thing she asked.'

'Go on,' Donna said.

'She asked Leggatt if he knew a woman from Stirling called, ah . . .'

he made a show of thinking '. . . ah, yes, Margaret Pope. Said she was an old family friend. He told her Scotland wasn't that small, made a joke about it.'

Donna felt the urge to step forward and slap Rodriguez, swallowed it. 'And you didn't think that was unusual?' she said. 'Christ, what type of reporter do they breed in America, or do they just drop you into a make-up chair, give you a script and hope for the best?'

Rodriguez puffed out his chest, anger in his eyes. 'What do you mean? I—'

'Codewords,' Donna said. 'Just like the code we were sent warning us about the bombs in Dundee and Edinburgh. Facts, Jonathan. They're what good journalism is based on. After the bombings I did a little research on codewords. And guess what? "Margaret Pope" was the code used as a warning before the Omagh bombing.'

Rodriguez's eyes went wide. 'Code?' he whispered. 'Are you telling me that she's – she's some kind of terrorist?'

Donna shrugged, irritation scratching at the back of her scalp. 'I don't know,' she said. 'But it's clear that she was sending Leggatt a message that led to two men being murdered and others put in danger.'

Rodriguez's head darted up. 'What do you mean?'

So she told him. About the firearms incident at Connor's flat. About not being able to get in touch with either of them. And as she spoke, she felt a desperate anger. Whatever Amanda Lyons had set in motion, Connor and Simon were at the heart of it.

She just prayed they would survive to understand what they had been drawn into.

CHAPTER 77

As Paulie had said, the warehouse stood at the back of a small industrial estate in the fields surrounding the village of Throsk. The estate had the tired, run-down look that was generated by the businesses on it dying slowly – from what Connor could tell, half of the units were shuttered and the rest had neglected frontages that looked out onto a road that was more pothole than tarmac.

They parked around the corner from the unit, used a large skip as cover as they peeked beyond it and surveyed the scene. A simple warehouse, one large roll door to let in vehicles, and a standard door beside it that Paulie had told him led to a small office. 'It's just a garage bay and the office,' Paulie had said. 'Duncan had the concrete floor dug out, set steel safes in it and relaid the floor. No idea what was in there when he died, but back in the day there were enough guns to supply an armed robbery at every bank in the Central Belt.'

Connor took another look, his desire to get into the building and to Simon warring with his caution over approaching a one-entrance building with armed hostiles inside.

What if you're too late? a voice whispered in his mind. *What if he's already dead?*

'Only way to play this is head-on,' Paulie said, as though reading Connor's thoughts. 'Though it would be a lot fucking easier if your ladyfriend would use some of her manpower and lend a hand.'

Connor gave a thin smile, thinking back to his roadside conversation with Amanda Lyons.

'Yeah, but at least she gave us some toys to bring to the party,' he said, shrugging the small backpack on his shoulder. Lyons had handed it to him almost apologetically, making it clear that she couldn't officially get involved in what was about to happen but wanted to help rescue Simon if she could. Her definition of help had been four small, remote-controlled magnetic explosive charges, flashbang grenades and two bulletproof vests for Connor and Paulie.

Paulie sighed. 'Aye. Right, let's get on with it. You get down there, plant the charges on the door. I'll follow you, watch your back. Then we blow the doors and storm the place.'

Connor nodded slowly. 'You don't have to do this, Paulie,' he said. 'If Walsh is in there, we need him alive.'

'You let me worry about that,' Paulie hissed.

Connor got moving, a low, crouched run to the door of the warehouse, his skin crawling with the certainty he was about to be shot at any minute. He reached the office door, held his breath as he attached one of the explosive devices, then shuffled along to the roll-up door and repeated the process.

'We set?' Paulie asked, face impassive, eyes gleeful.

'Set,' Connor said, the word sending a shiver of adrenalised fear down his spine as they retreated further up the building, away from the doors. He pulled out the detonator, held it in a hand that wasn't quite steady.

'Do it,' Paulie said.

So he did.

CHAPTER 78

Simon looked up, saw the two armed masked men standing side by side, the shorter of the two now pointing a shotgun directly at his face. Behind him, the third man stood with a phone held up, the torch on as he recorded. That was why they were wearing masks, Simon thought, so no one who saw the footage would see their faces.

'Night night,' the man said, as he adjusted his feet slightly, readying himself for the gun to kick.

Simon closed his eyes. Thought of Donna Blake and all the things he hadn't said when he'd had the chance. The moment seemed to drag out, Simon's nerves screaming to try something, anything, He tested his bonds, felt ice water flood through his stomach and his bladder threaten to release as he heard the shotgun being racked.

Donna—

The world exploded. It was like being caught in a sudden tsunami of heat and pressure and roaring, ear-splitting noise. A moment of weightlessness as he was flung forward by the force of the explosion behind him, and then, even over the shriek of noise that had filled the world, he heard the snapping of bone and the empty clattering of a gun hitting the floor as he was hurled into one of the gunmen.

Simon blinked, tried to roll away. He could hear shouting, the muffled, distorted sound of feet on the concrete floor. He felt the arm of the chair he was tied to give and managed to pull free. The man he had landed on was trying to disentangle himself, spitting and wheezing as he tried to kick Simon away. Simon swung his free arm as hard as he could, taking the splintered arm of the chair with him. Felt ribs crumple and snap as he connected with the gunman's body, heard a choked gargle as he saw the front of the mask he wore grow dark with a plume of blood.

'Fucker!' he spat, as he kicked back and away, somehow managing to stand up. And then he was looming over Simon, lifting his foot, and Simon realised it wasn't a bullet through his brain that would kill him, but a boot.

He moved, ignoring the agony in his muscles and back as he tried to shift himself while still tied to the chair, bracing for the blow. But then, the man looming over him was jerked violently right as a gunshot roared through the warehouse, his head exploding in a mist of blood and brain as he toppled over.

Simon whipped his head around, felt the urge to laugh surge through him again as he saw Connor looking down on him. 'Where the hell have you been?' he said, feeling tears of relief claw at the back of his eyes.

'Got a little sidetracked on the way here,' Connor said, crouching down to cut Simon free from what was left of the chair. He helped him up slowly, worry etching his face as his eyes skipped over the various injuries on Simon's face.

'I'm fine,' Simon reassured him, the lie of what he was saying evident in his tone. He took a breath, tried to steady himself. Smoke was wafting through the warehouse, escaping out into the day in lazy spirals through the hole that had been blown in the warehouse door. Then his gaze fell lower, to the lump of twisted flesh that had, until a few moments ago, been a man intent on kicking him to death. Blood and brains were spattered over the grimy concrete floor, and something in the sight of that weakened Simon's knees.

'Easy,' Connor said, grabbing him by the arm. 'Come on, let's get you out of here.'

'I'm okay, just a bit unsteady,' Simon said, his eyes drifting back to the body on the floor as a thread of alarm cut through his nausea. 'Hold on, that's one down. Where are the other two?'

'Back in the office,' Paulie said, as he stepped into the main warehouse. 'Miles took a bullet to the leg, and Walsh . . . Well, let's just say I rearranged his teeth when he tried to get past me.'

Simon gave the body on the floor a final glance. 'Night night, Dominic,' he whispered.

'You got Walsh tied up back there?' Connor asked, his voice low with a rage that Simon at once feared and found mirrored by his own.

'Yup,' Paulie said. 'I figured you'd want a word with him before, well, you know.'

Connor nodded, an expression Simon couldn't read passing over his face. 'Bloody right I would.'

CHAPTER 79

As Paulie had promised, Ryan Walsh was slumped in a chair in the office of the warehouse. Connor wanted to ask Paulie where he had found the zip ties that bound Walsh to the chair by the arms and feet, but let it go. After all, he had other, more important, questions to ask, and answers to get.

'Wrecker Ryan,' Simon said, sarcastic admiration in his voice. 'Fancy seeing you here.'

Walsh looked up, naked hatred in his eyes. He spat a wad of blood-flecked phlegm onto the floor. He was older, his beard a dull grey and his face more deeply lined and pinched, but Connor could see in front of him the man he had been in the picture with Balfour.

It was, he thought, in the eyes. It was always in the eyes.

'You'd best be cutting me free and letting me go,' Walsh said. 'Otherwise you're going to be in a world of shit.'

Paulie laughed, a harsh, humourless bark that made Walsh flinch. 'And how do you figure that after you killed two men, one of whom just happened to be a very close friend of mine?'

Walsh studied Paulie for a minute, then dropped his jaw, almost as if he had made some decision. 'MacKenzie,' he said. 'Yeah, I remember you. Paulie, isn't it? You worked with that two-faced cunt for years. He got off lightly. I should have made him watch me kill his wee girl before I gutted him for what he did.'

Paulie's hand flashed out so fast Connor almost didn't see it. The sound of the slap echoed through the room, and blood splattered across the wall. Walsh dropped his head to his chest, then his body started to jerk slowly. It took Connor a moment to realise he was laughing. He looked up at Paulie, lips pulling back into a dead, empty leer that exposed ragged stumps of bloodstained teeth.

'Truth hurts, doesn't it?' Walsh said.

'And what truth is that?' Connor asked. 'That you killed Duncan MacKenzie because he knew that Balfour was playing both sides off each other and was using the connections he made to sell guns. Or that you killed Balfour because you knew what he was doing for the security services? Or do you mean something else, like your relationship with Marcus Guthrie? He's the one who figured it out, isn't he?'

Walsh's gaze sharpened on Connor, hatred and something deeper than sorrow warring in his eyes. He took a deep breath and let it out slowly, his body seeming to collapse like a punctured balloon as he did so.

'Aye,' he agreed. 'It was that fucking dirk Balfour would wave around. The one with the Campbell motto on it. Marcus knew the story of the Glencoe massacre, how the Campbells slept with the MacDonalds before they turned on them and butchered them. Balfour must have thought he was a right funny cunt, waving around a symbol of Scot turning against Scot.'

'But that's not what did it, was it?' Connor said. 'Surely it must have been more than that dirk.'

'It was,' Walsh said, his voice growing wistful. 'Marcus went to visit Balfour late one night, saw he had a visitor in his office. So he listened at the door, heard him talking with Duncan MacKenzie, making a deal to ship the guns to paramilitary groups, see who was interested, then giving anyone who was anti-Union or anti-monarchy up to the intelligence services. Fucking traitor.'

'So you killed him? Dumped his body in the loch?' Connor said.

'Fucking right I did,' Walsh said, eyes bright with pride.

'But why stop there?' Simon asked. 'If you knew about what Duncan was doing back then, why wait until now to kill him?'

'But you didn't know about Duncan back then, did you?' Connor said. 'Marcus kept Duncan's part in everything quiet. He was only interested in Balfour betraying the cause. You only found out about Duncan years later, when this all started up again when Rodriguez announced his documentary.'

Walsh nodded, suddenly looking very tired. 'I only found out when Leggatt got in touch. He was panicking, almost feral, said some American woman had used an old codeword in a call. He was shitting it that she would find out he made all the claims about Balfour's death being a conspiracy to cover up what was really going on with the guns we were moving. He was terrified she knew about the camp, the group, Balfour being a government plant and Duncan growing fat off both sides, like the fucking parasite he was. I confronted Marcus and that was when he admitted Duncan was using the Vigil site in Edinburgh to meet people, republican and loyalist, and arrange arms deals.'

Connor nodded. 'That was why you bombed the Vigil. To get attention on to it, expose the story. But why now? Why after all this time?'

Walsh winced, as though Paulie had struck him again. 'No point in keeping secrets now, is there? Marcus and that guy who's an MSP now, MacRae, kept the truth about Balfour quiet at the time, not wanting it known that the nationalist movement had been infiltrated and led by the government, especially not under their noses. But when Marcus died, there was no point in keeping it quiet any more. The least I owed him was the truth, especially after all these years.'

'Why? Why did you owe him?' Simon asked.

'Because you loved him, right?' Connor said, thinking back to the picture with Walsh in it. It was obvious now, the way Marcus Guthrie was leaning in over Walsh's shoulder, chin touching it, one arm looped around his waist. 'It's why you blackmailed Donald Byrne to get you out of prison, set you up back in Scotland. To be with him. Is that why you killed his wife? Jealousy? Or to protect your secret?'

Walsh's face grew very still. 'It wasn't like that,' he said. 'She knew about us, had no problem with it. Only wanted to see Marcus happy. She had her own, ah, interests to pursue. When I came back to Scotland, I had a new identity, but I knew this story Balfour's kid was working on could ruin that. And she was always a smart woman, smart enough to put it together. And I couldn't risk that, couldn't risk being exposed.'

'So you decided to kill everyone who could identify you, expose Balfour then drift away into the shadows?' Paulie said, his voice devoid of emotion.

Walsh gave a cruel, empty smile but said nothing.

Connor felt a wave of exhaustion sweep over him, couldn't summon the energy to tell Walsh how wrong he was. How everything that had happened had been about him, and a very elaborate shell game to goad him into doing exactly what he had done – tidy up a very messy, very embarrassing problem for the state without it getting involved.

'It's very simple,' Amanda Lyons had said to him when she had pulled him and Paulie over. 'I've been working on this for months. You see, Walsh has been a wanted asset for years. We believe he's got some, ah, embarrassing information on a potential presidential candidate and his time in the Republic. We want that, so I made sure he felt enough pressure to raise his head above the parapet and expose himself.'

It was, she'd explained, why she couldn't help Paulie and Connor rescue Simon. 'How would it look, American assets putting boots on the ground in Scotland without the express permission of both the Scottish and UK governments?' she had asked him. 'Not great.'

So the deal had been simple. Connor would step in and rescue Simon, but Walsh was not to be harmed, and would be handed over when the dust cleared. In return, she would ensure Connor, Paulie and Simon would not face any charges.

'I may not be here officially,' she had told him, with a dead smile, 'but that doesn't mean I don't have pull.'

Connor sighed as he heard engines approaching: Amanda, or whatever the hell her name was, closing in to take her prize. A small, broken man who had killed indiscriminately, a man who could now help choose the next leader of the free world.

'Let me just get one thing clear,' Paulie said, snapping Connor from his thoughts. 'When you killed Duncan, you tortured him. That wasn't for the key to the arms cache, was it?'

Walsh blinked. 'What? No. The cache was only a message to Byrne, the Lord Advocate. Just a wee reminder of the shit I knew about him, a calling card to be played if I got into any trouble. It's always good to have a lawyer in your pocket, Paulie, you know that.'

'Aye,' Paulie said, 'It is. So the torture was what? For fun?'

Walsh's eyes blackened. 'He deserved it. He was a two-faced bastard. A traitor.'

'Yeah,' Paulie agreed, sadness in his voice. 'He was. But he was something else as well. He was my friend.'

Before Connor could move, Paulie drew his gun and shot Walsh in the head. At such close range, the damage was catastrophic, his head exploding in a crimson scream that arced up the wall and splashed back on Paulie. He turned to Connor, his face streaked with blood and gore, his eyes calm, smile empty.

'Paulie,' Connor whispered. 'What the fuck did you just do?'

CHAPTER 80

One week later

Connor stood back from the punchbag, chest heaving, eyes stinging as sweat dripped into them. He had been working out for about an hour, pushing himself as hard as he could, trying to drown his thoughts and feelings in the cracks of his fist hitting the bag and the jangle of the ceiling chain as it bucked and jerked under his assault.

So far, it wasn't working.

When Lyons arrived to find what was left of Walsh, she had taken in the scene silently, then left. She hadn't been seen since. It was as though she had never really existed. One moment there, the next not. But her influence could be felt. From what Donna told him and Simon, it was as though the hand of God had reached down from Heaven and scooped the whole story into its palm. Legal action was threatened against any news outlet that reported any allegations relating to the case of Professor Robert Balfour, links to Irish or Scottish nationalists or US intelligence assets operating on UK soil. Duncan MacKenzie's death was spun as gang-related, and stories relating to Duncan's less-than-legal activities began hitting the headlines. The bombings of Jamie Leggatt and of the site of the Vigil in Edinburgh were dismissed as the work of one of his students. A student who, conveniently, was found dead of an overdose when police broke down his door.

With no story to report, Rodriguez had returned to the US. From conversations with Ford, Connor knew that his relationship to Chief Constable Guthrie, who had suddenly developed a chronic medical condition and been placed on extended leave, was being closely investigated, and Rodriguez would probably have some serious questions to answer in the future.

And then there was Ronnie MacRae. The twenty thousand pounds Simon had found in his office safe, along with some accounting and passport checks Robbie ran, gave the reason for his career as an MSP and his polished hatred of the Union and the monarch. And, as with so many choices in politics, it boiled down to one thing: money.

Confronted by Simon, who was, understandably, looking to share some of the hurt he had endured at the hands of Walsh, MacRae had admitted that he had agreed to work with Balfour to identify nationalist threats. He had learned the speeches on independence and how out of touch the monarchy was in the modern age, then trotted them out at rallies and political gatherings. When the Vigil began in Edinburgh, he had used it as a platform to build his profile – and meet with MacKenzie to organise arms deals and swap information. But what no one, including the late Lord Advocate, Donald Byrne, had known was that MacRae and MacKenzie had maintained their relationship, carving out a very lucrative side business in post-Brexit exports and imports, with MacRae using his political clout to grant MacKenzie whatever permits and access he needed to make the deals and ship goods quietly into and out of Scotland. It was only when a financial scandal had rocked MacRae's party, and brought the threat of auditors to his door, that he'd decided to get out. So he upped his anti-royal rhetoric, made himself too extreme for his party. They had to boot him out and he stood as an independent.

An independent who wouldn't be audited by any party finance chiefs.

It was, Connor was forced to admit, a good plan. But now that everything had come to light, and with Simon determined to make sure everyone who could face charges would, MacRae was facing some long, sleepless nights and big troubles.

Connor found he didn't care. He had his own problems to deal with.

He knew what was coming the moment he had stepped into the flat. Jen had been there, and had rushed to greet him, but he could feel the void growing between them even as he took her into his arms.

'It's too much, isn't it?' Connor said, not wanting her to have to say it. 'All this. Paulie. People coming to our home looking for me.'

She looked up at him, mouth trembling as tears welled in her eyes. 'I just . . .' She stopped. 'I've already lost so much, Connor. Our baby. My health,' she held up a crutch, shook it angrily, 'and now Dad. I know I blamed you for that and I'm sorry. That was wrong. But I can't live in fear that I'll lose you too. I just can't.'

He had held her then, felt her tears soak into his chest, as though trying to soothe the heart that was breaking in it. They had talked for an hour and, although Connor had offered her the house they had bought with all its modifications to make her life easier, she had refused, saying she would move back to her own flat while they worked out what, if anything, the future held for them. Which left Simon in Connor's flat and Connor with an empty house that he wasn't sure he could ever live in.

He took a deep breath, started hammering into the bag again, dancing around it, throwing combinations of shots.

'You're dropping your left,' a voice called from the door.

Connor started, turned. Smiled despite himself when he saw Amanda Lyons standing there. 'Ms Lyons,' he said. 'Or whatever your name is. Didn't expect to see you again.'

'Oh, you didn't,' she said a coy smile on her lips. 'I was never here. And it's Gillian, by the way. Gillian Flint.'

'Flint?' Connor said. 'Really?'

'Maybe, maybe not,' she said. 'Not that a name matters, really. I've always found a person is more about their actions than their name.'

Connor turned back to the bag. 'Gillian, or whatever, I'm really not in the mood for games. You got what you wanted. Used Balfour to stir up some headlines, set Walsh on edge, forced him out into the open so you could grab him. I just hope the lives your little game cost were worth it. Now, if you'll excuse me.' He turned and threw a punch at the bag to underline his statement.

'Oh, do grow up, Connor,' she said. 'See the bigger picture. Grabbing a former terrorist who blackmailed your top lawyer to get his freedom was never going to be sanctioned through official channels or any cosy intergovernmental chats. So I improvised. But, more importantly, my employers and I have been very, very impressed by your actions in all of this. Okay, so your friend Paulie has caused us a significant headache, but it's one we can live with.'

'So you're going to leave him alone?' Connor asked.

She smiled. 'For now. I have more important matters to deal with than a small-time thug. But I wanted you to know that, if you ever wanted to explore them, there are many, many opportunities for a man like you in the United States.'

Connor laughed. 'A man like me? Thanks, but I'm happy here, and besides, my passport is out of date.'

'Two lies in one sentence. Not like you, Connor,' she said. 'Your call. But bear it in mind. You've still got my number. Call me one day.'

Connor watched her walk out of the gym. He stood there for a long moment, staring at the door. What did he have here other than his gran in a local care home, an empty house and a job that had probably cost him the woman he loved?

He shook his head, angry that he was even thinking that way. Started throwing punches again.

He was interrupted a few minutes later by the ringing of his phone. He stopped, took a hitching breath, then stepped over to his bag and fished it out. Felt a hammer blow in his chest as he read the caller ID, forced himself to breathe as he hit answer.

'Jen,' he said, heart hammering in his chest. And then, when there was no reply, just the sound of her breathing down the line, he added, 'I miss you. Can we meet? Talk?'

And then he waited for her answer.

ACKNOWLEDGEMENTS

Thanks to Gav Robertson (@gav_rab_pt) for helping me shed the book belly and making sure Connor's punches always land in the right places. Thank you, as well, to all the usual suspects who gather wherever a crime is committed, to the reptile boys, Ed and Derek, to Queen of the Bay Vic Watson, and to Douglas Skelton, who offered invaluable insight into the Glencoe Massacre. Thanks also to all the bloggers and booksellers who champion crime writing – in particular, the one and only Fiona Sharp at Waterstones Durham and @ scarletrix.

Special thanks to fellow writer and jute-snorting lunatic Mark Leggatt, who provided the stabilisers when I took my usual non-planning approach to writing this book and set off with nothing more than the first line and a vague idea. Next sherry is on me . . .